5-

D0708213

THE MAN WHO WAS THERE

On the airport at Beirut, Michael Locke is entrusted by an old friend, a Dominican priest, with a portfolio. He is asked to convey it to a certain Monsignor in London. Locke is a lecturer for a British cultural institution, under cover of which he does intelligence work in the Middle East. When he opens the portfolio, he releases a whole swarm of troubles on himself, and finds himself under the deepest suspicion of his employers. The secret it contains, which is virtually priceless, is from different motives sought by the Israeli Government, the Catholic Church, a notorious agent called Shafei, and Locke's own beautiful but enigmatic mistress.

THE MAN
WHO WAS THERE

by
Donald Barron

1969
CHATTO & WINDUS
LONDON

Published by
Chatto and Windus Ltd.
42 William IV Street
London W.C.2

*

Clarke, Irwin & Co. Ltd.
Toronto

SBN 7011 1445 2

Printed in Great Britain by
Cox & Wyman Ltd.
London, Fakenham and Reading

TO MY WIFE

Chapter 1

IT was four years since I had last met Gregory Swain, and seeing him again unexpectedly in a foreign country was no commonplace pleasure. It was an Occasion, a moment of rare anticipation.

My scheduled stop at Beirut was forty-five minutes, but that day it seemed they weren't keeping to schedules. There had been a delay in Abu Dhubi and now, long after we should have been soaring over the Aegean (in Icarus's slip-stream as one travel brochure put it with heavy whimsy) it was announced that our plane had engine trouble. It would be fixed soon.

But in these parts the word 'soon' is loaded with speculative content; it is by no means a promise of impending action but a mere comment on the subjective nature of time. In the case of Pan-Asian Airlines, the company that had brought me this far from Karachi, and whose services I had endured many times, the metaphysical nuances of the word 'soon' tend to be submerged into blatant cynicism. From experience I supposed that they didn't know, nor really cared, how long we would be stuck there.

I was familiar enough with the tedium that grows with prolonged delay in an airport; Beirut is no exception, and the spirits of the voyager wilt as quickly here as anywhere else with the passage of wasted time. It doesn't help to know that the big fat diamond of the Middle East is sparkling there at the end of the runway, in the palm of the hills a few minutes of taxi-ride away; for its six hundred bars and nightclubs, and the people I knew there, might as well have been on the moon for all the use they were on such an occasion.

Maybe there's a formula for dealing with these barren occasions, but I've never found it. Eventually one slips into that uncertain and unrestful sleep that comes of end-less ennui nurtured on drink and heat, and between crazy mini dreams that hover on the brink of reality, one remains sweatily conscious of being cheated by events. I woke from one such cat-nap determined to solve the two remaining clues in my crossword; my attention wandered from a quotation by Milton towards the bar as I consid-ered the attraction of another cold beer. And then it was that I saw Gregory Swain.

He was standing in profile to me at the other end of the passenger lounge, a tall angular-faced priest in the bil-lowing habit of the Dominican Order, talking earnestly with an elderly man possessed of a close-cut stubble of very white hair.

Gregory looked much as I remembered him, but then a man in his mid-thirties doesn't alter a great deal in the course of four years. We had met first as students at Ox-ford; to be precise, after a lecture given by a learned French professor on the significance of Montesquieu, and delivered in such atrocious English as to be barely com-prehensible. A private argument outside the lecture hall with a mutual acquaintance on the meaning of morality led to our first exchange of words, and an invitation to tea in my rooms.

From the beginning it had been both a demanding and a rewarding friendship; buffeted by clashes of temperament and conviction, and sustained almost as much by a shared enthusiasm for polemics and the sound of our own voices as by affection. Our battlefields stretched to a wide horizon in those days; Truth (Capital T and gold-leaf in those days) was the spur, history and philosophy our primary weapons (unblunted as yet by the rough of experience), and victory came not infrequently to the one who could talk the loudest. Yet at heart our disagreements were fundamental although we didn't appreciate it at the time. Gregory was already deeply religious and I was a practising atheist. His truth was not my truth, nor mine his. Where I saw cause and effect he saw revelation; when I said chance he said destiny, and when I wanted proof he was satisfied with faith. Yet youth was on our side, and mostly we cared more for the argument itself than for the viability of its content.

When Gregory took holy orders we saw much less of each other, and when we did the candid caprices of our debates suffered from the aura of his priesthood. I didn't feel free any more to support my arguments with cynical or facetious criticisms of his church, nor to prod the more obscure corners of his faith. And he too, I knew, felt constrained by the bondage of his obligations. We still talked a great deal when we met, but our relationship came to depend less on intellectual jousting and more on the simple satisfactions of sharing time with a good friend.

I watched the two men now, savouring the pleasure of meeting Gregory again, waiting for their intense tête-à-tête to abate before I intruded on them. The older man was like a foil to the priest, contrasting in all visible physical characteristics. He was short and stocky, and the cut of his light-grey suit tapered from disproportionately broad shoulders to spindly drainpipe trousers. His whole manner was one of quivering nervous excitement, and his face permanently raised towards the towering and impassive priest was animated by an uninhibited display of emotion. With his right hand he gesticulated violently and continuously; in his left hand he held a large and distinctive black bag, a curious mongrel affair that was part suitcase, part briefcase, and I thought it strange that he went on holding it instead of putting it down on the floor.

I waited for a lull in their ǀconversation, but it didn't come and I became impatient. I stubbed my cigarette out and walked over to them. I half expected Gregory to see me before I reached him, but his concentration on the older man never faltered until I stood by his side and addressed him by name. He turned round sharply. For a fleeting moment, while he was still on the threshold of recognition, I thought that I saw in those deep eyes of his the reflection of a wild fear. The impact of that dark agonized look was so strange, so unexpected, and it passed so quickly, that I was tempted to doubt my interpretation of its meaning.

"Well, this is a pleasant surprise," I said.

"Why Mike! What on earth are you doing here?" he exclaimed, producing a broad face-splitting smile. It was famous that smile, amongst his friends. It carried many things in its wake besides humour; a warm affection, certainly, and something else besides, less easily defined. The hallmark of inner confidence someone had once said. And yet as I looked at him, refreshing my memory, it seemed to me that I could still see in his face the residue of a deep unease.

"I'm on my way home, back to London," I said. "I've been in Pakistan and points East for six weeks."

"Sounds fascinating! Work or pleasure?"

"Work, every minute of it. Lecturing mainly, sponsored by the Canfield Foundation. Advice on higher educational know-how, and preaching Western intellectual superiority to the natives, outrageous conceit really."

We stared at each other. More than ever his long gothic face reminded me of the deeply chiselled apostles on the portals of Rheims cathedral. His skin, normally pale, was now deeply tanned and I supposed that he had been out East for some time.

"My dear Mike," he said, "it's been such a long time. We must talk, we must catch up on each other; this is terribly exciting."

He turned to the older man.

"Professor Ricardi, I'd like you to meet an old friend, indeed a fellow historian, Michael Locke. We did time together at Oxford. Mike, this is Professor Ricardi."

We shook hands and the professor inclined his head.

"It is a pleasure to meet you," he said in faultless English, but without enthusiasm. We exchanged a few polite words, and I was left in little doubt of his impatience with my interruption; and all the while I could see Gregory out of the corner of my eye fiddling nervously with his crucifix, rubbing its surface with the ball of his thumb in a quick repetitive circular motion, again and again.

I turned to him.

"I mustn't intrude on you any longer, Gregory, only I just had . . ."

"My dear Mike, I would never have forgiven you if you hadn't. Do I gather that you're flying on this Pan-Asian plane?"

"I am, if they ever get around to making it airworthy."

"Well, then, we shall have lots of time to chew the cud together. And there are still old scores to be settled you know."

I looked at him in surprise.

"You're on it, too?"

He nodded beaming.

"You're damned lucky," I said, "it should have left hours ago."

He went on smiling, but began fiddling with his crucifix again.

"I know," he said.

For a brief moment we stood there, the three of us, in an unrewarding silence. I put out a hand to the professor.

"I'll say good-bye then."

He nodded and we shook hands.

"Perhaps we shall meet again," he said politely.

I returned to my seat somewhat chagrined and frustrated. As a grand reunion the occasion had been something of a flop; as a diversion from boredom it had been sadly short-lived. I lit another cigarette, rested my head right back on the armchair, closed my eyes, and indulged myself with nostalgic thoughts of bygone days in Oxford. Fleeting memories blurred already at the edges by time, yet sufficient to perpetuate the desirable myth of one's happy youth. I could look back twelve years to those days, as I did sometimes, and speculate on why I had let myself be blown off course quite so much. The omens had been promising after all; a good degree followed quite quickly by a lectureship at London; the wake of my journey from that point should have been straight and placid, a gentle voyage on the way to some becalmed academic backwater. It was a reasonable conjecture, but it hadn't worked out that way. Sometimes, not often, I minded; I would see the cherished ambitions of a young man blown to the winds like an autumn leaf. Then I would hunt for explanations and excuses, but mostly I came back from the chase empty-handed. After all, some home truths one can do without.

Twice during the following twenty minutes, in between unwise reflections on things past, I half opened my eyes again to make sure that Gregory was still around. The first time both men were standing exactly as I had originally seen them, closeted with their animated whispered talk. In a moment of fantasy I saw them as conspirators, plotting some sinister theological heresy; activists of a secret consistory committed to some outrageous black dogma ... I drifted again into a dream; Savanorola was preaching in Trafalgar Square rousing the mob to reject Humanism and destroy the fleshpots, and a priest who looked like Gregory was standing by his side with a banner proclaiming that 'The End is Near'. But after a while I saw that Savanorola was really Gregory, and the mob turned on him and tied him to a stake, and a fellow student of ours put a torch to the faggots. . . .

The second time I looked for them, neither Gregory nor the professor were there any more. I got up to look around for them; I felt put out, unreasonably so perhaps, and was considering looking for Gregory beyond the confines of the passenger lounge when they began to broadcast the announcement of our impending departure. All around me the polyglot group of thirty or so despondent passengers began to shake itself out of its collective stupor, and slowly assembled at the departure point. Thoughts about home filtered back through my preoccupation with Gregory with renewed relevance; pleasant images of Louise, of familiar places, of my kind of world again. We received our boarding cards, and I looked around once more for a sight of Gregory, but he was nowhere in sight. It bothered me suddenly, that he had not troubled to say good-bye.

There was a flurry of movement, and we stepped out of the building towards our plane. It was already late in the afternoon, but the heat hit one full in the face like a physical blow, the way it does out there in summer after a prolonged stay in an air-conditioned building. The concrete apron shimmered, braised by the day's sunshine, a great white radiator stretched out in all directions. We had almost reached the plane when an air-hostess, her pretty conventional Lebanese face moist with perspiration approached us as fast as her tight skirt and high heels would allow her. It was me she came up to.

"You are Mr Locke?" she said.

"I am, yes."

"You are wanted, will you follow me, please."

"Now, just a minute," I said, "I've waited a long time to get on this plane . . ."

"The plane will not leave without you, Mr Locke. I understand you are wanted for a few minutes only."

For a brief moment I looked at her warily. There could be many reasons for my being wanted, not all of them pleasant. But her face was foolish and uninformative. I turned reluctantly to follow her, on the alert, seeking assurance in the probability that it was just another case of Middle East muddle. We did not return to the lounge, but made our way through another entrance into a broad corridor. Some ten yards along the air-hostess stopped at a door, knocked lightly, opened it without waiting for an answer and motioned me in.

I found myself in a small office, alone with Gregory. He stood facing me, gaunt and immobile; from the window just behind him a low oblique ray from the setting sun just caught the profile of his face in a thin golden line. I stood riveted by the absurdly romantic picture that he presented.

"Forgive me for delaying still further your departure my dear chap," he said, "but I need your help."

One could almost have supposed that a statue had come to life and spoken.

"Of course," I said.

He took a step towards me, and I noticed then that in his left hand he held the black case that Professor Ricardi had been holding in *his* left hand.

"I had understood you to say that we would by flying out on the same plane," I said.

My voice sounded stilted, as if I had caught something of his own strained and austere manner.

"I have been instructed not to proceed to London," he said.

"I'm sorry, I was looking forward to it."

He nodded slightly.

"As I was, but it has been decided otherwise. So I would ask you to take something to London for me, and to deliver it personally to the man I should have delivered it to. You would be doing me a great service."

"I will certainly do that for you."

He took another step towards me.

"This case," he said, stretching his left arm out. I put my hand out to take the black case but he hesitated, as if reluctant at the last moment to part company with it. I waited, my hand still outstretched.

"Please take great care of it," he said, and handed the case over to me. It was lighter than I had expected.

I smiled at him.

"May I ask whether I shall be embarrassed at the Customs?" I asked lightly.

But he did not smile back.

"No. There are papers and documents inside. The work of a friend of mine, mainly, which will not be of interest to them."

"That's all?" I said.

I had not really intended to ask a question that required a specific answer, but my words had an unhappy effect on Gregory. His hand moved slowly to his crucifix, trembling slightly, and stayed there, clutching the large silver cross. He looked unhappy.

"No," he said quietly, "it's not really all."

It crossed my mind that he would never lie to me, nor to anybody, because truthfulness was one of the corner stones of his creed.

I hesitated, fighting the demon of curiosity.

"What then?" I asked, in spite of myself.

For a long time I thought that he wasn't going to answer me; I even had time to regret my questioning. In the distance I could hear the urgent mounting shriek of jet engines, and I wondered if the plane was mine.

"It contains," he said, suddenly and unexpectedly, "something special as well. I should prefer you not to press me about it, but I assure you that it is of no interest to the customs men."

"I'm sorry. I had not meant to be nosey."

"You might say," he said softly, in the manner of a man talking to himself, "that you will be carrying the Testament of the False Witness."

The words drifted across my mind like wisps of cloud, tenuous, eluding reason. They could mean anything or nothing. A private monastoral joke, an obscure parable, the title of a religious tract. . . .

"Don't tell me you've taken to writing thrillers," I said.

For the first time he smiled, faintly, a mere shadow of what he was capable of.

"A thriller, yes, you could say that. But not written by me."

"We'll leave it at that then, Gregory. Tell me though, have you plans for returning to England, sometime?"

But before he could answer there was a knock at the door and the air-hostess reappeared.

"The plane is about to depart," she said. "You must come now, Mr Locke."

Gregory nodded. From the folds of his cloak he produced a long envelope, a key and a card.

"I should like the case and this letter to be delivered to the address on the envelope, to the man stated. His telephone number is also shown; and it would be better, by the way, if you rang first to make sure that he is in."

I took the envelope and looked at the writing on it. Mgr Wells, followed by an address and a telephone number.

"It's between Westminster Cathedral and Victoria Street," Gregory said.

"I'll find it."

He handed me the key and the card.

"This is for the case, and this is where you can write to me, if you care to. I should like to hear your news, you know."

"I shall certainly write," I said, stretching out my hand.
"God be with you," he said.

★　　　★　　　★

For five hours we flew westwards, chasing the setting
sun, monkeying with time, so that when we reached
London a high bank of cloud was still glowing pink against
the dusk. The lights of the great city were blinking into
life, and above, here and there, the first few stars were
bringing tidings from outer space. But my thoughts
were not with the mysteries of eternity, only with the
immediacy of the future. I was impatient for home-coming. No doubt it was unwise of me to expect to be met by
Louise at London Airport, after all those delays, but that
did not compensate for my disappointment at not finding
her there. I redirected my expectation to the locale of my
flat, and consoled myself with the thought that a reunion in private had much to commend it. But when my
taxi had turned off the Bayswater Road and deposited me
at my block of apartments, and I had opened the front
door, there was no familiar face or voice to greet me. I
switched the hall light on, brought my cases in and shut
the door.

An arrow on the hall mirror, drawn with lipstick,
pointed down to a sheet of writing-paper on top of a
sizeable heap of post. I picked it up.

"I am sorry but I have had to go to see my mother who
is ill in Leeds. Will be back at the office in time for
lunch tomorrow, I hope, unless things are worse than I

have been told. It would be nice to have lunch together, I'm longing to hear about the trip. I've stocked up the larder for you, and there's a new bottle of Scotch. Love, L."

I put the note down. Somewhere in the back of my head a little voice said, maybe she has a sick mother in Leeds.

I picked up my mail and strolled round the flat, switching on lights and drawing curtains, fighting off the threat of desolate thoughts. It was often like that, home-coming, after a mission for the Canfield; by and by little introspective demons would creep up on me, on the sly; demons called silence and solitude, old friends who made a habit of hanging around too long.

I went in search of the whisky, poured myself half a glass, and began to unpack; and every now and then, just to jolly things along, I treated myself to a session of hate therapy against the Canfield. But it was a poor substitute for the extravagant expectations I had been nursing. I sat by the telephone, opened my personal directory and spent a few shillings giving friends the glad tidings that I was back in circulation. I found no one eager to come and have a drink with me at that time of the night, but after half an hour or so my diary had acquired a reassuring busyness.

I sat back in my chair and began to read through six weeks' backlog of mail. Invitations to functions past, 'wish you were here' cards from friends who weren't there any more; circulars, bills. News from people who cared about me, or about the money that I owed them.

The local church clock was striking eleven as I put down the last of my post. I felt tired, yet the prospect of a solitary bed did not tempt me. I put on records and wandered around renewing acquaintance with favoured possessions. An early nineteenth-century ikon picked up in Istanbul on a previous trip, the two original cartoons by Daumier inherited from a favourite uncle, the long shelves of books. And as an alternative to the real thing, the large framed photograph of Louise, with her dark intelligent face, and her long straight black hair.

I picked it up, hesitant, touched by faint but familiar doubts. Discreet suspicions, like soft sighs, which I didn't have to hear, and yet did. "Hello," I said, but she had nothing to say to me. Her dark eyes looked at me, beyond me, through me as if to a private world of her own. They seemed full of tormenting mysteries, of tender half-truths, the way they always did. She would lie in my arms, sometimes, indulgent to the caresses of my mouth and my hands, her cheeks coloured by the ferment of our love-making, and somehow I would be left with the taste of a lie in my mouth.

It was often like that on those occasions when she let me make love to her. Yet, after two years, the thought of her in my bed could still leave me weak at the knees.

I put the photograph down and stood there, idling time, open to any interesting thought that cared to drift my way. But all that came was the recollection, so irrelevant, of an angry German at the Karachi customs who was being accused of smuggling dirty books into the country. He was gross and red in the face and had piggy

eyes; and he looked like a pornographer, and I didn't
care a damn about him; but the thought of him stirred
other memories of the sprawling city, suffocating in the
stagnant heat of summer days; of blue skies and brown
smells, of grey dust on one's clothes, and up one's nostrils
and in the soul of the people; of glistening flies clustered
round children's eyes; of women in veils to hide their
faces and their sadnesses. I thought of the things that I
had done out there, and not done, and done well, and
done badly.

And after a time I fetched my tape-recorder and put it
on my desk, collected my papers and my notebook, filled
up my glass again. I turned over the pages of my notebook and forgot about Louise and the ikon and the
paintings and books. I was back with Gumbar, sweating
it out in his hot humid room, trying to get his electric fan
to work, and wondering why the hell I was there, and
whether I really cared about our conspiracies . . .

"Report of Mission P.A.K. stroke eight two seven
stroke four. Classification: secret, grade B. Distribution:
Hughes only. Dictated by Michael Locke, Twentieth June.

"Part 1. The request for detailed information concerning
Shafei received only one week before the completion of
this mission, necessitated the abandonment of the pro-
gramme originally planned. Shafei's connection with the
Chinese Cultural Mission (C.C.M.) appears to be marginal. The appointment of Mrs L. Khan as a secretary to
C.C.M. has now yielded some interesting information,
but nothing of significance so far as Shafei is concerned.
This information may be summarized as follows . . ."

Chapter 2

THE Canfield Foundation resides in a fine Nash terrace overlooking Regent's Park, a building of cultured elegance for the dissemination of an elegant culture; or so they would have one believe.

Just for looking at, preferably from across the road and framed by the great trees, the Canfield and its sylvan environs can provide a rare visual delight at all seasons. On a November night, say, with the park stilled by autumnal mist and the old-fashioned street lights like so many watery yellow moons, the faintly seen columned façade acquires a haunting beauty, a mysterious backcloth to a world of shadowy melancholia. Once on such a night I passed that way and remembering Verlaine's *grand parc solitaire et glasse* regretted that I too was not a poet. It can get you like that sometimes.

But on the morning after my return to London the Canfield was sparkling handsomely in the sunshine against a clear blue sky. It smiled at the world and I for one was in a mood to smile back. Inside that splendid edifice, however, I have never been moved to write poetry. The patina of patronage, with its litter of expensive good taste, is too obtrusive; and one is discomforted by the material pretensions of an organization which claims concern with so many hungry millions.

I walked across the plush carpeted hall, past an Epstein bronze of Lord Canfield himself, a large Sutherland landscape, and substantial hunk of meat purveyed by Francis Bacon; climbed the fine sweeping staircase with its modern glass chandelier cascading down all four floors; made my way along a corridor on the second floor that had a pale ochre ceiling, and arrived at a figured walnut door with the number 219 in bronze. It was a little journey that I had made many times, and during which I had not infrequently said to myself, 'nevermore'. But 'nevermores' have a tendency to weather badly; they become malleable, somehow, with the passage of time. Or so I have found.

I knocked at the door and walked in. Miss Waterton was sitting behind her desk, a prim middle-aged dragon who had never contributed much to my enjoyment of life. She looked up at me and gave the impression that she didn't particularly like what she saw.

"Ah! Mr Locke," she said. "We were expecting you yesterday you know."

Her voice was brittle and accusing.

"Yes, I know. The plane got in six hours' late last night; it was a somewhat tedious and unsatisfactory journey I'm afraid."

"But you were supposed to arrive the day before, Mr Locke. Mr Hughes had kept the afternoon clear for you and he's a very busy man. He was most put out."

Be tolerant, I told myself, she's unhappy. The wind blows cold round Miss Waterton's soul and moustaches for women aren't in fashion this year. I produced a nice smile for her, for free, without obligation. "They have an inconsequential view of time out there, Miss Waterton," I said cheerfully. "I'm afraid it's rather catching."

But she went on frowning.

"Mr Hughes has someone in with him at the moment, you'll just have to wait."

"I'm in no hurry," I said, "it's on the firm's time."

I sat down in a chair facing her and thought about all the people whom I didn't like up and down that building. All told there are some eighty or so people at the Canfield and all but five or six are engaged in some way or other with the export of British culture, more especially to the so-called underprivileged countries. No doubt these countries would have preferred some wheat, or the odd steel mill, or a boat-load or two of the Pill, but apparently culture is all we can afford to give away nowadays. The top brass at the Canfield appears to have been selected almost entirely from a thin and somewhat eclectic layer of our social and educational strata; the aura of the place is one of well-bred scholarship.

The sour smell that sometimes bruises one's nostrils comes from patronizing condescension, but I don't think they are aware of it. As for the Founders' exhortation 'to establish ideological bridgeheads in the uncommitted countries', this phrase carries a flavour of militant purposefulness that is somewhat alien to their leisurely academic preoccupations. In the cold war for men's minds they are both amateurs and innocents.

The other five or six people at the Canfield wear the same kind of hats and look much the same underneath them, but the resemblance does not go much further than that. They lost their innocence a long time ago and they are nothing if not professional. Seconded either from the F.O. or Special Branch (and as I have never been a party to the inner cabal of British Intelligence the actual set up remains much of a mystery to me), their concern with the ideals of Lord Canfield is purely coincidental. Selected because they carry the same airs and graces as the others, they pursue their own special purposes under cover of a conformity that comes easily to them. And, to a large extent, it is they who pay my milk bills.

Of course, when I first strolled through the portals of the Canfield I too was an innocent, a greenhorn in search of a ladder to climb; for I had only been a lecturer at London University for two years when they asked me to do a short lecture tour in the Middle East. My first book had just been published (*British Policy in the Arabian Gulf, 1919–1959*, not everyone's favourite bedside reading but "a most valuable contribution" according to the *New Statesman*); I was fluent in Arabic and French and adequate in Italian and German; it seemed as if that combination of factors was sufficient compensation for my tender years.

It was some time later, when a second tour was mooted, that a Mr Hughes nobbled me by Lord Canfield's bronze bust in the entrance hall and proposed a spot of lunch. I failed to notice his forked tail at the time. They sold me the pass in penny packets, Mr Hughes and his friends did, until one day I discovered that I'd bought myself the whole deal. Even so, it took me some time to grasp that all of the Canfield was not as it appeared to be, and that they had in mind a bit of extra-curricular work for me, not at all on the official prospectus of that esteemed establishment.

I could do them a service, they said, filling my glass again. Them, and my professional prospects, and my Country, and NATO, and our Western Intellectual Heritage, and my overdraft. No particular order of preference I gathered, it was just that they liked to offer people a decent choice of motives. It was a matter of information, they said; information that I could obtain more easily than their own people in the Embassies; and the Consulates, and the Military Missions and the phony Commercial junketings. They needed better contacts in the Universities, the politico-literary world, in the top academic circles. Friendly contacts, with a few political professors, the odd student leader or so, even with some of the more promising intellectual rabble rousers. East of the Bosphorus, they said, it was in such circles that tomorrow's presidents tended to breed, and tomorrow's dictators and allies and enemies; and there seemed to be a case for sorting them out before tomorrow actually turned up. As a young but already well-known historian and specialist in the Middle East, with all the necessary languages, a gift of the gab, apparently popular in certain circles out there . . . perhaps I could see what they were getting at. They filled my glass up again. They were very courteous and only a bit evasive when I asked questions. Their little outfit at the Canfield was of course a very small affair they pointed out, with a strictly limited range of activities aimed at the Universities and the Cultural hot spots of certain countries. There were only seven other lecturers and specialists at the Canfield engaged on these activities, mostly part time, out of the many score that the Foundation actually sent out every year. It was inevitable, of course, that there had to be at times some contact and collaboration with the more professional side of the . . . er . . . Service. Not that I should suppose that this could involve me with the kind of romantic spy nonsense, ha! ha! that one read in books or saw in films. We all laughed. I would miss the beautiful blondes I said, which had them in fits. They might be able to fix me up with one or two they said, and that really had us rolling in the aisles; and it seemed churlish not to sign the bit of paper with the nonsense about official secrets.

They arranged for me to obtain six weeks' leave of absence from my College and sent me to stay at a fine country house in Bedfordshire (R. Adams, *circa* 1762) where they taught me some of the facts and tricks of their trade. It may not have been quite up to James Bond standard but nevertheless I came out of the place tolerably well equipped to take up any number of anti-social occupations. I went back to teaching of course – though on a more part-time basis – as an academic front was, after all, the whole point of the exercise.

That had been three years ago. And by and by I had been drawn into their shadowy disorientated world with its unkempt moralities and its precarious loyalties. A strange little esoteric world peopled by fugitives from normality, for it seems to me that the conspirator distorts reality with his obsession to deceive; and that in the long

THE MAN WHO WAS THERE

run he deceives no one so much as himself, for it is a way
of life that he comes to serve, rather than a cause or a paymaster.

A phone on Miss Waterton's desk rang, and though
she answered it briskly enough, her voice dropped perceptibly after a moment or two; she looked at me and
said that she would ring back in a few moments. Her
world, like mine in a lesser way, was conditioned by the
concept of secrecy; caution becomes a reflex action, and
most of it is unnecessary and absurd. And yet, with all its
absurdities, it is difficult to escape altogether from the
disturbing fascination that surrounds the whole apparatus
of conspiracy. You play it for kicks at first, tongue in
cheek maybe. You're young, the money's good, you're
seeing how the other half lives. And, of course, you'll
chuck it after a year or two.

And then one day you wake up in some crummy hotel
somewhere down the Gulf, and you lie there naked in the
heat on your bed, and look out on a hot blue sky through
a haze of flies and alien smells and somehow you know
that you're hooked. It tends to happen that way, suddenly,
for no good reason that you can think of.

The phone rang again on Miss Waterton's desk and she
picked it up.

"Mr Hughes will see you now, Mr Locke," she said,
"but he has another appointment in just over half an
hour." She got up, knocked at the door behind her desk
and showed me in. Hughes was waiting to greet me with
his customary courtesy, a tall distinguished looking man
with thinning grey hair, a rugged complexion, and a

smooth line in suits and silk shirts. It surprised some to discover on closer acquaintance that behind the elegance and the almost youthful charm, Hughes was tough and nudging sixty.

Looking him up in *Who's Who*, as I did early in our acquaintance, was like reading a digest of the mores of his class and generation. Son of a Bishop; Winchester, Trinity, Rifle Brigade; C.B., M.C.; Army and Navy Club, Travellers, Saville; fishing, golf and bees. Stir, pour into one of those old-fashioned moulds, and serve on guest night at the Mess with a glass of brandy and Corona. An English gentleman and an officer, one could say that of him, with respect or a sneer, depending on the viewpoint that one took.

"Ah! Locke," he said, striding towards me with his hand outstretched, "good to have you back. Sit down my dear chap . . . take that chair, it's more comfortable . . ." I sat down and accepted a cigarette from him.

"Well now, how was your trip? I gather that the gospel according to Michael Locke was well received in academic circles?"

"I talked, they listened. Nobody actually threw things."

"The paper cuttings and reports that we have received suggest a major success. People here are saying that you have established an enviable reputation out there . . ."

For a while we talked about the official Canfield part of my trip, about attendances at my lectures, University standards, the climate, a variety of topics that he didn't really care about. But I had been away for six weeks and it would have been ill-mannered of him to dispense with these customary preliminaries. So we talked of this and that and the impression grew on me that behind his easy self-assurance there lurked a certain nervousness; just for once the charm seemed mannered.

A few minutes later Miss Waterton appeared with coffee and biscuits on a silver-plated tray. She poured and passed the cups and plates round, a leisurely ritual of some importance to her I suspected, for she was both possessive and protective about her Mr Hughes.

"Thank you, Mary," he said gently as she departed. He sipped his coffee, his little finger stuck out the way actresses used to show duchesses doing it.

"I'm sorry about the sudden change of brief we sent you," he said frowning, "I hope that it didn't create too many difficulties for you."

"Not really," I lied.

He nodded.

"Were you able to get us anything?"

I took the box with the tape out of my pocket and handed it to him.

"I recorded this last night, I think it covers everything that might be of use to you."

He took the box, stared at it for a moment, and put it away in a drawer in his desk.

"Good. Carrington is coming round this afternoon and we'll go through it."

He offered me another cigarette and sat back in his chair.

"Briefly though, anything on Shafei?"

"Not much, I'm afraid. He's involved with the Chinese

Cultural Mission in Karachi, that's confirmed; and there's no doubt that Peking is using the C.C.M. as a base for general penetration in the Middle East. I've got quite a lot on their administrative arrangements, a few new names as well as some old familiar ones. An insight on some balmy Peking thinking, plans for a new Front journal. That kind of thing."

He was shifting a lot in his chair, and I could tell that it wasn't at all the kind of thing that he wanted from me.

"But Shafei himself? What's his role in all this, why is he involved in an outfit like the C.C.M.?"

His eyes were riveted on me, anxious, demanding, wanting something I didn't have.

"I should have thought he was merely advising them," I said, "putting them in touch with men who are prepared to do the donkey work. Gumbar's opinion is that he hasn't been in Karachi more than a couple of times."

"Look, right now I'm not interested in the C.C.M. Just the man himself. Anything you have on the man himself. Like who pays him?"

I stared back at Hughes.

"You mean apart from the Chinese?" I asked cautiously.

"Yes."

I wanted to ask him why the hell he hadn't asked me that kind of question when I was out there, but his politeness was catching. I shook my head.

"We only had six days you know," I said. "Not much time to dig deep."

He sighed slightly and sat back in his chair and blew smoke up towards the ceiling. It was a handsome ceiling, with delicate plasterwork, a heritage from a more elegant age, but right then I doubt if Mr Hughes was admiring it.

"You've met Shafei I believe?" he said.

"A couple of times, at Embassy receptions. And I've heard about him of course over the years."

"What do you make of him?"

I rummaged through my memory and a somewhat shadowy figure emerged.

"A clever man, sophisticated, sure of himself," I ventured. "Very Europeanized, speaks English and French like a native. Could be taken for a rich Arab playboy, Beirut-style."

I glanced at Hughes. It seemed unlikely that he was really interested in my observations about a man whom I hardly knew.

"Let me fill you in a bit, Locke. His father was a French officer in Syria in the late twenties and the thirties. He had his wife at home in France most of the time and he kept a Lebanese woman in Damascus all of the time. A fairly normal kind of set-up amongst French officers serving abroad, I understand. The Arab woman produced him a son and daughter, the son being our friend Shafei. The father was recalled to France just prior to the outbreak of war and brought his offspring with him, the Arab woman having by then died. What the wife thought about it the files don't reveal, but at any rate the whole family escaped to England from Brest in 1940 as the Germans were moving in. Shafei was ten years old at the time and spent the next five years at school in England. Hence his fluency in both English and French. His father was

eventually killed in Normandy in 1945 fighting with
the Free French. In 1946 Shafei left England and as far
as we are concerned vanished into thin air. We have
nothing on him for the next six years."

Hughes stopped talking. He opened a drawer in the
desk, took out a slim file and put it on his desk.

"You will appreciate, of course," he went on, "that
none of these facts was either known to us or of the
slightest interest to our department at the time. All this
information was collected later, much later. In fact Shafei
first came to our notice in the early fifties; our file on him
starts with a brief note dated November fifty-three. Nothing very special about it either, just another hot-head
riding the Arab nationalist bandwagon but apparently
also dabbling in political and military intelligence on the
side."

He opened the file and began flicking through it
casually.

"From then on we begin to bump into him all over the
place. Cairo, Amman, Damascus; even Moscow three
years ago. Smooth, urbane, everybody's friend, always
close to the people that matter."

Hughes was keeping something back of course, I knew
that. One had to wait with Hughes, until he had dealt out
all the cards and was ready to turn up his joker. Sometimes
you could see it up his sleeve all along, and then it was
polite to pretend, but that morning I didn't know what he
was getting at.

"There are a lot of Shafeis in this world," I said, "pedd-
ling information."

"Oh yes, in all colours and shapes, and when you left on your mission six weeks ago I'd just about heard of his name; damn it we've got about five hundred files like his."

"So?"

"He's in a class of his own now. Special, quite special."

I waited.

"He's special for three reasons. Firstly, he doesn't peddle as you've put it. He buys, buys every time. No sales, no exchanges, just information, bought, for cash. Every single record we have of a Shafei deal is in the same direction, a purchase, whether it's political information or military or economic. Sometimes he pays a lot of money. So much money that he has to be Government backed."

"Is that so special? After all, we're Government backed."

"Right. But we know which Government, and that's the second odd thing about Shafei. With all the stuff we have on him, nobody knows who he works for or who provides the money. Three years ago he was hobnobbing in the Kremlin, now you tell me he's helping to disseminate Chairman Mao's thoughts. Mortensen is convinced that he's a U.A.R. man. The F.O. says it's Saudi. No fixed loyalties and no proven paymaster, it bothers me, Locke."

"I shouldn't have thought there were so many paymasters to choose from. Half a dozen Arab countries, Moscow, Peking. I presume we can discount London and Washington."

But he wasn't in the mood for that kind of humour.

"The third reason why Shafei is special," he said quietly, "puts the other two in the shade."

He took a loose sheet of paper from the file and stared at it.

"Some two weeks ago, in Cairo, an American agent picked up an item of information and in due course it was passed on to us. It was so improbable that no one here took it seriously; but within forty-eight hours the same tit-bit came in from two independent sources, one backed by documentation, and both totally reliable."

He put the piece of paper back in the file, closed it and leaned back in his chair.

"A certain merchant in Beirut, one Ahmed Hamid, not unknown to us I may add, was approached by a friend who wished to purchase something. The price of that something was ten million dollars. American."

I lit a cigarette. As jokers went it was good, very good. Worth waiting for, I thought.

"And the man with the millions burning a hole in his pocket is Shafei?" I said.

"The man is Shafei, but what is he buying and whose money is he buying it with?"

I stared at him.

"Perhaps I'm being naïve, but why not ask Hamid?"

"Because Hamid doesn't know. He wasn't told. Nor were the other two people who have since let it be known to us that they, too, were offered ten million dollars. Ten million for what they asked, understandably. If you don't know you haven't got it, they were told."

"That's what Shafei said? No explanations?"

"Just that. If you've got it, I'll pay. Some think it's a joke, but you can take it from me that Shafei wouldn't waste either his time or his reputation on that kind of unfunny joke."

"So what's it all about?"

"You tell me, Locke."

It wasn't a question I could be expected to answer so I let it drift and allowed myself to be beguiled by the thought of ten million dollars. American. Too much, really, too big a feast, just for one man with just one life – time to indulge, even if he did have what Mr Shafei wanted to buy. Or maybe there were dreams to be bought for ten million, swollen purple dreams. . . .

"We had hoped that you might have picked up some kind of clue with the C.C.M.," Hughes said rather sharply.

I thought back at what I knew of Shafei, but somehow I couldn't see the man for dollars.

"The C.C.M. budget runs to about twenty thousands per annum," I said, "which hardly puts it in the same league. Not that that proves anything of course, if Peking wanted something all that much. But for what it's worth Gumbar doesn't believe that Shafei has been in Karachi for some weeks, and certainly there's been nothing about that kind of deal."

Hughes nodded.

"One further question," I said, "was your Mr Hamid being asked to sell information or a physical object?"

"My dear chap, it's faintly possible that the top scientist

in the United States or Russia might have information worth a few millions, but hardly a small-time trader in Beirut. What's the most you've ever been asked to pay for information East of Suez?"

I smiled at the recollection.

"One hundred and fifty Kuwaiti dinars," I said, "and it wasn't worth it."

Hughes sighed.

"The money was for an object, or objects, capable of being delivered by hand," he said. "That's all we know. From one unimportant Arab trader to another. For ten million dollars."

He frowned and stroked his chin.

"It may seem odd to you," he said reflectively, "but no one has yet ventured a plausible guess as to what it is that a man can carry about with him that could be worth ten million dollars."

"Not as odd as trying to buy something without saying what it is you want. Something stolen?"

"It's been suggested, yes, for even the fat Beirut merchants are unlikely to have a single object of that value; not without a lot of people knowing about it. And it would explain the secrecy, the 'you would know if you had it' line."

One of the three phones on his desk rang and he picked it up. He had his face half turned from me and I could see a nerve twitching on his cheek just above the mouth; he looked tired. He said 'yes' twice into the phone, put it down and turned to me.

"I have some people waiting to see me, Locke, but

there's one fact that I think I should tell you at this stage. It has seemed reasonable to us to assume that this business is connected in some way with the Arab–Israel balance of power. In the Middle East almost nothing else could explain away such a sum of money, in such circumstances. The Americans are afraid that it's military and that it's coming from Peking. As I said before that's a guess, and in my view not a convincing one, if as it seems Shafei is on the Peking pay-roll. But they say their Moscow hot line is reliable enough to leave the Russians out of anything really sinister, and so far nobody has come up with a better idea."

He stubbed his cigarette out and glanced at his watch.

"The point I'm making is that a lot of people have been concerned in this matter, at a high level. And because one of the few positive links with Shafei is the C.C.M., I'm afraid you're going to be involved rather more than has been our practice."

He looked at me solemnly but I wasn't prepared to offer him more than a faint nod.

"A meeting has been fixed for Friday morning ten o'clock," he said, "at Birdcage Walk, the usual room. Mortensen will be back from Cairo by then. All right?"

"Yes."

"We will have gone through your report, but I may wish to be in touch with you before the meeting. I take it you'll be around?"

"I will be, yes."

"Plans for summer leave?"

I thought about summer leave. I thought of Louise, of

cicadas making their crinkling music, and olive trees and cheap wine and games of boule being played in dusty market-places. A man needs to put on his rose-coloured glasses once in a while.

"I'm not sure," I said after a while, "I might drive through France, not too late in July perhaps, for a couple of weeks or so. Two or three days in Paris; there's some stuff I have to check for my new book."

Hughes smiled.

"That sounds very pleasant. You'll let Miss Waterton know the date of course, when you've decided that is."

He got up and made his way round his desk towards me.

"You know, Locke," he said, quietly, "I'm glad your work for us hasn't prevented you from pursuing your real interests. I mean your teaching and your writing. Perhaps it will encourage you to stay with us."

He looked at me quizzically. Twice that year I had tried to resign and allowed myself to be talked out of it; perhaps I hadn't been really trying.

"I shall carry on for a while yet, I suppose," I said amiably from the top of my fence.

"Good. Tell me, what is this latest book of yours?"

"The conflict of Anglo-French interests in the Eastern Mediterranean between the Wars. We rather hated each other's guts, you know, out there."

He nodded.

"Indeed, I remember. I did a spell in Palestine as a young captain, you know. My lord, it seems a long time now. The days of Empire and Imperial Fleets. It was something to be an Englishman in those days, a man could be proud . . ."

He sighed, walked over to the door and opened it.

"You know, we must take time off together sometime and talk about your work. I'd very much like that."

We shook hands.

"That would be nice," I said.

We often said things like that to each other, and I think we both meant them. Yet I had never met Hughes outside the line of duty.

Chapter 3

I LEFT Hughes's office and sat myself opposite Miss Waterton again and argued about the expenses claim that I had just presented to her. Money was a familiar subject of dispute between us, but then it didn't take much to re-kindle our mutual dislike for each other. Just meeting was usually sufficient.

On her side I believe that this antipathy stemmed from mistrust. Her attitude to the Department and to her superiors, especially Hughes, was one of devoted loyalty; and there was about twenty-five years of it behind her. A quarter of a century of service in and out of the corridors of power, but without the power. You had to be solemn about a thing like that; all those years of tea and biscuits for Mr Hughes, of duty to that same tight little in-group of civil servants. You couldn't joke about it. But in my early days at the Canfield I had made jokes about the job, and the people, and the files; I had, once or twice, and in front of her, adopted a cavalier attitude about matters which she took seriously. She hadn't liked that, nor the freedom of action, and non-action, available to myself and the other part-timers. Seen through her anxious watery but professional eyes I think she saw us all as untrustworthy amateurs.

But probably my worst offence had been to speak disparagingly, on occasion, about our brown-skinned brothers; for I discovered later that she espoused the English romantic view of the Arab and his desert lands. She nourished her lonely yearning soul, it seemed, on a heady diet of Lady Hester Stanhope, Lawrence, Freya Starke, Philby and the rest, and had apparently been seduced by her own fanciful visions of the world they described. She actually used phrases like 'the noble Arab'. But then, we are all duped by our dreams somewhere along the line.

"I cannot pass an item of eighty pounds for 'Private Payments', Mr Locke," she said severely, "unless it is properly substantiated."

"It is not normal, I must assure you Miss Waterton, to ask for a receipt when you are bribing an illiterate Karachi cab driver or the chambermaid in your hotel."

"That's as may be, but I have no means of knowing that the money was in fact spent that way. After all, this is the taxpayers' money . . ."

"May I suggest that the matter is referred to Mr Collins or to Mr Hughes himself."

She produced a haughty look.

"Mr Hughes has enough to worry about right now, without being bothered about such things as your expenses."

"Well, that's up to you, Miss Waterton."

I looked at my watch and discovered that it was twelve o'clock. Time to make my way to another part of the building, and my irritation evaporated just at the thought of it.

"I've supplied you with all the receipts that I was able to obtain," I said getting up, "and the rest you will have to take on trust I'm afraid."

She half opened her mouth, to say something indignant no doubt, but I had left the room before she managed to put words to her anger.

I can get from Hughes's office to Louise's in eighty-one strides, including twenty-four steps up the stairs. I counted them once, in one of my more besotted moments. I had met Louise some twenty months or so earlier, soon after she had joined the Canfield to run their Advanced Publicity Department, on the 'official' side. Mrs Poulson, as I then knew her, was thirty years of age, only recently divorced, and to my way of thinking beautiful, though not in an English way. Her skin had that soft tanned colour, like pale teak, which people seem to acquire from skiing in the sun. Her eyes, seen in a certain light, were almost as dark as her long straight black hair. Her nose was straight and fine, Greek classical; but there the Hellenic resemblance ended for her figure was modern, long limbed, slim waisted and slight. St Trop. style. In the Canfield hot-house of Oxbridge blue-stocking culture she was like a rare exotic flower.

Our reunion in her office was constrained by the presence of her secretary, fussing at her filing cabinet. I suffered ten minutes of polite talk about my journeyings, and the secretary took her time. Time enough for me to wonder again at the limpid sensuality of Louise's body, to be hypnotized again by the rippling rhythm of her hair when she moved her head; time enough, certainly for profligate thoughts. When at last the secretary had completed her filing and left us, I stood with my back to the door and we looked at each other. She sat on her desk facing me, her legs crossed, and lit a cigarette.

"Well?" I said.

She blew smoke towards me.

"You've lost weight," she said.

"It's not the welcome I had been hoping for."

"No?"

I shook my head and her left eyebrow moved up perceptibly.

"Flags and bunting?" she said, "ticker-tape motorcade?"

"*Je songe á la douceur*," I said.

She went on staring at me.

"*Tu songe trop mon cher*," she said, "try coming down to earth." But she stubbed her cigarette out and stood up. I put a hand out towards her. After a moment she came to me, a faint Mona Lisa smile about her lips. She let me draw her to me. I kissed her softly, then greedily, forcing her mouth open, indulging pleasures too long denied. I clung to her, unwilling to surrender the voluptuous taste of her mouth. For now at last, after all those empty weeks, I was no longer at the mercy of well thumbed memories and sterile fantasies.

She prised me away.

"I don't have to ask whether you are well, my dear," she said, sweetly, "you are obviously in rude good health."

"I've been rotten until about a minute ago."

She laughed lightly, a pleasant sound, and released her hand from mine.

"Tell me about it. You sounded so sorry for yourself in your letters."

"I only received two letters from you," I said, "about office gossip and the weather mostly."

She half turned her back to me, produced a lipstick and a mirror and began repairing her mouth.

"That wasn't kind," I said.

"Tell me about your trip to Kashmir," she said.

"For six weeks I lived in a great wilderness, a monstrous solitude, and only the postman could bring me solace, but he rarely came. That is why I've lost weight. I was emotionally starved. And you should be brimful with remorse, eager to make amends. Are you?"

I walked up behind her.

"We could have lunch at The George," she said, staring at the reflection of her face, "I have to be back not too late."

I put my hands round her and cupped her breasts and pulled her up against me.

"Busy this afternoon?" I whispered into her hair.

"Until six o'clock at least," she said, putting the mirror back into her bag.

"Pity. And this evening?"

She removed my hands and turned to face me.

"Maybe. What had you in mind?"

"Dinner, soft lights and sweet music. Seduction. Something on those lines."

She turned away and walked back to her desk.

"You have already seduced me, had you forgotten?"

She sat on her desk, and crossed her legs again and moved a strand of hair away from her cheek.

"We could pretend," I said. "It might be fun. It would put me on my mettle and you could . . ."

"You can call for me at eight, if you wish to take me out to dinner."

We stared at each other.

"You're so beautiful, I'd almost forgotten," I said, "*La femme au corps divin, promettant le bonheur.*" I stretched out a hand but she shook her head slightly.

"Let's go, Mike, I feel in need of a drink," she said.

I had envisaged a couple of leisurely hours or so together; an aperitif somewhere, a civilized lunch, a walk in the park; indolent time shared again with Louise, hand in hand in the dappled shade of trees on a hot summer's day. Real living, nice. But she had a meeting at two o'clock and it took a long time getting served at lunch, so I made the best of a crowded restaurant and a companion who had the gift – when she wished to dispense it – of making a man feel pleased with the sound of his own voice; or the colour of his tie for that matter, or the way he parted his hair, or anything. We ate, I talked, she listened, and it seemed sufficient for the time being just to be with her, coasting along on the swell of more ambitious expectations. We finished our meal and I walked her back to the Canfield. We stood for a moment or two in front of the building.

"I thought that we might dine at Marcel's this evening," I said. "For old times' sake."

"How lovely. I have a new dress that I shall wear for the occasion. And, by the way, there's a new Japanese film in the late night show at the Roxy; it's had rave reviews. It starts at eleven, we'd have lots of time."

She smiled too deliberately, with too much self-assurance.

"I hadn't thought of us going to the cinema after dinner," I said. She looked at me, her expression now quite neutral. I waited for her to say something. A little spiky barrier of silence grew between us.

She wrinkled her nose slightly and turned on her heels.

I watched her up the steps and through the entrance doors and she never looked back. I went on standing there. I sighed, saddened by incomprehension. She came and went, my Louise, a dancing star in a dark mysterious firmament of her own making.

The Australians were batting at Lord's in the Second Test and I bought an afternoon paper to see how the old enemy was faring. 'England Hammered' the headline said, but it was a smaller heading on the botton of the front page that held my attention . . .

'Famous Archaeologist Dead'

Professor Gino Ricardi, the well-known Italian Archaeologist, was found dead this morning in his hotel room in Beirut. A statement issued by the police said that the Professor appeared to have been killed the previous evening by an intruder thought to be a thief. Investigations are proceeding. For some years Professor Ricardi has been leading a joint Israeli-Italian team in Israel and there have recently been unofficial reports of some remarkable finds. Professor Ricardi was 63, and an authority on early Christian writings – Reuter.

I read the paragraph a second time without managing to squeeze anything more out of it and turned to the Stop Press. It informed me that the Australians had lost another wicket, but had nothing to add on Ricardi. I abandoned my half-formed project of going to Lord's, hailed a passing taxi, and went home.

The letter and the key that Gregory Swain had given me in Beirut I had put in my desk. I routed them out and dialled the telephone number on the envelope. It rang for a couple of minutes without anyone answering it, so I checked the number and tried again. But no one answered it that time either.

I put the phone down and sat there at my desk and tried to sort out a few relevant memories and facts; of a tall gaunt priest for instance, who talked in riddles and appeared to be all knotted up with some inner agony; of an ebullient fat Italian professor who clung to a fancy black suitcase as if his life depended on it. And maybe his life had depended on it, only it didn't matter any more, not to him. I went into my bedroom, took the black suitcase out of my wardrobe, put it on the bed, sat down beside it, and looked at it.

At the best of times I am not an enthusiast for 'coincidences'. It seems to me that they invite an irrational view of life, and I prefer to think that behind most so-called coincidences there is a progression of causes, a logic of inevitability, and if one cares to pursue the matter, a challenge to rational inquiry. I looked at the black suitcase and felt disinclined to shrug off its being there as a mere coincidence. So I took the key that Gregory had given me and trampled over a few outmoded scruples about the moralities of prying into a friend's personal belongings, and opened the case.

There were two things in it. A bundle of five quarto-sized notebooks, with hard covers, held all together by a thick rubber band; and a faded green metal box that looked as if it had seen better days. The name G. L. RI-CARDI painted in white capitals proclaimed the ownership of the box, if a dead man can be said to own anything beyond his solitude. I picked up the notebooks, slipped off the rubber band, and placed the top one on my lap.

On the cover the words BETH SHE'ARIM, POSTO 'C' were stencilled in black, and underneath that, in the same manner, TOMBA IV. The notebook itself consisted of forty-six pages of closely written notes in separately dated sections, and interspersed with frequent drawings and notations. Most of the writing was in Italian, but a few short sections were written in Hebrew.

All the remaining notebooks turned out to have the same main heading of BETH SHE'ARIM: the sub-heading of the second notebook was also TOMBA IV but was only two-thirds complete; the third and fourth notebooks were sub-headed TOMBA VII and TOMBA

VIII respectively, and the last one was sub-headed RIASSUNTO (Summary). It didn't take me long to establish that these notebooks were Ricardi's personal diary of excavations in Israel; that they covered a period of over three years; and that they were concerned with the site of a small necropolis dating back to the first century A.D. The occasional technical word in Italian had me guessing, and the Hebrew passages were of course beyond me, yet within minutes I had become totally absorbed.

The notebooks had, in the first place, a remarkable aesthetic quality about them, with an elegant well-mannered script and exquisite little sketches, all very precisely annotated. Aesthetic sensitivity is not, alas, a commonplace with historians, yet it gave one pleasure merely to look at Ricardi's diaries. But it was the literary style and its evocative imagery that led me to read through one book after the other; for what might have been merely a prosaic catalogue of archaeological finds turned out to be a book of revelation; a literary document full of vivid phrases that brought out ghosts from the past and made them live again. The hard facts of the professional were all there of course, the itinerary of history's left-overs, the pots, the clay tablets, the coins and trinkets, the fragments of this and that; numbered, codified, measured, classified; yet somehow the old man had illuminated mere facts with the penetrating and perceptive light of a poet's insight and wonder. And somewhere in his RIASSUNTO he had written the sentence, "I have seen rainbows in the dust of history." If men need epitaphs then I thought that would do for Gino Ricardi. It was in the RIASSUNTO book also that his imagination had, it seemed to me, begun to betray his historian's respect for the evidence at his disposal; that he began using his evidence as a launching pad for strange feverish speculations.

On the very last page of the RIASSUNTO, dated only three weeks back, he had written and underlined a single final short paragraph.

"Tomorrow we shall know. But if the choice is between Faith and Reason, what then?"

The choice between Faith and Reason. I repeated the words aloud, savouring the echo of some medieval dialogue, and the feeling grew on me that there was something distinctly odd about that last book of the old professor. I flicked back through the pages in search of clues to that cryptic final observation, but I could only find oblique references to some papers described in a notebook entitled GENIZA (APOCRYPHA), which I had already established was not in the collection in front of me. The word Geniza* had me fooled, but amongst a host of names that cropped up in the RIASSUNTO were those of the Procurator Coponius, the Essenes and Sadducees, and several cross references to the writings of Flavian Josephus. The central theme of the GENIZA book, however, appeared to be concerned with the Zadokite sect and documents referred to as "the so-called commentary of Zadok!" Professor Ricardi didn't like the Zadokites. The Orator of Falsehood he had written at one point,

*A secret place for the storage of writings not accepted as Canonical.

but without the original notebook the comments in the
RIASSUNTO didn't make all that much sense.

When I had finished reading the notebooks I put the
elastic band round them again and returned them to the
suitcase. It was five o'clock, and I had spent more than
two and a half hours with them. I went to the kitchen
and put the kettle on, but my thoughts remained with
Ricardi's post-mortem of the old necropolis. I had come
to feel in myself some of the fervour that had so obviously
sustained him for nearly three years.

Yet the real reason for that passion of his had eluded me.
There had to be something else, in the missing GENIZA
book perhaps, or even elsewhere. The record of those
relatively ordinary finds as described in the TOMBA
books was not sufficient to explain the emotions that had
gripped him. At some time, somewhere in that necropolis, Ricardi must have come across something really
significant, something very particular. Something that
had perhaps cost him his life?

I made myself a cup of tea, returned to the bedroom,
and took the green box out of the suitcase. On the side
of the box a small key was held in position by a strip of
sticky tape. I removed it and opened the box. Inside the
box I saw, and removed, a single brown-paper parcel
neatly tied up with string, and about eighteen inches long,
a foot wide, and some three inches thick. The knots gave
me trouble, but I took my time as I intended putting the
parcel back as I had found it, after examining the contents. I carefully unwrapped the brown paper.

The parcel contained twenty-six composite sheets.

In each one a page of parchment (or something that looked like parchment) was sandwiched between two thin sheets of a transparent material which I took to be perspex. The two sheets of perspex had been welded along all four edges, so that the parchment was totally protected from external contact.

In eighteen cases the pages of parchment were more or less intact and undamaged; four had parts missing, mostly at the corner; three were more seriously damaged with up to half a page missing; the twenty-sixth plate consisted only of a few isolated fragments mounted on a white card.

All the sheets were covered in faded Hebrew script, in some cases so faint as to be barely discernible. I picked them up and put them down again, one after the other, curious, regretful that through my ignorance their secrets remained inviolate. For I was in the mood to believe that they contained the clue to Ricardi's impassioned speculation and to Gregory's agitation in the airport lounge at Beirut. I wrapped the twenty-six sheets up again, and put them into my own briefcase.

It was now almost a quarter to six. I picked up the phone and dialled the number of one Robert Payne, photographer, and friend. A good friend, good enough to say that although he'd closed shop he'd open it again just for the pleasure of seeing my lousy face after all these months. Ten minutes then I said; time to get the glasses set up, he said. I picked up my briefcase and set out for Praed Street.

Friendship carries its own special penalties, not least

when one is in a hurry. Beer was Robert Payne's tipple, and talk his vice. It took some time before I was able to get down to business, four bottles of pale ale and a brief survey of our respective lives, going back several months. But he was interested enough when I eventually got round to showing him the twenty-six plates. Interested and not too pressing for hard facts about them.

"It's a question of time," I said, "I need them damned urgently."

"Sure, that's what they all say."

"One of each."

"Size?"

"Same size as the originals."

"It will mean blowing them up. I'll be using smaller plates. Twenty-six separate operations. Time and money, old son."

"Tomorrow evening?"

"Oh brother, you've no idea have you? Monday morning, and believe me I'll really be doing you a favour."

I considered Monday.

"Could you do any of them by Saturday?"

"I suppose so. Half a dozen, say."

"Right, I'll settle for that. Take six roughly from the middle in sequence; they're numbered as you see on the right-hand corner of the perspex."

I drank the rest of my beer. Two days to wait, and as long as I went on getting no reply from Monsignor Welles's number it didn't matter how long I kept Gregory's case. Alternatively I could be too busy to ring him, just for forty-eight hours.

"You're sure about Saturday?" I said.

"Sure I'm sure. Drop in just before I close at one o'clock and we can knock back a few at The Feathers before I go home for lunch."

I got up.

"O.K. You'll be careful, eh?"

"Careful, how?"

"With those papers. They're not mine and they could be precious."

★   ★   ★

I picked up Louise at eight and took her to Chez Marcel, and she seemed willing enough to be nudged into a sentimental frame of mind. Certainly we were subjected to a number of appropriate cliché-ridden situations; the friendly recognition of waiters at a favourite restaurant, the underlit corner table for two, a faintly ostentatious order for a bottle of champagne; good moments in any novelette.

Louise had brought with her her large grey handbag, an outsize in large handbags. I was very fond of that handbag and didn't see enough of it; for it signified that she intended to spend the night with me. I have never checked to see whether the handbag is an accredited sex symbol in the psycho-analysts' book of words, but for me that jumbo size bag was a promise of good things to come.

So we dined and talked, honeyed words and whispered extravagances, time laced with expectancy for she had never looked more beautiful, nor more desirable. I had brought my home-coming present with me wrapped in a large box that had provoked her curiosity, but I made her wait until we were having our coffee and brandy. It was a necklace made up of two rows of russet amber set in silver, which I had bought in Lahore. She took it out of the velvet-lined box and for a moment or two just looked at it without saying anything. Then she gave it to me, and bent her head towards me for me to put it round her neck. I fixed the clasp and she sat back for me to admire it. The stones and her eyes glowed faintly in the candle-light.

The night was warm, and when we left the restaurant I drove home the long way, through Hyde Park, with the hood down and her long black hair streaming away behind her.

Chapter 4

IT was eight o'clock in the morning. I had brought two mugs of coffee to bed and roused an unwilling Louise from her sleep. She had sat up frowning and silent and a bit wild looking, and held the mug in both hands, sipping every now and then. And after a few minutes she had handed it back to me half drunk and slumped down again.

I liked the lazy sensuality of those rare mornings when I woke to find Louise by my side. The warm scent of her body filled the bed and I could watch her sleeping face at my leisure, and maybe trace the line of her mouth or cheek with my finger-tip; or just lie there and indulge myself with agreeable thoughts. And there was a make-believe of domesticity about those mornings together, and I liked that, too. So I sat by her side, propped up by my pillow, and drank my coffee and pursued the not unpleasant fantasy of life with Louise.

The newspaper dropped through the letter-box and it broke the thread. Daydreams don't mix all that well with the world outside, and the world outside was on my doormat. Unsolicited worries filtered in and after a while they began to crowd me. There were things I wanted to know, curiosity that fed on speculation. I felt around for my slippers. Louise stirred.

"What time is it?" she murmured indistinctly.

"Gone eight. I'm going to fry some eggs and bacon. Want any?"

She shook her head. Her long black hair made patterns all over the pillow.

"Toast, anything?"

"Nothing."

I walked to the living-room and into the hall and collected my *Times* from the mat. I walked back slowly to the living-room, skimming over the front page.

"Any world-shattering events?" Louise said lazily. I glanced at her through the bedroom door and saw a solitary eye staring sleepily at me.

"Nothing much. I'm looking for details concerning the death of a man I met in Beirut."

Louise groaned.

"Lord, what a way to start the day!"

"Professor Ricardi; heard of him?"

"No," she said, after a long pause. "Should I?"

"Perhaps, if you're interested in archaeology."

"Tell me about him." She sounded alert, as if she really cared; I wondered why.

"I barely knew him."

The death of Ricardi was reported on an inside page. It confirmed that he had been murdered, shot by a revolver bullet through the heart; but the intriguing new aspect of the affair was contained in a statement issued by the Israeli Government. This said that the Israeli police had been looking for the professor for several days prior to his death, in connection with the disappearance of

historical documents that belonged to the State. Until then
Ricardi had been at his post in charge of the excavations
at Beth She'arim. In a brief comment on the man and his
work *The Times* archaeological correspondent referred to
recent rumours concerning discoveries of exceptional
significance. On the obituary page the professor rated over
half a column and a photograph that must have been
taken twenty years back. I read all there was to read to
Louise and went into the kitchen, leaving the door between us open.

"How did you meet him then?" Louise said.

I set about making myself my usual breakfast and told
her about my meeting with Gregory Swain and the black
suitcase that he had given me; and half-way through I began to wish that I'd kept my mouth shut. I saw her sit up,
wide awake now; her interest in Ricardi surprised me.

I faded the story out with my departure from Beirut.

"And?" she said.

"And what?"

"Well, for heaven's sake, what did you find in the suitcase?"

I brought my breakfast tray into the living-room and
sat down at the table facing her through the open doorway.

"I didn't find anything. Not being my suitcase, I didn't
look."

I'm not sure why I lied to Louise at that point, having
already told her so much. Delayed action caution perhaps,
or just that telling her lies about what I did had become a
habit.

"Have you delivered the suitcase to this Wells man?" she asked.

"No, not yet." I knew what was on her mind and wondered how blatant she would be.

She picked up her hairbrush from the bedside table and began to brush her hair with long slow movements. I watched her, captivated by the fluid rhythm of her naked brown arm, and the faintly seen up and down movement of a nipple through her nightdress.

"You've still got the case here then?" she said.

"Yes."

I poured some coffee and smiled at her and waited for the inevitable. About ten seconds.

"Let's look then, as you have the key," she said.

I counted another ten seconds, silently.

"I've made a fresh pot of coffee, would you like some?" I said.

She shook her head.

"Have you no curiosity?" she said.

I went on eating.

"Curiosity or noseyness?" I said, between mouthfuls.

"In view of Ricardi's death and everything the papers say I think you should look. It could be very important."

I sighed, wondering what the devil had got into her.

"Louise, my love, it's not my suitcase. It belongs to a very old friend of mine, a priest who can in no way be concerned with murders or thefts or anything improper. It's private and important, certainly, to him. And it's in my trust."

It didn't sound convincing, the fate of most hypocritical cant. Louise put a cigarette to her mouth and looked at me. I walked over and lit it with my lighter.

"Show me all the same," she said. "I'm unashamedly curious."

I turned away from the big black eyes and the soft mouth and the touch of her hand, and felt stronger at a distance.

"No," I said, and began to put the breakfast things back on the tray.

"You said the suitcase belonged to Ricardi, so why bring Brother Gregory into it?" Her voice had become unfriendly. "Besides, it could have been opened by any Tom, Dick or Harry at Customs," she persisted, "so why not, tell me?"

"Again," I sighed.

"You've opened it, haven't you, Mike? You've looked, you know what's inside, don't you?"

There was something out of character with her determination. Her eyes were fixed on me and they were cold and I could sense the Louise-type bitchiness building up. It was early in the morning but I reckoned that the best part of the day was over. "I'm going to wash," I said. I carried the tray to the kitchen and went to the bathroom.

I had a shower and shaved and griped to myself about Louise. It seemed as if she had to get bloody-minded with me every now and then, for her own obscure private reasons. It was typical of the kind of complication that she went in for, like refusing to live with me, and rationing sex as if there were a war on, and behaving emotionally like a yo-yo. It could get tiresome. I finished washing and returned to the bedroom feeling belligerent.

Louise was sitting on the side of the bed, dressed. The black suitcase was open in front of her, with the key that I had put in my desk drawer in one of the locks. The Ricardi notebooks were scattered about the bed and in her right hand she held the empty green metal box. She stood up and faced me.

"I'm sorry," she said, "but I had to make sure. Where are the pages of script?"

I stared at her blankly. The anger in me was suddenly submerged by stupefying incomprehension.

"They were in this box, I presume," she said. "What's happened to them?"

I struggled to work out and understand the implications of what she was saying. But it had come too quickly, too unexpectedly. I needed time and I clutched at the nearest time-wasting device.

"My dear Louise, what the hell are you talking about?" I said, dredging up a smile.

She walked towards me, up to me.

"I want to know what has happened to those pages Mike, please." Her face was taut but a note of pleading had softened her voice.

"Why did you open that case?" I said.

She shook her head impatiently, dismissing the futility of my question.

"They were in this case, weren't they? Tell me."

"You'll have to explain what you're asking me for. And why?"

"Mike, we don't have to pretend about what was in that case. What matters now is where they are, and what is going to happen to them. I'm asking you to tell me."

I tried hard to conjure up some explanation, a link, any improbable crazy connection between Louise and Gregory Swain. To see some sense in it. But I didn't have my crystal ball with me.

"And I'm asking you to tell me how you know about the contents of Ricardi's suitcase," I said.

She shook her head slightly again and frowned, and turned away from me. She went back to the bed and picked up her handbag and took out another cigarette.

"You haven't given them to Monsignor Wells, have you?" she asked.

I hesitated fractionally.

"I told you, he wasn't there when I rang him."

I walked over to her and put out my hand to her arm.

"Louise," I said softly, "why can't you tell me what this is all about?"

She drew hard on her cigarette.

"Those twenty-six pages," she said, "don't belong either to your friend Swain or to the man Wells."

"Are you saying this because of the Israeli news item, or because you know something apart from that?"

"Because I know that those documents are totally unique and precious and that they should be in the possession of people who understand about such things."

I let go of her arm and walked slowly towards the window and stood there looking out. I thought hard but no kind of an explanation seemed to be available.

"How do you know all this, Louise?" I said.

An invisible plane was defacing the clear sky with a long white streak. I watched it and waited for an answer to my question, but none came. After a long time, she said, "Don't let Monsignor Wells get those papers, Mike."

The white line in the sky was pushing its way slowly beyond the roof tops. I went on labouring in search of plausibility.

"I'll write to Gregory before I do anything," I said.

"Mike," she said, "either of those two men will destroy those documents. That's why they want them, so that they can be destroyed."

I floundered again, defeated anew by the implications of her words.

"For God's sake why should they want to do that?"

She turned away from me suddenly.

"Because they do, that's all. Can't you just believe what I'm telling you instead of asking all these questions?"

Frustration is a rich breeding ground for anger and I was beginning to feel very frustrated.

"Believe what?" I shouted at her back. "That a man like Gregory would steal a lot of archaeological papers just so that he could destroy them? Why the hell should I believe you?" But all the time I was aware that my irritation was misplaced. The essential fact was, inexplicable though it might remain to me, that Louise knew about the missing pages. And if she knew that much then she probably knew what they were and why they were wanted.

Louise sighed and looked at her watch.

"I can't tell you all that you want to know," she said. "Mostly that's because I don't know myself. I'm not playing hard to get, Mike. I can only say that these papers are what I've said they are, that certain people want to destroy them, that they should be returned to their rightful owners. That it matters very much. But there are others who do know. I will arrange for someone to get in touch with you this evening, someone who knows much more about it than I do and should be able to explain everything to you. I ask you only one thing Mike, not to do anything with these documents until you have heard from him. Don't give them to anyone; will you promise me that at least?"

She looked at me, earnest and anxious and appealing. I had a sudden wish to earn her gratitude, on the cheap, quickly. "If it will make you happy," I said, "I shall be at a meeting all day and I'll wait until I hear from your friend this evening before I do anything about the papers."

She smiled and picked up her bag.

"I'm going to be late for the office," she said.

I accompanied her to the front door, my hand on her arm, and the remnants of my sudden anger melted finally under the touch of her warm skin. We stood at the door facing each other and I sought reassurance in her face.

"When shall I see you again?" I said.

She gave a faint shrug of her shoulders.

"I don't know."

"It was marvellous having you here," I said, trying to spread a bit of enthusiasm around.

But her beautiful eyes remained grave and evasive.

"I'll ring you tomorrow," she said, "to find out what you have decided about the papers."

"Maybe we could go to see that Japanese film of yours. Monday evening say?"

"Perhaps. I'll ring you tomorrow anyway. I must go now, Mike."

I kissed her on the mouth, but neither of us got much out of it.

On the landing outside we waited together for the lift, and I mourned for the passion that had so recently united us.

"This man who will be ringing you," she said, "his name will be Nassim. He will probably want to come up and see you."

"Yes," I said, but I didn't care.

The lift came, the doors opened. Louise turned abruptly and kissed me fleetingly on the cheek.

"Thanks," she said, "it's been lovely."

The doors closed behind her, leaving me with the faint scent of Miss Dior for company.

I had an hour to dispose of before leaving for the meeting at Birdcage Walk. I kept telling myself that I should have shaken the truth out of Louise; but after a while I stopped trying to solve a puzzle of which I didn't appear to have any of the clues. I began instead picking up the threads of the work I had abandoned on my departure for Pakistan.

I had once tried to explain to a friend of the satisfaction that is to be found in historical research. But I don't think that I succeeded for it is not possible to explain away so much tedious time spent with the musty trivia of history, any more than one can justify a liking for, say, mangoes. For two years, mostly in London and Paris, I had been burrowing happily through official archives and private libraries, in search for those broad patterns of historical inevitability that give historians so much satisfaction. And, if hindsight can be dressed up with a theory that combines fashion with originality then certainly one is that much closer to a chair at some respectable university.

Flicking through one of my boxfiles full of photostat copies of letters, reports, inter-departmental memoranda, and the like, it occurred to me to consider whether there was anything there which might refer to Shafei's French father. My book on the politics of the Eastern Mediterranean naturally included Syria. I was concerned with the period between the Wars and according to Hughes, Shafei's father had been an officer there in the twenties and thirties. It was conceivable that I possessed some reference to the man, and if I could discover the name of Shafei's father it might be worth spending some time on a search.

I sat down at my desk and began selecting those papers which dealt specifically with Syria, until it was time for me to go.

*   *   *

For some months past, Mortensen had had the idea that there was an information leak at the Canfield. But Mortensen was young and just that bit fanciful at times, and nobody had taken it seriously. The Mortensen theory was that certain people in Cairo and elsewhere knew in advance of his various times of arrival in the Middle East. Pushed for proof he fell back on his intuition and the law of probability relative to certain coincidences. Not enough really, to justify a witch hunt. But on this occasion Mortensen had come back from Cairo with something more tangible than intuition, a nasty little package with all the loose ends tied up and it smelt so bad that nobody could ignore it. It was item one on the agenda.

There were nine of us round the table at the Birdcage Walk conference table, four facing four with Hughes at the head looking sick. From where I sat I could just see the tops of the trees in St James's Park. Hopkins – late thirties, and lecturer in Economics – sat next to me. Then Kendrick, middle forties, educationalist and author, part-time consultant to UNESCO; and Mortensen, a young thirty, Arabic studies, adviser to the Egyptian Government on a new Arabic–English Technical dictionary. Facing us, Hillcroft of the F.O., Jameson of Special Branch; Carrington, Deputy at the Canfield; and Miss Waterton, pencil poised over her notebook.

Mortensen's story was that on arrival at Cairo Airport the previous week he had spotted an Arab whom he felt sure had tailed him on a previous occasion. The man followed him again, by taxi to his hotel and there Mortensen confronted him. Indignant denials had given way to cautious reserve following the offer of £100 for the name of his employer. They haggled and settled for a further fifty. The name given by the Arab was Shafei.

First Extract from the Minutes of the Meeting

Mortensen: The man said that he and a friend had been doing this sort of thing for Shafei for over a year. From his description I rather think that Whitby was trailed when he came over before Easter.

Jameson: If these men have done their job well and if there is any kind of co-ordinated effort backing them, then by now Shafei must know most of our resident agents in Cairo.

Hughes: Perhaps. However, I think it's significant that none of our local people have been picked up by the Egyptian police.

Hillcroft: Meaning what?

Hughes: It suggests that Shafei is not working for the U.A.R.

Hillcroft: Which reduces the number of possibilities, but doesn't get us all that much more forward.

Jameson: With respect, may I recommend that we concentrate our efforts today on the London end of the problem. As I see it that problem is threefold. To consider the actual means by which Shafei is getting advance information from the Canfield, assuming that that is where he *is* getting it. To make an assessment of the damage that may already have been done to our network abroad. And to decide on what must be done now to deal with the situation. I need hardly add that a lot of people would like to know whether this leak is restricted to the Canfield or not.

Mortensen: On that last point there is a fact that seems relevant. According to what the Egyptian told me, and he was able to give me the dates, he did not meet me on the only two occasions when I flew in to Cairo from places other than London. Which suggests that Shafei's information does come from the Canfield.

Jameson: It's not proof, but it's as good a starting point as any. If Shafei has a pal in the Canfield that gives us some 80 candidates for treachery right away. The very nature of the Canfield set up is that your visits abroad are official and advertised. When any of you go on a lecture tour probably half the Canfield is involved one way or another in its planning.

Hughes: Hardly that.

Jameson: Nevertheless, it's no secret. Anybody can discover for himself who is going where and when.

Hughes: Certainly.

Jameson: Furthermore, the bitter truth is that we have no justification for thinking that these intelligence activities are restricted to Cairo. We have to assume, regretfully, that the whole of the Canfield network in the Middle East and beyond may have been breached . . .

End of Extract from Minutes

The Minutes do not record the unhappy silence that followed Jameson's statement. Nor the greyness of Hughes's face. I found it embarrassing to look at the old man – for he seemed old that day – so I looked out of the window at the treetops, and pondered on some of the legends that had grown round him. He'd had a good war, they said. He'd been Monty's blue-eyed boy from Alamein to Tunis, and the first British officer across the Rhine and a personal friend of Churchill himself. There were lots of legends about Hughes. He would be getting his knighthood any day now, the people in the know said.

But what would they say next year? After all his hard grind at the Canfield the organization appeared to have a leak big enough to sink him and his knighthood without a trace. Jameson went on to tell us that four of his people would be appointed to various official jobs at the Canfield within a matter of days, to help Special Branch with their investigation. A new check in depth of everyone at the Canfield was already in hand. For us there would soon be new directions on procedures. And so on. It all sounded like closing the stable door after the horse had bolted.

Second Extract from the Minutes

Kendrick: It seems one hell of a coincidence that this man, Shafei, should turn up suddenly from all directions. Last week we had this business of the ten million dollars, now we have a leak at the Canfield, and both involving this character.

Hughes: It's odd. As you know, our American friends believe Shafei is at the end of a string that ends up in Peking.

Kendrick: And Locke confirmed this, I understand?

Carrington: Locke confirmed Shafei's connections with the C.C.M. Yes. But he may well have been acting for them as a free agent.

Locke: Or a double agent, it's on the cards. May I ask by the way whether we know the name of Shafei's French father?

Hughes: Yes. Montagnard. Colonel Raoul Montagnard. Is it relevant?

Locke: Possibly. How much background have we on him?

Hughes: Not much more than I told you the other day. Dates of service, his stay in England and so on. Two or three pages maybe. All stuff we got from Drouet at the French Embassy. But why do you ask?

Locke: It seems curious to me that the son of a French officer who was educated in England should change both his name and nationality and go back to the Middle East; which after all he hardly knew, having left it as a child.

Hughes: It's a line of approach certainly, but long-term I should say. Right now there are one or two matters which need immediate attention. Locke, I'd like you to get in touch with Gumbar in Karachi and ask him to come here as soon as possible. The only known direct line to Shafei remains the C.C.M. and we must push harder. Mortensen, I'm afraid I'm going to ask you to return to Cairo . . .

End of Second Extract from Minutes

The meeting went on until well after four o'clock.

They brought us beer and sandwiches for lunch, and after six static hours my backside was sore and the view across the treetops had begun to pall.

Because Hughes wanted me to get through to Gumbar as soon as possible, I returned to the Canfield with him, sharing his official car with Carrington and Mortensen. It took me nearly an hour to get through to Karachi, and Gumbar seemed delighted at the prospect of a free trip to London. He would leave within forty-eight hours he said.

It was half past five when I got away from Hughes's office, and for most of the staff the trek homewards had already begun. However, it wasn't the done thing for the senior people to betray too much eagerness to get away, and there was a fair chance that I would be in time to catch Louise. I was half-way up the stairs to her floor when I passed her secretary on the way down. We both stopped. She was glad not to have missed me she said. She had a message, she'd had it all day in fact. Mrs Poulson's mother had died the previous evening, and Mrs Poulson had caught the first available train to Leeds and she wouldn't back for quite a few days. She had asked that I be told.

We walked down the grand stairway together exchanging polite platitudes about death and its sorrows.

Chapter 5

OUTSIDE the Canfield I saw Mortensen, on the look out for a taxi I supposed. I walked up to him.

"Time for a quick one?" I said.

"Damned good idea. I could do with one after that little session."

"Something of a record I guess."

"You can say that again. And worse to come, for me."

"Really?"

"I have a young and beautiful and tempestuous wife who has to be told that I'm off to foreign parts again. And brother, is she going to blow her top!"

I nodded sympathetically.

"A couple of whiskies might help then," I said.

We made our way towards Baker Street. Mortensen had married, a year or so back, a glamorous Greek girl whom he had met in Alexandria. Hughes had threatened to give him the push on discovering that she was the daughter of a Greek communist in exile. But Mortensen was a free-lancer like me and wasn't bothered all that much. In the end Hughes hadn't carried out his threat.

It was early for the regulars and The George was almost empty. We took our drinks and sat by ourselves, at the far end of the saloon bar. I liked Henry Mortensen.

He had a ferreting mind, not for the profundities of life but for its absurdities. Miss Waterton didn't like him any more than she did me. We had always got on well, and it helped at the Canfield to have a reliable colleague with whom one could let off steam once in a while, for a man can build up quite a head of neurosis when he gets to bottling up the truth about himself and his activities. We had a couple of drinks and talked shop. About Shafei and Mortensen's work in Cairo and my mission to Pakistan.

"This business of the ten million dollars has been getting around you know," Mortensen said, "there were some lunatic rumours circulating the embassies by the time I left."

"I can imagine."

"My favourite is that the Chinese are flogging germs to the Egyptians and that some keen Damascus entrepreneur got hold of the consignment. And then of course the usual joke to go with it. A Chinese agent offers a box of germs to an Egyptian General who complains of the high price. Ah, says the Chinaman, it is very expensive training the germs to be anti-semitic. The General hands back the box: I'm sorry, he says, but there are no Jews in the Yemen."

I refilled our glasses and we went on talking of this and that. And by and by I told him about Ricardi and Gregory Swain and the suitcase; but even with Mortensen there had to be secrets for he knew nothing of my relationship with Louise.

"I read about Ricardi's death yesterday on the plane

coming home," he said. "I met him once you know, Mike, at some official reception in Cairo."

"I didn't know that. What did you make of him?"

"Odd little man, with lots of bees in his bonnet. A devout Catholic it transpired. I remember asking him – I must have been a bit high – how he managed to reconcile his faith with an objective view of history. It was a great mistake, he was still telling me three cocktails later."

"Talking seemed to be his 'forte', the only time I saw him."

"Right. He told me that as a young man he had wanted to join a religious order but was not accepted. My guess is that the good fathers were horrified at the thought of having the young gas-bag around."

Mortensen looked at his watch.

"I must be thinking of going, old boy. Tell me, what's your theory about those Hebrew documents of yours?"

"I haven't any. I'm going to take the photographs to one of my old history professors, a Jewish scholar. He should be able to shed some light."

Mortensen got up.

"Well, it's the month for unresolved mysteries, that's for sure," he said.

We stood for a while outside the pub.

"I shall chuck this nonsense next year," he said. He would say that to me every now and then; and sometimes I would say it to him. It was comforting, somehow, to believe that we weren't stuck with the Canfield for keeps.

We parted. It was a pleasant summer's evening and I walked home. I got there around seven o'clock and tried once again to get through to Monsignor Wells, but the Monsignor didn't seem to be around these days. I sat at my desk and began working my way through the papers that I had set aside that morning, in search of Colonel Raoul Montagnard. Montagnard. The name rolled impressively off the tongue. I visualized a tall distinguished Frenchman, St Cyr probably, and the arrogance that used to go with it; with a taste for the cultured and the sensual, and a coffee-coloured Syrian girl; and maybe Shafei was *her* name.

I began my search briskly enough, but became distracted by irrelevances. It was like removing old newspapers from under a carpet or cupboard shelves; faded headlines catch the eye and lure one to read on. I picked up a long fiery letter from a prefect of Aleppo, long since dead, to General Weygand, on the subject of British intrigue with the Arabs. I read it aloud, just for the pleasure of recapturing again the passionate chauvenistic invective that had so moved that man over fifty years ago. And then a secret memorandum, dated April 1926, from a French Minister who wanted the troops to use dum-dum bullets against the Druse; a furtive, nasty little document. And many more. I must have been working for an hour on my Syrian papers when I came across the name Montagnard. The reference was very marginal. A provincial newspaper cutting from an article written in 1927 on the subject of Army morale in the Middle East referred to comments made by one Major Montagnard, on leave

at his home in Tulle, in Corrèze. The major's comments
were not in themselves particularly illuminating. I found
no other reference to him. I put the papers back in the
boxfile and thought about it for a bit, and decided to
send a telegram to my friend Armand Coty in Paris.

During the course of my researches in Paris for material
for my book I had been greatly helped by Armand. A
lecturer at the Sorbonne in Modern History and Politics,
we shared not only the same 'period' of history, but also
a general interest in things Middle-Eastern. He had
recently had published an excellent short book on the
1925 Jabal Druse revolt in Syria, which I had promised to
translate into English. It was, however, his specialized
knowledge of official French archives that had saved me
weeks if not months of tedium and frustration, and earned
him my deep gratitude.

I pulled out a sheet of paper and composed the telegram:

"Urgently require information concerning Colonel
Raoul Montagnard one-time officer in Syria killed Normandy nineteen forty-five with Free French. Information
received from French Embassy only refers to dates of
army service. Have established home was in Tulle,
Corrèze, please investigate. Any personal or family
information useful. Locke."

I phoned it through and was told that it should be
delivered by ten o'clock the following morning.

That evening two friends came to coffee and stayed
late. He wrote and she painted, and it was nice to be
talking again about things that really mattered; it would

have been nicer still if I hadn't been expecting Mr Nassim to ring me at any time. But in the event Mr Nassim did not ring and I assumed that Louise had been too preoccupied with her mother's death to get in touch with him.

On Saturday morning I woke late. I had breakfast and looked up Professor Joseph Abelson in the telephone directory and rang him up. It was ten years since I had last attended one of his boring lectures; as a young and aspiring historian of the Middle East I had felt the need to bolster up my knowledge of early Jewish history, and had suffered a course of lectures by him. I had given up half-way through, after a particularly ponderous effort of his on the Judaean Theocratic State.

I recognized his voice immediately, with its German accent and its Jewish mannerism. I explained that I possessed some old Hebrew manuscripts believed to be of exceptional interest, and wished to obtain his views on their significance and authenticity. He sounded only mildly interested.

"Well, certainly, young man; send them to me and I will look at them. Next week perhaps I will have the time."

"I would like to bring them to you today, it's rather an urgent matter, Professor."

"Today is Saturday," he said curtly, "I do not work on Saturday."

"Of course. It's just that I do not want to send them through the post. May I at least bring them to you?"

He wasn't keen. Probably people were always bringing him things to read.

"I would rather you saw them first, rather than Dr Cohen at the British Museum, that is," I said. It was a bit like telling Sotheby's that you were thinking of letting Christie's handle your collection of Impressionists. A curious grating noise came over the wire.

"Ach, very well," he said, irritably, "bring them along. But I can promise nothing you understand. I am a very busy man."

"I'll be around this afternoon," I said, "about three o'clock."

Around twelve-thirty I drove over to Robert Payne. Business seemed to be booming, and it wasn't until a quarter past one that he locked the door behind his last customer. He brought my briefcase from the back of the shop and took out two packets. The first consisted of the original Ricardi sheets, the second, of his six copies. We examined each of the photographs together; they were faultless. Ten pounds, he said, he'd been up until one o'clock the previous night. I wrote him out a cheque and he put the packages back in the briefcase. We were setting out for The Feathers when I stopped him.

"On second thoughts," I said, "would you mind keeping the originals?"

"If you like, it's no trouble."

"Somewhere safe?"

"With my life's savings under the mattress, if it will make you feel happier."

He took the originals to the back of his shop again, and we made a second start for the pub.

"This stuff of yours is on the level isn't it, Mike?" he said as we downed our first pints.

"As far as I'm concerned it is," I said, "it was given to me for safe keeping by a friend."

"That's a mighty evasive reply, old boy," he said, looking at me.

I grinned at him.

"To be frank, I'm beginning to have my doubts about the damned things. Just a hunch mind you, and I may know a lot more by early next week." Robert nodded.

"Just thought I'd like to know what to say when the police call," he said.

"I doubt if it will come to that," I said, "not as far as you or I are concerned at any rate."

We drank a couple more pints before he felt sufficiently fortified to go home to his loving family. I stayed on and had some lunch and listened to the start of England's innings at Lord's on the pub's radio. By ten to three, after forty minutes' batting, they had managed to lose both openers and it became too painful to hear. I got into my car and set off for Professor Abelson.

Professor Abelson lived in Willesden. For him and those around him, Willesden doubtless seems well endowed with visual delights; a plethora of favoured buildings and streets abound, one supposes, to stir the hearts of the borough's inhabitants. But for the outsider, unaffected by the treasured associations of youth or an esoteric taste for second-rate Edwardian domestic architecture, there is only the monotonous anonymity of those endless grey brick houses.

I got thoroughly lost looking for the Professor's house, for he lived somewhere in the heart of that desert. His street, when I got there, was like all the rest; his house sat heavy and four square on its plot behind a high privet hedge. I parked my car and walked up his glazed-tile pathway to a ponderous wood and stone porch. The panelled front door was bigger than they make them nowadays and the ugliness of the stained glass in the fan-light was quite arresting.

I pulled the old-fashioned brass bell knob and wished that a maid would come to open the door, just to complete the illusion of times past.

The door opened and a middle-aged woman stood there in a black dress and a dainty white apron and a cap to match. Her hair was grey and tied back in a bun and she wore shiny black boots. She looked very trim. No Holly-wood make-up man could have done better.

I smiled down at her.

"I have an appointment with Professor Abelson," I said, "my name is Locke."

She nodded.

"Oh yes. Do come in please, I'll tell the Professor that you are here." She too had that faint tell-tale accent that suggested, with people of her age, a childhood disrupted by Hitler.

She led me to a large drawing-room and disappeared unobtrusively. Inside the place was something of a period piece too, full of heavy old-fashioned furniture and ornate bookcases with glass doors, cream coloured lincrusta and a silk cover with tassels on the grand piano. There was even an aspidistra. The most obvious intrusion on another age was a large framed map of modern Israel in the place of honour over an ornate mantelpiece. I was looking at it when the Professor came in, accompanied by two little girls dressed in their best finery.

I had forgotten about his ugliness; the crumpled sponge-bag of a face, the disastrous nose; the frail body and the outsize hands. But the lenses of his glasses, I remembered those; they were thick, so absurdly thick. Mount Wilson would surely have found a use for them to explore the remoter periphery of outer space.

"Have you ever been to Israel, young man?" he said, as we shook hands.

"Once, quite a few years ago." Canfield men doing the Arab circuit weren't encouraged to visit Israel.

"It's a wonderful country. I have a son there you know, a mathematician; he teaches at Jerusalem University."

He beamed proudly. It's funny about Jews, the way they wear their pride, like medals. Maybe I'd go back some day and see what all the fuss was about.

"That's Uncle David," one of the little girls said to me. "He's terribly clever."

She also beamed at me, and it seemed only courteous to beam back at her. She had long shining black hair and vivid black eyes and she reminded me of Louise.

"Now go and play upstairs, girls," the Professor said. "I have some business to discuss with this gentleman."

The girls went obediently and the Professor motioned me to a chair.

"On Saturday afternoons," he said, with a smile, "I am sometimes allowed to have my grandchildren for tea."

"I shall not intrude for too long," I said.

He nodded. I opened my suitcase and took out the package and selected one of the photographs to give to him.

He took it, looking at it back and front, pushed back his thick glasses, and studied the script.

He said nothing for a few seconds, but frowned slightly.

"This looks quite interesting," he said, after reading quite a time. "Where does it come from?"

"I'm afraid I can't divulge that right now."

He looked up sharply and pushed his glasses back.

"I do not like unnecessary mysteries, young man. Besides, you must be aware that the significance and authenticity of documents depends largely on the circumstances of their discovery."

"I have not come to you for anything more than a translation of the context and your evaluation of that context."

He looked at me belligerently.

"Are these papers your own property?" he asked.

"They belong to a very good friend of mine who is abroad right now. I do not myself know their origin."

"Your friend must know," he said. His emphasis on the word 'friend' betrayed his continuing irritation. Undoubtedly I should have taken the hint about not calling on a Saturday.

"He has not told me. Look Professor Abelson, there are no mysteries I assure you. I have come here merely to show you the photographs of some Hebrew documents in the hope you can tell us what they are about."

He frowned and looked at the photograph again.

"There are five more," I said, handing them to him. He took them and looked at each one briefly.

"I see that there are numbers on each," he said, "eight to thirteen. What is the significance of that?"

I hesitated, and decided that the less he knew the better.

"I'm afraid I don't know that either," I said.

"Presumably there are at least seven other photographs."

"I have no idea."

He grunted. He was staring hard at the last photograph.

"It would be more interesting to see the originals," he said softly.

"I only have these six photographs."

"Your friend has the originals?"

"I believe so."

He looked at me, belligerent again.

"You believe so? You appear to know remarkably little."

"I'm sorry, but . . ."

"Yes, yes, you are just an intermediary, I understand. You say that this friend of yours is abroad, are you expecting him in England?"

"Some time soon, yes."

"I would like to meet him, to know a bit more about the origins of the papers."

"I might be able to arrange that," I lied.

The little girl with the black shiny hair burst into the room suddenly, demanding her grandfather's immediate arbitration in a quarrel with her sister, and the tension between us evaporated under the impact of her noisy intrusion.

I got up from my chair.

"My cue for taking my leave, I think," I said.

The Professor allowed the little girl to drag him towards the door.

"The duties of a grandfather are to be taken seriously," he said to me. "I shall read your documents, Mr Locke, and let you know. Perhaps you could leave me your address and telephone number with the maid."

The other little girl joined her sister, and with a look of happy martyrdom on his face the Professor was led noisily away. A moment or two later the maid came into the room. I left the Professor's house and drove westwards with the intention of taking a walk round the Serpentine; but the weather was spoiling fast and by the time I reached Hyde Park it had begun to rain, so I went home instead.

There was a telegram on my front door mat, and I picked it up. It was from Gregory. "Monsignor Wells in Rome stop Keep my bag stop Arriving London Tuesday and will contact you Swain."

I made myself a pot of tea and considered the implications of the telegram. As so often during that day my

87

thoughts on the subject of Ricardi's papers returned to the utterly perplexing fact that Louise knew all about them. It went on nagging away at me and I regretted increasingly that I had not managed somehow to bully the truth out of Louise.

A solicitor friend of mine had invited me to dinner that evening. But what promised to be a pleasant evening ended abruptly with his wife feeling ill and by ten-thirty I was on my way home again.

I opened the front door of my flat and stepped in and almost immediately saw the man behind the door. But not quite soon enough. The downward blow aimed at my head grazed my cheek and struck my shoulder, near the neck. I didn't know what the man had hit me with, but it was damned hard. The pain seemed to set fire to every nerve end of my body from the waist up. I struck out blindly with my right, but I was shaken and off balance and there wasn't much power behind it. I hit the man in the chest; simultaneously he kicked shut the front door and without the light from the landing I couldn't even see him. Fearing another blow like the first I closed on him and tried to get at his neck or face. For just a few seconds we grappled in the dark and I got my hand under his chin and pushed. I was about to bring my knee hard up against him when something hit me on the back of my head. Briefly I felt my head exploding in a roar of red lights, but I was out cold long before I hit the deck.

Chapter 6

As much as anything one resents a thief because of the intrusion on one's privacy. I walked about my room with a sore head and a black heart and took stock of the chaos.

Every drawer and every cupboard had been emptied on to the floor; my bed looked as if a prolonged orgy had taken place on it; the kitchen one could have supposed to have been ravaged by a starving mob; even the side bath panel had been removed. And in the middle of the bedroom floor as witness to the purpose of the assault on the flat, Ricardi's black case lay slashed and wrecked in a vain search for a secret hiding-place.

I took a couple of aspirins and began dealing with the worst of the damage. From my desk Louise's photograph stared dispassionately at the carnage, but then she had always been good at hiding her emotions. The paintings had been removed from the walls and I put them back first, and then started on the books. By the early hours it seemed clear that nothing had actually been stolen. I made my bed up and fell asleep in no time at all.

Some time around midday on Sunday I woke up. The pain in my head had become localized in a single blood-covered lump and there was a large bluish bruise on my shoulder where the first blow had struck me on the previous evening. I made myself a large pot of very black coffee.

There were to my knowledge four people who knew about Ricardi's case and its contents; Gregory Swain, Louise, Payne, and Mortensen. In addition Professor Abelson might well suppose that I had the originals of the photographs in the flat. I paraded them in turn in my mind's eye, five nice people who didn't at all add up to a rogues' gallery. Besides, Gregory was a few hundred miles away and was coming to collect his documents anyway; Louise was in Leeds burying her mother; Payne actually had the originals; Mortensen had been airborne for Cairo at the time; and Professor Abelson was a gentle old scholar who didn't work on Saturdays.

I drank some more coffee. Any one of the five could have spread the information around of course, and that opened the floodgates of conjecture beyond a level at which it was profitable to pursue the matter. I returned to the business of clearing up the flat.

I was having a late lunch in the kitchen when the phone rang. It was Hughes.

"I hope that I'm not disturbing you on your Sunday afternoon," he said politely. But the amiability sounded just a bit false.

"Not at all, I'm just tidying things up."

"Good. I'm at the office, and about to send a cable to Gumbar to stop him coming over. I first wanted to make sure that he hadn't been in touch with you personally. About the flight he was proposing to take for instance?"

"No, I haven't heard anything."

"There's been an unexpected development, Locke," Hughes said hesitatingly.

"Oh yes?"

"Yes. Late last night, quite fortuitously, an American agent in Beirut saw Shafei board a plane at the airport, London bound. He phoned through to his own people here, and they got in touch with us. He landed at Heathrow at six o'clock this morning and we had quite a reception party for him."

"You arrested him?"

"He's being tailed. We want to know what the hell he's doing here."

"Maybe it's founders day at his old school," I said, but he wasn't amused.

"How far has he gone so far?" I asked.

"He took a taxi to an address in Fulham, and about an hour ago he left again for Kings Cross. I'm waiting to hear whether he went to meet someone or to catch a train. And incidentally, does number sixteen Turner Road mean anything to you? According to the telephone people a man called Tomlin lives there."

"Not a thing. Sorry."

"We're watching the man anyway. Now, if Gumbar should get in touch with you, by phone, about his departure plans, you know what to say."

"Right."

"I expect to be in the office most of today, so you will be able to get in touch with me."

"Good. By the way, has Mortensen gone to Cairo?"

"Yes, we got the news too late to stop him. Why?"

"I just wondered."

I put the phone down, and sat down in my favourite armchair. I could imagine Hughes's incredulity on being told that Shafei, elusive Shafei, who was threatening not only his organization but his professional reputation had actually come to England, openly, without so much as a false beard. Cause for thanksgiving, the knighthood in focus again, for, undoubtedly Hughes believed that Shafei would lead him to the traitor at the Canfield.

But to my way of thinking, if that really was Hughes's expectation, it struck me as being optimistic. I didn't see Shafei as the man to leave a neat little trail for Hughes to sniff at. Clutching at a straw, I reckoned, but then maybe Hughes felt like a drowning man. I went on thinking about it and fell asleep again. It was past seven when I woke to the persistent ringing of the telephone. I dragged myself to my desk.

"Mr Locke?" Professor Abelson said, for there was no mistaking the voice.

"Yes, Professor."

I held the phone between my head and my left shoulder and began fiddling for a cigarette.

"Can you come round to see me this evening?"

"I could, yes."

"At about eleven o'clock, would that be too late for you? I have to go out to dinner unfortunately."

"Eleven o'clock tonight?" I repeated curiously.

"Yes, it is most important. I would not ask otherwise."

"I shall be there then."

"Thank you. May I ask you now, Mr Locke, whether

many people know about these pages of script that you have?"

"Not many," I said.

There was a slight pause. I managed to light my cigarette.

"Would you be prepared to tell me how you and your friend came into possession of these papers?" he said.

I drew on my cigarette.

"You would have to give me a very good reason for doing so," I said.

I could hear him breathing hard into the mouthpiece.

"I think that I shall be able to do just that when I see you this evening. Good-bye."

It was an unexpectedly sudden end to our conversation. He had sounded angry.

I put the phone down and went in search of a whisky and brought it back to the armchair. Or maybe he had sounded hysterical. One couldn't always be sure, not with German professors. At any rate he had read the papers, and he would be telling me what they were all about. Something important. I got up and switched the television on. It would be nice to have one little mystery in the bag, and it would still leave lots more around for a rainy day.

At ten to eleven I set off for Willesden in a mood of expectancy. Professor Abelson himself opened the door to me and led me to the sitting-room. The house was silent.

"Would you like a brandy?" he said after I had sat down in a large and comfortable old-fashioned armchair.

"Thank you."

He brought me my brandy in a fine globe glass, and sat himself in front of me with its twin. His eyes were fixed firmly on me. He raised his glass slightly and took a sip.

"You know, I'm sure," he said, "that the photographs you gave me yesterday are of papers that have recently been stolen from the Israeli Government."

I let that one settle a bit.

"No, I don't," I said. "Might I ask how you know, Professor?"

He had cupped his glass in both hands and was gently swirling his brandy round.

"The theft has been publicised by the Government," he said, his eyes still on me, "as an authority on the subject, with many friends in Israel, I naturally heard about the nature of the stolen papers. When I read the photographs you gave, I drew my own conclusions."

I nodded.

"Naturally I accept your assertion. But I would like to assure you that I was, and am, in no way connected with any such theft."

"I see; and you have the originals?"

"I know where they are."

"But you are not prepared to tell me either where those originals are, or how you came to possess them?"

"Not for the time being, no."

I lit a cigarette.

"Did you know Ricardi personally?" he asked me.

"Not really, I met him once; but, please, don't ask me where."

94

"He was a strange man. You know he was killed, of course?"

He looked up at me sharply, just a bit too speculatively, I thought. "Yes, I was in London when it happened."

He nodded faintly.

"He discovered these documents about a month ago. They were in superb condition, considering their age. Now, although Ricardi was the leader of a team, mostly Israeli, he was something of a vain man and when he realized what these papers were, he decided to deal with their translation and interpretation himself. Their uniqueness was, of course, appreciated by one or two others who had had a glimpse of them; and nobody minded if the old man himself wanted to keep the excitement of presenting his finds to the world for himself. And then he vanished, taking most of the papers with him, and nobody knew exactly what it was that he had actually discovered. For all I know, I may now be the only man who knows the full secret." He sipped some more of his brandy.

"I said most of the papers, because he left two half sheets behind, mere scraps, quite accidentally I'm sure. But they were enough to suggest the enormity of the theft. Through certain channels the Government let it be known that they would pay one million dollars for their recovery. Of course the people who knew Ricardi were baffled, at first."

"*One* million?" I said.

"Yes. And then, through a close personal friend of Ricardi's it was learnt that he was considering the destruction of the documents." I thought of Louise. She knew that too. I understood none of it.

"Are these facts generally known?" I asked.

"Not generally known, naturally not."

He spoke irritably, disappointed at my stupidity no doubt.

"The knowledge of Ricardi's intentions introduced a new sense of urgency. It was decided at Cabinet level that desperate measures were required. Many trained people were employed in trying to locate Ricardi, both inside and outside Israel. And the price for the return of the papers was raised to ten million dollars. I believe that a leading American Foundation was secretly involved in the offer. This offer was also leaked through the same channels, but not the object of the offer. It was assumed that Ricardi and anybody associated with him would know what it was all about."

He paused. I sipped my brandy. A solitary piece of the puzzle had dropped into place. It looked very lonely there all by itself.

"Why all the secrecy?" I said.

"The truth, if revealed, would have hit every headline of every newspaper in the world. It was essential that this should not happen. At this moment I doubt if there are more than twenty people who know that truth."

But I knew of two more.

"And what happened, after the offer was made?" I said.

"Nothing happened. The top Israeli intelligence drew a blank. Nobody came to collect the reward. Then Ricardi was killed and it was assumed that his murderer would turn up with the papers. They are still waiting, ready to pay cash."

He looked at me hard.

"Ten million. No questions asked."

I ignored the insinuation.

"For twenty-six pages of Hebrew script? Why?" I said.

"They are priceless, Mr Locke."

It wasn't a very satisfactory answer.

"Why then should Ricardi wish to destroy them?" I said.

The Professor stared at his brandy glass. It was some time before he answered me.

"Because of his faith, I suppose," he said, eventually. "Because those papers are what they are."

He frowned.

"It would be charitable to say that he died for his faith."

I sighed. The world seemed full suddenly of people who talked in riddles, who had to weave fancy words round the simplest of questions. I tried again.

"What are these papers then, Professor Abelson?" I said.

He smiled faintly at me, and I had the feeling that he was working hard at preparing another incomprehensible reply.

"Yes," he said, slowly, and began nodding his head, "that is really why you are here, isn't it?"

He walked over to the sideboard and brought the

G 97

bottle of brandy back. I had not finished my first ration, but I let him top me up. He returned to his armchair.

"You told me yesterday that some years ago you came to a course of lectures of mine, but had to give up before the end?"

Ye gods, I thought, what now?

"Yes, that's so," I said cautiously.

"Then I shall make up for it now, young man. I hope you will bear with me, but I want you to understand everything."

He leant back in his armchair and half-closed his eyes.

"People whose approach to God is through a simple faith like to believe in the immutability of their creed. Tradition is a comfort to them. They believe, they wish to believe, that their ritual and their dogma is God-given. They do not want to confuse faith with history. Not for them Arius and the dissension of Nicaea, or the struggles to formulate the doctrine of the Trinity, or the conflict between Alexandria and Antioch, or the repercussions of Chalcedon. I need not enumerate all the schisms that have rent the Church through the centuries.

"What is true of the Christian Church is true of Judaism, too. The tribes of Israel sought God in many different ways. There was orthodoxy and there were radical prophets, some of whom we would today call revolutionaries. And when we look back on these great debates and these struggles, Mr Locke, it is not God whom we doubt, but man's vision of God."

He stopped abruptly.

"Am I boring you?" he said.

"Not at all."

"You see, I wish you to understand the climate of religious thought as it existed during the tumultuous years when these precious papers were written."

"Please go on."

"Christ was born in an age accustomed to radical religious ideas. He quarrelled with the Pharisees, yes, but there is no evidence that he was reproved for his Messianic claims. It was his disrespect for the Establishment that angered the priests in the temples. And it was Paul, half a century later, who proclaimed Christ not merely a man but a second God. And that was a denial of the unity of the God of the Jews, and unacceptable to them. And the Christian Church was born.

"The point I'm labouring to make is that in the context of his time Christ was not unique. Which may explain why there is virtually no direct record of him, either Roman or Jewish, that dates from his lifetime, or for some years to follow."

He paused and sipped from his glass.

"For our knowledge of Christ we depend largely on men who never knew him. The Gospels of Matthew, Mark, Luke and John do not record history but hearsay. Besides, their objectivity is suspect. For nearly two thousand years Christ's historical credibility has depended on a few very frail factual papers, and a great deal of faith."

Unexpectedly, he got up, walked over to the fireplace and turned to face me. I could sense a mounting fervour within him, a landlocked excitement too long contained that was beginning to spill out.

"We have waited all this time for some tangible proof," he said, "but not in vain."

The glass in his hand had begun to tremble.

"Last month, digging in some unknown tomb at Beth She'arim, Professor Ricardi discovered that evidence. After all these centuries, it happened. The dating of the tomb is irrefutable, the tests on the paper and the ink have been checked many times over. And a single sentence in one of the two sheets left by Ricardi dates it to an exact year."

He stared at me; his face was flushed and he was breathing hard.

"A commentary on Christ by a man who knew him, a disciple, a companion. . . . He was there, he left his record, he wrote about the things he saw and heard and felt. A few fragile and faded pages, but it is enough. From the shadows of myths and speculation the historical Christ has emerged. At last."

He frowned.

"Do you understand the enormity of what I am telling you? Do you?"

His voice had risen.

"I understand," I said.

"A man who stood at Calvary. Who saw the nails driven into the flesh, who witnessed the agony on the cross. An ordinary man, but who could write, and who did write."

Slowly he took off his glasses. He held them in his left hand and began polishing them with a large handkerchief.

"He was there," he said softly, "that day. I read what he had to say about that day, about his sadness, his despair. And about his love. I understood; I read and I cried for the Man on the cross, for He was a man and they had crucified Him."

I had to look away from his face. I lifted my glass, and my hand was trembling too. It was a long time before either of us spoke.

"Those are the papers that you have, Mr Locke," he said quietly.

"Yes."

In a shabby little photographer's shop in Paddington, the testament of a man who had seen Christ on the cross.

A large bronze clock on the mantelpiece began striking midnight in quick sharp tones.

"Another day," he said, so softly that I hardly heard him.

I lit a cigarette.

"Time cuts a man down to size, don't you think, Mr Locke? We all aspire to divinity but endlessly suffer the humiliation of mortality. Time robs us of our illusions, so we seek in the Messiah, the man-God, the repository of our hopes. He is what we would wish to be ourselves and He is one of us. That is the meaning of Christ."

I nodded and drew hard on my cigarette.

"You said that Ricardi wanted to destroy these papers, I didn't really understand why," I said. But I was thinking of Gregory Swain, for Louise had said the same thing of him.

THE MAN WHO WAS THERE

"I cannot say for sure, but I can hazard a guess. I have only seen a fraction of those papers, but even in those . . ."

He hesitated.

"You see, even in that fragment there are significant differences. . . . The factual reporting of things seen and heard does not match up with the embroidered theology of the later-day Apostles."

"So?"

"Ricardi was a devout Catholic. I suspect, I am almost certain, that taken as a whole that testament denies the divinity of Christ, perhaps even records that Christ himself neither claimed nor believed Himself to be divine. It is not difficult to imagine the impact that such a revelation would have on the Christian world. Nor to guess at the agony of indecision that must have assailed Ricardi as the sole possessor of the knowledge contained in that testament."

I remembered suddenly the cryptic comment in the RIASSUNTO notebook about the conflict between Faith and Reason. But could an intelligent man shut out the truth by destroying the evidence of that truth?

"It is difficult to believe," I said, "that a man of such intellect, and who has devoted his life to historical research, could contemplate destroying those papers. After all, whatever there is in them, he knew, and destroying them would do nothing for his peace of mind."

Professor Abelson nodded.

"Yes, it is strange."

"Are you sure about it then?"

He shrugged his shoulders.

"At the best I have the information third hand."

"It just doesn't make sense, not to me, I'm afraid."

He looked at me sharply.

'No. But then I suspect that you are not a religious man, Mr Locke. I can believe that Ricardi may have been deeply distressed. Perhaps . . ."

He hesitated again.

"Perhaps what?"

"I was going to say that perhaps he was taking the historical view after all. The long view."

I looked at him blankly. We were back to riddles.

"What are you going to do with those papers, Mr Locke?" he said.

I considered his question.

"I'm not sure. Certainly there is someone I have to see before I do anything."

"You appreciate, of course, that they must be returned immediately. If you wish to hand them to me I give you my word that no questions will be asked, indeed I shall withhold your name. If it is the money you want I am prepared to act as your go-between with the Israeli authorities."

I sighed and stubbed my cigarette out.

"The tax angle would keep me awake at night," I said, "besides the papers are not mine to sell."

"I hope that is not your final word, Mr Locke, for unless you are prepared to guarantee the return of these papers, I shall have no alternative but to inform the British police and the Israeli authorities. I am just not prepared to leave a matter of this magnitude unresolved."

THE MAN WHO WAS THERE

"I understand your concern, but I can do nothing for at least forty-eight hours. The man who has given me these papers in trust is not yet in this country."

We haggled and in the end he agreed. He had no alternative really.

I got up and he prepared to show me out.

"I'd like the photographs back please," I said. He was half-way to the door. He stopped, and turned slowly.

"They at least are my own property," I said pleasantly. He didn't seem sure about it. Perhaps he needed re-assuring.

"Whatever happens," I said, "I shall not be giving *them* back to my friend."

"What possible use can they be to you?"

"Not of any use, but of considerable interest, I'm sure you can appreciate that."

"Possibly, but as things stand they are the only —"

"I know, but I want them back."

He glared at me, his eyes eloquent with dislike. And behind them he was doing his sums and getting unaccept-able answers.

"And if I refuse," he said with splendid dignity.

"I don't think you will refuse, not in the circumstances."

"I'm under no moral obligation to return them," he said sternly.

I nodded. I let him finish his calculations; his shoulders slumped a little.

"You say that you'll keep them yourself?" he said quietly, "whatever happens?"

"Yes, you have my word."

He turned away and walked slowly to a large bureau opposite the fireplace. He opened a drawer and turned to me with a large envelope in his hand.

"I have no choice but to trust you," he said. He wasn't angry any longer, just sad and worried. I wanted to say something nice and comforting to him.

"Don't worry," was all that I could muster.

I took the envelope from him and checked the photographs inside. He sighed, and showed me out. As we stood at the front door saying good night to each other he held my right hand in his and placed his left on my shoulder. It was an unexpected gesture.

"Take care," he said gently, "with those scraps of paper. Please."

I drove home through the empty silent streets. The sky was full of stars. Some people say that the star in the East was Halley's comet.

Chapter 7

I LAY in bed and watched the first pale flush of dawn creep up behind the jagged skyline of the buildings opposite. Another day, yes, one more behind, one less in front. . . . Night is the enemy, the hidden persuader, the distorting mirror, a man should sleep at night. I tried, I wanted nothing of my thoughts but they kept pace with my heart-beat and would not be denied. Shafei, Louise, Gregory, Ricardi, and the ghost of a man who had died a long time ago; they came and went and came again, unwelcomed.

I stared out at the new dawn and struggled once more with the intolerable coincidence that out of all the millions of women in England, I had as mistress probably the only one who knew of Ricardi's discoveries. And if one added to that the totally improbable circumstances that had led me to possess those papers? What then? I fumbled over my bedside table and picked up my packet of cigarettes. The combined odds were too great, the mere idea of it too fictional. Somewhere there had to be a pattern waiting to be revealed.

But all I had was one orphaned fact in search of a purpose in life. It clarified Shafei's role certainly. He'd picked up the scent and was after the big money, the purple dreams; a long shot no doubt but the alternative was bumming along with the C.C.M. or this and that Arab paymaster. Not much of a pattern, and no sight of Louise.

Louise. For no very good reason I found myself thinking of Abelson's little granddaughter, with the black eyes and the long black hair that had reminded me so forcibly of Louise. One could suppose them to share some common ancestry. A racial affinity even? Jew and Arab, it was possible. Two strands of destiny that thread their haphazard way through the past to a single font. Buff sands drifting towards a vacant horizon, the flaming desert sky at sunset, prophets' tombs haunting history amidst parched olive trees. It was not an inappropriate setting for that face. And she had a friend called Nassim, who should have called on me, not exactly an Anglo-Saxon favourite as names went . . . Nassim . . .

I woke with a start to the insistent ringing of the front door bell. I got up, slipped on my dressing-gown, and picking up my watch discovered to my surprise that it was coming up for ten o'clock.

A small pimply youth who looked as if he should still be at school handed me a telegram and grinned hopefully. I fetched two shillings for him, cheap at the price I reckoned when I read the message.

"Colonel Raoul Montagnard born Bergman in Lvov Poland eighteen ninety-five stop family emigrated France nineteen six naturalized French nineteen thirteen stop married Sarah Epstein nineteen twenty stop signed on as regular officer nineteen twenty one stop reached rank of colonel nineteen forty killed near Caen August nineteen

forty-five stop widow seventy last birthday stop pension
paid to Banque de Paris Lower Regent Street London stop
address of recipient unlikely to be given without authority
stop when are you coming to Paris Coty."

I went to the kitchen, opened a can of orange juice and
sat down. I read the telegram through a second time. *Né*
Bergman in Lvov. Died Montagnard in Normandy.
Shafei's father. A man could laugh till his sides ached. I
took another swig of orange juice. Hughes wouldn't be
laughing though, when I told him, that was for sure. He
was going to weep over this one, all those tidy facts in the
Shafei file, all those hopeful speculations. A Cairo man, a
Baghdad man, a Moscow man, a Peking man – non-
anthropological variety – and all wrong. Facts that had
failed to illuminate, guesses that had never hit the jackpot.
Né Bergman! I smiled, I laughed, I couldn't help myself.
Monsieur le Colonel, not St Cyr after all but Lvov. A
tailor *mon Colonel?* a *schneider?* in mantles? That's a
nice bit of cloth you've got there mon colonel, oh! ye
gods!

I phoned Miss Waterton. Mr Hughes was expected in
about half an hour she said. She supposed that he would
be able to see me, if it was really important. For a few
minutes, before his meeting at eleven thirty.

I washed and dressed and drove to the Canfield and
presented myself to Miss Waterton. But when she buzzed
through to Hughes he was closeted with Carrington and
unwilling to be disturbed.

"Please tell Mr Hughes that the matter is of extreme
urgency," I insisted.

"I'm sorry but Mr Hughes cannot see you now." She put the phone down and looked at me aggressively.

"Would you mind if I spoke to him myself, I'm sure . . ."

"I would mind very much. You will have to wait until he is free."

Perhaps I might have done just that but she was enjoying her authority too much. I turned round and walked to Hughes's communicating door, knocked, and went in. Miss Waterton leapt from her chair and came hot foot after me.

"I'm sorry, Mr Hughes," she shouted, "but I did tell . . ."

"That's all right, Mary," Hughes said angrily. "Why this intrusion, Locke?"

He was sitting at his desk with Carrington facing him.

"I'm sorry, but I have some information that I feel you would want to know about immediately."

"I see. What is it, then?"

He waved an imperious hand to the hovering Miss Waterton. I resisted the temptation to turn and watch her departure.

"It concerns Shafei," I said.

"Oh yes?" He was still cool, and there was no invitation to sit down.

"I know who he is working for."

Hughes took a cigarette from his silver-plated case and lit it, his eyes riveted on me the whole time.

"Go on then," he said.

"Shafei is a Jew."

"Really!" Carrington exploded. "What nonsense is this, we all . . ."

"Just a minute, John," Hughes interrupted. "Are you guessing, Locke, or do you know?"

"An hour ago I received a telegram from a friend of mine in Paris, in reply to one from me. A French historian and archivist. According to him Colonel Montagnard, Shafei's father, was originally called Bergman and came from Lvov in Poland just after the turn of the century. A Jew, I think one can assume, and certainly he married a Jewess. In spite of Shafei's natural mother being an Arab woman, his formative years, his childhood and youth, was spent with Montagnard and his wife. It seems equally reasonable to assume, I feel, that Shafei considers himself a Jew."

Hughes didn't laugh. He just sat there, silent and expressionless.

"Which would further suggest," I said, "that he works for Israel."

"You don't have to explain the obvious," Hughes said, with untypical viciousness. I shrugged my shoulders; you do a man a good turn and get kicked in the teeth for your trouble, that's how it goes.

"How do you know he married a Jewess?" Hughes said.

I took the telegram out of my pocket and gave it to him.

"Sarah Epstein," I said irritably, "it's not proof of course, she could be a lapsed Zen Buddhist for all I know."

Hughes read the telegram and passed it over to Carrington.

"Get on to Hedges and have him check this information with Paris. Urgently, tell him to drop everything. And then come back."

Carrington got up.

"Right," he said, and left us.

Hughes sat back in his chair.

"You have confidence in your informant?" he said.

"Absolutely. He would hardly have made this up."

"I meant confidence about keeping his mouth shut?"

"Certainly."

Hughes picked up his intercom phone and pressed one of the buttons.

"Mary, will you get me Drouet at the French Embassy; if he's not in then his assistant, I forget his name."

He put the phone down.

"That was a good bit of work, Locke, I should like you to know that it is much appreciated."

I felt mollified, I even basked a bit.

"We, on the other hand, have done badly. Very badly."

"In what way?"

"Our men lost contact with Shafei."

He said it in a matter-of-fact way, but I knew what it must mean to him, on top of everything else.

"I'm sorry to hear it; what happened?"

"He caught a late night train from King's Cross. Our follow-up chap checked with the ticket man and established that he'd bought one for Leeds. We had plenty of time to lay on a reception party at the other end, and we had three of our people on the train. At Leeds Central, in the early hours of the morning, he took a taxi and two cars trailed it. It was raining hard and as I understand it the leading police car contrived to get itself hit by a skidding lorry on a hill, and in the ensuing pile-up the taxi and the cars just got separated. As simple as that. They've got half the force on the alert now but so far nobody's had a smell of him."

I stared at him blankly.

"Leeds?" I said.

He merely nodded, but it was like a body blow. If Shafei had wanted to go somewhere he had the whole world to choose from; five continents, ten thousand cities and towns, lots of nice places. But he had chosen Leeds.

A phone on Hughes's desk rang and he picked it up.

"Yes, I'll hang on," he said, and turned to me.

"What does he do, this man Coty?"

"He's a lecturer at the Sorbonne. I've known him for years."

"I see. I'm on to Drouet's office and I'm going to ask him to authorize the bank to give us Madame Montagnard's address. She might be able to help us."

I nodded absent-mindedly. It's curious how insight comes to one sometimes, all at one go. Not just a part but the whole. Figures and landscape, seen in a flash of sudden revelation. It happened to me at that moment in a flash. Shafei seen in focus, meaningful, a rational man in a rational universe.

I could have told Hughes then that it was too late, that

Madame Montagnard wouldn't be helping anyone any-more. But I didn't. I held back. Absurdly I think that I wanted to believe in coincidences at that moment, to hide behind one, to use it as a shield against the truth. For I had seen the truth and hated it.

"All right then," Hughes said into the phone, "ask him to ring me as soon as he can."

"You won't want me any more?" I asked.

He looked at me and smiled.

"No, you've done your good deed for the day and we are deeply indebted to you. Can I get in touch with you later, if we need to?"

"I shall be at home, on and off."

He got up and opened the door for me.

I made the familiar journey upstairs to Louise's office. Her secretary was knitting when I knocked and went in, and looked guilty about it.

"Mrs Poulson not back?" I said amiably.

"No, things are rather slack," she giggled and pushed her knitting away.

"Any idea when she will be returning?"

"Oh yes, she rang Mr Partridge this morning to say that she would be returning to London tonight, and be back in the office tomorrow. The funeral was early this morning I understand."

I thanked her, and made my way out of the building again. I felt wary of returning to the flat, for left to my-self I knew that I would go on brooding; and I decided to go to Soho and to treat myself to a good lunch. I had my good lunch but it didn't stop me brooding. About the laws of probability mainly. After all, what the hell was the point of long odds if they didn't turn up just once in a while? Besides I was guessing all along the line, wasn't I? Well, wasn't I? But it's difficult to fool oneself when you're dead sober.

I drove home later with the intention of settling down to some serious work. I did some serious work. I checked the date of a foreign affairs speech by Mr Baldwin on party loyalties, a useful thing for me to do, but it only took five minutes. The sentiments and phraseology of the speech were outmoded, yet it set me thinking about my own loyalties, such as they were. One of the veneers of social man, yes, but there it is all the same. As dead as the epidermis if you like but it takes a snake to shed its skin. When it came to the push where were my loyalties going to lie? Because it was going to come to the push. Soon. At six o'clock I collected out of my desk a little flat box, wallet size, affectionately known at the Canfield as the Sesame Kit, as with Ali Baba. I got into my car and set off for Passmore Road, a little mews-like place to the west of Sloane Street. Louise's flat was on the third floor of a house in a pleasant early Victorian terrace. The house was narrow, and its staircase was narrow and served flats on one side only. One could stand at a landing and have reasonable warning of anyone coming.

I took my Sesame Kit out and got to work on the lock; it wasn't much of a challenge even to a part-time Canfield man, and I was in with the door shut behind me in about half a minute.

It was only the fifth or sixth time that I had been in

Louise's flat, and the others had been by invitation. She preferred us to meet elsewhere, it was one of her little foibles, part of the mystery game she went in for; but her behaviour made more sense to me now. Her flat was, I thought, a rather austere place for a young woman. True there were lots of books and gramophone records, but with the exception of one banal print of an alpine landscape the walls were bare. The furniture was sparse, there were few personal possessions. It didn't feel like a home.

To one side of a fireplace blocked up to accommodate an electric unit she had a writing-desk. I hoped to find what I wanted there as I had no wish to do to her flat what had been done to mine. I began searching it. It had four drawers. Three had nothing of interest to me and the fourth was locked. The lock was a small one and old-fashioned, and it took me considerably longer to get it open than the front door. I found in it a single passport, Louise's, and a fat sealed envelope about the size of a foolscap sheet of paper.

I took the passport and the envelope and sat down in one of her armchairs. The passport told me almost nothing I didn't know, except perhaps that she looked beautiful even in the lousiest of photographs. It was British, issued four years back; she was born in 1938, she had black hair and dark-brown eyes, and was five feet nine inches tall. It told me her maiden name, but then I'd known that for about six hours now. The contents of the envelopes, letters mostly, told me a lot more. Too much really, things I would rather not have known, private truths that were entitled to their privacy. They swept away the remnants of my faint hopes that maybe, after all, I'd made a mistake in adding up two and two.

I put the papers back in the envelope. I thought, an eyeful for an eyeful is the *mot juste*, but Louise won't appreciate the point. I looked at my watch and it seemed probable that I had a long wait in front of me. I walked over to her bookshelf and considered the choice available, which was not inconsiderable. I selected Camus' *L'Etranger*, because I had never read it in the French, and because it was short and I might even finish it before Louise arrived. I turned the armchair to face the door and began reading.

"Aujourd'hui, maman est morte. Ou peut-être hier, je ne sais pas!" I had forgotten the power of that objective detachment, of that solitary observer of the world about him, uncommitted to anything but his own integrity. One could envy such a man, his freedom from the moral heritage; not a real man of course, just a writer's speculation. Perhaps, as Abelson had said, we do aspire to divinity, and failing, seek our immortality in the images we make; writers like the rest of us.

I read till it was dark, and then pulled the curtains and switched the light on, and went on reading until I had finished the book.

I looked at my watch, and it was eleven o'clock. I got up and went to Louise's kitchen and rooted about for something to drink, and found a new bottle of Scotch in her larder cupboard. I poured myself a long one and brought it back to the living-room. I sat down again and lit a cigarette – Objective detachment, yes, an arrogant illusion, for who is born to take the solitude that goes with it? Man the God, God the man, of course; the favoured myth, superman dressed up by theologians; perhaps the only difference between Gregory and me was that we sought our myths in different books. . . . Time passed. I thought about this and that. I finished my cigarette and my whisky at about the same time and I went to the kitchen for a refill. I had another look at her bookshelves, but anything else after the Camus would have been an anti-climax. I picked a *Vogue* magazine from her coffee-table and brought it back to the armchair, and dipped into another kind of world, with its own brand of images and make believe.

At eleven-thirty I discovered that I only had two cigarettes left, and there didn't appear to be any around in the flat. I began to consider the possibility that Louise might not after all come back. I sat there, and waited. I lit my penultimate cigarette, and smoked it, and remembered a French film I had seen once, a long time ago. The hero was also waiting, for somebody or something, alone in a room hour after hour through the night; and he had lots of cigarettes but no matches, there's always something . . .

I heard footsteps coming up the stairs, and then a key in the lock. I stubbed my cigarette out and stood up.

"It's unlocked," I heard Louise say, and the door opened. She saw me immediately and stopped a step or two inside the hall. Behind her stood Shafei, tall, bronzed, smooth, much as I remembered him.

"It's been a long wait," I said.

Chapter 8

"WHAT on earth are you doing here, Mike?" Louise said.

Shafei came into the room and shut the door behind him. He carried a suitcase.

"Waiting for you," I said.

She smiled uncertainly, she hadn't yet noticed the passport and the envelope by the side of the armchair. I could almost see her struggling to be calm, to take things in her stride. She took a step towards me.

"I'd like to introduce you, Mike . . ." she said.

"I know," I interrupted, "your brother. We've already met."

The smile on her face vanished. Shafei put the suitcase down, locked the front door, and came into the room.

"What's this about, Mike?" she said softly.

"The old-fashioned word is treason, I believe."

Shafei took a couple of steps towards me.

"Could you manage to be a little more to the point," he said.

His voice was as cool and as calm as he looked. Either you were born with that kind of self-confidence or you had to do daily exercises. I bent down and picked up the passport.

"It's a pity about the British nationality," I said. "I

was hoping it wouldn't be; they would just have put you on the next plane out."

I handed the passport to her.

"Nowadays they're not nice to our kind; twenty years, even more. I wanted you to know that you haven't much time left to get out."

Louise looked at Shafei but he kept right on looking at me.

"Perhaps you would care to start at the beginning," he said, "it might help us to understand what you are talking about."

"You know what I'm talking about, and I know you know."

"Nevertheless, if it's not troubling you too much, Mr Locke. We might even sit down and have a drink, don't you think, Louise?"

I smiled faintly at her.

"The mice have been at the Scotch you keep in the larder," I said. But she had caught sight of the large envelope on the floor next to the armchair.

"He's found all my letters," she said woodenly to Shafei.

"All the more reason for a friendly chat, my dear," he said, "so please bring us something to drink."

She nodded and went to her kitchen. Shafei and I sat down facing each other; he offered me a cigarette.

"How did you get away from Leeds?" I asked. "I gather the police were thick on the ground looking for you."

He smiled.

"Yes, they've shown a great interest ever since I landed

at Heathrow, but I had a lucky break at Leeds. No doubt
you know."

I nodded. There was something disconcerting about his
amused detachment, like a man with a fistful of aces, only
I didn't see how that could be.

"I attended a funeral this morning, on the outskirts of
the city; we were not disturbed, naturally. From there we
took a car and drove to London; a tedious journey, but
untroubled."

Louise came back with a tray, the bottle of whisky,
and three glasses. She put it on the coffee-table and sat
down. She seemed to be making a point of not looking
at me.

"Good, just what I needed," Shafei said getting up.
He dispensed the drinks and returned to his chair.

"Mr Locke seems to know a lot about us, my dear," he
said pleasantly to Louise. She stared at her glass, silent.

"You will readily appreciate," he continued, "that I
am most curious to discover exactly how much you do
know, and even more whether your knowledge is shared
by others."

I drank some of my whisky.

"You are the son of one Colonel Raoul Montagnard," I
said. "For many years you have been an Israeli agent oper-
ating under cover of Arab nationality. The scope of your
activities suggests that your position is a very senior one.
Louise is your sister and has been feeding you with information about the Canfield. A lot of this information she
received directly or indirectly from me and our close
relationship was of course of considerable help to her. I

would suppose that by now you know all of the Canfield agents in the field, and most of their contacts in the Middle East."

Shafei blew a cloud of smoke towards the ceiling.

"All your own unaided work?" he asked softly.

"Mostly."

He nodded.

"Clever. One of these days you must explain to me where I went wrong. And tell me, how many people know about all this."

"About you, quite a few; but not about Louise, not yet."

"How d'you mean, not yet?"

"I shall be telling them, though given time they would get round to it themselves. There's an investigation in depth going on at the Canfield, and now that the name Montagnard means something to them . . ."

Shafei frowned.

"Could you spell it out for me, in simple language, why you haven't yet given your Mr Hughes this information? It puzzles me, after all I should say that you are taking quite a risk on your own account."

"I find the idea of Louise spending the next twenty years or so in an English jail rather repugnant."

It was now my turn to avoid looking at Louise. With-out saying anything Shafei got up and filled my glass again, and then his own. He stood by Louise with a hand on her shoulder.

"I see. And how long are you giving us?" he said.

"Twenty-four hours."

"It's not long, there are a lot of matters to be settled."

"It's long enough," I interrupted.

He sighed, and sat down again.

"I shouldn't like you to think that we are not grateful," he said, "because we are. Very much so. Which makes it all the more distressing for me to have to decline your request to leave the country so quickly."

He put his hand in his pocket, and it came out with a little black revolver. I looked at it, in his hand on his lap. It was almost dainty, a ladies' revolver, not a serious weapon, a limited range certainly. But it would manage the six or seven feet that separated us.

"I'm not a killer, Locke," he said, and I was conscious of the fact that he had dropped the 'mister', "but I would have to stop you if you tried to get away. Your leg or your shoulder, perhaps. I'd be sorry to have to do that, but I need more than twenty-four hours; and, above all, I need your co-operation."

"You're taking a chance with Louise," I said.

"I don't think so. You see, she didn't give Montagnard as her maiden name when she signed on at the Canfield, it would have been an unnecessary risk. She was neither born nor married in England, so there are no records at Somerset House. I grant you that if they dig deep enough they will get at the truth, but it will take time and there are, I believe, nearly one hundred other employees at your establishment. No, I think we have a few days, Locke, before they cotton on."

"If you want my co-operation," I said, "you're going about it in a curious way."

"True. But there comes a point in any situation like this when it is necessary to lay all one's cards on the table. And the best bargains are struck between equals."

He smiled. It was a pity, I thought, that the man was so likeable.

"I had the impression," he continued, "that you thought our relative positions were very unequal, but as you see we each have something the other hasn't got."

I took my packet with the solitary cigarette out of my pocket. I hesitated fractionally, and stretched out my hand towards Louise. She looked up at me then. Her face was drawn, she looked very tired.

"I was sorry to hear about your mother," I said.

She nodded.

"I'm sorry about a lot of things, Mike," she said. Her eyes were on me, she wasn't trying to evade anything any more. Shafei got up, silently, and drifted to look at the bookshelves. His back to me, his little revolver in his pocket, for he knew how it was now between the three of us. Not according to the regulations, but sometimes a man likes to make up the rules as he goes along.

She had taken the proffered cigarette and I got up to light it. She let her hand touch mine to steady it.

"It wasn't just because . . . because . . ." She fumbled for her words.

"Yes," I said.

"I didn't even know at first that you were tied up with Hughes."

"Sure, you don't have to explain."

"I tried not to let it . . . get out of hand but . . ."

She suddenly lay back in the armchair, her eyes closed, her body limp. A solitary tear grew at the corner of her right eye, like a pearl.

"I'm sorry, Mike," she whispered.

I stood watching her, looking at that tear, so rare, for I had never seen her cry; and after a while I returned to my armchair.

Shafei came back and sat down in front of me again.

"Of course you know why we cannot leave," he said, "not empty handed."

I looked at him.

"Ricardi's papers?"

He nodded.

"Naturally you are entitled to know why these papers are so important, and I will . . ."

"I know already."

Louise opened her eyes, and looked at Shafei.

"Oh?" he said.

"I had a few photographs taken and showed them to Professor Abelson. You doubtless know each other."

"We know of him, but he doesn't know of us. He told you?"

"Yes. What the papers were, about the ten million dollars, everything. He gave me forty-eight hours to return them before he went to the police."

Shafei laughed.

"Ultimatums are 'in' this year, it would seem. What was your answer?"

"Gregory Swain will be in London some time soon. In a few hours, I expect; I shall return the case to him, intact, with the papers, for as far as I'm concerned Ricardi gave them to him and he gave them to me. It's not for me to decide their legal ownership. Abelson and the police and the Israeli authorities can fight it out with Gregory, and good luck to them."

Louise sat up.

"Mike, I told you that Swain intends to destroy them," she said anxiously.

"So did Abelson. And as far as I can see, it's all based on some lunatic rumour of some so-called friend who . . ."

"It's no rumour," Shafei said sharply. "Ricardi and Swain have stated their intentions. Monsignor Wells is Swain's old confessor and friend and the only reason why they're not already just so much ash is that Swain felt that he needed his superior's spiritual support for what he was about to do."

"Forgive me for doubting you, but I don't see how you could know that."

"No? Tell me, did it never strike you as odd that in a matter of such concern to him Swain should have asked you to deliver these precious papers to a man who wasn't even in London? I'll tell you why that was. For some days before you met him that day in Beirut, Swain had been staying in a small cheap hotel in Beirut, the Palmyra. He had met Ricardi already and obviously they talked endlessly about what they should do. Swain wrote to Wells, and Wells wrote to Swain. Swain would give his letters to the bell-boy to post for him. A couple of hundred piastres went a long way with that bell-boy and we intercepted these letters. The last letter from Wells, telling

Swain that he was off to Rome, we kept. We wanted him to go to London, to bring the papers out of hiding as we didn't know where they were being kept. Two of my men were at the airport that day, they knew the papers were in the suitcase, we were ready to pounce. Unfortunately, nobody witnessed that little private meeting you and he had, and it was Swain we were waiting for, both in Beirut and at Heathrow. When Swain and Ricardi left the airport at Beirut without the case we realized that something had gone wrong with our plans.

"But the point I'm making is that the correspondence between Swain and Wells makes it clear beyond any doubt that it is intended to destroy those papers."

We sat looking at each other. I had nothing with which to refute his assertions, yet I could not believe them. Reason got in the way, reason which went on telling me that an honest man could not shut out the truth just by putting a match to it.

"So what's your answer?" he said. His voice, now hard and demanding, jabbed me like a fist. I was beginning to feel tired, and a shade resentful, but there were still things that I wanted to know.

"Did one of your men kill Ricardi?" I asked.

"No."

"Who then?"

"The murderer hadn't been found when I left Beirut. I would expect it to be some local man who had somehow heard about the papers and their value, and thought that he would like to get hold of them."

"I see."

"Now, would you mind getting back to the point. What are you going to do with the papers?"

"I intend to speak to Swain before I make any decision. I shall not give them to him until I know why he wants them. Nor to you."

Shafei said nothing.

"And when that's settled I shall go to see Hughes. Say, Wednesday morning. And may I suggest that you get yourself a one-way ticket back to Israel?"

Louise looked blankly at the fireplace, Shafei crossed his legs and put his right hand back into his pocket.

"I'm sorry, I thought we understood each other," he said.

"Oh, we do, I'm sure. You and Louise have got slightly over twenty-four hours to get out of the country. As for the papers, I'll decide after I've spoken to Swain, and I shall not be needing your assistance in coming to a decision."

Shafei smiled again, but this time his eyes weren't in on it.

"Diplomacy is the art of reasonableness, Locke, and you are not being reasonable. The alternative to us not coming to an accommodation would be unpleasant. I would have no alternative."

I stood up. Shafei's hand came up with the revolver in it. I took a step towards him and he tried to get up, but too late. I kicked hard at his arm, he fired and I made contact just about the same time. I felt a sharp sudden sting below my left elbow, the revolver went flying and Shafei, off balance, fell back in the armchair. The revolver clattered against the door that led to the kitchen and I ran for it. I picked it up and turned, and Shafei was still in the middle of the room.

"I shouldn't move, Shafei," I said. "I'm not fussy about using this on somebody who's shot me."

We stood facing each other, with Louise standing by his side. I could feel the blood coming down my arm, but it wasn't hurting much. I wondered how long it would be before one of the neighbours came to see what was up, or phone the police; it was a small gun but it made a big noise.

I began to walk sideways towards the front door, for I was at the wrong end of the room.

"A man should know when he's outstayed his welcome," I said, "so I'll be leaving you. I wouldn't waste your time trying to follow me."

"Get the gun, Louise," Shafei said softly, "he won't shoot you. Quickly."

I stopped. I hadn't a chance in hell in getting to the door first if Louise made a dash for me. I kept the revolver fixed on Shafei.

"If you try that Louise, I'll shoot your brother, first."

"He's bluffing, he isn't the type to shoot a man down in cold blood. Just get the gun, now."

He pushed her towards me, but she stayed where she was. I began moving round them again, slowly; I knew without looking that the blood had reached my hand and was dripping on the carpet.

"Louise, quickly," Shafei said.

"No, I can't," she whispered.

"For God's sake, he'll get away."

I could see him tensed, ready to throw himself at me. Two steps and Louise could be between us, and I wouldn't shoot, it was the only certain thing in life at that moment. She knew it too, but she stood where she was.

I had covered a third of the distance, and all the time I had the revolver pointed at Shafei's belly. Imperceptibly they turned as I moved round them.

"Louise, please," Shafei said. I could detect the desperation in his voice, and see the sweat on his brow.

She shook her head, and I knew that she was crying. I took two more steps sideways, and I was as close to the door now as I was to Louise. Shafei leapt forward and I took a step backwards, lowered the aim of the revolver and shot twice at his legs. Louise screamed, Shafei came at me in a flying tackle. I raised my hand and brought the revolver hard down on his head a fraction of a second before he collided with me.

We both went down but I was the only one to get up. It took some doing, a sense of urgent self-preservation whipping up an unwilling body. But I got up, and stood there swaying, as if a gale was blowing me, the revolver still in my hand. Shafei lay motionless on the floor, a patch of blood just beneath his knee, spreading.

There seemed to be a lot of blood spread around all of a sudden, over me, and a little trail marking my progress round the room, and it was still dripping away. I couldn't remember how much of the stuff a man can spare, a lot I seemed to remember, I would probably manage for a bit longer. It was just that I had the feeling that I was running to waste.

I went on standing there, the gift of decision-making somehow withheld, waiting for the return of purpose. Louise was on her knees turning Shafei round, getting a pillow under his head, pulling his trouser leg up. Somebody began banging at the door to her flat, trying the doorhandle, calling half a dozen times what was going on in a voice pitched high with suppressed hysteria.

"I don't think he's seriously hurt," I said to Louise, "a flesh wound in his calf, he'll come to soon." Nothing in her manner suggested that she cared for my views. I thought, the remnant of the dream is dying now and there will be no phoenix.

I turned away and walked to the front door, then turned to look at her, just once more. But from where I stood her long black hair hung like a shroud and I could see nothing of her face.

"You should ring for a doctor, you know," I said.

I waited a few seconds, they could be our last together, but she neither looked at me nor spoke to me.

"Good-bye," I said.

Nothing. The wild heart denied, forgot, that had set her blood astir and brought diamonds to her eyes.

I turned the key in the lock and opened the door. A stringy, balding middle-aged man in a bright green dressing-gown stared first at me, and then behind me.

"Oh, my God!" he muttered.

I walked past him, down the stairs, one at a time, clutching the handrail, and out into the street. For a moment or two the fresh air of the night sharpened my senses again. I got into my car and set off for St Mary's Hospital in Paddington, but after a time I knew that it was going to be a close thing; the wounded arm had gone dead on me, the smell of my own blood was making me sick. I got to St Mary's, but somewhere between my car and Casualty I finally passed out.

I woke up in a ward, slowly. For a bit I just lay there, thinking, remembering. A large clock on the wall opposite told me it was a quarter to seven; a passing nurse saw my eyes open. She stopped, she smiled, she produced a thermometer, a reflex action, I think.

It took me six hours to talk myself out of that ward and away from the hospital. I needed nursing they said, a rest, the wound had to be given time to heal, there was the possibility of infection. And, of course, they were curious. Even in Paddington you have to explain bullet wounds. However, it's a great help when one of the hospital consultants is an old family friend, and early in the afternoon he was back from my flat with a change of clothing; and had got me signed out.

They had my arm in a sling, and I didn't fancy trying to drive the car one-handed. I took a cab home and by the time I got to my front door I was beginning to think that probably they had been right at the hospital. I felt tired and dizzy again. On the hall mat there was a letter with just my name on it. I picked it up and took it with me into the living-room and lay down on my sofa. I tore open the envelope.

"Mike. I arrived in London with Monsignor Wells at

midday and rang you without success from the airport. Called now, two o'clock, still no luck. Staying tonight with him, could you telephone 361-4880 when you return. Gregory."

I let the note flutter to the floor. I wasn't sure that I was ready for dear Gregory, not quite yet. I lay there for half an hour or so, trying not to think about anything because I knew that I'd exhausted my credit in pleasant thoughts. And then I got up, and fetched a new packet of cigarettes from my desk, and rang Robert Payne. I told him that I needed the papers I'd left with him urgently, but that I had done a hurt to my arm and didn't feel up to coming round for them. The idea of his dropping them off at my flat on his way home didn't appeal to him. I reminded him of the business that I'd pushed his way in years past. He didn't like that either, but in the end he allowed me to talk him into it.

I poured myself a whisky and returned to the sofa but almost immediately the phone began to ring. I got up again.

"Where the blazes have you been all day?" Carrington said, irritably. "We've been trying to get hold of you since ten o'clock this morning."

Of course I could tell Carrington to go and take a running jump at himself any time.

"I'm sorry," I said. "I've only just come in."

"I know that. I've been ringing at half-hourly intervals."

"I see. What's the trouble then?"

"Shafei has been picked up following a shooting affray in a flat in Knightsbridge."

I wanted to make some comment, but nothing came.

"Did you hear me?" Carrington said loudly.

"Yes. When did this happen?"

"In the early hours of this morning, a neighbour got in touch with the police, and they found Shafei shot in the leg. He's been taken to a hospital."

"I see."

I waited for the bit I didn't want to hear.

"I doubt if you do. The extraordinary thing is that the incident happened in the flat of a Canfield employee. Mrs Poulson."

"Really," I said. I took a deep breath. "You've got Mrs Poulson then?"

"No. She was there all right, and another man, but they got away before the police came. Which is where you come in. We've been given to understand by Mr Pritchard and Mrs Poulson's secretary that you were friendly with her. That you saw a lot of her, in fact. Is that true?"

"Yes."

"I see. We'd like to talk to you straight away, Locke. Hughes is here and a couple of Special Branch men, we need to know everything you have on her."

"She's just a friend," I said. "I doubt if I can materially assist in . . ."

"Please don't argue, Locke, we've been waiting some hours for you and the position is extremely urgent."

"All right."

I looked at my watch.

"I won't be able to make it before seven o'clock," I said.

"Why the blazes not, it's only half past five now, you don't seem . . ."

"Don't push me too hard, Carrington," I said. "Any time you want my resignation I shall be pleased to give it. I can't make it before seven, O.K.?"

It wasn't in keeping, talking to Carrington like that. I didn't care, but he did. He blustered, but he had no option, not really. He said they would wait for me.

Chapter 9

AT five-thirty that afternoon England lost the Second
Test, by an innings and twelve runs, having followed on.
I sat watching the last few overs wondering rather why I
cared. With nothing to play for the tail-enders were
chancing their arm and every now and then, head high
and bat flaying, they made contact. It was something to
cheer for a change, for it had been a lean few days for
patriots.

The last wicket fell and the commentator began disin-
terring familiar excuses; there's an art in turning defeats
into moral victories but it doesn't make good viewing. I
switched off, picked the phone up and rang Gregory.

He sounded pleased to hear from me, in fact over-
flowing with untypical bubbling exuberance; heady stuff
I thought, and a flourish in his voice that I did not entirely
recognize. We didn't have long to talk, he was off to
church with Wells, he told me, but those three or four
explosive minutes left me disturbed. We arranged that he
would come to see me at my flat the following morning,
at eleven-thirty.

I put the phone down and stood thinking about
Gregory. Fervour he was certainly capable of, though I
had never known him as otherwise than in complete control of his emotions. He could even be demonstrative,

though strictly in a minor key. But on the phone he had
sounded . . . frenzied. It worried me.

Soon after six o'clock Robert Payne arrived somewhat
out of temper, with my briefcase and the Ricardi papers. I
would have liked to tell him that his journey had been a
worthwhile one, that for a few days he had harboured
one of the greatest historical finds of all time, he deserved
it, I thought. I brought a couple of cans of beer out of the
fridge instead, cold comfort one might say, but it was the
best I could do for him right then. One day perhaps I
would tell him, tell him something he could dine out on
for many a month, that he had had the treasure of Beth
She'arim, in his old shop off Praed Street, Paddington.
With a bit of practice it would make a good yarn. He
drank his beer but didn't linger. He was taking the wife
out he said, and it saved me the embarrassment of urging
him to be on his way. By a quarter to seven I was on my
way to Regent's Park in a taxi.

My reception in Hughes's office was not cordial. No
thanks for coming, no polite chit-chat, no cigarette from
Hughes's handsome silver case. As cosy as a slab of ice. In
reply to the inevitable question about my arm and the
sling I told them that I had a boil that had gone septic on
me; the information drew no solicitude from any of the
four men there; Carrington seemed quite cheered by it.
Jameson, of course, I had never liked; his colleague, Hall,
clearly viewed me with the greatest suspicion, and Carrington was still in a huff.

Hughes asked me to sit down, a chair was ready for me,
positioned so that I would face the four of them.

"Shouldn't there be a spotlight shining in my face?" I said pleasantly, but they all seemed to be practising their poker faces.

"Locke," Hughes said, "you've been told already that Shafei was found in Mrs Poulson's flat, in the early hours of this morning. We've been probing all day, and it has now emerged that her maiden name is Montagnard, that she is in fact Shafei's sister. No doubt that surprises you?"

He gave me an innocent guileless look of inquiry, but I didn't trust him.

"Very much," I said.

"We can assume that Mrs Poulson has been an active agent from the day that she started work at the Canfield, feeding Shafei with any information she could lay her hands on, from whatever source."

He paused, doubtless not wishing me to miss the significance of the last three words.

"We have not been able to trace Mrs Poulson so far, and we are eager to catch her before she gets out of the country. We need every lead we can get, but unfortunately it would seem as if she was something of a social recluse, at least as far as her associates at work are concerned. We have been interviewing people at the Canfield all day but no one could tell us anything remotely relevant about her." He looked at me, his eyebrows raised questioningly, but there wasn't anything relevant that I wanted to say either.

"We do understand, however, that you are the one exception, in that you have been a close friend of Mrs Poulson for some time. Or so we have been told, and naturally we would like to know all that you can tell us about her. Jameson has a few questions he wishes to put to you, and I would ask you to be completely frank with us."

I nodded and turned my attention to Jameson. He could have done without the Hughes's waffle, one could tell by the sour look on his face, it wasn't his kind of approach, too courteous, too democratic. 'Butch' Jameson, Mortensen used to call him which suited, for as faces go his lacked finesse. Big and broad yet thin lipped, strong bones and mean little eyes. Some years back he had switched to Special from the police force and to my way of thinking he must have looked more the part as one of the black booted toughs who ride police motor-bikes. One man's prejudice of course, no doubt there were those who thought him the salt.

He sat now next to Hughes with a file open in front of him and a couple more by his elbow. The phrase 'a few questions' can come in many sizes, Jameson stretched it almost beyond recognition. But it wasn't the duration of Jameson's inquisition that was noteworthy, but rather the fact that for the first half-hour he was concerned with me and not with Louise. My childhood, my education, my travels abroad, my political affiliations. It was all on the file they had on me, the one in front of his nose probably, and the irrelevance of his questions probably bored the others as much as they did me. But Jameson was a plodder who did things by the book and the book said that one should start at the beginning.

It gave me warning enough that I was suspect.

"When did you first meet Mrs Poulson?" Jameson asked, his fiftieth question, or thereabouts.

"Just under two years ago. She was handling the advance publicity on one of my trips."

"In her professional capacity only, how often would you expect to see her, on average?"

"Once or twice before each mission, and I usually do three missions a year. Of course one meets the staff in the canteen and . . ."

"How soon was it before you began to meet Mrs Poulson in a more personal capacity?"

"A few months."

"And then?"

"Quite frequently. Once or twice a week on average."

"Your relationship with Mrs Poulson became intimate?"

I felt in my pocket for my packet of cigarettes. I was starting to dislike his questions as much as I did his face.

"Yes," I said.

"You lived together?"

"No."

"A casual relationship then?"

I felt tempted to spit in his eye, the faintly bloodshot one to the left of his big squashed nose. I lit my cigarette and took my time over it.

"Would you mind replying to the question?" Hughes said curtly.

"Certainly I mind. What the hell is this anyway, a consistory court investigating moral turpitude?"

"Now look here . . ." Jameson exploded but Hughes interrupted him.

"Just a minute. Locke, this attitude of yours isn't going to get us very far. You are the only person who can help us with our investigation of Mrs Poulson, you may even be in a position to give us a lead on her whereabouts. I don't have to tell you how important a matter this is, so please answer the questions without making a fuss."

"I get the impression that I am the one who is being investigated, not Mrs Poulson."

Hughes fidgeted, frowned and looked irritable.

"That's nonsense," he said shortly and nodded to Jameson to get on with it.

Jameson started up again, and the questions were more on target. Louise. It took Jameson to ram home the truth about Louise and me, truth so long ignored, truth with the sharp edges filed down, for comfort. After two years, could I really know so little about her, could it all have been so frail? About her husband, Jameson said, but she had never talked to me about her husband, just a man she had married and it hadn't worked out. Relations? Yes, a mother in Leeds, whom I had never met and would never meet now. Friends? Yes, there had been the occasional reference to friends, once or twice, faceless, nameless; and one evening I had met a young couple in her flat, he had been a doctor, English I thought, and she had curly red hair.

"It strikes me as remarkable," Hall said, "that you are unable to tell us more about a woman who was a close friend of yours for nearly two years."

He didn't believe me, of course; none of them did.

"Yes, Mrs Poulson is a secretive person," I said, "and I understand why, now."

Secretive about the things that don't matter I told myself, but between us there had been something else surely, a different kind of truth, a breathless truth that left no room for real secrets and evasions.

Jameson tried again. But I didn't know where she had her hair done, or where she went for her grocieries, or at which garage she serviced her car; and after a time it got to be embarrassing all round.

"And you have absolutely no idea at all where she might be at the present moment?"

"None."

The little silence that followed was loaded with disbelief but I didn't care a damn. I wasn't wearing their colours any more.

"What will happen to Shafei?" I said. I was entitled to ask a question or two myself I thought.

"He is a foreign national," Hughes said. "When he has recovered he will be requested to leave the country and not to return. He has committed no crime in this country that we know of."

"And Mrs Poulson?"

"If we catch her before she manages to slip out of the country," Carrington barked, "we'll throw the book at her. She's British, she's committed serious treason, we shall go for the maximum penalty."

He looked at Hughes for support but Hughes wasn't all that pleased with the outburst.

"There is nothing more that you can tell us then, Locke?"

"I don't think so."

"I'll be frank, we had hoped for greater co-operation."

"I've told you all I know. It's a bit sparse, but would you expect one of your own agents to be expansive about himself? We're all a bit schizophrenic in this job aren't we, one half under permanent lock and key. How much do you tell your wife?"

"That's hardly relevant," he said, curtly.

"Mrs Poulson is a good agent, that's what it amounts to. She kept her mouth shut."

Hughes sighed.

"Well, if that's your last word I don't think that we need detain you any longer."

He got up – built-in politeness asserting itself whatever the circumstances – but the others didn't bother. He opened the door for me, we said good-night to each other; I made my way through the empty building out into the cool night air, and I was glad to get away from them.

A big ripe moon hung low in the sky and its reflection shimmered like silver foil on the lake. A light wind brought a murmur to the trees, a man and a woman walked slowly by, their arms entwined; a faint scent of mown grass laced the night air and only my thoughts intruded.

The host of vehicles that lined the road during daytime had mostly gone, but a few yards down a solitary car was parked with only one of its side lights shining. Shining

bright, a fearful asymmetry. I waited for a taxi, I didn't
mind waiting, not on such a night. In due course a taxi
came along. I got in and gave the driver my address. And
then, as if the magic of the night had been shut out when
I closed the cab door, my thoughts returned to Hughes's
room, to Jameson and all his questions. It's funny about
loyalty, but it takes time to opt out, to disengage from
the group identity. In spite of everything I found that I
still felt one of them, involved with their problems, seeing things their way. The self-transcendent need of the ego
to belong, or something like that. I could not only understand their suspicion of me, I could somehow share it
with them, be a part of their anger. It depressed me, a
schoolboy emotion of having let the side down, my own
side.

I wondered how much they knew; whether Abelson
had gone to the police after all; if Louise's neighbour, the
man in the green dressing-gown, had given an accurate
description of me; if Louise's secretary had told Hughes
that I had known of her visit to Leeds. There could be
many reasons for their suspicion, too many.

I sighed and lit a cigarette. A man can get intimidated
by circumstances I told myself, but the choice is his own.
I didn't have to cultivate my ulcers, not yet awhile. I
tried to think of something else.

The taxi turned away from the park and at the entrance
to Baker Street the traffic lights were red and we came to
a stop. I turned to look back one last time at the moon
hovering above the trees. The car with the permanent
wink came up slowly behind us; and picked up speed

again as the lights changed and we moved off. It followed us along Baker Street and was still there, some twenty yards or so behind, as we turned into Oxford Street. Circling Marble Arch we collected a tight little clutch of traffic and I lost sight of our one-eyed friend, and by the time we turned off the Bayswater Road I began to think that perhaps I had been suffering from 'Canfield *caffard*', a known professional hazard.

But my peace of mind was short-lived; as I got out of the taxi outside my flat old one-eye came round the corner. The car slowed as if to stop, then picked up speed again to pass me, slowed again, and after some hesitation took the first turning to the left and vanished.

I had never supposed that a car could look furtive but that one managed it.

I paid the cabby and went up to my flat; on the front door mat I found a note, two sentences scribbled on a page torn from a pocket diary and pushed through the letter-box.

"Hoped to find you in. Please ring me at home, at once, but from a public telephone box. Mortensen."

The words 'from a public telephone box' were underlined.

I screwed the paper up and threw it in a waste-paper basket. The only 'at once' I felt in the mood for was a drink. I went and got one and put my feet up. After all, it's not every day that a Canfield man gets tailed by his own side, it justified a bit of quiet meditation and the reassuring comfort of a Scotch or two. I had a drink and considered the absurd fallibilities of organizations like

the Canfield. So what did I care that they had put some
trainee to tail me, or of the half-baked logic that had led
them to suppose that I was 'in' on the Shafei set-up. Or
perhaps they didn't mind whether I knew that I was
being tailed? Perhaps, even, they wanted me to know. I
considered both possibilities but neither led me anywhere
that I liked the look of.

I finished my drink, checked Mortensen's phone
number, made sure I had a few sixpences on me, and set off
for the public telephone box in the entrance hall of the
building. It's a bleak, sterile kind of hall, not so much in
the hospital sense, but just as an environment for people.
A large bowl of plastic flowers selected at random from all
the seasons, dust-laden in lieu of pollen; an ugly marble-
topped table supported on curly wrought-iron legs; and
two uncomfortable upright armchairs. In the three years
that I had been a tenant there I had only once seen one of
those armchairs actually used, by an elderly, fat lady
who was suffering from asthma and who sat there getting
her breath back. You had to have a good reason to want
to linger in that hall.

But as I stepped out of the lift that evening I saw that
one of the armchairs was occupied, for a second time. By a
man I presumed as I could only see the lower half of dark-
blue trousers and black shoes. The rest of the person was
hidden behind a fully opened *Daily Telegraph*. I stood and
stared at that blatant cliché of a detective at work and
considered peeping over the top and pulling a face. I felt
entitled to take offence with this kind of amateurism.
However, I thought better of it and stepped into the

phone-box instead. I rang Mortensen and he answered it himself.

"Mike Locke," I said. "I got your note and am ringing from a public box."

"Good! I'm glad you're still around. I was beginning to wonder."

"Meaning what?"

"You should know, old boy. I got back from Cairo late last night and most of today I've spent at the Canfield being grilled about you. So as an old friend, I thought I'd let you know that your phone is being bugged."

"Thanks. I guessed when I read your note. I'm being tailed too as a matter of fact. What else is in store for me?"

"Well, I'm neither Hughes's nor Jameson's favoured confidant, but I rather gather that you're their public enemy number one right now. You've had your little chat with them by now, no doubt?"

"Yes."

I gave him an outline of what had been said to me, and by me.

"You've still got your passport?" Mortensen said at the end of it.

"Sure."

"I'd consider a quick impromptu holiday. Tristan-da-Cunha, lower Patagonia, something on those lines." But I was discomforted to discover that in spite of his wisecracks Mortensen believed not only that I was in serious trouble, but also that I was not entirely innocent of some kind of double-dealing with the Canfield. He didn't say so in so many words, but then he didn't have to. He hedged, and that was enough.

"Look, Henry," I said irritably, "this is nonsense and you know it. Why should I pass on information to Louise Poulson which she could obtain herself? We are all agreed that almost anybody at the Canfield could find out your times of arrival at Cairo, you said so yourself at the Bird-cage Walk meeting."

"No, we overlooked something. Late last autumn, I went to Cairo specifically to meet your pal Gumbar. You fell sick at the last moment, remember?"

"Well?"

"There was no publicity, quite the contrary. But Shafei's man was there all the same."

I started fumbling with a cigarette.

"It seems that there has to be somebody else," Mortensen said unhappily.

"So why me? I should have thought..."

"Mike, when they line up the five possibles you stick out like a sore thumb. You must see that surely?"

"But good God, it was me who told them who Shafei was!"

"I know, I know. I don't get it, honestly..."

"Who are the five?"

There was a short silence.

"Hughes, Carrington, Miss Waterton, you and me," he said apologetically. "We worked it out, there wasn't anybody else who could have known."

Put that way there wasn't much scope for argument.

Hughes's and Carrington's loyalty couldn't be doubted, nor Miss Waterton's hatred of Israel.

"I'm sorry," I said, "but there must be somebody else. A secretary, the man who issued your plane ticket, somebody."

I should, I suppose, have been grateful that he had troubled to warn me but instead I found myself getting angry. I remained angry five minutes later when we had finished our little chat and I stepped out of the telephone box.

The man in the blue trousers was still reading his newspaper. On an impulse I went up to him.

"I'm going to bed now," I said. "I thought that you would like to know."

The paper came down suddenly. A youngish man with sallow skin and large protruding ears stared anxiously at me, his mouth slightly agape.

"It will comfort me to think of you here, O faithful watchdog, O eternal sentinel."

The mouth dropped a bit more, showing yellow teeth.

"Vindicating your existence in this mean place," I added.

He seemed to be having some difficulty in breathing and beads of sweat were forming on his brow. I stared at him blankly. On second thoughts he didn't at all look like a Special Branch man.

"Good grief!" I muttered, "Don't tell me that you're just another asthmatic?"

He was looking quite frightened now. I turned away

and walked back to the lift. I thought, damn it, he *must* be one of Jameson's boys, but I didn't have the nerve to look back at him.

There was a late night film on the goggle box and I settled down in front of it in search of some badly needed entertainment and distraction. It provided me with little of either, being an old cheaply made murder melodrama of the early fifties. Its plot centred round a crime that appeared to be motiveless; the *dénouement* revealed that the murderer had been deliberately deceived as to the character and activities of the victim. What seemed meaningful to him therefore appeared meaningless to the outside world. One could have wished for some good existentialist director to exploit that interesting if familiar paradox, but the film remained soggy and banal to the end.

However, it told me who the real traitor at the Canfield was.

Chapter 10

IN the morning I decided that I was ready to give up my wounded hero disguise; the fashion was for black eye-patches anyway. The arm was still a bit sore but it didn't seem to make much difference whether I wore the sling or not.

I was having breakfast when the doorbell rang. I looked at my watch and thought, Gregory is early, perhaps he's skipped Matins or something for it had only just turned nine o'clock. But it wasn't Gregory.

A tall young man with a pleasant grin stood outside the door.

"My name is Halpern," he said. "I have a message for you."

He didn't look like a Halpern, not with all that blond hair and the rosy cheeks and the pale-blue eyes.

"You're sure you've got the right place? Locke is my name."

"Yes, I know," he said, and grinned some more. He had a curious hybrid accent, Commercial Road cockney and a touch of the Bronx, I thought.

"Come in then," I said.

I shut the door behind him and led him to the kitchen.

"Forgive me if I finish my breakfast but I hate cold eggs. Take a chair."

We both sat down.

"How do you know me?" I asked. "I don't know you that I'm aware of."

"I hit you over the head, a couple of nights back," he said pleasantly. I looked at him and nodded.

"So you're the louse," I said, and went on eating.

"I'm sorry, I hate hitting a man from the back, but you weren't being nice to my friend."

He pulled out a packet of cigarettes, stuck one in his mouth and put the packet back in his pocket.

"That coffee smells the way I like it," he said.

"You've got a damned nerve."

"No hard feelings, I hope, I was just doing my job."

"Hard feelings, that's an apt way of putting it. There's a mug on the dresser behind you."

He brought the mug and I poured him some coffee. If all the people on one's own side were nice and all those on the other side were nasty, life could be that much simpler.

"You made a hell of a mess of my flat too, and all for nothing."

"Yeah. We tried not to damage anything, we took trouble, but I'm sorry about that too."

I spread some marmalade on my toast.

"You don't look all that sorry," I said between mouthfuls.

"Yeah. I reckon I gotten past the crying stage by now, but you should have seen me yesterday . . ."

"You say you've got a message for me?"

He pulled out a letter from his breast pocket.

"From a man called Nassim, I don't think you know the guy."

I took the envelope from him.

"Nassim? Sounds vaguely familiar."

"We all have a friend in common I guess," he said, but I had already remembered.

"How is Mrs Poulson then?" I said.

"She's O.K. She asked me to say hullo and good-bye to you."

"You've got her out of the country yet?"

"No, these things take time; you've got to be smart."

"They'll make it tough for her if they catch her, a British subject and all that."

"You don't have to tell me, but thanks all the same. For giving her a break I mean; we know it meant sticking your own neck out."

I nodded and opened the letter. It was written in ink in a generous flowing hand.

"One last appeal to reason, to common sense, and to your integrity as an historian. As it is not money you seek, nor notoriety, it can only be some very personal concept of loyalty to a friend that stops you from returning the Beth She'arim papers to their rightful ownership. I beg you to believe me that this loyalty is misplaced. Swain wants this unique record destroyed, and destroy it he will if he is given the opportunity. You must accept this as true and I cannot believe that you wish such a thing to happen.

"In spite of the fact that an approach to the British authorities would be an embarrassment to us, for reasons

which you will readily understand, we now have no
alternative. We must prevent the possibility of your
handing over the papers to Swain when he comes to
London.

"Unless, therefore, you are prepared to hand them over
to Halpern within one hour of your reading this letter, I
shall immediately get in touch with the Foreign Office and
the police. Nassim."

I folded the letter and put it back in the envelope.

"There's one more thing," Halpern said. "Something
that Nassim couldn't write. If he has to go to the police he
will make no effort to suggest that you were not involved
with Shafei, these last two or three years. You get my
meaning?"

I lit a cigarette.

"Yes, I get your meaning. He'll see that I'm stuck with a
double agent tag."

Halpern just grinned.

"I have to wait for your answer," he said after a while.
I thought about it. It's curious about double agents,
how the law hates them. For murder or rape or robbery
with violence you can scrape through with ten or
twelve years more often than not. But if they catch a
double agent flogging the plans of a local NAAFI
canteen for the price of a new suit they put him away
for thirty."

"He must be all mixed up, your friend, Nassim," I said.
"First he invokes my integrity, then he tries blackmail, all
in one breath."

"It's just that he cares a lot about those papers."

"Perhaps, the way women care about diamonds. For the pleasure of possession; because they are valuable, rare, prestigious."

"Is that so wrong?"

"There are other ways of caring, the way Swain cares for instance. A different kind of integrity, something of a joke I suppose in our acquisitive society, but I'm not sure I want to laugh."

"They didn't tell me that you talked so much. So what's your answer?"

"I have to see Swain, he gave them to me and I want to know what he wants them for. Curiosity, put it down to that."

"For a clever guy you don't show much common sense, knowing what you've been told."

"Common sense isn't everything. A man needs something else in life; just for flavour you might say . . ."

"Look, do me a kindness will you, a single Yes or No; how about it?"

"I don't see why I should sell Gregory short just for you, or Nassim, or anybody else."

"Just in one word, please."

"No."

Halpern sighed, stubbed his cigarette out and got up.

"If I have to wait as long for my funeral I shan't complain," he said.

I got up too, and led him out of the kitchen.

"Maybe you're wrestling with shadows, huh?" he said, "just a bit, what d'you say?"

"Could be, there are lots around. Sometimes one can't see one's way for shadows."

He laughed.

"I should have known better than to ask," he said.

I opened the front door for him.

"If there's a man sitting in one of the armchairs in the hall," I said, "spit in his eye for me, will you?"

"It's not gentlemanly," he said, "but I'll do that."

I saw him out and returned to the kitchen. The heat of another warm summer's day was beginning to build up, shirt-sleeves and strawberries, one could tell by the powder-blue haze. I opened a couple of windows. The hum of the traffic thundering down Bayswater Road was louder than usual, wind from the south I supposed. The woman upstairs had begun shouting at her nice husband, the way she did every now and then, and someone some-where was making a hash of a Chopin nocturne. But my own little world was suddenly losing touch with the background buzz of everyday things. It happens that way when one starts worrying about self-preservation, all you can think of is the life-belt. I began clearing up, through restlessness rather than any feeling for domestic order. For it seemed to me that I was in trouble, 22 carat trouble.

If Nassim set off his little booby trap for me, as Halpern said he would, then I could book my accommodation with one of H.M. prisons right there and then. It was on the cards, a deal to get Jameson's co-operation in locating the Beth She'arim papers. It was no skin off Nassim's nose to say that I'd been tied up with Shafei all these years, no trouble at all. He'd buy a lot of gratitude from Butch Jameson with that. I didn't like to speculate on what it would buy me. I wiped the table-top and listened to the old girl upstairs, still shouting away, the words themselves lost in the floor between us, but the tone of indignation and anger coming through clear enough. I never heard the man, I guess he just sat there wishing the world at large would let him be. And that made two of us.

Of course a man doesn't have to just sit around waiting for the arrows of outrageous fortune to make another St Sebastian of him. I began to consider what I should do to avoid premature martyrdom. I could take Mortensen's advice and get out. Or I could try to prove that I was no kind of a traitor. One or the other. Either way time was the enemy.

I looked at my watch. Half past nine. At eleven-thirty Gregory would be coming to collect the Beth She'arim papers; at about the same time I could expect somebody to come to collect me.

I picked up the relevant telephone directory and looked up Waterton, Miriam, Miss. I wrote the address down in my diary, picked up the Sesame Kit, and made my way out of the flat. There was no sign of anyone around keeping a watch on me. I tried to work up a bit of optimism about my mission but the needle stuck at zero. Probably there was no proof, not in her flat, not anywhere. I told myself that I had nothing to lose but even that thought didn't carry much conviction. I drove myself to Belsize Park.

Miss Waterton lived in an old-fashioned-looking block of flats, nineteen thirties vintage, designed on the external corridor principle. Outside the lift a bronze plate allocated flat numbers to each floor and number twelve was on the first; I walked up and made my way out on to the access balcony.

Outside her door I stopped. I rang the bell and waited, wondering what I would say to her if she had decided to take the day off instead of going to the office. After a couple of minutes I rang again. Nothing. I looked around, casually, then pulled out my Sesame Kit and started to work on the lock. It presented no problem and I let myself in, shutting the door quietly behind me. I stood there for a moment, listening.

The hall was planned as a corridor serving half a dozen doors; close carpeted, free of furniture except for a narrow table against the left wall. A bowl of flowers on the table, two pictures on opposite walls. One of the doors was glazed and I made my way to it, and entered the living-room. It was quite a room. The immediate impression was of a film property store for some desert epic, except that everything was too orderly. Trinkets and *objets d'art* of all kinds were crammed on to every available shelf, table and wall, and one could suppose that Miss Waterton was a familiar and welcome figure in the souks of the Middle East.

Figurines, amulets and little objects weighed down with history covered several shelves of a glass-fronted bookcase; above the fireplace a small faded oriental carpet hung, from a brass rail; to its left six Persian tiles, framed in wood, enticed the eye to admire a wonder of exquisite turquoise and cobalt blues; metal, clay and faience pieces of all kinds met the eye wherever one turned; amongst the books *The Seven Pillars of Wisdom* bound in white calf took pride of place; on the wall facing the fireplace a large photograph of Nasser, his bright eyes staring away at some pan-Arabian Utopia no doubt; a map of Luxor; an amateur's water-colour of Baalbek against an impossible mauve sunset. There seemed no end to it, the loot, one supposed, of many memory-laden journeys, deployed here to promote instant recall and ward off the emptiness of long winter evenings.

I walked round, just looking, resisting the temptation to linger over things that caught my interest, surprised every now and then at the quality of some of the items there. It wasn't the Miss Waterton I had chosen to see over the years; not just the infatuated romancing of a middle-aged schoolgirl. I felt a twinge of guilt.

A large ornate Japanese type bureau stood by the wall facing the window. The telephone rested on it and it contained several drawers. I suspected that if I was to find anything of use to me it would be there, but decided to make a quick survey of the flat before examining anything in detail. A door facing the one I had entered by led to the kitchen. I looked in briefly and then returned to the entrance corridor. I opened the first door on my left. It was Miss Waterton's bedroom.

I could tell because both Miss Waterton and her bed were in it.

I stood in the doorway and looked at her across the width of the room. She lay on her bed, fully dressed, one hand clutched in a tight fist just under her chin, the other hanging down to the floor. Her eyes were closed, her mouth slightly open, and a wisp of grey hair curled across her puckered brow. A bedlight on the wall was switched on. From where I stood she looked dead.

I walked slowly across to her and put my hand to her pallid cheek. It was very cold. On her bedside table were three objects. An empty glass, an empty medicine bottle and a small framed photograph. I picked up the photograph. It showed an elderly couple in a flower garden, dressed in the fashion of the twenties. 'From Mummy and Daddy' someone had written at the bottom. They were smiling, faded sepia smiles full of indulgent hope for their Miriam. I put the photo down again. Miss Waterton's face was turned towards it, the last thing she had seen before closing her eyes, their look of love, arrested for ever on that summer's day long ago. I returned to the living-room, to the bureau and began opening the drawers, flicking through papers, diaries, a personal address book. I spent ten minutes doing that, and it was sufficient. I put the things back where they had come from and rang up the Canfield. I asked for Hughes but was told that he wasn't expected till later that morning. I asked for Carrington but Carrington had gone to Portsmouth for the day. I hung up.

I drove home, my thoughts with Miss Waterton. Nobody's bride yet she had found a passion for the long petty years, a mute passion to make a ferment in her blood. A traitor they would call her, yet she had not been false to herself. The wrong deed for the right reason, maybe that doesn't need any excuses.

I reached home and rang Hughes again, but he still hadn't arrived. I put the phone down and went to sit in an armchair. I lit a cigarette and shut my eyes. The front door bell rang. I got up again and went to see who it was. Gregory stood outside and gave me his big smile, the one with sunbeams at the edges.

"Mike," he said, "it's good to see you again!"

We shook hands warmly and I led him into the flat; it was always nice seeing Gregory again, whatever the circumstances. It was his first visit to me there and the interest that he showed in it was, I knew, more than politeness. He had once confessed to me that one of the most difficult adjustments he had had to make on entering his Order was the forsaking of private possessions. At college he had been something of a magpie, cluttering up his room with every kind of bric-à-brac.

"Ah yes, the Daumier cartoons," he said standing in front of them, "how well I remember them. But this is new, isn't it?"

He picked up a large Anatolian plate with blue and green plant motifs, admired it, put it down again; and wandered over to my books.

"I was thinking of making some coffee," I said.

"That would be nice." He was engrossed reading book titles, turning his head sideways every now and then. I went to the kitchen leaving the door open between us. We talked and he wandered about the living-room, and after a time I wasn't sure whether it was curiosity or nervous tension that kept him on the move like that.

I brought the coffee in and we sat down facing each other.

"How's the writing, Mike, anything new that I should be reading?"

I brought him up to date on my work, and all the time he kept fidgeting, shifting in his chair, fumbling with his crucifix, his eyes restless. I saw no point in boring him for too long.

"And how was Rome?" I said.

He brightened up then.

"Ah! Wonderful as ever. So much visual delight, Mike, so much of man's history and genius at every turn. I'm always at peace with myself there you know, it's like coming home, for me."

He sipped his coffee.

"You had no difficulty with my suitcase," he said. At last.

"Not through Customs, no. But later."

He seemed to freeze in his chair.

"Don't worry, the contents are safe, only the case is a wreck."

"What happened?" he said, softly, his eyes now riveted on me.

"Lots of things. I've been hit on the head, shot in the arm, threatened, spied on. My flat has been broken into; that's when your case was ripped to shreds."

"What are you saying, Mike? Is this all true?" Both his

hands were clenched, and the sudden change in his appearance worried me.

"Yes. You see, I'm afraid that quite a lot of people seem to know about your suitcase, and what was in it. They know and they want to have these papers."

"How – how do they know, how could they? Mike, what is all this?"

"It's quite a story, not all of it convincing and some of it I can't tell you anyway. You know, of course, that a great deal of publicity was given to Ricardi's death, not least the statement issued by Israel about his having taken something special out of the country."

"Mike, all I want to be told is how and when and why that case was opened and its contents removed."

"I'm doing just that, Gregory. When I got back home I met an old friend and not unnaturally we talked about my trip. I happened to mention that I had met Ricardi in Beirut; you know how it is, 'I know somebody who is in the public eye', that kind of thing. And about you, and the case; it was just something to talk about, I didn't know it was so special, then. Unfortunately it turned out that the person concerned was an Israeli agent and . . ."

"What on earth do you mean, 'turned out to be an Israeli agent'? How does an old friend 'turn out' to be an Israeli agent?"

He was angry now, it was understandable enough. I explained, as best I could. Truth and lies, cheek by jowl; a quagmire of deception through which I trod laboriously and carefully, but mostly he was too upset to pick up all the loose ends.

"Are you telling me that you're some kind of a spy?" he said, when I had finished.

"The word is dated, but something like that, yes."

"I see. All this comes as a great shock to me, I had no idea, I would never have given you the case. You should have told me, Mike."

I lit a cigarette.

"You were a shade less than honest with me yourself, you know," I said. "Besides, I had no reason to anticipate the kind of situation that emerged."

He slumped back in his chair and fell silent.

"The important thing," I said, "is that the Beth She'-arim papers are here, quite safe."

He nodded.

"Yes. I'm sorry. I am very much in your debt, I see that, and you've suffered a great deal on my account. I should be thanking you, not bawling you out. Forgive me."

"There's nothing to forgive."

"There is, but I will take advantage of our friendship." He smiled.

"I'd like to see the papers now, if I may."

I drew hard on my cigarette.

"Gregory, before I hand them over to you, there is something I would like to know. That I must know. I have been told repeatedly that it is your intention to destroy these papers, and I need your assurance that this is not true."

For a few seconds we just stared at each other, then he lay back in his armchair again and shut his eyes. With his right hand he held his crucifix, his left hand flopped down to the carpet and he sat there, quite still. A minute passed, and then another. He remained quite motionless, withdrawn. More time passed by, unnoticed . . .

I didn't mind, time is for such a purpose, to share silence with a friend. I wondered, what strange despair assails him now, what sense of sin erodes his conscience . . . dear Gregory, struggling along the long stony path to his heaven, so solitary. . . . And I thought of another solitary, her struggles over, her sins paid up, unassailable now. I would have to get hold of Hughes, soon.

Gregory sat up, slowly, and opened his eyes.

He smiled, faintly.

"Yes," he said softly, "it is true that at one time I had thought to destroy the papers of Ricardi's. But I have changed my mind."

I waited for him to say something more. But he didn't.

"Is that all?" I said, after a moment or two.

"That is what you wanted me to say, isn't it?"

He forced a smile.

"I wish to know why you want those papers, Gregory, and what you intend doing with them?"

He kept the smile going but it wasn't fooling anyone.

"Those are your conditions for returning them to me?"

"Yes. I'm sorry but I cannot give them to you unless you convince me that you do not intend to destroy them."

He nodded.

"I see. Then I shall have to try to convince you, an

objective I have rarely achieved during the course of our friendship."

"But this time I want to be convinced, Gregory."

"My word is not enough for you then?"

"I shall believe what you tell me, it's just that so far you haven't told me very much."

He sighed.

"Then I shall tell you, for there are no mysteries, no devious designs. The papers that Ricardi discovered relate to the life of our Lord. They contain much that is new, much that is . . . different. Yes, there are aspects there that are in contradiction with the Gospels. I am concerned that the first authorized publication of this testament should be undertaken by the Church. Even more, I consider it essential that the theological implications of these papers should be fully considered by the Church before they are made public. They require interpretation. You will readily appreciate the distress and the bewilderment that would be created if the testament was given to the world by an atheistic, or some anti-Christian body, if it were presented as a Denial . . ."

His voice was rising, animated by a growing fervour.

". . . which it would be, oh yes. And those of simple faith would not understand, they would be vulnerable to the distortions of an ignorant and opportunist Press, eager only for sensationalism. The lies and the mockery of those who have never known God's love would be a great hurt to them. Don't you see, you must see, Mike, that this is a job for the Church, for the Church alone."

He leant towards me, bright-eyed, demanding my acceptance.

"That is really your purpose?" I asked.

"Yes, it really is. That they should be kept from the Israelis."

I hesitated, not because I thought him implausible; it made sense, Gregory always made sense even when one disagreed with him, but somehow I couldn't quite shake off a lingering taste of uncertainty. It was no more than a faint intuitive doubt, a feeling that there was something else, something that still remained unsaid, unrevealed. I couldn't put my finger on it; but that inner tension of his was still there, tightening the skin over the sharp structure of his face. And mostly his eyes were evasive, which wasn't like him.

"Who will you be giving the papers to?" I asked.

He considered the question.

"John Wells, in the first place. Then Rome, I imagine. It will be out of my hands by then."

I nodded. And after a while I got up and went to my desk. I unlocked one of the drawers and took out the bundle that included both the originals and the envelopes with the photographs. I took the elastic band off, put the envelope back in the drawer and turned to Gregory. He was watching me intently.

I could think of no reason now for not giving the papers to him. But I just didn't want to, and my hesitation betrayed me.

"You don't believe me?" he said softly.

I looked at him. We stared at each other.

"I give you my word," he said, "as a friend, an old friend."

I had to turn away from him. I hated my doubts, not being able to trust him after all these years. Gregory of all people, a man whose integrity I had always respected. What justification could I offer for denying him? That I preferred the word of a stranger called Nassim to his?

"Would you like me to swear on the crucifix?" he said gently.

I almost winced. In refusing to trust either his word or our friendship I was humiliating both of us; he had become a suppliant for his honour and I couldn't take it. I picked up the parcel and handed it to him.

"I'm sorry, Gregory, but so many people have told me that your intentions were different."

"Mike, I understand. It's so reasonable that you should be so concerned."

He put the parcel on his lap and unwrapped it. Then carefully he took each sheet in turn and looked at it, and put it back, until he had gone through them all. I stood watching him. He held each one delicately between his finger-tips, as if they were fragile. And once he trembled slightly.

"Satan's hand," he murmured, "faded, stretching out across time. So delicate too."

"What do you mean?" I said uneasily.

He put the sheets together and began wrapping them up again.

"His ways are also strange and mysterious," he said. He looked up at me suddenly. "You have been a good

167

friend, and more besides. One day perhaps you will understand . . . you will see."

He got up.

"You know I haven't really followed all that you have told me, Mike, all those extraordinary events. Violence, even guns. But I do appreciate the part you played. I want you to know that. And now I must go."

"Well, if you must. Will you be staying in London long, we might meet again?"

"It would be nice, but I am expected back soon."

"A pity."

I was about to accompany him to the door when I remembered something.

"You might as well take Ricardi's diaries with you while you're about it."

"If you wish."

"I've been reading them when I go to bed, they're quite fascinating."

I went into my bedroom, collected them from my bedside table, put the fat rubber band round them, and brought them back to Gregory.

"Can I give you a lift somewhere, Gregory?"

"Thank you, but no. I feel like a walk across the park on such a nice day, and then I shall go and pray."

I opened the door. We shook hands, we said good-bye, I watched him walk down the corridor, clutching his loot.

I shut the door and returned to the living-room. I shook off an unreasonable yet persistent flicker of doubt, picked up the phone, and rang Hughes. This time he was in, and bellicose by his standards.

"This is Locke," I said. "I've been trying to get you for some time."

"Where are you?" he said sharply.

"At my flat. I have some bad news for you." I paused.

"Go on," he said.

"Miss Waterton is dead."

It was some time before he answered.

"Is this true?" he asked quietly.

"I'm afraid so. I've been trying to get hold of you for some time. I broke into her flat earlier this morning and . . ."

"My God!" Hughes exploded, "you've got a lot to explain, Locke."

"It's not important any more, Miss Waterton has been dead for quite a few hours, and it's almost certainly suicide."

"Suicide?" he whispered, "but why?"

"She had her reasons," I said.

There was a short silence.

"I think you had better explain that," Hughes said.

"She made a mistake. When she found out I think the irony of it was too much for her to bear. Too bitter, not something that she could go on living with. You see Mrs Poulson was only the post office in the Shafei set-up at the Canfield, the go-between. And it wasn't me who passed on the information but Miss Waterton."

"You're mad, Locke," Hughes said angrily. "Miss Waterton was not only a loyal Englishwoman but she had a genuine affection for the Arabs. I'd go so far as to say that it was one of the driving forces of her life. The very idea of her acting as an Israeli agent would have struck her as monstrous."

"Yes, it did. That's why she killed herself."

"What d'you mean?"

The anger had subsided, and I could sense the deep unease that had replaced it.

"I mean that like you, and like Carrington, and like the F.O., she thought that Shafei was an Arab. For two years she betrayed her job and her country in the belief that she was serving the Arab cause. I would suppose that she met Shafei on one of her annual holidays to the Middle East and . . ."

"Locke," he interrupted, "this is all supposition, isn't it, and you've no evidence for all these allegations, have you?"

I sighed.

"You'll find all the evidence you need in her flat; and it wasn't only departure times that she passed on. Mrs Poulson's private number is in her telephone book, she wasn't all that careful; she had no need to be really."

I could hear him breathing hard.

"Stay where you are, Locke, until someone comes to fetch you," he said.

I put the phone down.

Every crisis has its turning point, and it seemed to me that I had passed this one. Had the circumstances been different it might even have been the occasion for a celebration. A toast, to Michael Locke none other; who had suffered Doubt and Despair and mortification of the flesh, but had now reached the sunny side. Gregory had his precious papers and in due course the Vatican would certainly be returning them to Israel. Smiles all round. Nassim wouldn't need to tell lies about me, Miss Waterton's private diaries would see the light of day, Hughes would be offering me cigarettes once more from his silver case; I might even contrive to meet Louise again, no strings attached, just to rub memories together. All that and a shiny conscience too.

I poured myself a drink and thought about Louise, and felt only regret. Not about the past, not the bitter regret of betrayal for I didn't see it that way. But regret for an impoverished future, the hopes I had worn with everyday life discarded; orchids in the dustbin. I thought about Louise, perplexing Louise, because it was a nice thing to do. I turned the memory tap on and let it all bubble out, the hot and the cold, fun times and bitchy times, triumph and torment. Two years, tempestuous, alive, no regrets certainly, except for its ending.

I picked up my glass. The phone started to ring, scattering my scrapbook of images. I let it ring, I doubted whether it would be anything pleasant. Besides, I had a yen to keep the outside world at bay, just for a while longer. I got up and wandered over to my desk eager to indulge the return of normalcy, to do something ordinary again. The phone stopped ringing at last. I felt gratified with my resolution for mostly I am a compulsive answerer of telephones.

I found the place where I had previously stopped writing and re-read the paragraph; and gradually slipped back through the years, into a little enclave of events that I had not experienced myself but found all the more interesting for that. History beguiles I suspect, because time erodes the validity of personal experience, and the recording of history is really a process of imagination. I sat there at my desk, content, bringing the past to life, giving it faces, voices, purpose. Knowing that it was I and not the past that was making history. A vanity, but it fitted my mood.

The phone began ringing again. I said 'damn' and picked it up.

"Mr Locke? Michael Locke?" a man's voice said. A gentle, kindly voice, rather elderly.

"Yes."

"Ah! Good! You don't know me, Mr Locke, I've never had the pleasure of meeting you. My name is Wells, Father John Wells; we have a friend in common, Gregory Swain."

"Indeed, he has mentioned you several times."

"And he has often spoken to me of you, he holds you in great esteem. Mr Locke, I am telephoning you on a matter of some delicacy. You see, I have reason to believe that Gregory will be calling on you at any time now and it is most important that I speak to you before he does, because there is something . . ."

"Father Wells, Gregory has already called, and departed."

There was a little silence at the other end.

"I see. May I ask, did you by any chance give him the black suitcase he gave you in Beirut?"

"I gave him the contents, yes."

Another silence.

"Oh! I'm sorry about that, I was hoping to be in time."

I was beginning to have a sick feeling in the pit of my stomach.

"In time for what?" I asked.

"To warn you, not to give him those papers, not on any account."

Chapter 11

I SQUIRMED under the hateful implication of his words, my skin prickled, sweat gathered on my brow. I drew hard on my cigarette.

"Why shouldn't I have given Gregory the papers?" I asked.

"Those papers were very special, of inestimable . . ."

"I know what the Beth She'arim papers are about," I interrupted.

"I see. I didn't appreciate that Gregory had told you . . ." He hesitated fractionally.

" . . . Yet you gave him the papers? I would have thought that, under the circumstances. . . . Are you sure that you understand the significance of those documents Mr Locke, forgive my insistence but . . ."

"Yes, I do. And I saw no reason for withholding them. They were his, given to me for safe keeping. He offered me a perfectly reasonable and rational explanation of his intentions."

"Rational? No, I think that Gregory has passed that stage. Convincing up to a point perhaps, but not rational."

"What do you mean?"

"He is unwell. You are an old friend of his, you noticed surely?"

"Unwell?" I repeated woodenly.

"I think so, I can find no other explanation. Something

shut up inside, an absurd obsession, it has been a source of great concern to me."

I remembered the airport at Beirut, the heat in Gregory's eyes; the alien excitement of his voice on the telephone the day before, his restlessness earlier in the morning. But I had been unwilling to draw any uncomfortable conclusions.

I took a deep breath.

"Why shouldn't I have given him the papers?" I asked again.

"Because I regret to tell you he intends to destroy them, he . . ."

"He assured me that he intends to do nothing of the kind. He merely wants their publication to be organized by your Church."

Monsignor Wells sighed audibly.

"Ah! I'm afraid he has not told you the truth," he said. "I have been with him for three days, here and in Rome. I have reasoned with him, we've talked about it, we've prayed together for guidance, long into the night. I've tried everything, but now I know that I have failed; and because what he has in mind to do is such a terrible thing, I had decided that I could no longer honour his confidence. But it would seem that I am too late after all, and it grieves me deeply."

I felt depressed by what he said. Words that despoiled the future credibility of a long friendship.

"Thirty minutes," I said, "if you had only rung me up earlier, he was still here."

"Yes. I had meant to get in touch earlier this morning, but I had to leave, I have been travelling."

We fell silent, an unhappy quiet.

"I had six pages photographed," I said, "at least they are still in existence."

"Six? Out of twenty-six?"

I heard him sigh.

"It's something," I said.

"You have no idea where he has gone, I suppose," Wells said, after a while.

"A walk in the park. Hyde Park I presume. It's a big place."

He sighed again.

"This is a terrible thing, I feel so much to blame. Yet he came to me for help and advice, I had to listen, he was so troubled. He saw it all as a personal spiritual challenge. A Divine intervention, I could not make him see it otherwise."

"Tell me," I said, "if Gregory wanted to pray, here in London, this morning, is there a particular church that he would seek out? Within walking distance of Hyde Park say?"

"Did he say that he was going to Church?"

"He said he was going to pray after his walk."

"I see. He would go to a church then. St Anthony's, Wootton Street, perhaps. Yes, quite possibly . . ."

Colour returned to his voice, a faint hope on the wing.

" . . . I think it would be more than likely, it is a church that has special associations for him I believe; he never fails to go there when he visits London."

"Where is Wootton Street?"

"It's a very small church, little more than a chapel

really." He described its location, in Pimlico, not far south of Victoria Street.

"Are you going to see if you can find him there?" he asked, and I warmed to the sudden excitement in his voice.

"It might be worth a try, just in case he has gone there. I could make it in about fifteen minutes, and if he decided to walk it all the way . . ."

"Oh yes, certainly it is worth a try. Anything would be, to save those documents."

"Could you meet me there? With the two of us it might be easier to talk some sense into him."

"Alas, I am speaking from Islington, and I have no car. I could never get there in time. But you, Mr Locke, you should go now, every minute could make a difference, such an important difference."

We said good-bye to each other and I put the phone down. I stood there, uncertain whether I really wanted to go in pursuit of Gregory; uncommitted still to the belief that he was going to destroy the Beth She'arim papers, in spite of Wells. It's curious how the mind works, the absurd self-deceptions. An hour earlier I had been reluctant to believe Gregory; now in the face of everything I felt unwilling to jettison the faith that I resurrected; unwilling to cross again that Rubicon of doubt. It was a crazy proposition anyway, expecting to find Gregory waiting for me in some remote Pimlico church. And if he were there, then what would I say to him this time?

Out of the corner of my eye I saw that one of the drawers in my desk wasn't shut properly; the one which

I had kept locked with the Beth She'arim papers, the one where I had put back the photographs. I put one hand in my pocket for my keys and opened the drawer with the other. It was empty. I stared down at that hateful emptiness, riveted, stunned; agonizing through a long improvident moment that left me helpless with the sour anger of defeat.

I didn't have to look anywhere else for the envelope; I knew that I had put it there. I knew that Gregory had watched me take it out with the originals; that he had been curious, suspicious perhaps. That while I was in my room getting the Ricardi diaries he had looked into the drawer; found the photographs, acted according to his lights. There wasn't any room for conjecture.

So there would be no record of any kind. Nothing left from the witness who had stood at Calvary; the Scribe of Beth She'arim, Christ's friend. Not even six photographs to recall a fragment of what he had written. They would go the way of the originals, I couldn't doubt that: the slate with the offensive words wiped clean. Nothing left but a few speculations, a professor desperately trying to remember exactly what he had read.

I stood looking at the empty drawer. I finished the drink in my glass. "Hell!" I said aloud. Did I care all that much? The sun would rise tomorrow all the same. Twenty-six tattered remnants, the testament of another historian. History had been robbed before . . .

I put on my jacket, walked out of the flat and locked the door behind me.

I began to run along the corridor. The lift was not at

my floor and I reckoned that I could make the five floors down quicker by foot than wait for it. I took the stairs two at a time, then three, finally four, consumed suddenly by an overwhelming sense of urgency. For I knew that I did care, that I cared greatly, for ordinary commonplace reasons, platitudinous sentiments I would not have wished to put words to, a mindfulness distilled from so many things. . . .

I ran down the five floors and with a last flourish of a leap reached the entrance hall. Jameson and a police officer came through from the street at the same time, and the three of us came to a sudden stop some ten feet apart. Out of arm's reach but close enough to see a mean look in a man's eye.

"Going somewhere?" Jameson asked. His face was expressionless, the voice was coated in sneer.

"Just going to church," I said. I needed time, to get my breath back, to come to some decision or other.

"Quit clowning, Locke. I asked you a question."

"I gave you an answer, I'm sorry you don't like the sound of it." They took a step towards me, first Jameson and then the officer, and he was a big boy too.

"You are coming with us, Locke, there are one or two matters we would like to talk over with you."

"When did you speak to Hughes last?" I asked.

"Earlier this morning. What's that to you?"

"I rang him half an hour ago. He's got all the answers, he doesn't need to see me now."

Jameson sneered a bit more.

"That's not up to your usual standard, Locke. But then maybe you didn't know that a Mr Nassim has been telling us quite an interesting story about you?"

I moved back a bit.

"That was before I spoke to Hughes," I said.

"Could be. Let's go and talk it over with him then. Without making too much of a damned fuss about it."

I tensed myself.

"Sorry," I said, "I have a previous engagement."

Jameson shook his head slightly. His eyes were mean all right, now. A hungry cobra who had spotted an easy kill.

"It can't wait," he said softly.

"You have some authority, a warrant, perhaps?"

He allowed himself a faint smile, it didn't do much for his face though.

"You should know better than that, Locke," he said. They came at me, together.

I took a step back, turned sharply to run, and knew at once that I had left it too late. For a big man the officer moved fast, shooting out a hand that was just able to grip my jacket. I swung round, my right hand back and clenched, and aimed at his chin. It was ill-considered, at odds with the swing of my body. I hit a lot of friendly air and took his own punch to my belly without being able to do a thing about it. It was quite a punch, sixteen stones of power at least, and just that extra bite that comes when you do something for pleasure. It folded me up like a book being snapped shut, and if Jameson hadn't held me I would have hit the floor, head first.

For a few seconds I just stood there, rocking slightly, staring at three pairs of feet and a patch of blue carpet, concentrating on not vomiting, nursing a great hate, waiting for the pain to ebb, and for my strength to return.

Then they jerked me up, one on each side of me, and started dragging me along towards the entrance doors.

"C'mon you bastard," the officer muttered.

"Reckon he's passed out," Jameson grunted. "You hit him bloody hard."

They dragged me along a couple more yards.

"I'll get Norton to help us to the car," Jameson said. "We don't want any trouble in the street. You just hold him up till we get back."

The officer got both his arms round me, under my arms. Jameson let go and pushed his way through the doors. I heard his footsteps fading away. We would have a few seconds alone together now, the officer and I, ten seconds, perhaps twenty, not more. I shifted my position slightly and took the weight off my right leg. The officer hoisted me up, adjusting my weight load. I moved my right leg forward, and with all the strength I could muster I kicked backwards, bringing the heel of my shoe sharply into the shin of his left leg. Immediately he lost his balance, let go his hold, then grabbed me again to stop himself falling. It was my wounded arm that he caught and held on to, the whole weight of his body suddenly transferred to it in a sharp downward thrust. A jab of pain flashed from my wrist to my shoulder and I knew that the bullet wound had opened up again. For a brief moment he was bending forward, his head level with my stomach. I hit him on the side of the neck, right-fisted, too close for real power. But it was sufficient. He fell clinging to my arm as if his life depended on it and pulled me down with him.

He shouted "Jameson" at the top of his voice, and he

went on holding my arm, down against the floor, and struggled to turn me over. I put my knee on his upturned wrist and applied my weight to it. He grunted and let go my arm. I jerked away from him and got to my feet.

Through the glass entrance doors I saw Jameson and a uniformed policeman coming up the steps at a run. I turned and made for the staircase. Taking an optimistic view I had a ten yard start on them.

I made for the underground car park in the basement, two flights down and past a fire door. Briefly I considered a fancy Le Mans type leap into my car, but I would have had to reverse and negotiate a tight three-point turn, and my ten yard start just wasn't enough for that. I made for a small side door opposite, an escape-way out to the tradesmen's entrance. I pushed the door open, slipped inside the passage, and waited. If they assumed that I had gone for the main car exit I could look forward to a peaceful getaway, if not I had a good deal more running ahead of me.

Almost immediately I heard them burst into the garage, a lot of feet clattering across the concrete floor.

"I'll take that door," I heard Jameson shout. "You and Norton take the ramp up to the street."

The sound of running feet started up again, one pair undoubtedly making for my door. There are those who say that man is master of his own fate, jokers all I reckon.

I turned and ran up the narrow steps, out into the service yard. It is a square canyon-like place overshadowed by high walls and fire-escape staircases, cluttered with dustbins and accumulated rubbish. Half-way across the yard I heard a door crash open and Jameson shouted, "Stop that man." But there were no takers, just an echo. I ran on, out into a long narrow road, a couple of hundred yards or so long, a seedy place with old terraced houses and one-man shops, something of a relic in these parts. Not far behind I could hear Jameson, his heavy boots clacking away on the pavement, level pegging with me by the sound of it.

"Stop that man," he shouted again. A milk float stood by the kerbside and by it a youth with long hair. But he wasn't made in the heroic mould and he smiled amicably as I sped past him. Not far ahead a young coloured girl was getting off a half-sized bicycle. She stood by it, and stared towards me, her mouth open, looking scared. I began running in her direction and she backed hastily as I reached the bike.

"Sorry about this," I shouted to her and leaped on to it. It felt even smaller than it looked; I pedalled away for all I was worth, my knees working like pistons in front of me, good for a laugh if anybody was watching, but I wasn't feeling bothered about my image right then. And by the time I reached the end of the road and turned left I could see that I had more than doubled my distance from Jameson. Somewhere, not far, I heard a police car siren.

I turned left again when I reached Bayswater Road, pedalling away hard. People stared at me smiling, thinking it was some kind of stunt perhaps. Fifty feet or so along I stopped, parked the bicycle against a wall, and looked down the endless flow of oncoming traffic for a taxi. I waited. A police car, its siren wailing came down the other way at speed, and then began slowing down with the obvious intention of turning into the street I'd come from. A few more swollen seconds ticked over, each one hatefully disguised as a minute. I began keeping an eye on the road corner, and walked slowly away from it, not looking where I was going most of the time, ready to start running again.

A taxi came into view, hugging the kerbside, its yellow 'for hire' sign lit up. I stuck my arm out, the good one, and almost simultaneously Jameson appeared in the distance, on the trot. And with him two other men, one in uniform, perhaps from the police car that had driven by a minute or two earlier. They didn't see me at first, not until the taxi had actually stopped in front of me and I was halfway in it. They put on a spurt then and shouted but the actual words got lost on the way amongst the roar of the traffic.

"Wootton Street, off Victoria Street," I said to the cabby and shut the door.

We made a leisurely start, travelled slowly for a few seconds, and came to a stop at the end of a long queue of vehicles. Quite some way ahead I could see red traffic lights. I looked back through the rear window but a lorry behind us reduced my angle of vision, and I could only speculate on the progress of my pursuers. I looked at the traffic lights, and they had turned green, but I reckoned the damage had been done. There was too much stuff in front of us waiting to go. I fished half a crown out of my pocket and gave it to the driver.

"I've changed my mind," I said, and got out on the right side. Edging my way between the taxi and a large petrol tanker, I waited for a break in the opposing flow of traffic, and crossed the road.

I stood there waiting for a cab again; out of breath, feeling sick, the red patch on my jacket sleeve growing;

hoping one would come before the big tanker moved on and exposed me to Jameson's view. For I had done all the running I was capable of that day.

A taxi came. I stopped it, got in, and gave the address; sat back with a sigh of thankfulness, wiped the sweat off my brow with the back of my hand, closed my eyes and listened to my heart-beat. I felt the taxi turn but by the time I realized what was happening it was too late. The driver completed his U-turn and we were back in the up-town stream. Somewhere ahead, not far, Jameson and his pals would be searching for me, sharp-eyed, and eager.

I bent forward, my head well down, and stared at a couple of drops of fresh blood on the floor. The taxi kept on the move, a bit faster, a bit slower, but never stop-ping; and I kept my head down until I felt so dizzy that I had to straighten up.

We were nearing Marble Arch, going briskly, and not a policeman in sight. I fished out my cigarettes and lit one. My hands were shaking, a thin trickle of blood had reached my left wrist. I felt lousy.

We arrived at Wootton Street, and St Anthony's. I got out of the taxi and struggled to pay the cabbie, my left hand indifferent to the proceedings.

"Are you all right, mate?" the driver said anxiously.

"Sure, it's nothing."

"You look bad, I could take you to a doctor y'know."

"Thanks. The blood makes it look worse than it really is. I can manage."

I turned to face the church.

Chapter 12

ST ANTHONY'S was a small narrow-fronted church, hemmed in and overlooked by taller buildings; in the Early English manner, its stone blackened and worn by nature's elements and civilization's dirt. I walked uncertainly up the steps and pushed my way through the doorway.

I stood inside, enveloped by a neglectful silence and looked across rows of empty pews. A single nave but no aisles; narrow windows high up towards the vaulted roof, a chaste light that filtered, tinted, through pre-Raphaelite stained glass, emphasizing pools of darkness. Guttering candles broke the illusion of a cold empty world transfixed, four or five clustered together in one shadowed corner, and to the left of the altar a large single candle flickered in an ornate candlestick.

There was only one other person there. He was kneeling on a step in front of the altar, a lonely figure, his broad cloaked back bent in prayer, motionless, seeking I knew not what through his solitary communion. By his side lay the Beth She'arim papers, unwrapped, unmistakable even in the half-light. The altar itself was a simple thing, set against a plain wall. And on that wall there hung a great bronze crucifix with an emaciated El Greco-like Christ, looking down; forgiving, or reproachful perhaps, who could tell.

I took a couple of steps forward, rubber-kneed, and gripped one of the pews for support.

"Gregory," I called out.

Instantly he rose to his feet and turned to face me. We looked at each other across the length of the small church, at opposite ends of the nave, at opposite ends of so many things.

"Are you hurt?" he said. His voice echoed slightly.

"A little. It seems to have become a national pastime, being beastly to Locke."

"How did you know I was here?"

"Wells rang me up, we had a little talk, he said that you often came here to pray."

"A little talk?"

"He told me that you intend to destroy the papers."

I had no confidence in my ability to take them away from him by force, not the way I felt. I wasn't even sure that I could manage to walk the distance that separated us.

He said nothing.

"I'd like to know," I said.

"Yes, they have to be destroyed."

He spoke defiantly.

"Why? It seems so meaningless, so unreasonable."

I wanted to talk him out of it, I sought some valid argument, a logic, an appeal to his rational self. Yet I didn't believe in my ability to reach him. Faith always has the edge on reason, it seems to me. It is part of our failure, a built-in defect.

"What good will it do you, or anybody, destroying this record of history?" I insisted. He shook his head.

"I am not thinking of myself. I am concerned with the millions who have died with Christ's name on their lips. Shall they all be betrayed by a few scraps of paper? Shall we say it was all in vain, their sacrifices, their love, their prayers? Men on their knees, for twenty centuries, a thousand million voices calling to the Saviour. All for nothing? A mockery? Just to satisfy the ego of a few uncaring men?"

I felt provoked to argument, in spite of myself, unable to stomach such a defence of obscurantism.

"If that is the line you wish to pursue," I said, "you might at least consider the other side of the picture, after all . . ."

"I know," he interrupted, "I am familiar with the history of man's inhumanity to man. Twenty centuries littered with bones broken on the wrack, the smell of flesh burnt and torn by the Inquisition. Is that also to be redeemed you are asking."

"Well?"

"Yes, the martyrs and the innocent, their sacrifices above all must be saved from the intolerable tragedy of being futile."

I took a step or two forward. Perhaps I might reach the papers after all, call out for help, somehow get them away from him. There would be no other way.

"The dead are beyond caring, Gregory, the living are entitled to the truth. Either the truth is contained in these papers or it is not. If it is, and you believe it is, then by destroying them you are perpetrating a deception, a great deception, and certainly your own knowledge of that truth will not be destroyed at the same time. And if the message is false, palpably untrue, then what have you to fear?"

Beginners' logic. It wasn't much of an argument, poor stuff to assail his kind of resolution, to lay siege to his kind of faith.

"It is the devil's truth, that is why I am afraid," Gregory said, his voice rising. "Written by his acolyte nearly two thousand years ago. A monstrous lie. The lie that Christ is not the son of God, not the Saviour, not the Hope of Man, not the Redeemer . . ."

He stood there, his arms stretched out, his eyes ablaze, his voice filling the church in a great crescendo of sound. The raw wound of madness, I could see it now.

". . . Yes, the testament of the False Witness, hibernating all these centuries in the hot dry sand of the desert, waiting for the right moment, for this moment, oh yes, a world sick with doubt, blinded by greed, ready now for Satan's call to despair and self-destruction."

In a sudden movement he stooped and picked up the papers and held them up, high above his head.

"Is it not fitting that it be committed to this holy flame," he shouted. "This lie sent to defile Man and his faith?"

He turned to one side and grasped the great candle and placed it in front of the altar. He held the papers close to the flame.

"For God's sake, Gregory," I shouted, "you can't do that!" I walked unsteadily towards him.

"You invoke God's name," he cried out, "but know Him not. Yet what is Man without God, a moment not reckoned in the infinite. Less than nothing, lost, unless he can build a bridge to life eternal. Christ is that bridge and those who would destroy Him must be themselves destroyed."

I willed up the ebbing strength in my body and swayed towards him. As I did so he put the papers to the flickering flame of the candle. I stumbled and half fell on to one knee, and struggled up again.

"You and your damned myths," I cried out.

The bottom corner of the treasure of Beth She'arim caught fire slowly. I ran the last three or four steps and fell clutching his robe, trying to pull him down, staring up at him. He held the burning papers high up above the altar, a bright fire that seemed to envelop his hand.

"Don't you understand," he said quietly. "Man needs his myths to save himself from a mean fate."

The face of the Christ in agony glowed faintly in the light of the flames.

After a while I heard Gregory walk away, slow measured steps echoing through the church like the beat of a slow requiem. A requiem for the comforting belief that there is something durable beyond the hesitant inner voice. I sat there at the foot of the altar staring at the ashes of the Beth She'arim papers, and saw a truth obliterated by the little flame of a candle, surviving only in the mind of a priest who didn't believe it.

Too bad, really. Truth as mortal as man himself; just the inner voice after all, solo, kidding one along. While the breath lasts.

Epilogue

I WAS sitting in Hughes's office, facing him across the big desk; just the two of us, wearing our best smiles, working hard to whitewash the stain on our beautiful professional friendship. It was past six o'clock in the evening.

I was smoking one of his cigarettes, and soon he would be offering me a dry sherry; not a minute too early, but then his drinking habits were more conventional than mine. In his right hand he held my letter of resignation.

"This is so unnecessary," he said softly. "I should like to think that you wrote it in a moment of understandable pique, and that it is now open to reconsideration?"

His eyebrows lifted questioningly. As understatements went I thought that 'pique' was worthy of an Oscar.

"It's been on my mind a long time, I think you know that. Besides, I would suppose my value to you in the Middle East to be seriously debased now. A bit too familiar in certain circles, wouldn't you say?"

"Of course, but I wasn't thinking of the Middle East." I looked at him blankly, he squeezed a bit more out of his smile.

"Ours is a large parish," he said, "there's a wide choice."

"I suppose so, it's just that I don't see myself as one of your incumbents right now."

He laughed and stood up.

"Well, perhaps not immediately. In the meantime, let me pour you a glass of sherry."

He poured out two glasses, gave me one, and returned to his chair.

"Did you know that I received a letter from Mrs Poulson a couple of days ago?" he said casually.

I shook my head, and stared into my glass; and saw dancing images in the mind's eye, released anew by the mention of her name.

"A very nice letter."

He sipped at his sherry. I waited, the way one had to with Hughes.

"She assured me," he said, "that you had not been involved in the Shafei set-up, whatever anyone else had said. Of course by then we knew the truth, but that hardly detracts from her generosity."

For a moment or two we looked at each other, but I doubt if we were thinking about the same things.

"This isn't a bad set-up you know, Locke," he said quietly, "for a man like you. Seems a pity to chuck it, now that we know each other so well."

I said nothing.

"Something has cropped up," he said, "which I think might interest you. Let me tell you about it."

I thought, maybe she will write to *me* one of these days. Just a picture postcard perhaps, having fun, wish you were here . . .

New Casebooks

APHRA BEHN

EDITED BY JANET TODD

First published 1999 by
MACMILLAN PRESS LTD
Houndmills, Basingstoke, Hampshire RG21 6XS
and London
Companies and representatives throughout the world

ISBN 0–333–72020–2 hardcover
ISBN 0–333–72021–0 paperback

A catalogue record for this book is available from the British Library.

This book is printed on paper suitable for recycling and made from
fully managed and sustained forest sources.

10   9   8   7   6   5   4   3   2   1
08   07   06   05   04   03   02   01   00   99

Typeset by EXPO Holdings, Malaysia

Printed in Hong Kong

Published in the United States of America 1999 by
ST. MARTIN'S PRESS, INC.,
Scholarly and Reference Division,
175 Fifth Avenue, New York, N.Y. 10010

ISBN 0–312–21858–3

Contents

Acknowledgements

My thanks to Ros Ballaster, Derek Hughes, Jessica Munns, Jacqueline Pearson and Jane Spencer for help in the selection of these articles.

The editor and publishers wish to thank the following for permission to use copyright material:

Ros Ballaster, for material from *Seductive Forms: Women's Amatory Fiction from 1684 to 1746* (1992), pp. 100–13, by permission of Oxford University Press; Carol Barash, for material from *English Women's Poetry, 1649–1714: Politics, Community, and Linguistic Authority* (1996), pp. 124–9, by permission of Oxford University Press; Laura Brown, for 'The Romance of Empire; *Oroonoko* and the Trade in Slaves; in *The New Eighteenth Century*, ed. Laura Brown and Felicity Nussbaum, Methuen (1988), pp. 40–61, by permission of the author; Elin Diamond, for '*Gestus* and Signature in Aphra Behn's *The Rover*', *ELH: English Literary History*, 56 (1989), 519–41, by permission of the Johns Hopkins University Press; Margaret W. Ferguson, for 'Juggling the Categories of Race, Class and Gender: Aphra Behn's *Oroonoko*' in *Women, Race and Writing in the Early Modern Period*, ed. Patricia Parker and Margo Hendricks (1994), pp. 209–24 by permission of Routledge; Catherine Gallagher, 'Who was That Masked Woman? The Prostitute and the Playwright in the Comedies of Aphra Behn', *Women's Studies*, 15 (1987), 23–42, by permission of Gordon and Breach Publishers; Jessica Munns, for '"But to the touch were soft": Pleasure, Power and Omnipotence in "The Disappointment" and "The Golden Age"', in *Aphra Behn Studies*, ed. Janet Todd (1996), pp. 178–96, by permission of Cambridge University Press; Susan J. Owen, for '"Suspect my loyalty when I lose my virtue":

Sexual Politics and Party in Aphra Behn's plays of the Exclusion Crisis, 1678–83', *Restoration*, 18 (1994), 37–47, by permission of Restoration: Studies in English Culture, 1660–1700; Jacqueline Pearson, for 'Gender and Narrative in the Fiction of Aphra Behn', *Review of English Studies*, 42, 165–6 (1991), 40–56, 179–90, by permission of Oxford University Press; Ellen Pollak, 'Beyond Incest: Gender and the Politics of Transgression in Aphra Behn's *Love Letters between a Nobleman and His Sister*', in *Rereading Aphra Behn: History, Theory and Criticism*, ed. Heidi Hutner (1993), pp. 15–66, by permission of the University Press of Virginia; Janet Todd, for material from *Gender, Art and Death* (1993), Polity Press, pp. 49–61, by permission of Blackwell Publishers.

Every effort has been made to trace the copyright holders but if any have been inadvertently overlooked the publishers will be pleased to make the necessary arrangement at the first opportunity.

General Editors' Preface

The purpose of this series of New Casebooks is to reveal some of the ways in which contemporary criticism has changed our understanding of commonly studied texts and writers and, indeed, of the nature of criticism itself. Central to the series is a concern with modern critical theory and its effect on current approaches to the study of literature. Each New Casebook editor has been asked to select a sequence of essays which will introduce the reader to the new critical approaches to the text or texts being discussed in the volume and also illuminate the rich interchange between critical theory and critical practice that characterises so much current writing about literature.

In this focus on modern critical thinking and practice New Casebooks aim not only to inform but also to stimulate, with volumes seeking to reflect both the controversy and the excitement of current criticism. Because much of this criticism is difficult and often employs an unfamiliar critical language, editors have been asked to give the reader as much help as they feel is appropriate, but without simplifying the essays or the issues they raise. Again, editors have been asked to supply a list of further reading which will enable readers to follow up issues raised by the essays in the volume.

The project of New Casebooks, then, is to bring together in an illuminating way those critics who best illustrate the ways in which contemporary criticism has established new methods of analysing texts and who have reinvigorated the important debate about how we 'read' literature. The hope is, of course, that New Casebooks will not only open up this debate to a wider audience, but will also encourage students to extend their own ideas, and think afresh about their responses to the texts they are studying.

John Peck and Martin Coyle
University of Wales, Cardiff

Introduction

JANET TODD

Aphra Behn was an author who disliked arrogant, overeducated and elitist critics. In the preface to her third play, *The Dutch Lover* (1673), she showed her irritation at being reproached for writing in an unregulated manner. She presumed that this was because she was deemed an uneducated woman who did not know the classical rules of drama, the three unities of time, place and action. Her play, the critic had implied, failed because of its crowded, disordered nature. Behn's answer to this charge was to mock the rules of drama as absurd pedantry devised by learned but nonsensical men who had failed to understand that pedantry had no place in the popular theatre. The unities had to do with learned critics, not professional writers, sensible playwrights who sought only to please. She herself had clearly not 'hung a sign' of pedantic seriousness over her play but rather of 'Comedy' which she had 'inscrib'd … on the beginning of my Book'.

Despite the absurd pretensions of some educated men, the writing of plays was no great thing in Behn's view: drama was not worthless, but neither was it the most serious enterprise of life, being found rather 'among the middle if not the better sort of Books'. She had written her plays for money and she supposed others had done so too. As she became more famous and the political times more alarming, Aphra Behn changed her opinion about the triviality of plays. She then came to see them no longer as entertainments that wiled away the time for the leisured but more as powerful instruments of political instruction, and herself as mistress of the form. But she did not repudiate her earlier scorn of pedantic, university-educated critics.

1

Although the kind of criticism now currently read and produced in universities, colleges and schools may be useful in illuminating Behn, especially considering the profound difference between the late seventeenth and the late twentieth centuries, it will be as well to keep in mind Behn's robust views on critical opinion as we rightly struggle with our own shifting critical environment. What Behn brought to the august literary critical tradition of her time, which tended to treat literature as timeless, was a very real awareness of historical contingency and specificity, of the economic foundations of literature, and, of course, of fashion.

In her moment, Behn received the mixed reviews the public meted out to most of her fellow dramatists and she, like them, responded accordingly. From her angry defences of herself we learn that she was much attacked for plagiarism and bawdiness, the latter charge borne out by lampoons of Robert Gould, her political antagonist, Thomas Shadwell, and even her colleague William Wycherley. Yet the increasing enthusiasm for her works in some circles at least is evident from the growing importance of the dedicatees of her plays and by the large number of puffing poems she could provide for the collections of her verse. Since her death came just after the completion of many of her best works, *Oroonoko*, *The Fair Jilt*, *The Luckey Chance* and *The Emperor of the Moon*, one might expect considerable honouring of her memory. Unfortunately she died just after the coronation of William and Mary, which ended the line of Stuart kings she had so generously hymned. So her political standing, as well as the changing morals and taste of the new regime, meant that she was not much noticed in her death, and her two posthumous plays were shoddily performed and indifferently or hostilely received.

In 1696, however, she was given a new lease of life when Thomas Southerne turned her short story *Oroonoko* into a famous stage play. The success suggested to the men who had control of her literary legacy, Charles Gildon, Thomas Brown and Samuel Briscoe, that the dead woman might yet be exploited. Consequently there was a rush to publish Behn's outstanding unpublished works, including a large number of short stories the authenticity of which cannot easily be proved, given the forging habits of the age. Brown, Gildon and Briscoe all helped to float Behn anew, at first with the respectable likeness of a generous cavalier lady and then increasingly, as times became stricter concerning the presentation of women, with a naughtier, more titillating and disreputable image.

This latter image, along with the eighteenth-century tendency to demonise the Restoration as a period of arbitrary rule and courtly licentiousness, meant that Behn's plays slowly left the repertoire, despite the considerable popularity of *The Rover* in particular during the first quarter of the century. Simultaneously, her more respectable poems (excluding both the erotic and the political) arrived in the anthologies of women poets, usually with a caveat about her appalling life and the impossible obscenity of most of her writing. Occasionally she was again saved by *Oroonoko*, now seen as an abolitionist text, often expurgated or much changed – especially in France. When severed from her licentious times and life, then, Behn could sometimes enter the sentimental realm of fiction in which ladies were allowed to be supreme.

In the nineteenth century, Aphra Behn had an even harder critical time. Both male and female anthologists and historians of women writers routinely condemned her, finding in her the antithesis of the moral and spiritually superior woman they hoped to discover among the 'poetesses'. The nineteenth century emphasised the domestic sphere for women and for women writers, and it encouraged them to consider subjects involving children, marital and filial relations, and helpless victims. At the beginning of the century Anna Laetitia Barbauld wrote a poem called 'On a Lady's Writing' which stressed that propriety should be women's goal in art and life.

The emphasis was thoroughly felt in the various compendia of women's writing throughout the nineteenth century, from Alexander Dyce who brought out his *Specimens of British Poetesses* in the 1830s. He included Behn, judged her poetry as spirited, but found the plays examples of an essential 'grossness'. An idea of the tone of such compilers can be gauged from Frederic Rowton, who, in 1848, published his edition of *The Female Poets of Great Britain*. He took from three centuries of English women's writing and declared that his anthology was designed to 'supply a want which must have been frequently experienced by every student of our literary annals; – the want of a History of our Female Poets'; he would provide 'the memorials of the Female Mind'.

Rowton was steeped in the Victorian ideology of art as ameliorating morals and he saw his enterprise as part of a general cultural one: 'the great task of enlightening and elevating the whole family of man'. In his view, women were intellectually equal but different from men, being rulers of the heart working through influence where men were of the mind and ruled through force. Consequently, he had a gallant attitude to women as readers and writers, considering that, had women operated more widely in the world, 'humanity would have been far wiser, and better, and happier than it is'. Woman would have softened and tempered 'Man's coarser spirit' which had made the world 'too gross, material, sensual, and violent'. Inevitably his women poets conformed in the main to his conception of the female and did indeed address the feelings not the understanding. They wrote to increase virtue and influence morality not politics.

Rowton had some difficulty in fitting Aphra Behn into his scheme. She was, he wrote, 'one of the most prominent, but one of the least estimable, of the British Female Poets'. She was a 'A Female Wycherley' – not a compliment in the nineteenth century – and both lived in a 'wicked era'. At the same time, Rowton could not but admire some of the poems and, although he firmly judged her plays as 'amongst the grossest productions ever given to the world', he none the less considered that Behn's verses had a 'liveliness and pointedness of fancy' and an 'aptness and happy expressiveness'.

The early twentieth century saw a flutter of interest in Aphra Behn. The Victorian disapproval of her had given her some champions such as John Pearson, who had published an anthology of favourable comment on her and, although she was not rescued as a playwright, she was assuming a new role as fictionist, seen now as important in the development of the novel. So she could occasionally be studied and considered as a whole by respectable scholars who were presumed to be immune to contamination from her grossness and indelicacy. The site of rehabilitation was again *Oroonoko*, now delivered not only as an emancipatory novel but, more importantly, as a remarkable mixture of fact and fiction, on the cusp between genres.

Once the latter case had been made, Behn was open to a rather different form of abuse from the usual one of indecency: that of being a liar. Eager to condemn Behn, Ernest Bernbaum attempted to disprove the accuracy of her depiction of Surinam in *Oroonoko* and indeed doubted that she had ever visited the colony. His accusations were fertile ground for the scholars of *Notes and Queries*, who pointed out specific accuracies they had discovered in Behn's work and provided parallels with other contemporary accounts.

Then in 1915 came a major event in Behn scholarship when the eccentric Montague Summers, learned Restoration scholar and believer in vampires, produced a six-volume edition of her works. The footnotes were sometimes useful, sometimes wildly tangential, showing that fascination with the exotic erotic that Summers frequently displayed in his occult studies. Summers published only the secure plays of Behn, seventeen in all, not the attributed ones, and he omitted the poems which Behn separately printed and did not include in her anthologies, such as her state poems to the Stuart kings. He also omitted her *Love-Letters between a Nobleman and His Sister*. None the less, this edition with its full biographical and critical introduction was immensely useful and it allowed more informed comment on Behn in the early twentieth century than had been possible during the nineteenth.

The effect was clearly seen over the next years with the end of the First World War, the residual feminist interest from the suffrage movement, and the Bloomsbury concern for writers not much appreciated by Victorian and Georgian predecessors. In the 1920s, the friends Vita Sackville-West and Virginia Woolf both discovered Aphra Behn. Their interest suggested that, in advanced circles at least, a respectable woman might now utter the name of Behn without apology.

In 1927 Vita Sackville-West published a brief biography entitled *Aphra Behn: The Incomparable Astrea*. Although condescending and irritatingly dismissive of Behn's artistry, it followed Summers in appreciating the occasional power of the fictional works. Yet, despite some critical praise, Sackville-West was concerned to present Behn robustly as a woman, not a writer. For her, Behn was both an impecunious, vulgar hack, zestful, with naturally coarse tastes, and a woman capable of sincere passion and suffering. Sackville-West saw Behn as sometimes driven by necessity and a loose pleasure-loving temperament into the kind of cynical incidental liaisons of which at heart she disapproved. Her Behn was, then, coarse and vulgar on the one hand and moral and idealistic on the other. She remained significant not for artistic skill and generic transformations but for her place in the history of women's writing:

> although her language is not to be recommended to the queasy, and although in her private life, she followed the dictates of inclination rather than of conventional morality, Aphra Behn, in the history of English letters, is something much more than a mere harlot. The fact that she wrote is much more important than the quality of what she wrote. The importance of Aphra Behn is that she was the first woman in English to earn her living by her pen.

A very similar view was taken by Virginia Woolf in her extremely influential *A Room of One's Own* in 1929. In the memorable phrases that have graced many a cover of Behn reprints, she wrote, 'All women together ought to let flowers fall upon the tomb of Aphra Behn, for it was she who earned them the right to speak their minds'. As with Sackville-West, the fact that Behn had supported herself by writing was again more significant than any consideration of what she wrote; so Woolf, like her friend, lost sight of any literary merit. Perhaps this was inevitable, for both Woolf and Sackville-West were writing when literature was thought able to transcend its historical moment and when it had to refuse the contamination of politics. Romantic notions of art as self-expressing were not, however, current in the Restoration, Aphra Behn's literary moment; at that time many men wrote openly for money and political purpose, as did Behn.

Interestingly, the woman artist whom Virginia Woolf praised in Aphra Behn's place was an invented one, a sister Judith for the great literary icon, William Shakespeare. Judith Shakespeare was a failed Romantic, a woman who grew suicidal under her injuries and failed even to enter the theatre in her quest to write plays like her brother. Behn, who did manage spectacularly to enter, was reduced by Woolf and Sackville-West to a hack – her mind unfree because she wrote for money. For Woolf, with almost as much snobbish sense of class as the aristocratic Sackville-West, Behn became a 'middle-class woman with all the plebeian virtues of humour, vitality and courage; a woman forced by the death of her husband and some unfortunate adventures of her own to make her living by her wits'. The fact of her writing 'outweighs anything that she actually wrote'. Here the very professionalism which prevented Behn from ending up suicidal kept her from the ranks of the great artists.

After the Second World War, when Behn's stock had again declined, she found a new champion in the anarchist George Woodcock. In opposition to the class-bound and feminist Woolf and Sackville-West, Woodcock saw Behn as a radical in a culturally revolutionary age and he appreciated what she wrote as much as the fact that she wrote. He especially commended Behn's prose style, used fluently to develop the fictions that he saw as the precursors of the eighteenth-century English novel. Although, in a reprinting of his work 40 years on, Woodcock rather doubted his youthful enthusiasm for the Restoration wits as revolutionary, he still continued to see Behn as a 'free spirit, a woman liberated by nature and circumstances from the customary inhibitions of her age, and for that reason able to make one of the great innovatory leaps in the history of women's emancipation – and to do it alone'.

From the 1940s to the 1970s Behn was little considered, except in fragmented biographical form. By the 1970s the feminist movement was drawing attention to early women writers and Behn was included, for example, in my *Dictionary of British and American Women Writers 1660–1800*. Yet, in its excited phase, early American feminist criticism largely passed Behn by. The great icons were from the nineteenth century and their important books were delivered as the experiences of every woman reader by groundbreaking studies such as Elaine Showalter's *A Literature of their Own* and Sandra Gilbert and Susan Gubar's *The Madwoman in the Attic*. There was not much room for Aphra Behn in the search for suffering sisters, and indeed Gilbert and Gubar's otherwise brilliant study dismisses her in the traditional terms of the rake and freak. Behn did not fit into the sort of scheme feminism was demanding and, as a political propagandist for much of her writing life, she did not present works suitable for the feminist method of reading against the grain, so applicable to the nineteenth-century lady writer. Firm in her demand for fame, Behn appeared not to require the kind of scrutiny that found aggression in disclaimer and longing in assurances of modesty.

Yet, preparations were already being made for Behn's entry into a later phase of feminist criticism, one more concerned with the female manipulator than with the victim. In the late 1970s and early 1980s, two major biographies appeared within three years of each other. Over the next decade they would help transform Behn from being a fairly unknown minor Restoration writer into one of the major resources of feminist and new historicist scholarship, a gift for doctoral students wanting to combine study of women writers with the increasingly fashionable mode of gender and race analysis.

Maureen Duffy's *The Passionate Shepherdess 1640–89* (1977) laid the foundation for future biographical work on Aphra Behn by establishing the most likely provenance of Aphra Johnson Behn and fully using the few hints of Behn's early life from such private sources as Thomas Colepeper's unpublished 'Adversaria'. This careful scholarship helped to quell the antiquarian obsession with the authenticity of Behn's accounts, especially in *Oroonoko*, and, although it did not itself make great claims for Behn's literary importance, it did allow this to emerge in the dense texture of literary people that surrounded her.

Angeline Goreau's *Representing Aphra* of 1980 was more securely feminist in the American mode than Duffy's, less historical and more literary critical and cultural, more readable and less detailed. Copiously referring to other women writers of the time, Goreau made Behn a symbolic figure for authorship in the Restoration, a writer and a strumpet muse combined. In her pages Behn became a complex woman indeed, but also thoroughly generous and loving, developing an ideal of masculine sexual freedom for her heroines which matched her own desires. Goreau's study was less concerned than Duffy's with the political and literary scene in which Behn acted, and the background it provided for Behn through her connections with the proprietor of Surinam, Lord Willoughby of Parham, was more glamorous and less convincing.

The phase of preparation for Behn's critical adoption was concluded by Mary Ann O'Donnell's 1986 bibliography of both primary and secondary material, which helped Behn towards the 'Fame she longed for'. This bibliography listed 106 titles of works written, edited or translated by Behn and 661 critical commentaries. Carefully describing the editions of Behn's writings, sifting attributions and banishing ghosts, it cleared up many misdatings, identified faulty texts and established Behn scholarship on a firm basis. The scholar following O'Donnell's meticulous lead can only marvel at her accuracy across continents and libraries, although inevitably the odd omission was later noted.

By the late 1980s, Behn was appearing in overviews of early women's writing, for example, Jane Spencer's *The Rise of the Woman Novelist: From Aphra Behn to Jane Austen* (1986), Elaine Hobby's *Virtue of Necessity: English Women's Writing 1649–88* (1988), and my own *The Sign of Angellica: Women, Writing, and Fiction 1660–1800* (1989). Jane Spencer provided a full assessment of Behn, noting the high praise of her in her lifetime and her comparisons with Sappho and Orinda (Katherine Philips). She also noted how quickly Behn became a problematic model for the aspiring woman writer, although she was hard to ignore because of her commercial success. In her plays Behn showed concern for women's freedom, Spencer argued, but it was outside them, through her claims for women's writing ability, that she supported her sex most thoroughly. Although many eulogists declared Behn especially feminine in love, Spencer noted that she herself did not see love as an essentially female theme, simply as an important poetic one: 'it was as a poet, simply, that she wanted to be remembered'.

Elaine Hobby's study delivered a rather different Behn. With its enthusiasm for radical women, it distrusted those espousing conservative or Tory values. The overall thesis was that, after a very lively Civil War and Interregnum period, women were, in the Restoration, driven back into quiescence. Behn therefore assumed that the world could not change, where the women of the 1650s had been lobbying for it to do so. Yet, accepting that Restoration women were largely confined to love and romance, Hobby did admire Behn for the wit and humour of her response, and she noted the dilemmas that she and other women faced in a debauched and bleak age. My own history of early women's fiction, *The Sign of Angellica*, took its name from Behn's *The Rover*, where the painting or the sign of the prostitute Angellica Bianca is hung out to advertise the wares within. Like Angellica Bianca, whose initials she shared, Behn too had problems with representation and her image in the market place. The emphasis in the work was primarily on *Love-Letters between a Nobleman and His Sister* with its extraordinary picture of an aristocratic woman transforming herself into a whore and its narrator watching the transformation with horror and admiration.

Out of the general studies on women's writing including Behn, I have chosen as essay 8 an extract from Ros Ballaster's *Seductive Forms: Women's Amatory Fiction from 1684 to 1740* (1992), which deals with the English women fictionists, Behn, Manley and Haywood, and places them within a context of developing French and English romance. Ballaster's emphasis on the narrative devices in the fiction complements the analysis by Jacqueline Pearson in 'Gender and Narrative in the Fiction of Aphra Behn' (1991) (essay 7). Writing at a later date, Carol Barash (essay 6), included Behn in a study of women writing between the public execution of Charles I in 1649 and the death of the last Stuart monarch, Queen Anne, in 1714; these women explored the complicated and often conflicting ways in which changes in political and linguistic authority affected the lives and writing of women.

It was in the 1990s that Behn scholarship vastly expanded. As a result she started to make appearances in rather extraordinary places. The long eighteenth century often stretched back to include her in eighteenth-century conferences while the elastic category of the English Renaissance stretched forward to take her into itself. She made constant appearances in interdisciplinary studies of the period increasingly called early modern. Also she fitted easily into the late 1980s and 1990s kind of feminist and new historicist criticism, which turned from old historical readings as essentialist and responded to a new emphasis on representation, generic mutation and discursive parallels. The important influence here was Catherine Gallagher's 'Who was That Masked Woman? The Prostitute and the Playwright in the Comedies of Aphra Behn', published in 1988, which is essay 1 of this selection. It has become one of the most quoted and reprinted articles on Aphra Behn. In similar mode, but concentrating on Behn's most famous play, *The Rover*, Elin Diamond's '*Gestus* and Signature in Aphra Behn's *The Rover*' of 1989 (essay 2) explores the self-authoring of a playwright through her encoding of the conditions of her own literary and theatrical production, while Ellen Pollak's 'Beyond Incest: Gender and the Politics of Transgression in Aphra Behn's *Love-Letters between a Nobleman and His Sister* (1993) (essay 9) reads Behn's first and longest novel as an investigation of gender, desire, identity and representation. In essay 5, '"But to the touch were soft": Pleasure, Power and Impotence in "The Disappointment" and "The Golden Age"' (1996), Jessica Munns takes up similar issues of gender and desire with reference to two of Behn's most famous poems.

Even beyond her suitability for new historicist criticism, however, Behn was coming to appeal to the critics of gender and race. *Oroonoko* had often saved Behn's reputation in the past; now it would thoroughly establish it and make of its author a wonderful early exemplar of western culture's fascination with race and gender. The former had been a predominant American interest since Black Studies had been founded in the late 1960s, but both gained such impetus in the late 1980s and 1990s that, in many colleges, the taught canon of literature came to consist largely of those works which gave rise to critiques foregrounding them. Among these was now Behn's *Oroonoko*. Prime examples of such critiques are Laura Brown's 'The Romance of Empire: *Oroonoko* and the Trade in Slaves' (1987) and Margaret Ferguson's 'Juggling the Categories of Race, Class and Gender: Aphra Behn's *Oroonoko*', essays 10 and 11. They reveal the robust belief that the effort of interrogating modern notions of race, class and gender, by comparing them to earlier historical versions and vice versa, is, in Ferguson's words, 'crucial to the intellectual work of US feminism in the 1990s'. Brown and Ferguson laid out many avenues of research for later critics, especially in their emphasis on blackness, on Imoinda, and on the uncertain status of the narrator.

Many British and American critics followed the same sort of reading and provided stimulating studies of Behn's works, but in recent years in Britain there has been greater emphasis on the historical moment of

Behn, her political position and the shifting views that parallel shifting moments in the culture of which she was a part. My own biography of Behn, *The Secret Life of Aphra Behn* (1996), creates a primarily political Behn, who saw her cultural moment as peculiarly enabling for her sort of masked writing and who regarded herself as an increasingly important player on the public stage. Essays 3 and 4 – Susan J. Owen, '"Suspect my loyalty when I lose my virtue"; Sexual Politics and Party in Aphra Behn's plays of the Exclusion Crisis, 1678–83' of 1994, and Janet Todd, an extract from 'Spectacular Deaths: History and Story in Aphra Behn's *Love Letters, Oroonoko* and *The Widow Ranter*' (from 1993) – are examples of the kind of criticism that stresses a more political and historical context for Behn's works.

Behn is probably here to stay, but she would no doubt be unsurprised if this were not the case. One of her last published poems, a pindaric to Gilbert Burnet, propagandist of the new regime of William of Orange, revealed that she well knew that literary reputation depended on political fashion and that works were valued as 'Current Coyn' only when the stamp of political approval was placed on them. In this poem, the fame that Behn so frequently declared she wanted – or in modern terms entry into a taught canon – was, she saw, predicated on acceptance by an elite that controlled culture. Probably this still remains so.

(NOTE: The spelling of names for and from Behn's work is not fixed, so they may be different in each essay or extract.)

1

Who was That Masked Woman? The Prostitute and the Playwright in the Comedies of Aphra Behn

CATHERINE GALLAGHER

Everyone knows that Aphra Behn, England's first professional female author, was a colossal and enduring embarrassment to the generations of women who followed her into the literary marketplace. An ancestress whose name had to be lived down rather than lived up to, Aphra Behn seemed, in Virginia Woolf's metaphor, to obstruct the very passageway to the profession of letters she had herself opened. Woolf explains in *A Room of One's Own*, 'Now that Aphra Behn had done it, girls could go to their parents and say, You need not give me an allowance; I can make money by my pen. Of course the answer for many years to come was, Yes, by living the life of Aphra Behn! Death would be better! and the door was slammed faster than ever.'[1]

It is impossible in this brief essay to examine all the facets of the scandal of Aphra Behn; her life and works were alike characterised by certain irregular sexual arrangements. But it is not these that I want to discuss, for they seem merely incidental, the sorts of things women writers would easily dissociate themselves from if they led pure lives and wrote high-minded books. The scandal I would like to discuss is, however, with varying degree of appropriateness, applicable to all female authors, regardless of the conduct of their lives or the content of their works. It is a scandal that Aphra Behn seems quite purposely to have constructed out of the overlapping discourses of commercial, sexual, and linguistic exchange. Conscious of her historical role, she introduced to the world of English letters the professional woman writer as a new-fangled whore.

This persona has many functions in Behn's works: it titillates, scandalises, arouses pity, and indicates the vicissitudes of authorship and identity in general. The author–whore persona also makes of female authorship per se a dark comedy that explores the bond between the liberty the stage offered women and their confinement behind both literal and metaphorical vizard masks. This is the comedy played out, for example, in the prologue to her first play, *The Forced Marriage*, where she announces her epoch-making appearance in the ranks of the playwrights. She presents her attainment, however, not as a daring achievement of self-expression, but as a new proof of the necessary obscurity of the 'public' woman.

The prologue presents Aphra Behn's playwrighting as an extension of her erotic play. In it, a male actor pretends to have escaped temporarily the control of the intriguing female playwright; he comes on stage to warn the gallants in the audience of their danger. This was a variation on the Restoration convention of betraying the playwright in the prologue with an added sexual dimension: the comic antagonism between playwright and audience becomes a battle in the war between the sexes. Playwrighting, warns the actor, is a new weapon in woman's amorous arsenal. She will no longer wound only through the eyes, through her beauty, but will also use wit to gain a more permanent ascendency. Here, woman's playwriting is wholly assimilated to the poetic conventions of amorous battle that normally informed lyric poetry. If the male poet had long depicted the conquering woman as necessarily chaste, debarring (and consequently debarred from) the act of sex itself, then his own poetry of lyric complaint and pleas for kindness could only be understood as attempts to overthrow the conqueror. Poetry in this lyric tradition is a weapon in a struggle that takes as its most fundamental ground-rule a woman's inability to have truly *sexual* conquest: for the doing of the deed would be the undoing of her power.

Aphra Behn's first prologue stretches this lyric tradition to incorporate theatre. However, the woman's poetry cannot have the same *end* as the man's. Indeed, according to the prologue, ends, in the sense of terminations, are precisely what a woman's wit is directed against:

> Women those charming victors, in whose eyes
> Lie all their arts, and their artilleries.
> Not being contented with the wounds they made,
> Would by new stratagems our lives invade.
> Beauty alone goes now at too cheap rates
> And therefore they, like wise and politic states,
> Court a new power that may the old supply,
> To *keep* as well as gain the victory:
> They'll join the force of wit to beauty now,
> And so *maintain* the right they have in you.[2]

Writing is certainly on a continuum here with sex, but instead of leading to the act in which the woman's conquest is overturned, playwriting is supposed to extend the woman's erotic power beyond the moment of sexual encounter. The prologue, then, situates the drama inside the conventions of male lyric love poetry but then reverses the chronological relationship between sex and writing; the male poet writes before the sexual encounter, the woman between encounters. She thereby actually creates the possibility of a woman's version of sexual conquest. She will not be immediately conquered and discarded because she will maintain her right through her writing. The woman's play of wit is the opposite of foreplay; it is a kind of afterplay specifically designed to prolong pleasure, resuscitate desire and keep a woman who has given herself sexually from being traded in for another woman. If the woman is successful in her poetic exchange, the actor warns the gallants, then they will no longer have the freedom of briskly exchanging mistresses: 'You'll never know the bliss of change; this art Retrieves (when beauty fades) the wandring heart.'

Aphra Behn, then, inaugurated her career by taking up and feminising the role of the seductive lyric poet. The drama the audience is about to see is framed by the larger comedy of erotic exchange between a woman writer and a male audience. That is, this prologue does what so many Restoration prologues do, makes of the play a drama within a drama, one series of conventional interactions inside another. But the very elaborateness of this staging of conventions makes the love battle itself (the thing supposedly revealed) seem a strategic pose in a somewhat different drama. After all, what kind of woman would stage her sexual desire as her primary motivation? The answer is a woman who might be suspected not to have any: a woman for whom professions of amorousness and theatrical inauthenticity are the same thing: a prostitute. Finally, just in case anyone in the audience might have missed this analogy, a dramatic interruption occurs, and the prologue stages a debate about the motivation behind all this talk of strategy. The actor calls attention to the prostitutes in the audience, who were generally identified by their masks, and characterises them as agents of the playwright, jokingly using their masks to expose them as spies in the amorous war:

> The poetess too, they say, has spies abroad,
> Which have dispers'd themselves in every road,
> I' th' upper box, pit, galleries; every face
> You find disguis'd in a black velvet case.
> My life on't; is her spy on purpose sent,
> To hold you in a wanton compliment;
> That so you may not censure what she's writ,
> Which done they face you down 'twas full of wit.

At this point, an actress comes on stage to refute the suggestion that the poetess's spies and supporters are prostitutes. She returns, then, to the conceits linking money and warfare and thus explicitly enacts the denial of prostitution that was all along implicit in the trope of amorous combat. Unlike the troop of prostitutes, she claims,

> Ours scorns the petty spoils, and do prefer
> The glory not the interest of war.
> But yet our forces shall obliging prove,
> Imposing naught but constancy in love:
> That's all our aim, and when we have it too,
> We'll sacrifice it all to pleasure you.

What the last two lines make abundantly clear, in ironically justifying female promiscuity by the pleasure it gives to men, is that the prologue has given us the spectacle of a prostitute comically denying mercenary motivations. The poetess like the prostitute is she who 'stands out', as the etymology of the word 'prostitute' implies, but it is also she who is masked. Indeed, as the prologue emphasises, the prostitute is she who stands out by virtue of her mask. The dramatic masking of the prostitute and the stagey masking of the playwright's interest in money are exactly parallel cases of theatrical unmasking in which what is revealed is the parallel itself: the playwright is a whore.

This conclusion, however, is more complex than it might at first seem, for the very playfulness of the representation implies a hidden 'real' woman who must remain unavailable. The prologue gives two explanations for female authorship, and they are the usual excuses for prostitution: it alludes to and disclaims the motive of money; it claims the motive of love, but in a way that makes the claim seem merely strategic. The author–whore, then, is one who comically stages her lack of self-expression and consequently implies that her true identity is the sold self's seller. She thus indicates an unseeable selfhood through the flamboyant alienation of her language.

Hence Aphra Behn managed to create the effect of an inaccessible authenticity out of the very image of prostitution. In doing so, she capitalised on a commonplace slur that probably kept many less in- genious women out of the literary marketplace. 'Whore's the like re- proachful name, as poetess – the luckless twins of shame',[3] wrote Robert Gould in 1691. The equation of poetess and 'punk' (in the slang of the day) was inescapable in the Restoration. A woman writer could either deny it in the content and form of her publica- tions, as did Catherine Trotter, or she could embrace it, as did Aphra Behn. But she could not entirely avoid it. For the belief that 'Punk and Poesie agree so pat,/ You cannot well be *this*, and not be *that*'[4] was held independently of particular cases. It rested on the ev- idence neither of how a woman lived nor of what she wrote. It was, rather, an a priori judgement applied to all cases of female publica- tion. As one of Aphra Behn's biographers, Angeline Goreau, has as- tutely pointed out, the seventeenth-century ear heard the word 'public' in 'publication' very distinctly, and hence a woman's public- ation automatically implied a public woman.[5] The woman who shared the contents of her mind instead of reserving them for one man was literally, not metaphorically, trading in her *sexual* prop- erty. If she were married, she was selling what did not belong to her, because in *mind and body* she should have given herself to her husband. In the seventeenth century, 'publication', Goreau tells us, also meant sale due to bankruptcy, and the publication of the con- tents of a woman's mind was tantamount to the publication of her husband's property. In 1613, Lady Carey published (anonymously, of course) these lines on marital property rights, publication and female integrity:

> Then she usurps upon another's right,
> That seeks to be by public language graced;
> And tho' her thoughts reflect with purest light
> Her mind, if not peculiar, is not chaste.
> For in a wife it is no worse to find
> A common body, than a common mind.[6]

Publication, adultery, and trading in one's husband's property were all thought of as the same thing as long as female identity, self-hood, remained an indivisible unity. As Lady Carey explained, the idea of a public mind in a private body threatened to fragment female identity, to destroy its integrated wholeness:

> When to their husbands they themselves do bind,
> Do they not wholly give themselves away?
> Or give they but their body, not their mind,
> Reserving that, tho' best, for other's prey?
> No, sure, their thought no more can be their own
> And therefore to none but one be known.[7]

The unique, unreserved giving of the woman's self to her husband is the act that keeps her whole. Only in this singular and total alienation does the woman maintain her complete self-identity.

We have already seen that it is precisely this idea of a totalised woman, preserved because *wholly* given away, that Aphra Behn sacrifices to create a different idea of identity, one complexly dependent on the necessity of multiple exchanges. She who is able to repeat the action of self-alienation an unlimited number of times is she who is constantly there to regenerate, possess, and sell a series of provisional, constructed identities. Self-possession, then, and self-alienation are just two sides of the same coin; the alienation verifies the possession. In contrast, the wife who gives herself once and completely disposes simultaneously of self possession and self alienation. She has no more property in which to trade and is thus rendered whole by her action. She *is* her whole, unviolated womanhood because she has given up possessing herself; she can be herself because she has given up *having* herself. Further, as Lady Carey's lines make clear, if a woman's writing is an authentic extension of herself, then she cannot have alienable property in that without violating her wholeness.

Far from denying these assumptions, Aphra Behn's comedy is based on them. Like her contemporaries, she presented her writing as part of her sexual property, not just because it was bawdy, but because it was hers. As a woman, all of her properties were at least the potential property of another; she could either reserve them and give herself whole in marriage, or she could barter them piecemeal, accepting self-division to achieve self-ownership and forfeiting the possibility of marriage. In this sense, Aphra Behn's implied identity fits into the most advanced seventeenth-century theories about selfhood: it closely resembles the possessive individualism of Locke and Hobbes, in which property in one's self both entails and is entailed by the parcelling out and serial alienation of one's self. For property by definition, in this theory, is that which is alienable. Aphra Behn's, however, is a gender specific version of possessive individualism, one constructed in opposition to the very real alternative of staying whole by renouncing self possession, an alternative that had no legal reality for men in the seventeenth century. Because the husband's right of property was in the whole of the wife, the prior alienation of any part of her had to be seen as a violation of either actual or potential marital propriety. That is, a woman who, like Aphra Behn, embraced possessive individualism, even if she were single and never bartered her sexual favours, could only do so with a consciousness that she thus contradicted the notion of female identity on which legitimate sexual property relations rested.

Publication, then, quite apart from the contents of what was published, ipso facto implied the divided, doubled, and ultimately unavailable person whose female prototype was the prostitute. By flaunting her self-sale, Aphra Behn embraced the title of whore; by writing bawdy comedies, which she then partly disclaimed, she capitalised on her supposed handicap. Finally, she even uses this persona to make herself seem the prototypical writer, and in this effort she certainly seems to have had the cooperation of her male colleagues and competitors. Thus, in the following poem, William Wycherley wittily acknowledges that the sexual innuendoes about Aphra Behn rebound back on the wits who make them. The occasion of the poem was a rumour that the poetess had gonorrhea. Wycherley emphasises how much more public is the 'Sappho of the Age' than any normal prostitute, how much her fame grows as she loses her fame, and how much cheaper is the rate of the author–whore than her sister punk. But he also stresses how much more power the poetess has, since in the world of wit as opposed to the world of sexual exchange, use increases desire, and the author–whore accumulates men instead of being exchanged among them:

> More Fame you now (since talk'd of more) acquire,
> And as more Public, are more Mens Desire;
> Nay, you the more, that you are Clap'd to, now,
> Have more to like you, less to censure you:
> Now Men enjoy your Parts for Half a Crown,
> Which, for a Hundred Pound, they scarce had done,
> Before your Parts were, to the Public known.[8]

Appropriately, Wycherley ends by imagining the whole London theatrical world as a sweating-house for venereal disease:

> Thus, as your Beauty did, your Wit does now,
> The Women's envy, Men's Diversion grow;
> Who, to be clap'd, or Clap you, round you sit,
> And, tho' they Sweat for it, will crowd your Pit;
> Since lately you Lay-in, (but as they say,)
> Because, you had been Clap'd another Way;
> But, if 'tis true, that you have need to Sweat,
> Get, (if you can) at your New Play, a Seat.

If Aphra Behn's sexual and poetic parts are the same, then the wits are contaminated by her sexual distemper. Aphra Behn and her fellow wits infect one another: the theatre is her body, their wits are their penises, the play is a case of gonorrhea, and the cure is the same as the disease.

Given the general Restoration delight in the equation of mental, sexual, and theatrical 'parts', and its frequent likening of writing to prostitution and playwrights to bawds, one might argue that if Aphra Behn had not existed, the male playwrights would have had to invent her in order to increase the witty pointedness of their cynical self-representations. For example, in Dryden's prologue to Behn's *The Widow Ranter*, the great playwright chides the self-proclaimed wits for contesting the originality of one another's productions and squabbling over literary property. Drawing on the metaphor of literary paternity, he concludes:

> But when you see these Pictures, let none dare
> To own beyond a Limb or single share;
> For where the Punk is common, he's a Sot,
> Who needs will father what the Parish got.[9]

These lines gain half their mordancy from their reference to Aphra Behn, the poetess–punk, whose offspring cannot seem fully her own, but whose right to them cannot be challenged with any propriety. By literalising and embracing the playwright–prostitute metaphor, therefore, Aphra Behn was distinguished from other authors, but only as their prototypical representative. She becomes a symbolic figure of authorship for the Restoration, the writer and the strumpet muse combined. Even those who wished to keep the relationship between women and authorship strictly metaphorical were fond of the image: 'What a pox have the women to do with the muses?' asks a character in a play attributed to Charles Gildon. 'I grant you the poets call the nine muses by the names of women, but why so? ... because in that sex they're much fitter for prostitution.'[10] It is not hard to see how much authorial notoriety could be gained by audaciously literalising such a metaphor.

Aphra Behn, therefore, created a persona that skilfully intertwined the age's available discourses concerning women, property, selfhood and authorship. She found advantageous openings where other women found repulsive insults; she turned self-division into identity.

The authorial effect I'm trying to describe here should not be confused with the plays' disapproving attitudes toward turning women into items of exchange. *The Lucky Chance*, which I am now going to discuss, all too readily yields a facile, right-minded thematic analysis centring on women and property exchange. It has three plots that can easily be seen as variations on this theme: Diana is being forced into a loveless marriage with a fop because of her father's family ambition. Her preference for the young Bredwell is ignored in the exchange. Diana's father, Sir Feeble Fainwood, is also purchasing himself a young bride, Leticia, whom he has tricked into believing that her betrothed lover, who had been banished for fighting a duel, is dead. Julia, having already sold herself to another rich old merchant, Sir Cautious Fulbank, is being wooed to adultery by her former lover, Gayman. That all three women are both property and occasions for the exchange of property is quite clear. Diana is part of a financial arrangement between the families of the two old men, and the intended bridegroom, Bearjest, sees her merely as the embodiment of a great fortune; Leticia is also bought by 'a great jointure', and though we know, interestingly, nothing of Julia's motives, we are told that she had played such a 'prank' as Leticia. It is very easy, then, to make the point that the treatment of women as property is the problem that the play's comic action will set out to solve. Whether she marries for property, as in the cases of Leticia and Julia, or she is married *as property* (that is, given, like Diana, as the condition of a dowry), the woman's identity as a form of property and item of exchange seems obviously to be the play's point of departure, and the urge to break that identification seems, on a casual reading, to license the play's impropriety. One could even redeem the fact that, in the end, the women are all *given* by the old men to their lovers by pointing out that this is, after all, a comedy and hence a form that requires female desire to flow through established channels.

Such a superficial thematic analysis of *The Lucky Chance* fits in well with that image of Aphra Behn some of her most recent biographers promote: an advocate of 'free love' in every sense of the phrase and a heroic defender of the right of women to speak their own desires. However, such an interpretation does not bear the weight of the play's structure or remain steady in the face of its ellipses, nor can it sustain the pressure of the play's images. For the moments of crisis in the play are not those in which a woman becomes property but those in which a woman is burdened with a selfhood that can be neither represented (a self without properties) nor exchanged. They are the moments when the veiled woman confronts the impossibility of being represented and hence of being desired and hence of being, finally, perhaps, gratified.

Before turning to those moments, I'd like to discuss some larger organisational features of the play that complicate its treatment of the theme of women and exchange. First, then, to the emphatic way in which the plots are disconnected in their most fundamental logic. The plots of Diana and Leticia rely on the idea that there is an irreversible moment of matrimonial exchange after which the woman is 'given' and cannot be given again. Thus the action is directed toward thwarting and replacing the planned marriage ceremony, in the case of Diana, and avoiding the consummation of the marriage bed in the case of Leticia. Julia, however, has crossed both these thresholds and is still somehow free to dispose of herself. The logic on which her plot is based seems to deny that there are critical or irremediable events in female destiny. Hence in the scene directly following Leticia's intact deliverance from Sir Feeble Fainwood's bed and Diana's elopement with Bredwell, we find Julia resignedly urging her aged husband to get the sex over with and to stop meddling with the affairs of her heart: 'But let us leave this fond discourse, and, if you must, let us to bed' (p. 135). Julia proves her self-possession precisely by her indifference to the crises structuring Diana's and Leticia's experiences.

On the one hand, Julia's plot could be seen to undercut the achievement of resolution in the other plots by implying that there was never anything to resolve: the obstacles were not real, the crises were not crises, the definitive moment never did and never could arrive. Julia's would be the pervasive atmosphere of comedy that keeps the anxieties of the more 'serious' love plot from truly being registered. But on the other hand, we could argue that the crisis plots drain the adultery plot not only of moral credibility but also of dramatic interest, for there would seem to be simply nothing at stake in Julia's plot. Indeed, Julia's plot in itself seems bent on making this point, turning as it so often does on attempts to achieve things that have already been achieved or gambling for stakes that have already been won. These two responses, however, tend to cancel one another, and we cannot conclude that either plot logic renders the other nugatory. *The Lucky Chance* achieves its effects, rather, by alternately presenting the problem and its seeming non-existence. The imminent danger of becoming an unwilling piece of someone else's property is at once asserted and denied.

The alternating assertion/denial emphasises the discontinuity between the two 'resolutions' of the woman's sexual identity that I discussed earlier: one in which the giving of the self intact is tantamount to survival; the other in which an identity is maintained in a series of exchanges. This very discontinuity, then, as I've already pointed out, is part of an overarching discursive pattern. The proof of self ownership is self sale; hence, Julia has no exculpating story of deceit or coercion to explain her marriage to Fulbank. But the complete import of what she does, both of what she sacrifices and what she gains, can only be understood against the background of a one-time exchange that involves and maintains the whole self.

The disjunction between the plot exigencies Leticia is subjected to and those that hold and create Julia (our inability to perceive these plots within a single comic perspective) reveals the oppositional relationship between the two seventeenth-century versions of the female as property. Built into this very disjunction, therefore, is a complicated presentation of the seeming inescapability for women of the condition of property. In the play, the exchange of women as property appears inevitable, and the action revolves around the terms of exchange. The crisis plots, of which Leticia's is the most important, posit wholeness as the precondition of exchange and as the result of its successful completion. The unitary principle dominates the logic of this plot and also, as we are about to see, the language of its actors and its representational rules. Julia's plot, on the other hand, assumes not only the fracturing and multiplication of the self as a condition and result of exchange, but also the creation of a second order of reality: a reality of representations through which the characters simultaneously alienate and protect their identities.

This split in representational procedures can be detected in the first scene, where it is associated with the characters of the leading men. In the play's opening speech, Bellmour enters complaining that the law has stolen his identity, has made him a creature of disguise and the night. His various complaints in the scene cluster around a central fear of de-differentiation, of the failure properly to distinguish essential differences. Thus it is the 'rigid laws, which put no difference/'Twixt fairly killing in my own defence,/And murders bred by drunken arguments,/Whores, or the mean revenges of a coward' that have forced his disguise, his alienation from his own identity. That is, the denial of the true, identity ensuring, difference (that between duellers and murderers) necessitates false differences, disguises and theatrical representations that get more elaborate as the plot progresses. The comedy is this series of disguises and spectacles, but its end is to render them unnecessary by the reunion of Bellmour with his proper identity and his proper wife.

The very terms of Bellmour's self-alienation, moreover, are identitarian in their assumption that like must be represented by like. Bellmour has taken a life in a duel, and for that he is deprived of the life he thought he would lead. He has destroyed a body with his sword, and for that a body that belongs to him, Leticia's, will be taken from him also through puncturing. Even the comic details of Bellmour's reported death are consonant with this mode of representation:

> **Ralph** Hanged. Sir, hanged, at The Hague in Holland.
> **Bellmour** For what, said they, was he hanged?
> **Ralph** Why, e'en for high treason, Sir, he killed one of their kings.
> **Gayman** Holland's a commonwealth, and is not ruled by kings.
> **Ralph** Not by one, Sir, but by many. This was a cheesemonger, they fell out over a bottle of brandy, went to snicker snee, Mr. Bellmour cut his throat, and was hanged for't, that's all, Sir.
>
> (p. 81)

The reductio ad absurdum of like representing like is the commonwealth in which everyone is a king. It is within this comically literalist system of representation that Bellmour is imagined to have had his neck broken for slitting the throat of a cheesemonger. It is no wonder that the climax of Bellmour's performance is a simulation of the exchange of like for like. As Sir Feeble Fainwood approaches the bed on which he intends to deflower Leticia, asking her, 'What, was it ashamed to show its little white foots, and its little round bubbies?', Belmour comes out from between the curtains, naked to the waist. And, all the better to ward off that which he represents, he has Leticia's projected wound painted on his own chest and a dagger ready to make another such wound on Sir Feeble. The whole representational economy of this plot, therefore, has an underlying unitary basis in the notion that things must be paid for in kind. Even Leticia's self sale seems not to be for money but for the jewellery to which she is often likened.

Like Bellmour, Gayman also enters the first scene in hiding, 'wrapped in his cloak', but the functional differences between the two kinds of self-concealment are soon manifested. The end of Gayman's disguises is not the retrieval of his property, but the appropriation of what he thinks is the property of others: 'Are you not to be married, Sir?' asks Bellmour. 'No Sir', returns Gayman, 'not as long as any man in London is so, that has but a handsome wife, Sir' (p. 77). His attempts are not to re-establish essential differences, but rather to accelerate the process of de-differentiation. 'The bridegroom!' exclaims Bellmour on first seeing Sir Feeble. 'Like Gorgon's head he's turned me into stone.' 'Gorgon's head,' retorts Gayman, 'a cuckold's head, 'twas made to graft upon' (p. 79). The dizzying swiftness with which Gayman extends Bellmour's metaphor speaks the former's desire to destroy the paired stability of exchanges. Looking at the bridegroom's head, Bellmour sees an image of destructive female sexuality, the Gorgon. Thus, the bridegroom represents the all-too-available sexuality of Leticia. Gayman's way of disarming this insight is to deck it with horns, to introduce the third term, taking advantage of Leticia's availability to cuckold Sir Feeble. But for Bellmour this is no solution at all, since it only further collapses the distinction between lover and husband, merging him with Sir Feeble at the moment he alienates his sexual property: 'What, and let him marry her! She that's mine by sacred vow already! by heaven it would be flat adultery in her!' (p. 80). 'She'll learn the trick,' replies Gayman, 'and practise it the better with thee.' The destruction of the 'true' distinctions between husband and lover, cuckold and adulterer, proprietor and thief is the state for which Gayman longs.

Bellmour's comedy, then, moves towards the re-establishment of true difference through the creation of false differences; Gayman's comedy moves toward the erasure of true differences through the creation of false and abstract samenesses. Gayman is in disguise because he cannot bear to let Julia know that he is different from his former self. He wishes to appear before her always the same, to hide the new fact of his poverty. He tries to get money from his landlady so that he can get his clothes out of hock and therefore disguise himself as himself in order to go on wooing Julia. On the same principle of the effacement of difference, Gayman later tries to pass himself off as Julia's husband when he, unbeknownst to her, takes the old man's place in bed.

Moreover, just as the false differences of Bellmour's comedy conformed to a unitary like-for-like economy of representation, the false samenesses of Gayman's plotting are governed by an economy of representation through difference. The most obvious example of this is the use of money. Money in this plot often represents bodies or their sexual use, and what is generally emphasised in these exchanges are the differences between the body and money. For example, in the scenes of Gayman's two prostitutions (the first with his landlady and the second with his unknown admirer), the difference between the women's bodies and the precious metals they can be made to yield is the point of the comedy. The landlady is herself metamorphosed into iron for the sake of this contrast: she is an iron lady who emerges from her husband's blacksmith's shop. She is then stroked into metals of increasing value as she yields 'postle spoons and caudle cups that then exchange for gold. However, Gayman's expletives never allow us to forget that this sexual alchemy is being practised on an unsublimatable body that constantly sickens the feigning lover with its stink. Even more telling is the continuation of this scene in which Gayman receives a bag of gold as advance payment for an assignation with an anonymous woman. Here the desirability of the gold (associated with its very anonymity) immediately implies the undesirability of the woman who sends it: 'Some female devil, old and damned to ugliness,/And past all hopes of courtship and address,/Full of another devil called desire,/ Has seen this face, this shape, this youth,/ And thinks it's worth her hire. It must be so' (p. 94). Of course, as this passage emphasises, in both cases the women's money stands for Gayman's sexual worthiness, but as such it again marks a difference, the difference in the desirability of the bodies to be exchanged. Hence the unlike substance, gold, marks the inequality of the like biological substances.

The freedom and the perils, especially the perils for women, that this comedy of representation through difference introduces into erotic life are explored in the conflict between Julia and Gayman. And this conflict returns us to the issue of authorial representation. Julia, like many of Aphra Behn's heroines, confronts a familiar predicament: she wishes to have the pleasure of sexual intercourse with her lover without the pain of the loss of honour. Honour seems to mean something wholly external in the play; it is not a matter of conscience since secret actions are outside its realm. Rather, to lose honour is to give away control over one's public representations. Hence, in the adultery plot, as opposed to the crisis plot, women's bodies are not the true stakes; representations of bodies, especially in money and language, are the focal points of conflict.

Gayman's complaint against Julia, for example, is that she prefers the public admiration of the crowd, which she gains through witty language ('talking all and loud' p. 99), to the private 'adoration' of a lover, which is apparently speechless. Julia's retort, however, indicates that it is Gayman who will betray the private to public representation for the sake of his own reputation. It is Gayman who will 'describe her charms', 'Or make most filthy verses of me/Under the name of Cloris, you Philander,/Who, in lewd rhymes, confess the dear appointment,/What hour, and where, how silent was the night,/How full of love your eyes, and wishing mine.' (We have just, by the way, heard Gayman sing a verse about Cloris's wishing eyes to his landlady.)

To escape being turned into someone else's language, losing the ability to control her own public presentation, Julia subjects herself to a much more radical severance of implied true self from self-representation than Gayman could have imagined. At once to gratify her sexual desire and preserve her honour, she arranges to have Gayman's own money (in some ways a sign of his desire for her) misrepresented to him as payment for sexual intercourse with an unknown woman. That is, Julia makes the anonymous advance earlier discussed.

Julia, then, is hiding behind the anonymity of the gold, relying on its nature as a universal equivalent for desire, universal and anonymous precisely because it doesn't resemble what it stands for and can thus stand for anything. But in this episode, she becomes a prisoner of the very anonymity of the representation. For, as we've already seen, Gayman takes it as a sign of the difference between the woman's desirability and his own. Apparently, moreover, this representation of her undesirability overwhelms the private experience itself, so that when the couple finally couples, Gayman does not actually experience Julia, but rather feels another version of his landlady. As he later reluctantly describes the sightless, wordless encounter to Julia (whom he does not suspect of having been the woman), 'She was laid in a pavilion all formed of gilded clouds which hung by geometry, whither I was conveyed after much ceremony, and laid in a bed with her, where, with much ado and trembling with my fears, I forced my arms about her.' 'And sure,' interjects Julia aside to the audience, 'that undeceived him.' 'But,' continues Gayman, 'such a carcass 'twas, deliver me, so shrivelled, lean and rough, a canvas bag of wooden ladles were a better bedfellow.' 'Now, though, I know that nothing is more distant than I from such a monster, yet this angers me,' confides Julia to the audience. ''Slife, after all to seem deformed, old, ugly.' The interview ends with Gayman's final misunderstanding, 'I knew you would be angry when you heard it' (p. 118).

The extraordinary thing about this interchange is that it does not matter whether or not Gayman is telling the truth about his sexual experience. The gold may have so overwhelmed his senses as to make Julia feel like its opposite: a bag of wooden ladles rather than precious coins; and, indeed, the continuity of images between this description and Gayman's earlier reactions to women who give him money tends to confirm his sincerity. The bag of ladles reminds us of the landlady, who was also a bag, but one containing somewhat more valuable table utensils: 'postle spoons and caudle cups. However, Gayman may be misrepresenting his experience to prevent Julia's jealousy. Either way, Julia was missing from that experience. Whether he did not desire her at all or desired her as someone else is immaterial; what Julia experiences as she sees herself through this doubled representation of money and language is the impossibility of keeping herself to herself and truly being gratified as at once a subject and object of desire.

By participating in this economy of difference, in which her representations are not recognisably hers, then, Julia's problem becomes her state of unexchangeability. The drive for self-possession removes her 'true' self from the realms of desire and gratification. Because she has not given herself away, she finds that her lover has not been able to take her. Surprisingly, however, the play goes on to overcome this difficulty not by taking refuge in like-for-like exchanges, but by remaining in the economy of difference until Julia seems able to adjust the claims of self-possession and gratification.

The adjustment becomes possible only after Julia has been explicitly converted into a commodity worth three hundred pounds. The process leading up to this conversion merits our scrutiny. Gayman and Sir Cautious are gambling: Gayman has won 300 pounds and is willing to stake it against something of Sir Cautious's

> **Sir Cautious**   I wish I had anything but ready money to stake: three hundred pound, a fine sum!
> **Gayman**   You have moveables Sir, goods, commodities.
> **Sir Cautious**   That's all one, Sir. That's money's worth, Sir, but if I had anything that were worth nothing.
> **Gayman**   You would venture it. I thank you, Sir. I would your lady were worth nothing.
> **Sir Cautious**   Why so, Sir?
> **Gayman**   Then I would set all 'gainst that nothing.

Sir Cautious begins this dialogue with a comical identification of everything with its universal equivalent, money. Everything he owns is convertible into money; hence, he believes that money is the real essence of everything that isn't money. Hence, everything is *really* the same thing – money. For Sir Cautious the economy of difference collapses everything into sameness. The only thing that is truly different, then, must be 'nothing', a common slang word for the female genitals. One's wife is this nothing because in the normal course of things she is not a commodity. As Sir Cautious remarks, 'Why, what a lavish whoremaker's this? We take money to marry our wives but very seldom part with 'em, and by the bargain get money' (p. 126). Her normal nonexchangeability for money is what makes a wife different from a prostitute; it is also what makes her the perfect nothing to set against three hundred pounds. We could say, then, that Julia is here made into a commodity only because she isn't one: she becomes the principle of universal difference and as such, paradoxically, becomes exchangeable for the universal equivalent.

The scene provides a structural parallel for the scene of Gayman's prostitution, in which, as we have seen, money also marks difference. But the sequels of the two scenes are strikingly dissimilar. Gayman is once again back in Julia's bed, but his rather than her identity is supposedly masked. Whereas in the first encounter, Gayman went to bed with what he thought was an old woman, in the second, Julia goes to bed with what she thinks is her old husband. But the difference between these two scenes in the dark as they are later recounted stems from the relative inalienability of male sexual identity. Even in the dark, we are led to believe, the difference of men is sensible: Gayman says, 'It was the feeble husband you enjoyed. In cold imagination, and no more./Shyly you turned away, faintly resigned. ... Till excess of love betrayed the cheat' (p. 139). Gayman's body, even unseen, is not interchangeable with Sir Cautious's. Unlike Julia's, Gayman's body will undo the misrepresentation: no mere idea can eradicate this palpable difference and sign of identity, the tumescent penis itself. Hence, when Gayman takes Sir Cautious's place in bed, he does not really risk what Julia suffered earlier: 'after all to seem deformed, old, ugly'. Gayman's self will always obtrude into the sphere of representation, another version of the ladle, but one that projects from the body instead of being barely discernible within it.

This inalienable masculine identity, although it seems at first Gayman's advantage, is quickly appropriated by Julia, who uses it to secure at once her own good reputation and complete liberty of action. Once again we are given a scene in which the speaker's sincerity is questionable. When Gayman's erection reveals his identity, Julia appears to be outraged at the attempted deception: 'What, make me a base prostitute, a foul adult'ress? Oh, be gone, dear robber of my quiet' (p. 139). We can only see this tirade as more deceit on Julia's part, since we know she tricked the same man into bed the night before. But since her deceit was not discovered and his was, she is able to feign outrage and demand a separation from her husband. The implication is, although, once again, this cannot be represented, that Julia has found a way to secure her liberty and her 'honour' by maintaining her misrepresentations.

It is, then, precisely through her nullity, her nothingness, that Julia achieves a new level of self-possession along with the promise of continual sexual exchange. But this, of course, is an inference we make from what we suspect Julia of hiding: her pleasure in Gayman's body, her delight that she now has an excuse for separating from her husband, her intention to go on seeking covert pleasure. All of this is on the other side of what we see and hear.

It is this shady effect, I want to conclude, that Aphra Behn is in the business of selling. And it is by virtue of this commodity that she becomes such a problematic figure for later women writers. For they had to overcome not only her life, her bawdiness and the author-whore metaphor she celebrated, but also her playful challenges to the very possibility of female self-representation.

From *Last Laughs: Perspectives on Women and Comedy*, ed. Regina Barreca (New York, 1988), pp. 23–42.

NOTES

[Examining the scandal of Aphra Behn's life, Catherine Gallagher argues that, in her first prologue to *The Forc'd Marriage* in 1670, Behn made female authorship into a kind of dark comedy and introduced to English Literature 'the professional writer as a newfangled whore'. Behn and her female characters were empowered by splitting their identities and selling them bit by bit. The process of female ownership through the fracturing and multiplication of the self was, however, problematised because occasionally the woman confronted the impossibility of 'being, finally, perhaps gratified'. The fracturing might elide female desire, since the female character achieved self-possession through her very nothingness. Ed.]

1. *A Room of One's Own* (London, 1929), p. 67. Woolf here no doubt exaggerates the deterrent effects of Behn's scandal. We know that hundreds of women made some sort of living as writers in the late seventeenth and early eighteenth centuries. Indeed, there was no consensus that Behn was infamous until the second half of the eighteenth century. Nevertheless, in an age that loved scandal, she seems willingly to have obliged her audience's taste.

2. 'Prologue', *The Forc'd Marriage or the Jealous Bridegroom* (London, 1671), n.p.

3. This quotation is from Robert Gould's *Satirical Epistle to the Female Author of a Poem called 'Sylvia's Revenge'* (London, 1691). The poem acknowledges that the lines are a paraphrase from Rochester's 'Letter from Artemisia in the Town to Chloe in The Country'. The sentiment is presented as a commonplace.

4. Ibid.

5. This discussion is heavily indebted to Angeline Goreau's *Reconstructing Aphra. A Social Biography of Aphra Behn* (Oxford, 1980), especially pp. 144–62. Goreau has gathered much of the evidence on which I draw; however, we reach very different conclusions on the basis of the evidence. Goreau writes that Behn 'savagely resented' the charge of immodesty and makes no references to the playwright's own sly uses of the author-whore metaphor. For a discussion of Behn's self-presentation that recognises her use of this trope, see Maureen Duffy, *The Passionate Shepherdess. Aphra Behn 1640–89* (London, 1977), especially pp. 94–104.

6. Lady Elizabeth Carey, *The Tragedy of Mariam, the Fair Queen of Jewry* (London, 1613), Act III, unpaginated. Quoted in Goreau, *Reconstructing Aphra*, p. 151.

7. Ibid.

8. William Wycherley, *Miscellany Poems*, vol. III, *The Complete Works of William Wycherley* (London, 1924), pp. 155–6.

9. 'Prologue', *The Widdow Ranter or The History of Bacon in Virginia* (London, 1690), n.p. The prologue was, in fact, first spoken to Shadwell's comedy, *The True Widow*, in 1678, yet another reminder that the author–whore metaphor was ready-made for Behn's appropriation.

10. Quoted at the opening of Fidelis Morgan, *The Female Wits. Women Playwrights of the London Stage 1660–1720* (London, 1981), n.p.

11. *The Lucky Chance or An Alderman's Bargain* (performed first in 1686) in *The Female Wits*, p. 76. All further quotations are from this edition of the play, and page numbers are given in the body of the essay.

2

Gestus and Signature in Aphra Behn's *The Rover*

ELIN DIAMOND

> Where the dream is at its most exalted, the commodity is closest to hand.
>
> (Theodor Adorno, *In Search of Wagner*)

Near the end of Act II of *The Rover*, after the wealthy virgins and hungry gallants have been introduced, and the reader-spectator is made aware that comic symmetry is pressing toward chase and final reward, mention is made of a beautiful courtesan whom the gallants, including the affianced ones, are trying to impress. Angellica Bianca would seem to be a supplement to the intrigue plot – a supplement since one need not intrigue to visit a whore. Yet before the virgins are rewarded with the husbands they desire, they will traverse this whore's marketplace. In 'scenes' and 'discoveries', they will market themselves as she does, compete for the same male affection, suffer similar abuse. The courtesan herself enters the play not in the way the audience might expect, behind an exotic vizard, or 'discovered' in her bedchamber after the parting of the scenes, but as a portrait, as *three* portraits, a large one hung from the balcony and two smaller ones posted on either side of the proscenium door designating her lodging. Willmore, the play's titular rover, arrives at her door, and in the absence of the courtesan he cannot afford, he appropriates her in representation – he reaches up and steals a portrait.

Willmore's gesture, I will suggest, contains information beyond the local revelation of one character's behaviour. We might read

Willmore's gesture as a Brechtian *Gestus* or 'gest', a moment in performance that makes visible the contradictory interactions of text,
theatre apparatus, and contemporary social struggle.[1] In the unravel-
ling of its intrigue plot, Aphra Behn's *The Rover* not only thematises
the marketing of women in marriage and prostitution, it 'demonstrates', in its gestic moments, the ideological contradictions of the
apparatus Behn inherited and the society for which she wrote.
Brecht's account of the *Gestus* is useful for alerting us to the vectors
of historical change written into dramatic texts, but he makes no
provision for gender – an unavoidable issue in Aphra Behn's own
history. Educated but constantly in need of money, with court connections but no supporting family, Aphra Behn wrote plays when
female authorship was a monstrous violation of the 'woman's
sphere'. Since the reopening of the theatres in 1660, Frances
Boothby and the Duchess of Newcastle each had had a play produced, but no woman had challenged the Restoration theatre with
Behn's success and consistency.[2] Indeed, that she could earn a living
writing for the theatre was precisely what condemned her. The
muckraking satirist Robert Gould wrote typical slander in a short
piece addressed to Behn that concluded with this couplet: 'For Punk
and Poetess agree so Pat, / You cannot be This and not be That.'[3]

In her suggestive 'Arachnologies: The Woman, The Text, and the
Critic', Nancy Miller implicitly proposes a feminist version of the
Gestus; texts by women writers, says Miller, encode the signs or
'emblems of a female signature' by which the 'culture of gender
[and] the inscriptions of its political structures' might be read.[4] In a
woman-authored text, then, the gestic moment would mark both a
convergence of social actions and attitudes, and the gendered
history of that convergence. Robert Gould's verse, with its violent,
unequivocal equation of 'poetess' and 'punk', provides some evidence of the culture of gender in Restoration London. Like her male
colleagues, Behn hawked her intrigue comedies and political satires
in the literary and the theatrical marketplace, and, like them, she suffered the attacks of 'fop-corner' and the sometimes paltry remunera-
tion of third-day receipts. In her case, however, the status of
professional writer indicated immodesty: the author, like her texts,
became a commodity.

Deciphering Behn's authorial 'signature' obliges us to read the
theatrical, social, and sexual discourses that complicate and obscure
its inscription. I am aiming here to open the text to what Brecht

calls its 'fields of force' (p. 30) – those contradictory relations and ideas that signify in Behn's culture and are, as this reading will indicate, symptomatic of our own. Like Brecht, in his discussion of Shakespeare's *Coriolanus* (pp. 252–65), I am interested less in interpretative truth than in exploring a complex textual system in which author, apparatus, history, and reader-spectator each plays a signifying role. The following section will consider Behn's authorial contexts, the Restoration theatre apparatus, with its proto-fetishist positioning of 'scenes' and actresses; the next two sections focus on multivalent signs of gender in *The Rover*; and the final section, returning to the theatre apparatus by way of Behn's unique obsessions, poses the question of the woman dramatist's signature: How does Aphra Behn encode the conditions of her literary and theatrical production? How does she stage the relationship between female creativity and public calumny – between what Robert Gould, in darkly humorous euphemisms, refers to as 'this' and 'that'?

I   THE APPARATUS

The term 'apparatus' draws together several related aspects in theatre production: the hierarchy of economic control, the material features of machinery and properties, and, more elusively, the social and psychological interplay between stage and audience. When Aphra Behn wrote her seventeen plays (1670–1689), the theatrical hierarchy, like all cultural institutions, was patriarchal in control and participation. Charles II invested power in the first patentees, Thomas Killigrew and William D'Avenant; aristocratic or upper-class males generally wrote the plays, purchased the tickets, and formed the coteries of critics and 'witlings' whose disruptive presence is remarked on in countless play prologues and epilogues. In its machinery and properties, the Restoration stage was not unlike Wagner's theatre in Adorno's critique: dreamlike, seductive, and commodity-intensive. Though the technology was well established in Italian and French courts, and in English court masques before the Interregnum, the two new Restoration theatres gave Londoners their first view of movable painted 'scenes' and mechanical devices or 'machines', installed behind the forestage and the proscenium arch. Actors posed before elaborately painted 'wings' (stationary pieces set in receding rows) and 'shutters' (flat painted scenes that moved in grooves and joined in the centre). When the scenes parted, their characters were 'discovered' against other painted scenes that, parting, produced further discoveries.[5] Built in 1671, The Duke's Theatre, Dorset Garden, the site of most of Behn's plays, was particularly known for its 'gawdy Scenes'.[6]

The movement of painted flats, the discoveries of previously unseen interiors, introduced a new scopic epistemology. Seated and unruly in semicircular areas of pit, boxes, first, middle, and upper galleries, Restoration spectators, unlike their Elizabethan counterparts, were no longer compelled to imagine the features of bedchambers, parks, or battlefields. Like Richard Flecknoe, they could rely on scenes and machines as 'excellent helps of imagination, most grateful deceptions of the sight. ... Graceful and becoming Ornaments of the Stage [transport] you easily without lassitude from one place to another, or rather by a kinde of delightful Magick, whilst you sit still, does bring the place to you.'[7] Assuming that Flecknoe's reaction is typical, and there is evidence that it is, Restoration stagecraft seems to have created a spectator-fetishist, one who takes pleasure in ornaments that deceive the sight, whose disavowal of material reality produces a desire for the 'delightful Magick' of exotic and enticing representations.[8]

I am deliberately conflating two uses of 'fetishism' in this account of Restoration reception: one, Freud's description of the male impulse to eroticise objects or female body parts, which derives from a disavowal of a material lack (of the penis on the mother's body); and two, Marx's account of the fetishisation of the commodity: at the moment of exchange, the commodity appears to be separate from the workers who produce it; the 'special social character of private labours' is disavowed.[9] Nowhere are these meanings of fetishism more relevant than in discourse generated by that other ornament of the stage, the Restoration actress. In his preface to *The Tempest*, Thomas Shadwell links the new phenomenon of female performers with painted theatrical scenes, both innovative commodities for audience consumption:

Had we not for yr pleasure found new wayes
You still had rusty Arras had, and thredbare playes;
Nor Scenes nor Woomen had they had their will,
But some with grizl'd Beards had acted Woomen still.

That female fictions were to be embodied by beardless women would, Thomas Killigrew promised, be 'useful and instructive'.[10] What the signifying body of the actress actually meant in the culture's sexual economy is perhaps more accurately suggested by metatheatrical references in play prologues and epilogues. The actress playing Flirt in Wycherley's *The Gentleman Dancing Master* satirically invites the 'good men o' th' Exchange' from the pit into the backstage tiring-room: 'You we would rather see between our Scenes'; and Dryden, in the Prologue to *Marriage A-la-Mode*, has the actor Hart refer to passionate tiring-room assignations.[11]

The private writings of Samuel Pepys are even more suggestive of the sinful pleasures afforded by actresses. On October 5, 1667, he visited the Theatre Royal in Bridges Street:

> and there, going in, met with Knipp [Mrs Knep], and she took us up into the Tireing-rooms and to the women's Shift, where Nell [Gwyn] was dressing herself and was all unready; and is very pretty, prettier than I thought; and so walked all up and down the House above, and then below into the Scene-room. ... But Lord, to see how they were both painted would make a man mad – and did make me loath them – and what base company of men comes among them, and how lewdly they talk – and how poor the men are in clothes, and yet what a show they make on the stage by candlelight, is very observable.
>
> (p. 834)

Candlelight has the ideological function of suturing contradictions between 'lewd' actors and an alluring 'show', and even a habitual playgoer like Pepys is disturbed when the seams show. That actresses were pretty women was not surprising, but the transformation of women into painted representations beautifully exhibited by candlelight was both fascinating and disturbing. Pepys went behind the painted scenes, but the paint was still there. He hoped to separate the pretty woman from the painted actress, but it was the actress he admired – and fetishised – from his spectator's seat.[12]

For Pepys and other Restoration commentators, the actress's sexuality tended to disavow her labour. Rather than produce a performance, she is a spectacle unto herself, a painted representation to lure the male spectator. In her professional duplicity, in her desirability, in her often public status of kept mistress, she is frequently equated with prostitutes or 'vizard-masks' who worked the pit and galleries of Restoration theatres during and after performances. In Wycherley's *The Plain Dealer*, Mrs Hoyden is disparaged for being 'As familiar a duck ... As an Actress in the tiring-room' (p. 407).

The epistemological link between the theatre apparatus and illicit female signs is not of course new to the Restoration. Jonas Barish, documenting the antitheatrical prejudice, notes that Patristic condemnation of the theatre, typified in tracts from the third-century Tertullian's to those of Renaissance Puritans Phillip Stubbes and William Prynne, builds on the Platonic condemnation of mimesis as the making of counterfeit copies of true originals. Actors in paint and costume contaminate their true God-given identities: 'Whatever is *born*', writes Tertullian, 'is the work of God. Whatever ... is *plastered on* is the devil's work.'[13] To the Puritan mind the presence of women on stage was an affront to feminine modesty, but more damning was the fact that the means of illusionism – use of costume, paint, masking – involved specifically female vices. The nature of theatrical representation, like the 'nature' of woman, was to ensnare, deceive, and seduce.

Given this cultural legacy, and the metonymic connection between painted female performer and painted scenes, it is not surprising that the first woman to earn money circulating her own representations had a combative relationship with the theatre apparatus. As we will see, Aphra Behn, more than any other Restoration playwright, exploits the fetish/commodity status of the female performer, even as her plays seek to problematise that status. She utilises the conventional objects of Restoration satire – the marriage market, sexual intrigue, masquerade, libertine flamboyance – even as she signals, in 'gestic' moments, their contradictory meanings for female fictions and historical women.

II VIRGIN COMMODITIES

The Rover (1677) and *The Second Part of The Rover* (1681), both drawn from Killigrew's *Thomaso, or The Wanderer* (1663), are Behn's only plays to label a character a courtesan; in her wholly original *The Feigned Curtezans* (1679), witty virgins impersonate famous Roman courtesans and near-debauches occur, but, as befits the romantic intrigue, marriages settle the confusion of plots and the financial stink of prostitution is hastily cleared away.[14] If courtesans figure by name in only three plays, however, the commodification of women in the marriage market is Aphra Behn's first and most persistent theme. Beginning appropriately enough with *The Forced Marriage; or The Jealous Bridegroom* (1670), all of Behn's seventeen known plays deal to some extent with women backed by dowries or portions who are forced by their fathers into marriage in exchange for jointure, an agreed-upon income to be settled on the wife should she be widowed.

There was a lived context for this perspective. The dowry system among propertied classes had been in place since the sixteenth century, but at the end of the seventeenth century there were thirteen women to every ten men, and cash portions had to grow to attract worthy suitors. As the value of women fell by almost 50 per cent, marriage for love, marriage by choice, became almost unthinkable.[15] Women through marriage had evident exchange value; that is, the virgin became a commodity not only for her use-value as breeder of the legal heir but for her portion, which, through exchange, generated capital. If, as Marx writes, exchange converts commodities into fetishes or 'social hieroglyphics', signs whose histories and qualitative differences can no longer be read (p. 161), women in the seventeenth-century marriage market took on the phantasmagoric destiny of fetishised commodities; they seemed no more than objects or things. As Margaret Cavendish observed, sons bear the family name but 'Daughters are to be accounted but as Movable Goods or Furnitures that wear out'.[16]

Restoration comedy, from the earliest Etherege and Sedley through Wycherley, Dryden, Vanbrugh, D'Urfey, and Congreve, mocked the marketplace values of marriage, promoting the libertine's aesthetic of 'natural' love, verbal seduction, and superiority over jealous husbands and fops. But Aphra Behn concentrated on exposing the exploitation of women in the exchange economy, adding vividly to contemporary discourse on the oppressions of marriage. 'Wife and servant are the same / But differ only in the name,' wrote Lady Mary Chudleigh.[17] 'Who would marry,' asks Behn's Ariadne (*The Second Part of the Rover*), 'who wou'd be chaffer'd thus, and sold to Slavery?'[18] The issue arises repeatedly in plays and verse of the period: not only are marriages loveless, but, once married, women lose both independent identity and control of their fortunes. Ariadne again:

> You have a Mistress, Sir, that has your Heart, and all your softer Hours: I know't, and if I were so wretched as to marry thee, must see my Fortune lavisht out on her; her Coaches, Dress, and Equipage exceed mine by far: Possess she all the day thy Hours of Mirth, good Humour and Expence, thy Smiles, thy Kisses, and thy Charms of Wit.
>
> (1:152)

The feminist philosopher Mary Astell would have had no sympathy for the sensuous appetites of Behn's females, but Ariadne's sentiments receive astute articulation in Astell's *Some Reflections Upon Marriage*. The money motive for marriage produces in the man contempt and

'Indifferency' which 'proceeds to an aversion, and perhaps even the Kindness and Complaisance of the poor abused'd Wife, shall only serve to increase it'. Ultimately, the powerless wife ends up 'mak[ing] court to [her husband] for a little sorry Alimony out of her own Estate'.[19] Two centuries later Engels merely restates these comments in his observation that forced marriages 'turn into the crassest prostitution – sometimes of both partners, but far more commonly of the woman, who only differs from the ordinary courtesan in that she does not [hire] out her body on piecework as a wage worker, but sells it once and for all into slavery'.[20]

Yet in order to launch *The Rover*'s marriage plot and to provoke sympathy for her high-spirited aristocrats, Behn dissimulates the connection between virgin and prostitute. When Florinda, Hellena, and Valeria don gypsy costumes – assume the guise of marginal and exotic females – to join the carnival masquerade, they do so explicitly to evade the patriarchal arrangement of law and jointure laid down by their father and legislated by their brother Pedro: Florinda shall marry a rich ancient count and Hellena shall go into a convent, thus saving their father a second dowry and simultaneously enriching Florida. The opening dialogue of *The Rover* is also implicitly 'gestic', raising questions about women's material destiny in life as well as in comic representation:

> **Florinda** What an impertinent thing is a young girl bred in a nunnery! How full of questions! Prithee no more, Hellena; I have told thee more than thou understand'st already.
> **Hellena** The more's my grief. I would fain know as much as you, which makes me so inquisitive.[21]

Hellena dons masquerade because she desires not a particular lover but a wider knowledge. Given the conventions of Restoration comedy, this wish to know 'more than' she already understands is troped as a wish for sexual adventure. But if we hear this dialogue dialogically – in its social register – other meanings are accessible.[22] Women's lack of access to institutions of knowledge spurred protest from writers as diverse as Margaret Cavendish, Bathsua Makin, Mary Astell, and Judith Drake. Aphra Behn mocks a university fool in *The City Heiress* and a learned lady in *Sir Patient Fancy*; she criticises neoclassical aesthetics in 'Epistle to the Reader', appended to *The Dutch Lover* (1:221–5), for having nothing to do with why people write or attend plays.[23] When she translates Bernard de

Fontenelle's *A Discovery of New Worlds*, however, she reveals as passionate a hunger for esoteric knowledge as these early English feminists. Unfortunately, the controlling conceit of Fontenelle's work – a mere woman is informally taught the complexities of Copernican theory – produces an untenable and revealing contradiction for Behn: 'He [Fontenelle] makes her [the Marchioness] say a great many silly things, tho' sometimes she makes observations so learned, that the greatest Philosophers in Europe could make no better.'[24] Insight yet silly, wise yet a *tabula rasa*, Fontenelle's Marchioness oscillates between intellectual independence and slavish imitation. She is perhaps less a contradictory character than a projection of a male intellectual's ambivalence about female education.

Aphra Behn's Hellena seeks knowledge 'more than' or beyond the gender script provided for her. She rejects not only her brother's decision to place her in a nunnery, but also the cultural narrative of portion, jointure, and legal dependency in which she is written not as subject but as object of exchange. Yet Hellena, too, oscillates – both departing from and reinforcing her social script. Her lines following those cited above seem, at first, to complicate and defer the romantic closure of the marriage plot. To have a lover, Hellena conjectures, means to 'sigh, and sing, and blush, and wish, and dream and wish, and long and wish to see the man' (p. 7). This thrice-reiterated wishing will result in three changes of costume, three suitors, and three marriages. As with the repetitions of 'interest', 'credit', and 'value' – commodity signifiers that circulate through the play and slip like the vizard from face to hand to face – this repetition invokes the processes underlying all wishing, to desire that will not, like a brother's spousal contract, find its 'completion'.

If we incorporate insights from feminist psychoanalytic theory, the virgins' masquerade takes on added significance, or rather this discourse helps us decode what is already implied – namely, that in an economy in which women are dependent on male keepers and traders, female desire is always already a masquerade, a play of false representations that covers over and simultaneously expresses the lack the woman exhibits – lack of the male organ and, concomitantly, lack of access to phallic privileges – to material and institutional power. Unlike the theatrical mask, which conceals a truth, the masquerade of female sexuality subverts the 'Law-of-the-Father' that stands 'behind' any representation.[25] Underneath the gypsy veils and drapes of Behn's virgins, there is nothing, in a phallic sense, to see; thus no coherent female identity that can be co-opted into a repressive romantic narrative. Willmore, titillated by Hellena's witty chatter, asks to see her face. Hellena responds that underneath the vizard is a 'desperate ... lying look' (p. 56) – that is, she, like her vizard, may prevaricate; represented may mingle with representer – for the spectator (Willmore) there will be no validating stake.

Yet, as Behn well knew, there is means of validation, one that guarantees patriarchy's stake in portion, jointure, and the woman's body: the hymen. In Restoration comedy no witty unmarried woman was really witty unless she had property *and* a maidenhead. Behn's virgins may re-'design' their cast of characters but they cannot change their plot. Ultimately their masquerade is dissimulation in the classic representational sense, a veil that hides a truth. Hellena's mask merely replicates the membrane behind which lies the 'true nature' of woman: the equipment to make the requisite patrilineal heir. Thus Willmore's masterful response to Hellena's 'lying look' is a mock-blazon of her facial features, ending in a fetishistic flourish: 'Those soft round melting cherry lips and small even white teeth! Not to be expressed, but silently adored!' (p. 56). The play in Hellena's discourse between knowing and desiring, which extends through the masquerade, completes itself in the marriage game. She exercises her will only by pursuing and winning Willmore, for as it turns out he has the 'more' she 'would fain know'.

Wilmore acts not only as the rover but as signifier for the play's phallic logic. His name metaphorises the trajectory of desire as he roves from bed to bed 'willing more', making all satisfactions temporary and unsatisfying. Desire's subject, Willmore never disguises himself (he comes on stage *holding* his mask); until enriched by the courtesan Angellica Bianca, he remains in 'buff' or leather military coat. In another sense, though, Willmore is already in disguise, or rather the entity 'Willmore' covers a range of linguistic and social signifiers. Behn's model for Willmore (like Etherege's for Dorimant) was reputedly the womanising courtier, the Earl of Rochester, whose name, John Wilmot, contains, like the rover's, the word ('mot') 'will'. Rochester was also the lover and mentor of Elizabeth Barry, the actress who first played Behn's Hellena. In Tory mythology Charles II, on the verge of fleeing England, disguised himself in buff – a leather doublet.[26] Indeed, Willmore's first lines refer to the offstage Prince who, in exile during the Commonwealth, was also a rover. Doubled mimetically and semiotically with both Rochester and the Merry Monarch (who attended at least one performance of *The Rover* before the play was restaged at Whitehall), Willmore needs no mask to effect his ends: his libertine desire is guaranteed and upheld by patriarchal law. Hellena's playful rovings, on the other hand, and her numerous disguises, signal both ingenuity and vulnerability.[27] Ironically, the virgins' first costume, the gypsy masquerade, represents their actual standing in the marriage market – exotic retailers of fortunes (or portions). Their masquerade defers but does not alter the structure of patriarchal exchange.

In contrast to the virgins' 'ramble' are the stasis and thralldom that attend the courtesan Angellica Bianca. While the virgins are learning artful strategies of concealment, Angellica's entrance is a complicated process of theatrical unveiling. She arrives first through words, then through painted representation, then through the body of an actress who appears on a balcony behind a silk curtain. She is also the site of a different politics, one that explores desire and gender not only in the text but in the apparatus itself.

The first references to Angellica situate her beyond the market in which we expect her to function. According to Behn's gallants, she is the 'adored beauty of all the youth in Naples, who put on all their charms to appear lovely in her sight; their coaches, liveries and themselves all gay as on a monarch's birthday' (p. 28). Equated thus with sacred and secular authority, Angellica gazes on her suitors and 'has the pleasure to behold all languish for her that see her' (p. 28). This text in which desire flows from and is reflected back to a female subject is immediately followed by the grouping of the English gallants beneath the courtesan's balcony. They wait with the impatience of theatre spectators for Angellica to appear – not in person but in representation, as 'the shadow of the fair substance' (p. 29).

At this point the problematic connection between shadow and substance preoccupies them. Blunt, the stock country fool, is confused by the fact that signs of bourgeois and even noble status – velvet beds, fine plate, handsome attendance, and coaches – are flaunted by courtesans. Blunt is raising an epistemological issue that Behn and her colleagues often treat satirically – the neoclassical assumption regarding mimesis that imitated can be separated from imitator, nature from representation, truth from falsehood, virgin from gypsy. By suggesting that whores are indistinguishable from moral women, Behn revives the problematic of the masquerade casting doubt on the connection/separation of sign and referent. Significantly, when Hobbes constructed his theory of sovereign authority, he employed theatre metaphors to distinguish between '*natural*' and '*feigned* or *artificial*' persons. But he noted that 'person' was itself a slippery referent:

> The word Person [persona] is Latin ... [and] signifies the *disguise*, or
> *outward appearance* of a man, counterfeited on the stage; and some-
> times more particularly that part of it, which disguiseth the face, as
> a mask or vizard: and from the stage, hath been translated to any
> representer of speech and action, as well in tribunals, as theatres. So
> that a *person* is the same that an *actor* is, both on stage and in
> common conversation.[28]

Since, as Christopher Pye notes, everyone is already a 'self-imperson-
ator, a mediated representation of himself', the difference between
'natural' and 'feigned' rests on highly unstable assumptions about
identity which, both 'on stage' and 'in common conversation' are
capable of shifting.[29] Blunt's confusion about the true status of apparently noble women may also be read as an extra-textual reference
to the Restoration actress and her female spectators. As kept mistresses, actresses often displayed the fine clothing and jewels of aristocrats like the notorious Duchess of Cleveland, who regularly
watched the play in vizard-mask from the king's box. Yet the respectable Mrs Pepys also owned a vizard-mask, and on her frequent
visits to the theatre occasionally sat in the pit near the 'real' vizards.[30]

Given the theatricality of everyday Restoration life, and the ambiguity of signs representing the status and character of women,
Angellica's three portraits allow Aphra Behn to comment on the
pleasures and politics of theatrical signification. Though I have
ignored the specifics of Behn's adaptation of her source play, it is
helpful here to compare her handling of the paintings with that of
Killigrew in his ten-act semi-autobiographical closet drama,
Thomaso, or The Wanderer. In both plays, one portrait is prominent
and raised, and two smaller versions are posted below, one of which
is snatched by the rake – Thomaso in the source play, Willmore in
Behn's. But there is an important difference in the disposition of the
paintings vis-à-vis the woman they represent. In *Thomaso*, 2.1,
anonymous parties of men pass in front of the paintings, react
scornfully to the courtesan's high price, and wander on. But in 2.2,
with the arrival of Killigrew's main characters, Angellica Bianca is
sitting on the balcony in full view of her prospective buyers. Her
bawd challenges the men to 'compare them [the paintings and the
woman] together'.[31] With neoclassical correctness, the men agree
that the woman exceeds her representation: 'That smile, there's a
grace and sweetness in it Titian could never have catch'd' (p. 333). By
the time the English Thomaso and his friends arrive, the viewing of
the paintings and the viewing of Angellica are almost simultaneous:

Harrigo That wonder is it I told you of; tis the picture of the famous Italian, the Angellica; See, shee's now at her Window.
Thomaso I see her, 'tis a lovely Woman.

(Killigrew, p. 334)

Aphra Behn's Angellica Bianca never invites such explicit comparison. In fact, Behn prolongs the dialogue between titillated suitors and suggestive portraits: Angellica's simulacra, not Angellica, preoccupy her male audience. When the English cavaliers first view the paintings, Belvile, the play's fatuous moral figure, reads them as 'the fair sign[s] to the inn where a man may lodge that's fool enough to give her price' (p. 33). That is, the iconicity of the paintings, their likeness to Angellica, which so impresses Killigrew's cavaliers, is in Behn's text suppressed. Gazing on the portraits, the gallants rewrite the courtesan's monarchial description, now figuring her as a thing, a receptacle for depositing one's body. To underscore the point, Behn has Blunt ask the ontological question to which there is a ready answer in commodity discourse: 'Gentlemen, what's this?' **Belvile**: 'A famous courtesan, that's to be sold' (p. 33). The infinitive phrase is curious. To be sold by whom? Released by her earlier keeper's death, Angellica and her bawd seem to be in business for themselves. At this point, however, Blunt reminds us again of the object status of the woman, as of her painted signs: 'Let's be gone; I'm sure we're no chapmen for this commodity' (p. 33).

Willmore, however, monarchy's representative, succumbs to the lure of the signs, believing not only in their iconicity but in their value as pleasurable objects – for the original one must pay one thousand crowns, but on the portraits one can gaze for nothing. Penury, however, is not the real issue. Willmore seems to understand that the appeal of the paintings is precisely that they are not the original but an effective stand-in. After the two Italian aristocrats draw swords in competition for Angellica, Willmore reaches up and steals one of the small paintings, in effect cuts away a piece of the representation for his own titillation. His intentions, like his actions, are explicitly fetishistic:

This posture's loose and negligent;
The sight on't would beget a warm desire
In souls whom impotence and age had chilled.
This must along with me.

(p. 38)

This speech and the act of appropriation occur *before* Willmore sees Angellica. Only in Behn's text do the paintings function as fetishes, as substitute objects for the female body. When challenged why he has the right to the small portrait, Willmore claims the right 'of possession, which I will maintain' (p. 38).

At the outset of this paper I described Willmore's acquisitive gesture as a Brechtian 'gest' – that moment in theatrical performance in which contradictory social attitudes in both text and society are made heuristically visible to spectators. What does this gest show? Willmore removes Angellica's portrait the way a theatre manager might lift off a piece of the set – because without buying her, he already owns her. Her paintings are materially and metonymically linked to the painted scenes, which were of course owned, through the theatrical hierarchy, by patentee and king – who, in Behn's fiction, validates and empowers Willmore. This 'homosocial' circuit, to use Eve Sedgwick's term, extends into the social realm.[32] As innumerable accounts make clear, Restoration theatre participated in the phallic economy that commodified women, not in the marriage market, but in the mistress market: the king and his circle came to the theatre to look, covet, and buy. Nell Gwyn is the celebrated example, but Behn's biographer Angeline Goreau cites other cases. An actress in the King's Company, Elizabeth Farley, joined the royal entourage for several months, then became mistress to a Gray's Inn lawyer, then drifted into prostitution and poverty.[33] The answer to the question, 'Who is selling Angellica?' is, then, the theatre itself, which, like Willmore, operates with the king's patent and authorisation. When Angellica sings behind her balcony curtain for her Italian admirers, and draws the curtain to reveal a bit of beautiful flesh, then closes it while monetary arrangements are discussed, she performs the titillating masquerade required by her purchasers *and* by her spectators. This is mastery's masquerade, not to demonstrate freedom, but to flaunt the charms that guarantee and uphold male power.

If Angellica's paintings stand for the theatre apparatus and its ideological complicity with a phallic economy, what happens when Angellica appears? Is illusionism betrayed? Interestingly, Aphra Behn chooses this moment to emphasise presence, not only of character but of body; Angellica emerges in the flesh and offers herself, gratis, to Willmore, finding his scornful admiration ample reason for, for the first time, falling in love. In their wooing/bargaining scene it becomes clear that Angellica wants to step out of the exchange economy symbolised by the paintings: 'Canst thou believe [these yielding joys] will be entirely thine, / without considering they were mercenary?' (p. 45). The key word here is 'entirely'; Angellica dreams of full reciprocal exchange without commerce: 'The pay I mean is but thy love for mine. / Can you give that?' (p. 47). And Willmore responds 'entirely'.[34]

A commodity, Marx writes, appears as a commodity only when it 'possess[es] a double form, i.e. natural form and value form' (p. 138). Angellica's name contains 'angel', a word whose meaning is undecidable since it refers simultaneously to the celestial figure and to the old English coin stamped with the device of Michael the archangel, minted for the last time by Charles I but still in common circulation during the Restoration. By eliminating her value-form, Angellica attempts to return her body to a state of nature, to take herself out of circulation. While the virgins of the marriage plot are talking 'business' and learning the powers of deferral and unveiling, Angellica is trying to demystify and authenticate herself. She wants to step out of the paintings, to be known not by her surface but by her depth.[35] As she 'yields' to Willmore upstairs, the portraits on the balcony are removed – a sign that the courtesan is working. In this case, not only does the (offstage) 'natural' body supplant its painted representation, but the courtesan, who has been in excess of, now makes up a deficiency in, the marriage plot: Angellica (with Willmore) labours for love.

Though the paintings disappear in Act III, however, the signs of commodification are still in place, or are metonymically displaced through properties and scenes to other characters in the marriage plot. We learn that Hellena's portion derives from her uncle, the old man who kept Angellica Bianca; thus the gold Willmore receives from the courtesan has the same source as that which he will earn by marrying the virgin. Like Angellica, too, the virgin Florinda uses a portrait as a calling card, and at night in the garden, '*in undress*', carrying a little box of jewels – a double metonym for dowry and genitals – she plans to offer herself to Belvile (p. 65). Unfortunately Willmore, not Belvile, enters the garden and nearly rapes her.

Florinda's nocturnal effort at enterpreneurship takes place in the upstage scenes, where Aphra Behn, like her fellow Restoration dramatists, situated lovers' trysts and discoveries. The thematic link between commodified 'Scenes' and females is particularly crucial, however, in *The Rover*. In IV.iv, a disguised Florinda flees from

Willmore by running in and out of the scenes until she arrives in
Blunt's chamber, where another near-rape occurs. Blunt has just
been cozened by a prostitute and dumped naked into the city sewer;
he emerges vowing to 'beat' and 'kiss' and 'bang' the next woman
he sees, who happens to be Florinda, but now all women appear to
be whores. In fact Willmore, Frederick, and even Belvile arrive soon
after to break open the door and 'partake' of Florinda. If Angellica
Bianca makes a spectacle of herself through balcony curtains and
paintings, Florinda's 'undress' and her proximity to the painted
scenes signify a similar reduction to commodity status.

IV 'I ... HANG OUT THE SIGN OF ANGELLICA'

Angellica's paintings, I have argued, are the bright links in a
metonymic chain joining the text of *The Rover* to the apparatus of
representation. Angellica's portraits represent the courtesan in the
most radical sense. They produce an image of her and at the same
time reduce her to that image. Notwithstanding her passionate
address, Angellica cannot exceed her simulacra. In effect she is
doubly commodified – first because she puts her body into exchange, and second because this body is equated with, indeed interchangeable with, the art object. When Willmore performs the 'gest'
of appropriating the painted image of Angellica, he makes visible,
on the one hand, the patriarchal and homosocial economy that controls the apparatus and, on the other hand, the commodity status of
paintings, of their model, and, by metonymic extension, of the
painted actress and the painted scenes.

Flecknoe and Pepys, we noted earlier, testify to the intensity of
visual pleasure in Restoration theatre. It is a fascinating contradiction of all feminist expectation to discover that Aphra Behn, more
than any of her Restoration colleagues, contributed to that visual
pleasure by choosing, in play after play, to exploit the fetish/com-
modity status of the female performer. The stage offered two
playing spaces, the forestage used especially for comedy, where
actor and audience were in intimate proximity, and the upstage or
scenic stage, where wing-and-shutter settings, as much as 50 feet
from the first row of spectators, produced the exotic illusionistic
discoveries needed for heroic tragedy. Writing mostly comedies,
Aphra Behn might be expected to follow comic convention and use
the forestage area, but as Peter Holland notes, she was 'positively

obsessive' about discovery scenes (p. 41). Holland counts thirty-one discoveries in ten comedies (consider that Sedley's *The Mulberry Garden*, 1668, uses one; Etherege's *The Man of Mode*, 1676, uses two), most of which are bedroom scenes featuring a female character '*in undress*'. Holland reasons that such scenes are placed upstage so that familiar Restoration actresses would not be distractingly exposed to the audience (pp. 41–2). We might interpret Behn's 'obsession' differently: the exposed woman's (castrated) body must be obscured in order to activate scopic pleasure. Displayed in 'undress' or loosely draped gowns, the actress becomes a fetish object, affording the male spectator the pleasure of being seduced by and, simultaneously, of being protected from the effects of sexual difference.

Is it also possible that this deliberate use of fetishistic display dramatises and displaces the particular assault Behn herself endured as 'Poetess/Punk' in the theatre apparatus? The contradictions in her authorial status are clear from the preface to *The Lucky Chance* (1686). Behn argues that 'the Woman damns the Poet' (3:186), that accusations of bawdy and plagiarism are levied at her because she is a woman. On the other hand, the literary fame she desires derives from a creativity that in her mind, or rather in the social ideology she has absorbed, is also gendered: 'my Masculine Part the Poet in me' (3:187).[36] In literary history, the pen, as Gilbert and Gubar have argued, is a metaphorical penis, and the strong woman writer adopts strategies of revision and disguise in order to tell her own story.[37] In Behn's texts, the painful bisexuality of authorship, the conflict between (as she puts it) her 'defenceless' woman's body and her 'masculine part', is *staged* in her insistence, in play after play, on the equation between female body and fetish, fetish and commodity – the body in the 'scenes'. Like the actress, the woman dramatist is sexualised, circulated, denied a subject position in the theatre hierarchy.

This unstable, contradictory image of authority emerges as early as Behn's first play prologue (to *The Forced Marriage, or The Jealous Bridegroom*, 1670). A male actor cautions the wits that the vizard-masks sitting near them will naturally support a woman's play and attempt to divert them from criticism. He is then interrupted by an actress who, pointing '*to the Ladies*' praises both them and, it would seem, the woman author: 'Can any see that glorious sight and say / A woman shall not prove Victor today?' (3:286). The 'glorious sight', is, once again, the fetishised, commodified representation of the female, standing on the forestage, sitting in the pit, and soon to be inscribed as author of a printed play. If this fascinating moment – in which a woman speaking a woman's lines summons the regard of other women – seems to put a *female* gaze into operation, it also reinforces the misogynist circuitry of the theatre apparatus: that which chains actress to vizard-mask to author.

At the outset of this essay we asked how Aphra Behn encodes the literary and theatrical conditions of her production. Behn's 'Postscript' to the published text of *The Rover* provides a possible answer. She complains that she has been accused of plagiarising Killigrew simply because the play was successful and she a woman. Yet while claiming to be 'vainly proud of [her] judgment' in adapting *Thomaso*, she 'hang[s] out the sign of Angellica (the only stolen object) to give notice where a great part of the wit dwelt' (p. 130). This compliment to Killigrew may also indicate what compelled Behn to embark on this adaptation. The 'sign[s] of Angellica' both constitute and represent the theatre apparatus, serving as metacritical commentary on its patriarchal economy, its habits of fetishistic consumption. They may also constitute Behn's authorial signature, what Miller calls the 'material ... brutal traces of the culture of gender' (p. 275). As a woman writer in need of money, Behn was vulnerable to accusations of immodesty; to write meant to expose herself, to put herself into circulation; like Angellica, to sell her wares. Is it merely a coincidence that Angellica Bianca shares Aphra Behn's initials, that hers is the only name from *Thomaso* that Behn leaves unchanged?

The 'signs of Angellica' not only help us specify the place of this important woman dramatist in Restoration cultural practice, they invite us to historicise the critique of fetishisation that has informed so much feminist criticism in the last decade.[38] Certainly the conditions of women writers have changed since the Restoration, but the fetishistic features of the commercial theatre have remained remarkably similar. Now as then the theatre apparatus is geared to profit and pleasure, and overwhelmingly controlled by males. Now as then the arrangement of audience to stage produces what Brecht calls a 'culinary' or ideologically conservative spectator, intellectually passive but scopically hungry, eager for the next turn of the plot, the next scenic effect. Now as then the actor suffers the reduction of Angellica Bianca, having no existence except in the simulations produced by the exchange economy. The practice of illusionism, as Adorno points out above, converts historical performers into commodities which the spectator pays to consume.

If Restoration theatre marks the historical beginning of commodity-intensive, dreamlike effects in English staging, Aphra Behn's contribution to contemporary theory may lie in her demonstration that, from the outset, dreamlike effects have depended on the fetish-commodification of the female body. When Willmore, standing in for king and court, steals Angellica's painting, Behn not only reifies the female, she genders the spectatorial economy as, specifically, a male consumption of the female image. Reading that confident gesture of appropriation as a *Gestus*, the contemporary spectator adds another viewpoint. Angellica Bianca's paintings appear to us now as both authorial 'signature' and 'social hieroglyphic', signs of a buried life whose careful decoding opens up new possibilities for critique and contestation.

From *English Literary History*, 56 (1989), 519–41.

NOTES

[In Behn's most famous play, *The Rover*, Elin Diamond defines the hero Willmore's gesture of stealing down the picture of the whore Angellica Bianca as a Brechtian *gestus*, a moment of phallic logic that marks the convergence of social action and attitude and the gendered history of that convergence. The article goes on to explore the complex textual system in which the author, history, apparatus and reader-spectator play signifying roles, and asks in the end how Behn encodes in the play the conditions of her literary and theatrical production. Ed.]

1. John Willett's translation of *Gestus* as 'gest' (with the adjective 'gestic') has become standard English usage (see *Brecht on Theatre; The Development of an Aesthetic* [New York, 1964], p. 42). Further references will appear in the text. Like many concepts in Brecht's epic theatre theory, *Gestus* is terrifically suggestive and difficult to pin down. Words, gestures, actions, tableaux all qualify as gests if they enable the spectator to draw conclusions about the 'social circumstances' (p. 105) shaping a character's attitudes. The gest should be understandable, but also dialectical, incomplete: '[the] expressions of a gest are usually highly complicated and contradictory ... ' (p. 198). In an excellent essay the semiotician Patrice Pavis describes *Gestus* as 'the key to the relationship between the play being performed and the public, [as well as] the author's attitude [toward] the public'. See *Languages of the Stage* (New York, 1982), p. 42.

2. Margaret Cavendish's play was produced under her husband's name. See Maureen Duffy, *The Passionate Shepherdess: Aphra Behn 1640–1689* (London, 1977), pp. 95–104, and Angeline Goreau, *Reconstructing Aphra: A Social Biography of Aphra Behn* (New York, 1980), pp. 115 ff.

3. Robert Gould, cited in George Woodcock, *The Incomparable Aphra* (London, 1977), p. 103.

4. The full citation from Nancy K. Miller is as follows: 'When we tear the web of women's texts, we may discover in the representations of writing itself the marks of the grossly material, the sometimes brutal traces of the culture of gender; the inscriptions of its political structures'. See 'Arachnologies: The Woman, The Text, and the Critic', in *The Poetics of Gender*, ed. Nancy K. Miller (New York, 1986), p. 275. Further references appear in the text.

5. I am indebted to the detailed discussion of Restoration theatre practice in Peter Holland's *The Ornament of Action: Text and Performance in Restoration Comedy* (Cambridge, 1979), particularly the first three chapters. Further references will appear in the text.

6. See Dryden's Prologue to *Marriage A-la-Mode in Four Comedies*, ed. L. A. Beaurline and F. Bowers (Chicago, 1967), p. 284.

7. Richard Flecknoe, 'A Short Discourse of the English Stage', in *Critical Essays of the Seventeenth Century*, vol. 2, ed. J. E. Spingarn (Oxford, 1908), p. 96.

8. The Prologue to *Tunbridge-Wells*, produced at Dorset Garden, February–March, 1678, chastises the audience:

> And that each act may rise to your desire
> Devils and Witches must each Scene inspire,
> Wit rowls in Waves, and showers down in Fire. ...
> Your souls (we know) are seated in your Eies. ...

Cited in Montague Summers, *The Restoration Theatre* (London, 1934), p. 42. Pepys remarks frequently on scenes and costumes. On 8 March 1664, he saw *Heraclius* at Lincoln's Inn Fields (the home of the Duke's Company before Dorset Garden was built): 'But at the beginning, at the drawing up of the Curtaine, there was the finest Scene of the Emperor and his people about him, standing in their fixed and different postures in their Roman habits, above all that ever I yet saw at any of the Theatres' (*The Shorter Pepys*, ed. Robert Latham [Berkeley, CA, 1985], p. 362). Further references will appear in the text. See also Hugh Hunt, 'Restoration Acting', in *Restoration Theatre*, ed. John Russell Brown and Bernard Harris (London, 1965), pp. 178–92, on competition between theatre companies over spectacular displays. Hunt makes the point, too, that as comedies often closed after one day, or ran no more than eight or ten performances, scenery was restricted to what was available (p. 187). I comment on Behn's use of scenes and discoveries in the final section of this essay.

9. Karl Marx, *Capital*, trans. Ben Fowkes (New York, 1977), p. 167. Further references will appear in the text.

10. Shadwell and Killigrew are cited in Arthur H. Avey and Arthur H. Scouten, 'The Audience', in *Restoration and Eighteenth-Century Comedy*, ed. Scott McMillin (New York, 1973), pp. 445, 442.

11. William Wycherley, *The Gentleman Dancing Master*, in *The Complete Plays of William Wycherley*, ed. W. C. Ward (London, 1902), p. 242. Further references to *The Complete Plays* will appear in the text. John Dryden, *Marriage A-la-Mode*, p. 283. More damning are Dryden's lines to the playhouse 'gallants' (probably a mixture of country squires, London aristocrats, and young professionals) in the epilogue 'To The King and Queen, At The Opening Of Their Theatre Upon The Union Of The Two Companies In 1682' (Summers, *The Restoration Theatre*, p. 56):

> We beg you, last, our Scene-room to forbear
> And leave our Goods and Chattels to our Care.
> Alas, our Women are but washy Toys,
> And wholly taken up in Stage Employs:
> Poor willing Tits they are: but yet I doubt
> This double duty soon will wear them out.

12. On 2 March 1667, Pepys admired Nell Gwyn as Florimell, a 'breeches part' in Dryden's *Secret Love, or The Maiden Queen*, which allowed her to show her legs. He was so impressed he saw the play two more times. Breeches grant Behn's heroines the independence to fulfil their romantic destiny and simultaneously encourage the processes of fetishism. As Hugh Hunt, 'Restoration Acting', so quaintly puts it: 'to the Restoration gallants the public display of a woman's calf and ankle was little less than a "bombshell"' (p. 183).

13. Jonas Barish, *The Anti-Theatrical Prejudice* (Berkeley, CA 1981), p. 158.

14. *The Town Fop* (1676) and *The City Heiress* (1682) contain two practising bawds, and Behn creates several adulterous wives; the latter, however, all claim a prior love attachment that was cut off by a forced marriage. *The Lucky Chance* (1686) is most concerned with what Eve Kosofsky Sedgwick calls the homosocial bonds between husbands and lovers. See *Between Men: English Literature and Homosocial Desire* (New York, 1982).

15. See Angeline Goreau, *Reconstructing Aphra*, pp. 77–8. See also Lawrence Stone, *The Family, Sex, and Marriage in England, 1500–1800* (New York, 1979), pp. 77–8.

16. Margaret Cavendish, cited in Hilda Smith, *Reason's Disciples: Seventeenth-Century English Feminists* (Urbana, IL, 1982), p. 79.

17. Lady Mary Chudleigh, 'To the Ladies', from *Poems on Several Occasions*, in *First Feminists: British Women Writers 1578–1799*, ed. Moira Ferguson (Bloomington, IN, 1985), p. 237.

18. Aphra Behn, *The Second Part of the Rover*, in *The Works of Aphra Behn*, ed. Montague Summers, 6 vols (London, 1915), 1:152. With the exception of *The Rover*, all references to Behn's plays are cited from this edition.

19. Mary Astell, cited in Smith, *Reason's Disciples*, pp. 133, 135.

20. Frederick Engels, *The Origin of the Family, Private Property and the State* (New York, 1985), p. 134.

21. Aphra Behn, *The Rover*, ed. Frederick Link (Lincoln, NE, 1967), p. 7. All subsequent references are to page numbers in this edition.

22. 'Dialogism', associated with the writings of M. M. Bakhtin and V.N. (a cover name for Bakhtin), implies that utterance is always social; any single utterance interacts with meanings in the larger discursive field. As Volosinov puts it: 'A word is a bridge thrown between myself and another. ... A word is a territory shared by both addresser and addressee, by the speaker and his interlocutor.' (See *Marxism and the Philosophy of Language*, trans. L. Matejka and I. R. Titunik [Cambridge, 1986], p. 86.) Though Bakhtin has little to say about theatre texts, the notion of shared verbal territory has obvious relevance for speaker-audience interaction. How to describe and analyse the relationship between text and cultural context has long been the preoccupation of cultural materialists. See especially Raymond Williams, *Marxism and Literature* (London, 1977), Jonathan Dollimore, *Radical Tragedy: Religion, Ideology and Power in the Drama of Shakespeare and His Contemporaries* (Chicago, 1984), Peter Stallybrass and Allon White, *The Politics and Poetics of Transgression* (Ithaca, NY, 1986), and essays in *Rewriting the Renaissance: The Discourses of Sexual Difference in Early Modern Europe*, ed. M. W. Ferguson, M. Quilligan, N. J. Vickers (Chicago, 1986), particularly feminist readings of women writers, for example Ann Rosalind Jones's 'City Women and Their Audiences: Louise Labé and Veronica Franco', pp. 299–316.

23. Until Act V of *Sir Patient Fancy*, the prevailing view of the learned Lady Knowall seems to be best expressed by the real Sir Patient: 'that Lady of eternal Noise and hard Words ... she's a Fop; and has Vanity and Tongue enough to debauch any Nation under civil Government' (4.32); indeed, like a female version of the old senex, Lady Knowall pursues her daughter's lover. Act V, however, reveals her 'design'; she has been testing the lovers and scheming to wrest from Sir Patient a fabulous jointure for them. The signs of Lady Knowall's learning (such

as abstruse vocabulary) remain in place to the end but are rendered benign through her assumption of her proper gender role.

24. Cited in Smith, *Reason's Disciples*, p. 63.

25. According to Lacanian psychoanalyst Michele Montrelay, masquerade has always been considered 'evil' because, in flaunting the absent-penis, it sidesteps castration anxiety and repression, thus threatening the Father's law (incest taboo) and all systems of representation. See Montrelay,'Inquiry Into Femininity', *m/f*, 1 (1978), 83–101.

26. See Susan Staves, *Players' Scepters: Fictions of Authority in the Restoration* (Lincoln, NE, 1979), p. 2.

27. My view that Hellena is fully recuperated into the economy she rebels against contrasts with, among others, Frederick M. Link's interpretation in his Introduction to *The Rover* (see note 21) and, more recently, to DeRitter Jones's in 'The Gypsy, *The Rover*, and the Wanderer: Aphra Behn's Revision of Thomas Killigrew', *Restoration*, 10 (Fall 1986), 82–92. Both Link and Jones argue that Hellena represents a positive alternative to both the ingenuous Florinda and the rejected Angellica; her contract with Willmore is 'no marriage for "portion and jointure", no marriage arranged to perpetuate a family's name or increase its wealth, but a contract between two free and like-minded people' (Link, p. xiv). Even from a humanist perspective, this view is dubious: Hellena's freedom is inconceivable outside the market economy; from a historical or gestic perspective, Hellena's 'identity' is at the very least divided and ambivalent.

28. Thomas Hobbes, *Leviathan*, ed. Michael Oakeshott (New York, 1962), p. 125.

29. Christopher Pye, 'The Sovereign, the Theater, and the Kingdom of Darknesse: Hobbes and the Spectacle of Power', *Representations*, 8 (Fall 1984), p. 91.

30. Cited in Summers, *The Restoration Theatre*, pp. 85–6. The self-theatricalising nature of the audience produced enormous chaos, as indicated in this satirical speech from Betterton's *The Amorous Widow; or The Wanton Wife*: 'to see a Play at the Duke's House, where we shall have such Sport. ... 'Tis the pleasant'st Thing in the whole World to see a Flock of wild Gallants fluttering about two or three Ladies in Vizard Masks, and then they talk to 'em so wantonly, and so loud, that they put the very Players out of countenance – 'Tis better Entertainment than any Part of the Play can be' (Summers, p. 68). See also the often-cited passage in Pepys in which he complains that dialogue between Sir Charles Sedley and two vizarded women both entertained – one was 'exceeding witty as ever I heard woman' – and distracted him from viewing the play (*The Shorter Pepys*, ed. Lathem, p. 728).

31. Thomas Killigrew, *Thomaso, or the Wanderer*, parts 1 and 2, in *Comedies and Tragedies* (London, 1663), p. 333. All references in the text are to this edition.

32. See Sedgwick's *Between Men* (note 14 above), particularly her analysis of Wycherley's *The Country Wife* (pp. 49–66). Interestingly, when cuckoldry drives the plots of a Behn play, as in *The False Count*, the wife's passion, trammelled by her forced marriage, is given as much weight as homosocial competitiveness.

33. See Goreau, *Reconstructing Aphra*, p. 174.

34. What Angellica desires is the fantasy described by Luce Irigaray in 'Commodities among Themselves' (*This Sex Which is Not One*, trans. Catherine Porter with Carolyn Burke [Ithaca, NY, 1985], pp. 192–7): 'Exchanges without identifiable terms, without accounts, without end.' But such nonmaterialist exchange is possible, Irigaray implies, only in a lesbian sexual economy, while Behn's Angellica remains (and fails) within the heterosexual economy of the intrigue plot. Compare these representations to Margaret Cavendish's utopia for aristocratic women in *The Convent of Pleasure* (pub. 1668). Cavendish bans husbands but offers her women unlimited access to commodities – 'Beds of velvet, lined with Sattin ... Turkie Carpets, and a Cup-board of Gilt Plate' (see Ferguson, *First Feminists*, p. 91).

35. Behn intensifies the motif of the honest whore in *The Second Part of The Rover*. In the sequel, Hellena has died and Willmore is once again a free rover. Angellica's counterpart, La Nuche, is pursued by Willmore precisely because to deal with a prostitute is plain dealing, yet he also berates her: 'Damn it, I hate a Whore that asks me Mony' [sic] (1:123). Nevertheless, in this play the 'women of quality' envy the courtesan; Willmore and La Nuche reject marriage but swear undying love, while the virgin and gallant accept the less interesting but pragmatic fate of marriage.

36. The Prologue to *The Rover*, 'Written by a Person of Quality', dramatises that ambivalence; the lines indirectly addressed to Behn use the pronoun 'him': 'As for the author of this coming play, I asked him what he thought fit I should say' (p. 4). This is unusual. In Behn's prologues the masculine pronoun is used only as a general referent for poets/wits, as in the last line to the prologue to *Sir Patient Fancy*: 'He that writes Wit is the much greater Fool' (4:9).

37. See Sandra M. Gilbert and Susan Gubar, *The Madwoman in the Attic: The Woman Writer and the Nineteenth-Century Literary Imagination* (New Haven, CT, 1979), pp. 3–92.

38. Feminist film theorists have taken the lead, with Laura Mulvey's pathbreaking article on the fetishist position produced by Hollywood narrative cinema ('Visual Pleasure and Narrative Cinema', *Screen*, 16,

no. 3 [1975], 6–19. For a full elaboration of this and other psychoanalytic concepts in film, see Mary Ann Doane's *The Desire to Desire:
The Woman's Film of the 1940s* (Bloomington, IN, 1987). In literary
study, see Naomi Schor's 'Female Fetishism: The Case of George Sand'
(in *The Female Body in Western Culture: Contemporary Perpectives*,
ed. Susan R. Suleiman [Cambridge, MA, 1986], pp. 363–72). For
fetishism in theatre as well as in film and fiction, Roland Barthes's work
is particularly useful; see 'Diderot, Brecht, Eisenstein' in *Image, Music,
Text*, trans. Stephen Heath (New York), pp. 69–78.

3

'Suspect my loyalty when I lose my virtue': Sexual Politics and Party in Aphra Behn's Plays of the Exclusion Crisis, 1678–83

SUSAN J. OWEN

Aphra Behn was the first woman professional dramatist in England, and so it is fruitful to consider her work in terms of sexual politics. However, Behn, as a dramatist, also intervened in 'high' politics which began in the Exclusion Crisis to be 'party' politics. I want to look at the way sexual politics and party politics interacted in Behn's drama in the Exclusion Crisis. My starting point is the existence of striking complexities and contradictions in the sexual politics of Behn's Exclusion Crisis drama. I would suggest that these complexities and contradictions might be accounted for in terms of the precise historical moments in the party political struggle in which the particular plays are located.

The Exclusion Crisis is a particularly appropriate period to observe the intersection of party politics and sexual politics. In the earlier Restoration period various phenomena had led to a questioning of gender relations in the theatre: the influence of court libertinism, the coming of actresses, the very existence of a female playwright. The Exclusion Crisis led to the questioning of other certainties, as the fragile post-Restoration political consensus was shattered, and modern party-political methods began to be seen in England for the first time. As is well known, the Popish Plot scare which broke out in autumn 1678 led to attempts by the Parliamentary Opposition, later to be called the Whigs, to exclude the Catholic James, Duke of York, from the succession to the crown. What is less well known, perhaps, is that many at the time thought they might succeed.[1] This political battle was often conducted in the language of sexual politics.[2] For example, both sides used rape as a trope of monstrosity, associated by Tories with rebellion, and by Whigs with popery.[3] It is in this context that Behn, like all other dramatists at this time, was working. In order to explore the complexities of the sexual politics of Behn's drama at this period, I want first to compare the contradictions between three plays which appear to belong to the early part of the Crisis, falling within the 1678/79 and 1679/80 theatrical seasons, namely *The Feign'd Curtizans, The Revenge*,[4] and *The Young King*.[5] Then I shall examine the dichotomy in outlook between two 1681 plays, *The Second Part of the Rover* and *The Round-heads*.

In *The Feign'd Curtizans* and *The Revenge* we find witty heroines similar to those in earlier plays such as *The Rover*. There is a power-ful resonance, particularly in *The Feign'd Curtizans*, in the spectacle of these women evading an oppressive destiny of arranged marriage and enforced celibacy, plotting to take control of their lives, civilis-ing rakes, and winning marriage choice and freedom of sexual ma-noeuvre. When necessary these heroines dress as men and fight alongside men. The feminist force of this[6] is increased by the fact that actresses now played the parts. In both plays Behn evokes sym-pathy for the victims of sexual double standards, and the double standards are subjected to explicit critique. She also extends qualified sympathy to prostitutes, women who find themselves vic-timised outsiders through meeting men's needs. This is particularly true of *The Revenge*. Behn's source for this play is Marston's *The Dutch Courtesan*. Marston's whore, Franceschina, is a laughing-stock, set apart by a ridiculous way of speaking, and finally subjected to what is portrayed as a deserved humiliation. In Behn's play the prostitute, Corina, is made a native rather than a foreigner, and the ending is altered to permit her to repent of her revenge and find a husband.

This enables the full force of hostility in the play to be directed to the citizen, Dashit. The citizens of London provided the social base of the Whig Opposition[7] during the Exclusion Crisis, and Behn gives

topical force to the humiliation of Dashit at the hands of a dispos-
sessed young aristocrat, Trickwell. Dashit is made credulously and
ridiculously anti-popish, which accords with the Tory view that the
Popish Plot scare was a fabrication.[8] Dashit demonstrates the 'busy'
nosiness and credulity for which London's citizens are often criticised in Tory prologues and epilogues. He laps up a tale told by
Trickwell, disguised as a barber, of monstrous whales coming ashore,
turning into elephants, then cockatrices, then into 'Giants in Scarlet,
with Triple Crowns on their heads, and forked Tongues that hiss so
loud, the noise is heard to the Royal Exchange; which has put the
Citizens into such a Consternation, that 'tis thought the world's at an
end'.[9] For Dashit 'this must portend right-down Poperie, that's
certain' (p. 24). Later, the worst revenge Dashit can think of for his
tormentor is, 'I'll hire a Priest to make a Papist of him before
Execution; and when he's dead, I'll piss on's Grave' (IV.iv, p. 45).
Unjustly hounded into Newgate himself, he exclaims, 'To Newgate,
amongst the prophane Jesuits too? oh, oh!' (IV.iv, p. 48).

Dashit's puritan hypocrisy is satirised, which fits well with Tory
attacks on dissenters who supported the Whigs. In Act II, scene iii
he fears that Heaven is displeased because he has disguised English
Protestant wines with 'heathenish names' (p. 22). Quite apart from
the malpractice involved, the very idea of 'Protestant' or 'heathenish' wine is ridiculous. In Act III, scene ii Dashit remarks that 'a
Punch-bowl is a most fashionable thing, now French Wines are prohibited' (p. 30). In Act V, scene iv anti-Popery is mocked ironically
by reference to wine as Trickwell, disguised as a dissenting preacher,
reminds Dashit of his sins:

> ... but Brother, you must remember your sins too, and iniquities; you
> must consider you have been a Broacher of prophane Vessels, you
> have made us drunk with the juice of the Whore of *Babylon*: for
> whereas good Ale, Perry, Syder, and Metheglin, were the true
> Ancient *British* and *Trojan* Drinks, you have brought in Popery, meer
> Popery – *French* and *Spanish* Wines, to the subversion, staggering,
> and overthrowing of many a good Protestant Christian.
>
> (p. 67)

Thus the fear of French influence and imports which fuelled
Whiggery becomes mere boorishness and stupidity.

Similarly, in *The Feign'd Curtizans* Behn satirises 'cits', parvenues,
and puritans. The Englishman, Sir Signall Buffoon, boorishly apes
Italian manners and language, though his father sent him into Italy

with a puritan chaplain as a safeguard against 'the eminent danger that young Travellers are in of being perverted to Popery'.[10] This puritan father is 'a fool and knave' who 'had the attendant blessing of getting an Estate of some eight thousand a year' (I.i, p. 5), so presumably he is an upstart, sequestrating puritan of the type satirised in Howard's *The Committee* (1662) and Behn's own *The Round-heads*. The tutor, Tickletext, is tasteless and mercenary, making his pupil trade in gloves, stockings, and pins on the Grand Tour. He is also crudely anti-papist and foolishly proud of being English. In the Exclusion Crisis, patriotism and hostility to the influence of Popish countries were weapons in the Whig arsenal.

Tickletext is hypocritically glad to exploit Roman custom to get a whore. He is a philistine, condemning Roman church architecture for reasons of religious bigotry. He believes 'harmless Pictures are Idolatrous' (I.ii, p. 12). He himself aspires to a literary style which combines puritan plainness, bathos, and credulity about portents: 'April the Twentieth, arose a very great storm of Wind, Thunder, Lightening, and Rain' – which was a 'shrewd sign of foul weather' (III.i, p. 31). Behn thus associates anti-Popery and patriotism with hypocrisy, folly, and pretension, as well as philistinism and low-class money-grubbing. Tickletext's faults are generic: 'we have a thousand of these in *England* that go loose about the streets, and pass with us for as sober discreet religious persons' (IV.i, p. 45). Satire of him is satire of the Protestant, mercantile middle class which was the Opposition's chief base of political support. It is also satire of the prevailing mentality in 1679, as seen by royalists.

Thus in *The Feign'd Curtizans* and *The Revenge* royalist satire of Whiggish citizens and puritans coexists quite comfortably with feminism. Women scheme for greater freedom and control within the framework of upper-class solidarity and shared values. In *The Feign'd Curtizans* Behn emphasises that, whilst middle-class patriots are to be derided, upper-class good taste is international. She seems in her prologue to be making a political point of the conventional Italian setting: '*To what a wretched pass will poor Plays come, / This must be damn'd, the Plot is laid in Rome*' (Sig A4r). The play opens with hospitable exchanges between the Italian Julio and the English Fillamour. Later, English gentlemen court Italian ladies. Wit and good taste cross national boundaries, and hostility to Catholic countries is misconceived.

However, in *The Young King*, Behn switches from comedy to tragi-comedy and offers a much more profound engagement with the Exclusion Crisis. This political engagement involves the use of gender and sexuality as political discourse in a way which involves a radical departure from the feminism of the other plays I have discussed. The full title of the play is *The Young King; or, The Mistake.* The mistake is the Queen's exiling of the heir to the throne, her son, Orsames, and her training of her daughter, Cleomena, to rule in his stead. Just as the contemporary Whig Opposition wanted to exclude James from the throne due to fear of popery, and of his temperamental intransigence and 'arbitrariness', the play's Queen exiles her son, Orsames, because she believes an oracle which has foretold his tyranny. At the end of the play she repents of this 'superstitious errour'.[11]

Female cross-dressing is made to do a job of political work in this play, emphasising the unnaturalness of the Queen's actions. Cleomena has no problem with dressing and fighting as an 'Amazon' until she falls in love, whereupon her true womanly nature asserts itself. Therefore the spectacle of a woman dressing and fighting as a man is a temporary reversal of roles which are not fundamentally questioned in this play. The effects of enforced and unnatural passivity on Orsames are harder to undo.[12] Even though his restoration to the throne comes about as a natural process, there are some residual doubts about his suitability to rule. His early tyrannical posturings do not survive the mellowing influence of the love of his family and future wife. However, because he has been excluded from Court life, he is characterised by a lack of political sagacity. He announces his intention of relying for political advice upon his country's erstwhile enemy, the King of Scythia (V.iv, p. 63). His exile has engendered a lack of human sympathy, political judgement, or political propriety, and an associated absence of sexual decorum. In Act II he tries to grab a woman's breasts, and his last action at the end of the play is to bestow a maiden upon a soldier with naïve high-handedness, without consulting the wishes of either party. Behn's point might well be that the much criticised faults of the Stuart brothers – Charles's licentiousness and perceived passivity, James's arbitrariness – are attributable to their respective exiles at the hands of an ungrateful and misguided nation. Behn's depiction of the disastrous results of political exclusion on the royal personality reflects fears expressed by Parliamentary opponents of the Exclusion Bills that excluding James from the succession might make him desperate and lead to civil war.[13] Behn associates sexual inversion and unnatural motherhood with political exclusion; Tories argued that Charles would be unnatural if he consented to the Exclusion of his own brother.[14] The play thus mobilises traditional gender values and family values in the interests of political conformity.

Now I want to contrast Behn's feminist interrogation of the libertine ethos prevalent in Court circles in *The Second Part of the Rover* with the sexual conservatism of *The Round-heads*. At first sight these plays appear similar. Both are set in the Interregnum and both appear to counterpose the jolly rakishness of royalists to the hypocrisy of parliamentary puritans. *The Second Part of the Rover* was published with a Dedication to James, Duke of York, in which Behn identifies James with her hero, Willmore. Royalist politics and cavalier sexual mores are contrasted to the hypocrisy, *'ingratitude'* and *'Arbitrary Tyranny'* of the *'seeming sanctifi'd Faction'* in the Civil War and their Whig descendants in the Exclusion Crisis.[15] In the play the verb 'Cavaliering' is used to convey both adherence to the royalist cause and sexual adventurism: cheated out of sexual fulfilment and otherwise discomfited, the character Fetherfool resolves: 'If this be the end of travelling, I'le e'ne to old *England* again, take the Covenant, get a Sequestrators place, grow rich, and defie all Cavaliering' (V, p. 84). It should be noted that James was himself a rake. As Bishop Burnet put it, he 'had always one private amour after another'.[16] During the Exclusion Crisis his seduction of Catherine Sedley was probably a factor in driving her father, Sir Charles Sedley, from support for the Court to moderate Whiggery.[17] So James is likely to have found the glorification of cavalier behaviour congenial.

The connection between politics and sexual politics in *The Second Part of the Rover* is spelled out by the play's royalist hero, Willmore. In Act II he contrasts his own libertinism with the sexual habits which typify a parliamentarian. He expects free sex, both in the sense that he wants to be open about it and because he wants it without monetary or social cost: 'Let the sly States-man, who Jilts the Commonwealth with his grave Politiques, pay for the sin that he may doat in secret' (p. 18). In Act III he says of his pursuit of a large woman, 'better to be Master of a Monster / than Slave to a damn'd Commonwealth' (p. 43). In other words, the royalist rake has a control in the sexual sphere which is denied to him in the political sphere. The play would seem to end with rakishness triumphant, there being no reformation of the rake, as in *The Rover*.

Yet I would argue that this play contains as profound a questioning of libertinism as is to be found in any other Restoration comedy.

Despite her avowed intention of celebrating cavaliers, Behn comes close to the excoriation of libertinism which in the Exclusion Crisis was receiving explicitly Whiggish colouration in the plays of Shadwell. Firstly, the callousness of the rake is stressed. He speaks of his wife's death 'With a Sham sadness' (I, p. 5) and seems to be as much concerned with the loss of her fortune as with the loss of her. This mercenary motivation competes with sex for priority in his mind, for 'money speaks sense in a Language all Nations understand, 'tis Beauty, Wit, Courage, Honour, and undisputable Reason' (III, p. 43). Desire for wealth (as opposed to mere bewailing of poverty) is usually associated with grasping cits like Dashit in *The Revenge* or, in Exclusion Crisis tragedies, with villains who thirst for reward, so it is disconcerting to find the royalist hero so mercenary.

Secondly, it is emphasised that libertinism not only renders woman an object but renders the identity of the object secondary: several characters, including Willmore, pursue two rich jewesses, one of whom is a dwarf and the other a giantess. The function of 'these Lady Monsters' (I, p. 8) is to show the monstrousness of libertinism itself: its object is so irrelevant that it can even be a freak (in Restoration terms), so long as there is the spice of novelty. In Act V the poor giant is pushed and pulled to and fro by the various men as if she were literally an object. In the dark in Act IV, scene ii Willmore sees the maiden, Ariadne, and the courtesan, La Nuche, just as two women, and remarks, 'no matter which, so I am sure of one' (p. 51). In Act IV, scene iv he issues instructions to another man's servants to serenade whatever lady is to be pursued, for he neither knows nor cares who it will be. The object of Willmore's pursuit changes constantly. His aim is simple: 'I must dispose of this mad fire about me' (IV.ii, p. 58). The lack of closure at the end reinforces our sense of unregenerate cavalier predatoriness. Willmore disguises himself as a mountebank to further his love plots, and we cannot help feeling that the guise is symbolically appropriate.

Thirdly, we are distanced from the action in a way which encourages us to reflect upon the various sex plots rather than to engage with the characters. Thus in Act I we watch Ariadne and Lucia watching Willmore watching La Nuche watching her bawd, Petronella, gull Fetherfool. Similarly, in Act II Ariadne and Lucia follow Willmore and Blunt who follow Fetherfool and La Nuche's 'bravo'. This leads to my fourth point: there is much dizzying farcical by-play and endless confusion of identity as men carry off the wrong woman and climb into bed with other men by mistake, and women dress as men and (for various devious reasons) pursue each other as well as men. The effect is to engender mockery rather than royalist sympathies. Fifthly, and most disturbingly, the misogyny beneath the surface of libertinism is explicitly revealed. Willmore hates the women he desires for their beauty and wealth and for their power over himself: 'by Heaven, I will possess this gay Insensible, to make me hate her – most extremely curse her' (I, p. 13). The wit which is generically supposed to excuse all often wears rather thin.

Since Behn has explicitly coupled royalism and cavalier sexual mores, it is disturbing from a Tory point of view that rakishness is seen to be so obnoxious in *The Second Part of the Rover*. The tone of *The Round-heads* is very different. *The Round-heads* works much better as Tory drama because, as in *The Young King*, Behn chooses to abandon feminist anatomisation of libertinism in favour of a more conventional Tory association of royalism with virtue and rebellion with sexual monstrosity.[18] She sharpens the satire of Interregnum Parliamentarians and puritans in her source, Tatham's *The Rump*, and makes it more topical. She adds cavalier heroes, Loveless and Freeman, who attempt to cuckold the Parliamentarian leaders, Lambert and Desboro'. Yet, Lady Desboro', though a royalist at heart, and happy to mock her husband, refuses to be unfaithful to him: 'No, I'm true to my / Allegiance still, true to my King and Honour. Suspect my loyalty when I / lose my virtue.'[19] Behn thus specifically associates royalism and 'virtue'. This bizarre yoking of cavalier mores and the virtue of chastity somehow succeeds, so thoroughly does Behn link lust and secret sex with canting, hypocritical puritans. We learn that Lambert has colluded in Cromwell's affair with his wife. In Act III, scene ii Lady Desboro' exposes the sexual hypocrisy of the puritan Ananias Gogle, who has been feeling her breasts and making sexual suggestions while talking of the sins of the flesh: 'How, this from you, the Head o' th' Church militant; the very Pope of Presbytery?' (p. 28). She can then exploit his fear of scandal to make Gogle procure her suitor Freeman's release from a room full of enemies behind Gogle's cloak, which enables Freeman to respond, 'So this is the first Cloak of Zeal I / ever made use of' (IV.i, p. 35).

In Lady Lambert and Lady Cromwell, Behn makes conservative use of the figures of the shrew and the upstart woman aping the great Lady. Lady Lambert beats up and bosses her husband, and interferes in political meetings. Lady Cromwell is jealous of her dignity and indignant when other women encroach on what she calls 'our Royal Family' (V.ii, p. 49). The gender transgression reinforces the social presumption, typifying a world upside-down. Lady Lambert's capacity for love – and the superior sexiness of the cavaliers – eventually restores her to the 'sanity' of political and sexual submissiveness. Behn also inserts the comic interlude of a Council of Ladies, infiltrated, and satirised 'aside', by the heroes in drag. Here Behn constructs a paradigm of presumptuous folly and impropriety which both reflects and typifies the rebel world; she also focuses on a peculiarly female propensity for pettiness. She shows women in power behaving in a way which anti-suffragists were to depict two centuries later, elevating private grievances, bitchy, competitive, and silly. Thus Behn's habitual – and liberating – depiction of women who are wiser and wittier than their husbands coexists with and is overdetermined by a conventional Tory rhetoric of gender difference and female subordination.

How may we account for these shifts in Behn's treatment of sex and gender issues? It seems to me that it is no accident that the shifts parallel changes in the political situation. *The Feign'd Curtizans* was performed early in the Exclusion Crisis period, at a time when few dramatists had taken sides. This is not to say that political concerns are not apparent in the drama. Concerns about popery predated the Popish Plot scare. James's marriage to the Catholic Mary of Modena had led to parliamentary protest in 1673. Marvell's 'An Account of the Growth of Popery and Arbitrary Power in England' had been published in 1677. Dryden responded to the situation in the 1678/79 theatrical season by demonising political rebellion in *Oedipus*, and by suggesting in *Troilus and Cressida* that the government might have to use machiavellian means if necessary to secure order and deal with trouble-makers. In *Oedipus*, as in *The Feign'd Curtizans*, class is a stable referent: the Thracian Prince Adrastus is Oedipus's worthy enemy and then his ally, the populist Creon and the people themselves are to be mistrusted and kept down. Yet *Oedipus* is coloured by a sense of darkness and of the difficulty of right action, as are other plays in this season with a royalist colouration, such as Crowne's *The Ambitious Statesman*. In *Oedipus, The Ambitious Statesman*, and *Troilus and Cressida* royal lust is problematised alongside rebellion. It is no surprise then that Behn's royalism emerges in the form of satire of fairly safe targets, upstarts and puritans, and in celebration of upper-class good nature and good taste across national boundaries.

The Young King was a response to a new situation of deepening polarisation and of vigorous royalist response to the Opposition's successful exploitation of the Popish Plot scare. In the autumn of

1679 the Government really began to go on the offensive against
the Opposition.[20] The clergy 'seem now to lay down all fears and
apprehensions of Popery; and nothing was so common in their
mouths as the year forty-one, in which the late wars began, and
which seemed now to be near the being acted over again.'[21]
Shadwell's *The Woman Captain* was produced around the same time
as *The Young King*. In this play Shadwell begins to give Whiggish
colouration to his habitual excoriation of the immorality and folly
of the times, by focusing upon the lust, degeneracy, and extrava-
gance of an aristocratic youth who wastes the inheritance from his
decent, puritan father. He also has the eponymous woman captain
chastise the unmanly male characters and threaten to send them to
the war in Flanders, a war against Louis XIV which Charles reluctantly supported only under strong pressure from the Parliamentary
Opposition. It is also in this season that William Whitaker produced
The Conspiracy, one of the most fervent and idealistically royalist
plays of the Crisis, if not of all time, and Elkanah Settle produced a
scathing satire of the Catholic Church in *The Female Prelate: being
the History of the Life and Death of Pope Joan*. Whitaker and Settle
use female monstrosity to demonise rebellion and popery respectively. In this climate Behn is inspired to produce (or exhume or
rework) a piece which can offer a more thoroughgoing and explicitly topical critique of contemporary Exclusionists. She turns from
comedy to tragi-comedy in order to do this, and in the process (temporarily) abandons feminism in favour of a much more reactionary
use of sexual inversion to invoke moral and political horror.

Not all plays produced at this time are political or partisan.
D'Urfey's *The Virtuous Wife*, also premiered in this season, seems to
be offered as a humorous distraction in difficult times, though some
extraneous political allusions are thrown in for good measure.
Behn's own *The Revenge* is a less politically 'engaged' piece than *The
Young King*, despite the satire of anti-papist 'cits' referred to above.
It is also a slighter piece, bearing signs of hasty composition: *The
Young King* is a more substantial reworking of Calderon and of
Fletcher's *Love's Cure; or, The Martial Maid* than *The Revenge* is of
The Dutch Courtesan. We might speculate that *The Revenge* was
published anonymously for reasons of literary insouciance rather
than political strategy.[22]

In *The Second Part of the Rover* Behn is 'back on form' with what
I have argued represents a profound commitment of dramatic
energy to the anatomisation of libertinism. This coexists oddly with

her expressed commitment to cavalier politics in the Dedication. However, the Dedication was supplied upon publication.[23] The play itself was produced earlier in 1681: references in the epilogue suggest that it was performed before the dissolution of Parliament in January. This means that it was performed in the period before the Oxford Parliament in March 1681, during a period of apparent Whig ascendancy. The repeated success of the Whigs in the elections and in the House of Commons encouraged the Earl of Sunderland and even the King's hated Catholic mistress, the Duchess of Portsmouth, to fraternise with them.[24]

At this time many dramatists made concessions to Opposition sentiment. Perhaps they were motivated in part by a desire to cater to a more Whiggish audience, as the second Exclusion Parliament was sitting at this time. Lee offers a critique of royal effeminacy and irresponsibility in *Theodosius* and a politically emotive dramatisation of the expulsion of the Tarquins in *Lucius Junius Brutus*. Shadwell, in *The Lancashire Witches*, gives a sweeping indictment of the decay of old-fashioned, Protestant, parliamentarian, gentry values. He satirises not only popery but collusion with popery and misplaced lust within the Church of England. Perhaps more surprising are the shifts made by Dryden in *The Spanish Fryar* and Crowne in *Henry the Sixth, the First Part*. Dryden said in later life that he offered *The Spanish Fryar* 'to the people'.[25] The play has anti-Catholic satire in the 'low' plot and a main plot which offers a message of moderation, and of reconciliation of royalists and parliamentarians around the values of 1660.[26] Crowne makes an astounding shift in this season from the triumphant and successful Toryism of *The Misery of Civil War* in the previous season to an attack primarily directed at corrupt, effeminate, and popish courts in *Henry VI: The First Part*.[27] There is a striking shift in the tone of prologues and epilogues in this season: the sneering at Whiggery, anti-popery, and newsmongering which predominated in the previous season is almost entirely absent, replaced by jocular misogyny or mock-deference to the ladies, or by apolitical complaints of the hardship suffered by poets, and of the philistinism and folly of the age.

Such shifts were not necessarily opportunistic: as I have argued elsewhere, it was unfashionable to be a zealot after 1660.[28] It may have seemed both logical and rational for dramatists to foreground those aspects of their vision of society most in accordance with the spirit of the times. We could equally well argue that the shift in the political situation empowered the dramatists to be more explicit in criticising royal lust and impropriety, and court corruption, than they might otherwise have been.[29] Dryden and Crowne make their political shifts explicit in their Dedications to Whiggish patrons, whereas Behn boldly dedicates *The Second Part of the Rover* to James. Yet it might well be the case that Behn has space in this season to offer a critique of libertinism which would have been misplaced or misapplied a little earlier or a little later in the Exclusion Crisis.

Although *The Round-heads* was produced later in the same year as *The Second Part of the Rover*, the situation was very different indeed. In the autumn of 1681, it had become clear that the Oxford Parliament had been a victory for the King. In the theatres, as in society, the 'Tory Reaction' set in with a vengeance. The dramatists atoned for their apostacy by writing fervently royalist plays, vigorously declaring their allegiance in Dedications and Prefaces, and writing Tory prologues and epilogues which were published as broadsides in the pamphlet war. The Whigs were satirised in plays like *Sir Barnaby Whigg* and *Mr. Turbulent*, and Whig plays could no longer be performed in the theatres.[30] Of course this is not to say that tensions, anxieties, and contradictions did not persist in the drama. However, what seems clear is that there was a specific context and a substantial motivation for Behn to make a vigorous effort at this time to subordinate her capacity for feminist insight to the sexually conservative tropes of Toryism in order to demonise the Whigs' attempt to 'turn the world upside-down'.

My argument, then, is twofold: Behn, like her fellow dramatists, responds to the needs of the particular historical moment, and the moments at which it becomes most urgent to give ideological affirmation to Toryism produce the plays in which there is least space for feminism.[31] Feminist anatomisation and critique of the libertinism associated with the Court must give way to the invoking of conventional gender values to justify the established order.

From *Restoration*, 18 (1994), 37–47.

NOTES

[Susan Owen argues that, in her plays, Behn responds to the needs of a political moment. In *The Revenge* and *The Feign'd Curtizans*, she combines her feminism with royalist satire of Whiggish citizens and puritans. In *The Young King*, however, she engages with the Exclusion Crisis, mobilising gender and family values in the interests of political conformity. In *The Second Part of*

SEXUAL POLITICS AND PARTY *69*

The Rover she questions libertinism – associated firmly with Tory-cavalier values – and its reduction of women to objects of pursuit; the questioning is made possible by the play's production during Whig ascendancy. In contrast, *The Round-heads*, produced during the Tory reaction, emphasises conventional Tory rhetoric, gender difference and female subordination. Ed.]

1. K. H. D. Haley, *The First Earl of Shaftesbury* (Oxford, 1968), pp. 588–9; J. R. Jones, *Country and Court* (London, 1978), pp. 215–16.

2. This was not a new phenomenon: for the association of political and sexual misconduct in earlier Restoration literature and political writing see Susan Owen, '"Partial Tyrants" and "Freeborn People" in *Lucius Junius Brutus*', SEL, 31 (1991), 463–82, and Paul Hammond, 'The King's Two Bodies: Representations of Charles II', in *Culture, Politics and Society in Britain, 1660–1800*, ed. Jeremy Black and Jeremy Gregory (Manchester, 1991), pp. 13–48.

3. For example, rape is associated with rebellion in Dryden's and Lee's *Oedipus*, Crowne's *The Misery of Civil War*, and Otway's *Venice Preserv'd*, with royalism in Lee's *Lucius Junius Brutus*, and with popery in Settle's *The Female Prelate*.

4. This play was published anonymously. Attribution to Behn was made by Narcissus Luttrell in a note on his copy, bought in July 1680. A later attribution to Betterton is probably erroneous. The political slant of the play accords with Behn's Toryism, and the sympathy accorded to the prostitute character, which I discuss below, might be internal evidence to support the attribution to Behn, who had expressed more sympathy for sexually compromised women than was customary in previous plays such as *The Rover* and *The Feign'd Curtizans*. See also William Van Lennep et al. (eds), *The London Stage, 1660–1800, Part 1, 1660–1700* (Carbondale, IL, 1965), p. 287; Leo Hughes and A. H. Scouten, *Ten English Farces* (Austin, TX, 1948), pp. 203–4; and Judith Milhous and Robert D. Hume, 'Attribution Problems in English Drama, 1660–1700', *Harvard Library Bulletin*, 31 (1983), 5–39, p. 29.

5. Information on dating may be found in Van Lennep et al., *The London Stage*; Judith Milhous and Robert D. Hume, 'Dating Play Premières from Publication Data, 1660–1700', *Harvard Library Bulletin*, 22 (1974), 374–405; Pierre Danchin, *The Prologues and Epilogues of the Restoration, 1660–1700* (Nancy, 1981–8); and in Susan Owen's PhD thesis, 'Drama and Politics in the Exclusion Crisis: 1678–83' (University of Leeds, 1992), which is the basis of a forthcoming book. Probable première dates are: *The Feign'd Curtizans*, early 1679; *The Young King*, autumn 1679; *The Revenge*, early 1680; *The Second Part of the Rover*, January 1681; *The Round-heads*, autumn 1681. Behn states in her dedication to *The Young King* that this play was her first: one might speculate that it was staged (and probably reworked somewhat) at this time because of the topicality of the material. The statement might be intended partly

as a cautious (and disingenuous) denial of topicality, as was common at this early and uncertain stage of the Crisis.

6. I use the word 'feminist' not to imply similarity to modern feminism but to suggest that conventional restrictions upon women are challenged. As Catherine Belsey has put it, 'Even while it reaffirms patriarchy, the tradition of female transvestism challenges it precisely by unsettling the categories which legitimise it': see 'Disrupting Sexual Difference: Meaning and Gender in the Comedies', in *Alternative Shakespeares*, ed. John Drakakis (London, 1985), p. 180. On the de facto feminist effect of cross-dressing in Behn's plays see Jacqueline Pearson, *The Prostituted Muse: Images of Women and Women Dramatists, 1642–1737* (New York, 1988), pp. 154–9.

7. I use the terms 'Whig' and 'Tory' for convenience, but it should be borne in mind that they were only current from 1681: see R. Willman, 'The Origins of "Whig" and "Tory" in English Political Language', *Historical Journal*, 17 (1974), 247–64. This may seem a trivial point, but it has force in terms of my subsequent argument about the dramatic shifts which accompanied the deepening political polarisation to which this terminology is related.

8. The tide of anti-popery began to ebb in autumn 1679: J. P. Kenyon, *The Popish Plot* (Harmondsworth, 1974), ch. 2. However, there was scepticism about the Popish Plot in Court circles from the earliest stages: Kenyon, p. 86.

9. First edition (London, 1680), II.iii, p. 23.

10. First edition (London, 1679), I.i, p. 5.

11. First edition (London, 1683), V.iv, p. 62.

12. Pearson says love reveals Orsames's 'innate kingliness and manliness', but this is true only to a limited extent, and ignores residual contradictions which she notices in the case of Cleomena: 'To a certain extent the play accepts conventional sex roles: love reveals the real femaleness of the masculine woman. But sex roles are still more fluid than is the case in most plays by male authors: even the perfect Woman Cleomena can continue to show a manly strength' (*The Prostituted Muse*, p. 159).

13. Haley, *Shaftesbury*, p. 483; John M. Wallace, 'Otway's *Caius Marius* and the Exclusion Crisis', *MP*, 85 (1988), 368.

14. See Roger L'Estrange, *The Case Put Concerning the Succession* (1679), p. 17.

15. First edition (London, 1681), Sig A3v–A4r.

16. *History of My Own Time*, ed. Osmund Airy, 2 vols (Oxford, 1897), I, 405. See also Antonia Fraser, *The Weaker Vessel: Women's Lot in Seventeenth-Century England* (London, 1984), p. 453.

17. For the affair with Catherine see Fraser, *The Weaker Vessel*, p. 453. For Sedley's moderate Whiggery, see Vivian de Sola Pinto, *Sir Charles Sedley, 1639–1710: A Study in the Life and Literature of the Restoration* (London, 1927), pp. 168 ff., and Basil Duke Henning, *The History of Parliament: The House of Commons, 1660–1690*, 3 vols (London, 1983), III, 409–10. *DNB* seems to be wrong in describing Sedley as a moderate Tory but notes his alienation from the Court: Sedley is said to have re-marked in 1690 that he was 'even in civility with King James, who had made his daughter a countess, by helping (through his vote [for William] in the Convention parliament) to make the king's daughter a queen'. A rhyme circulated in 1688: 'But Sedley has some colour for his Treason / A daughter Ravished without any Reason' (Finch MSS, III, p. 347, cited Pinto, *Sir Charles Sedley*, p. 174). Kenyon says that James mixed with 'swordsmen and rakes' (*The Popish Plot*, p. 38).

18. We might compare the use of female monstrosity to demonise rebellion in Whitaker's ultra-royalist *The Conspiracy*.

19. First edition (London, 1682), IV.i, p. 33.

20. Kenyon, *The Popish Plot*, p. 210.

21. Burnet, *History of My Own Time*, II, 215–16.

22. For a discussion of some of the strategic reasons for anonymity, see Paul Hammond, 'Anonymity in Restoration Poetry', *Seventeenth Century*, 8.1 (1993), 123–42.

23. The play was entered in the *Term Catalogues* under June 1681, so was probably published by then.

24. Haley, *Shaftesbury*, pp. 588–9; Jones, *Country and Court*, pp. 215–16.

25. Preface to *De Arte Graphica, The Works of John Dryden*, ed. H. T. Swedenberg et al., 20 vols (Berkeley, CA, 1956 onwards), XX, 76, 1.16.

26. It has not been sufficiently noticed that the royalist hot-head, Raymond, is as misguided as the apparent plotter, Bertran, or the usurper Queen, Leonora. No one is all bad or always right. What is stressed is unity, family values, forgiveness, providential 'restoration', and the need to avoid hasty action. Most critics have followed Louis I. Brevold, who argued in 1932 that the play was Tory, refuting an older notion that Dryden had written a Whiggish piece in a mood of disenchantment with the court: 'Political Aspects of Dryden's *Amboyna* and *The Spanish Fryar*', *University of Michigan Publications, Language and Literature*, 8 (1932), 119–32. My work on the drama of the Exclusion Crisis leads me to disagree strongly with Phillip Harth's view that Dryden was politically uncommitted prior to 'Absalom and Achitophel': 'Dryden in 1678–1681: The Literary and Historical Perspectives', in *The Golden and the Brazen World: Papers in Literature and History, 1650–1800*, ed. John M. Wallace (Berkeley, CA, 1985), pp. 55–77.

27. Crowne describes in his Dedication his methods of foregrounding anti-Catholicism by additions to his source material. Matthew H. Wikander couples this play with *The Misery of Civil-War*: 'The Spitted Infant: Scenic Emblem and Exclusionist Politics in Restoration Adaptations of Shakespeare', *Shakespeare Quarterly*, 37 (1986), 340–58. His title refers to the fact that, as the hero, Gloucester, is led off by plotters, Crowne replaces Shakespeare's image of Henry as a mother cow bereft of her calf with the image of a mother whose infant is carried off on a soldier's spear (IV, p. 45). It is true that slaughtered children functioned to demonise rebellion in *The Misery of Civil-War*, but here the substitution of woman with panting breasts for mother cow still leaves Henry embarrassingly passive and unable to protect his loyal subject, especially by comparison with Gloucester, whose 'manliness' is stressed. The spectacle of a weak 'effeminate' king surrounded by corrupt courtiers and plotting papists has pointed topical application. In *The Misery of Civil-War* Henry's weakness was changed to saintly recognition that Edward's accession would restore the true line.

28. Owen, '"Partial Tyrants" and "Freeborn People"', p. 477.

29. The shift from royalism to moderation and / or critique is the more striking since the dramatists took political – and financial – risks: *Lucius Junius Brutus* was banned after a short run, following complaints from influential members of the audience. *The Lancashire Witches* was cut by the censor, following similar complaints. Crowne says of *Henry VI* in the Dedication to *The English Frier* (1690), 'my aversions to some things I saw acted [at Court] by great men, carried me against my Interest, to expose Popery and Popish Courts in a Tragedy of mine … which pleas'd the best men in *England*, but displeas'd the worst; for e're it liv'd long, it was stifled by command' (Sig A3v).

30. The Dedication to the Whig leader Shaftesbury of *Rome's Follies; or, The Amorous Fryars* (1681) states that the play had to be performed at a private house because 'the Subject being not a little Satyrical against the Romanists, would very much hinder its taking, and [it] would be … difficult to get play'd' (Sig A3r).

31. I do not consider these arguments anti-feminist. On the contrary, we do Behn as a woman dramatist a great disservice by not considering her as a Tory dramatist whose political commitment was equal to that of Dryden and others. I consider that my argument about the incompatibility of Toryism and feminism may serve as a corrective to the extraordinarily pervasive but mistaken assumption that royalism, libertinism, and, by extension, Toryism, offered a liberating space to women which was brutally curtailed with the demise of the Stuart dynasty. This view was widely expressed at the Conference, 'Voicing Women: 1500–1700' at the University of Liverpool, England, in April 1992, and I consider that it does feminism – and indeed scholarship – no service whatsoever.

4

A Spectacular Death: History and Story in *The Widow Ranter*

JANET TODD

Aphra Behn largely avoided theatrical tragedy; consequently she rarely depicted heroic death. Her one tragedy, *Abdelazer*, which, if her poem to the tragedian Sir Francis Fane can be taken as autobiographical, she felt 'cold' and 'feeble', has a remarkably villainous pair at its centre; both die in discourses that trivialise their dying, the woman talking of lust, the man of cruelty.

Outside the tragic theatre, however, Behn frequently and lengthily represented death. Both in theatrical tragicomedy and in her prose works she could mitigate the simplicity of tragedy, tempering rather than destroying the heroism of a violent conclusion. The represented death might, for example, be noble and honourable, yet at the same time involve grotesque mutilation or absurd blunder. The tempering or mitigating is most obvious when Behn's fictional narrative approaches historical narrative, when artistic representation interacts with historical event.

Such representation is tempered also by another ingredient: life as represented pretending to copy or actually copying a literary event. Against the confusions of experience, the fictional dying hero tries to approximate his death to the satisfying simplicity of tragedy (the masculine possessive pronoun is intentional: women die violently in Behn's work, but men are the usual centres of fatal political theatre). The effort, which necessitates some literary self-consciousness, does not diminish the heroism of the death for the agent, but it adds a tinge of the absurd for the spectator.

Towards the end of her life, in the 1680s, Behn created several heroic and oddly anachronistic figures, who form a commentary on the conflicted politics of the period, especially on the part played in them by the last Stuart king, the personally heroic but politically inept James II, whom she never openly criticised or questioned. The Civil War pressed heavily on the decade, constantly expecting a repetition of the royal tragedy of 1649. In this political context, her stories of humbled princes and ingenuous heroes achieve a kind of typological power.

Two of Behn's heroes, Oroonoko of the short story and Bacon of *The Widow Ranter or Bacon in Virginia*, are set in the New World. The third, perhaps in part the inspiration for the other creations, was James Scott, Duke of Monmouth, 'Cesario' of the closing pages of her novel, *Love-Letters between a Nobleman and his Sister*, set in a European context. All three are gentlemanly, idealistic and romantic men. They are quite distinct from the witty, sexy, opportunistic and roving cavaliers of her earlier works, such as Wilmore of *The Rover* or Loveless of *The Roundheads*, both plays set before 1660, when the glitter of restoration could be imagined for the future. The later heroes, simple, decent men, exist in a decadent world after disillusionment and are distanced by the narrator or by other characters who are part of a cynical society and wryly contemplate their heroic simplicity. The spectators marvel at their admirably naïve inability to separate words and meaning, for example, or to desire sex and money above romantic love, or food and drink over death. Each hero is theatrical in the sense that some aspect of his actions is inspired by gestures in the theatre; he acts and speaks more suitably for the heroic stage than for the grubby political life in which he is involved.

Love-Letters, *Oroonoko* and *The Widow Ranter* each have a substantial amount of historical parallel. They fictionalise history, as do Behn's earlier works, but they add the new theme of interacting history and formal fiction. At the centre of these artistic constructions, the 'historical' hero consciously presents and projects himself. The relationship between fiction and fact, fiction and faction, fact and faction, literary faction and political faction comes to the fore, not only in Behn's choice of subjects from life, but also in her simultaneous definition of them in political and dramatic terms. The heroes fashion themselves, but they need the models from the past and the audience from the present. The author ironically revamps history to fit it for fiction; in similar fashion but with a contrasting result, her characters absurdly remake their misunderstood lives into the stuff of art.

The climax of the self-consciously shaped life is a violent and voluntary death, an artificial process outside natural decaying and ending. The experienced event is almost pure theatre for the inexperienced watcher and is intended as theatre by the voluntary agent/victim. Behn's three heroes all have a death that is brought about before nature can intervene; all of them wish to kill themselves and become direct agents of their own deaths. Bacon, Behn's last hero, alone among them is allowed the kind of ending his self-presentation demands, even though this appears to contradict historical record. Unhappily for him it is laughably at odds with the rest of the play in which he has been condemned to act by his knowing author.

The only popular British uprising in colonial America took place in Virginia in 1676; its leader was Nathaniel Bacon, who had come as a young man from England in 1674 to set up as a gentleman planter on the James River. Like his neighbours he suffered various Indian raids on his servants and property; soon he concluded that the governor, Sir William Berkeley, was too lenient on the Indians and too unconcerned for the lives and livelihoods of the lesser planters. Consequently he took up arms against the raiders without waiting to be commissioned for such activity. The rebellion that commenced with this act and included the sacking of James Town has been seen variously as a popular protest against the older aristocratic hegemony, which was accused of appeasing Indians and strangling trade in the colonies, and as one episode in the long struggle of puritanism and royalism, democracy and centralism. On a personal level it was a fight between an ageing legitimate governor and a young populist would-be hero, not unlike that between Monmouth and his ageing uncle, James II. The rebellion was fierce but short. Within a few months Bacon died and it fizzled out. Reprisals by the governor foreshadowed the alleged severity of James to the hapless followers of Monmouth. Probably in the final year of her life, Behn turned this colonial material into a play which was performed posthumously in 1690: *The Widow Ranter*, the first play to be set in colonial America. In contrast with the Monmouth story, which she wrote into *Love-Letters*, the historically recorded death of Bacon needed modification to fit it for fiction.

As in the case of *Oroonoko*, it is important for Behn's narrative that her hero be acting within a vacuum of authority. In the short story, Byam the villain is given as little legitimating status as possible, while the real governor, Lord Willoughby, is absent throughout the tale; in the Virginia of the play, the governor and the King's deputy, Sir William Berkeley, who in history struggled against Bacon, is also absent, so that the rebel can assume something of royal authority himself. This accords with the historical Bacon who repeatedly made his appeals direct to King Charles.

In *The Widow Ranter*, Bacon is presented as a tragic masculine hero sited not in the unreal exoticism of Renaissance Spain or pre-Columbian America, the proper home for the heroic male in early Restoration drama, but instead in the disgruntled 1670s in a mismanaged colony. He is thus forced from being a glowingly simple hero destroyed by social forces in the manner of Dryden's early heroes into becoming a commentary on a murkily complex reality that does not so much destroy as sully and diminish him. In this context, masculine heroism and its aesthetic come under closer scrutiny than ever before in Behn's works.

The play is a tragicomedy, a form Behn had not used in her original plays since her first dramas twenty years before. In the absence of a governor, Bacon is rebelling against the debased but nonetheless legal political authority of the vulgar, uneducated Virginians who, he and his followers believe, have failed to defend the people against the Indians. Like the fictional Oroonoko, he has a strong sense of what he can accomplish: one of his opponents calls him

> a man indeed above the common rank, by nature generous; brave, resolved, and daring; who studying the lives of the Romans and great men, that have raised themselves to the most elevated fortunes, fancies it easy for ambitious men to aim at any pitch of glory. I've heard him often say, 'Why cannot I conquer the universe as well as Alexander? or like another Romulus form a new Rome, and make myself adored?[1]

It is clear that such ambition now belongs in the theatre, since little can be achieved in a world where an admiring man, such as this speaker shows himself to be, will go on to declare himself an enemy of Bacon, simply because of an 'Interest' he has in the new governor.

Bacon, who has a strong sense of the theatrical heroic, loves and is beloved by a tearful Indian queen, whose virgin heart he had apparently conquered before she married the Indian king. Cynical onlookers within the play, young men who know that marriage and love are partly affairs of money and ease, declare that Bacon needed a princess to love to complete his image. In the course of the play Bacon defeats and kills the Indian king; after her husband's death, the queen dons male attire to escape, but she has no heart for cross-dressing; she is as 'timorous as a dove', she declares, and she admits that 'I have no Amazonian fire about me'. Consequently, she simply causes confusion in the battle. In the end she is mistakenly killed by Bacon before he can sully her by physical love. He responds to his fatal error and a sense that he is losing the battle against the authorities by imagining a heroic classical suicide for himself like Cleopatra's – he is well read in the *Lives of the Romans* – accompanied with the correct heroic dying words and followed by an equally heroic funeral: 'make of the trophies of the war a pile, and set it all on fire, that I may leap into consuming flames – while all my tents are burning round about me.'[2]

After much talk that almost falls into a surprising blank verse in this most prosaic of plays, Bacon does kill himself in the mistaken belief that he has lost the battle. He is provoked into it by fear of what one of his followers describes as 'a shameful Death'. Suicide for Bacon becomes 'a noble remedy for all the ills of life' and he is sure that he will thereby secure himself 'from being a public spectacle upon the common theatre of death'. Like Monmouth on the scaffold, he is more concerned with earthly reputation than with repentance, but, dying by his own hand rather than by another's, unlike Monmouth he feels able to utter on his own account the proper political words: 'never let ambition – love – or interest make you forget as I have done – your duty – and allegiance.'[3]

Like the Indian queen, however, Bacon is seemingly in the wrong play and in the wrong time. He has actually won the battle, as Cleopatra had not when she purposed to die in 'high Roman fashion', and no one is making a spectacle of him except himself. (Happily his erroneous death can suggest another Latin parallel and one of his followers stoutly declares that Bacon has fallen like Roman Cassius 'by mistake'.) No legal death is ever performed in the play: no one achieves public hanging in the chaotic colony, although many are condemned to it. Without Bacon, his former followers compromise, make peace and are pardoned. His heroic, futile death and his beloved's ineptly romantic one are juxtaposed with the feasting to celebrate the opportunistic marriage of one of his followers with a wealthy, tobacco-smoking woman of the town, the widow Ranter, who shares with him the title of the play.

Characters within *The Widow Ranter* comment on Bacon's stagi-
ness. He insists, despite the inglorious times, on achieving glory by
playing chivalrous roles, uncommon outside the theatre: he demands
a personal duel with the Indian chief, whom others simply dismiss as
a 'mad hot-brained youth', to fulfil his 'romantic humour', and he
treats those he conquers with elaborate courtesy. The glamorous and
glorious conception of personal power Bacon holds resembles that of
heroic drama and indeed of the glamorous Stuart kings, Charles and
James. Both Bacon and the Stuarts inspire followers with this
glamour and amaze others with their anachronism.

Bacon talks of empire while his contemporaries seek simple sol-
vency. He has the consciousness of the mythologised 1640s, when
cavaliering was swashbuckling, or of the 1660s, when such myths
were fashioned, the early jubilant years of the Restoration with their
fantastic hopes of a heroic golden age and incorruptible power. He
also believes in a kind of transcendental politics, true for all times
and places. This political belief is based on heroic myths and is
deeply embedded in masculine classical literature which he takes to
be true.

Bacon has faith in the integrity of language: the oath and word
of honour. In an obsessively plotting age like the 1680s it was no
longer clear that there was any real reference for words at all, or
that anything out there in any way corresponded with the verbal
representation. This worrying disjunction of words and things was
the theme of many pamphlets by Behn's political associates such as
Roger L'Estrange. Even more strongly than Oroonoko, Bacon
believed that, if addressed to him or by him, the word must still be
true like himself. So, when a clearly false letter arrives from the
Virginian council, Bacon assumes it is sincere where his followers
observe its falseness. This easy deception makes Bacon absurd in a
world where even his staunchest admirers can see that the personal
heroism of a 'great soul' is not the answer to duplicitous statecraft.
So with death: he trips himself into it with heroic rhetoric.

The historical versions of Bacon occur in several sources. The
most accessible to Behn would have been a pamphlet, *Strange News
from Virginia; Being a full and true Account of the Life and Death of
Nathaniel Bacon Esquire, Who was the only Cause and Original of
all the late Troubles in that County. With a full Relation of all the
Accidents which have happened in the late War there between the
Christians and Indians*, published in 1677. This has Behn's tone only
in the beginning: 'There is no Nation this day under the copes of

Heaven can so experimentally speak the sad Effects of men of great Parts being reduc't to necessity, as *England*'; Bacon's ambition acted out on the colonial stage is called indulgently 'the general lust of a large Soul'. But there are other tones: 'when men have been once flusht or entred with vice, how hard is it for them to leave it. In the last two pages, which record the providential death of Bacon, the tone is harsher: he is 'the great Molester of the quiet of that miserable Nation'. His death is downgraded by the rumour that he was a hard drinker and died of 'two much Brandy'; though the author does not believe this slander, it has been repeated. The pamphlet ends more positively with praise of his 'natural parts', learning and sense:

> Wherefore as I am my self a Lover of Ingenuity, though an abhorrer of disturbance or Rebellion, I think fit since Providence was pleased to let him dye a Natural death in his Bed, not to asperse him with saying he kill'd himself with drinking.

The official view which Behn might have read in manuscript if she were still working directly with government intelligence in the 1680s was *A True Narrative of the Late Rebellion in Virginia, by the Royal Commissioners, 1677*. This included *A True Narrative of the Rise, Progresse, and Cessation of the Late Rebellion in Virginia, Most Humbly and Impartially Reported by His Majestyes Commissioners Appointed to Enquire into the Affaires of the Said Colony*. The report arose out of a commission sent to Virginia after news of the rebellion had reached London in September 1676. The commissioners arrived in the beginning of 1677 and returned in July to make their report to the Privy Council in October. In this they present themselves as transparent observers, allowing the 'most knowing, credible and indifferent Persons in Virginia' to speak through them and basing their narrative on the 'most authentique Papers, Records, Reports …'.[4] Like Byam in his letter and Behn in *Oroonoko*, they claim truth: they wrote what they 'thought most consonant to Truth and Reality'. A source of the Indian queen may be found here in the historical Queen of Pamunckey, who feels the dual allegiance to Indians and settlers which is given in romantic terms to the young Indian queen in *The Widow Ranter*. But this woman flees from Bacon and swerves decidedly from the timorous fictional character in playing a subtle diplomatic part, more concerned with supplies and troop movements than with romance.

The commissioners give Bacon the old-world status of an illustrious family, which Behn's character assumes. Like Behn's creation,
this one is ambitious, arrogant and imperious, but unlike hers he
manages to hide these qualities till he grew 'powerfull and popular'.
He is closer to Monmouth than to Behn's Bacon when he is pre-
vailed on to lead the revolt by appeals to the vanity of leadership,
when he seduces 'the Vulgar and most ignorant People' to believe in
him, and when he uses the appearance of magic to impress the credulous. He has notions quite beyond the times or his capabilities: 'he
pretended and bosted what great Service hee would doe for the
country in destroying the Comon Enemy, securing their Lives and
Estates, Libertyes', called by the commissioners 'such like fair
frauds'.[5] He is a fantasist who returns from a campaign 'with a thousand braging lyes to the credulous Silly People of what feats he had
perform'd' and he speaks to them after he had caused 'the Drums to
Beat and Trumpet to Sound'; in his rousing words the rebels
become the true guardians of 'his majestyes country'.[6]

Like Behn's heroes and their historical equivalents the Commissioners, Bacon is not impressed with Christianity: he is 'of a pest-
ilent and prevalent Logical discourse tending to atheisme ...'; the
germ of the classically suicidal Bacon described by Behn may exist
here. His death is physical and ignoble:

> But before he could arrive to the Perfection of his designes (w'ch
> none but the eye of omniscience could Penetrate) Providence did that
> which noe other hand durst (or at least did) doe and cut him off.
> Hee lay sick. ... of the Bloody Flux, and ... accompanyed with a
> Lousey Disease; so that the swarmes of Verymn that bred in his Body
> he could not destroy but by throwing his shirts into the Fire as often
> as he shifted himself.
> Hee dyed much dissatisfied in minde. ...[7]

With this death, close to the physical realism of Oroonoko's man-
gling, Behn's character in *The Widow Ranter* has nothing to do,
unless it be in the 'dissatisfied' mind.

Holding less to the particulars of history than in *Love-Letters*, Behn
in *The Widow Ranter* manages to create a death for Bacon that both
celebrates and anatomises a masculine heroics embodying and
flouting authority. It becomes a statement of her ambivalent attitude
to the politics of glamour and personal power, seen as both naïve and
splendid. The depiction of Bacon's death gains some of its absurdity
through the usual posturing and self-dramatising of the protagonist

and some from its deviation from history. Where the heroic, romantic-ally inspired death of Cesario is made absurd by the token of the tooth-pick case and the fiercely heroic death of Oroonoko by the pipe-smoking and the grotesque physical failure, in *The Widow Ranter* Bacon's heroic death is senseless in the circumstances of the play and absurd in its replacement of physically disgusting disease with clean suicide.

It seems that it is the interpenetration of history and story, fiction and faction (in both its senses), that intrigues Behn in her last years. The self is taken outside itself through the ideals of love and heroic politics. The self fictionalised in and outside of history, the self that is annihilated in death, is the mobile, shifting self of Lucretian atomism, a momentary voyeur of itself, taking an anticipatory plea-sure before death in the contemplating of its assumption in death into heroic art or after death into folk mythology.

In Behn's presentations, there seems no concept of a personal or political grand narrative as context, no concept of history as Christian and providential, often a feature of the purportedly histor-ical accounts which parallel her fictions; instead she allows her pro-tagonists a sense of the aesthetics of a willed or anticipated death. This moment, contextualised more in classical philosophy than in Christian religion, gives an artistic if not a political authenticity to the otherwise unstable selves of the protagonists. They achieve their greatness by moving out of history into myth, in the manner of Mircea Eliade's heroes who transport themselves into a mythical epoch for the moment of their 'exemplary gesture'.[8]

The intrusion of the grotesque and absurd from history into the magnificent causes a coexistence of myth and its undercutting. These moments in which history and fiction involve each other, in which history interrupts generically formal art with precise physical and social circumstances or shadows its effort by simple contradic-tion, insist that reference be made beyond the fiction and that pre-sentation be known as representation. This insistence is aided by the self-consciousness in the protagonists, caused by their reaching out to classical literary images or tokens. In the context Behn provides, the aesthetic moment of organised death is not a Burkean aesthetic-ising of political truth in a fetishised body, but more an anarchic moment, destabilising political and literary categories.

The represented, planned and orchestrated deaths of great men are both private and public. They refuse to conform to any Renaissance notion of didactic virtue and instead hold to an anachronistic Roman sense of manly honour. At their ends Oroonoko, Bacon and Cesario are buoyed up by a concept of classical masculine behaviour, not by any need to be an exemplar of Christian virtue. All three depicted men refuse Christian death and its inevitable contingency and, dreaming of Roman suicide, try to achieve the Lucretian power to act as they will. Refusing like Lucretius to accept the hidden divine power that 'treads human grandeur down' or like Behn to see life's constant deflations, they create a self that they appear to believe for the moment is not manipulated by others, ironically taking a kind of freedom at their supreme moment of impotence.

Beyond the aesthetics of what might be called the heroic grotesque is the spectating life that continues. The spectators live on in the Lucretian flux, momentarily exalted as by great art rather than edified by exemplary behaviour; these men and women are written into Behn's accounts as, with their ordinary selves intact, they leave on the next boat, learn new proverbs or make political compromises. There is a gender division too: at the close of the *The Widow Ranter*, the heroic man is dead and the pragmatic widow lives on to die from the 'Toils of Sickness'.

The public deaths make a political, as well as an aesthetic and individual, point: they interrogate order and a doomed aristocracy. The heroes exist in worlds largely without proper authority. The worlds outside England – the colonies of Oroonoko and Bacon – are simpler than England; there is a sense almost of childish make-believe in them and people can declare themselves of any class and sex. The proper authority will come from outside and is not represented: the governors are awaited in *Oroonoko* and *The Widow Ranter*. In such circumstances, there can be a fantasy of proper authority and order, never quite to be portrayed. Perhaps in this depiction of England through what is not England, there is a desire once again to inhabit the promising world of the late Interregnum, of *The Rover* and *The Roundheads*, where political idealism was still possible. In this aspect alone, the works would then become a kind of rewriting of the Restoration as a perpetual future restoration.

Perhaps, though, the doomed leaders have a more cynical message in themselves for authority; perhaps they speak less of the historical rebels they represent than of legitimate authority. In many respect Cesario, Oroonoko and Bacon seem an amalgam of the heroic and theatrical Charles I, whose great death on the scaffold so dominated Restoration politics, and of his two sons: the cynical, charismatic

Charles II and the doomed idealist James II, about to be deserted by most of the followers Behn had resplendently described in her *Coronation Ode*. After all her public support for the Stuarts, are these late works ways of suggesting the anachronistic, 'fictional' nature of what she purportedly admires, a more open expression of that political exasperation to be found in her last published poems, the *Pindaric Poem to Dr Burnet* and the *Congratulatory Poem to Queen Mary*? Is the imagined spectator of public deaths a displaced image of the subject-spectator of the death of a dynasty?

Public deaths and suicides from apparent failure affirm the legal order and serve power; as a failed rebel, Bacon is in a way destroyed by legally constituted authority. But his death is marked less by the re-establishment of order than by a resumption of semi-order. The new governor has after all not arrived and colonial confusion can easily reassert itself. In proportion as their social context is debased, each of the three heroes becomes heroic and tragic, so that Oroonoko in a colony governed by evil deputies is the most heroic and Monmouth in a country with standards of literary expression and proper behaviour the least. Bacon, the most politically justified, kills himself and suggests that authority, in almost Hobbesian terms, remains to be obeyed even when corrupt and base. Power needs constant victims and constant spectacles. There is nothing left politically for the decent knowing character to do but to obey the dubious law and contemplate the image of art: as one admirable character in *The Widow Ranter* laments, 'What pity 'tis there should be such false maxims in the world, that noble actions, however great, must be criminal for want of a law to authorise them.'[9]

From Janet Todd, *Gender, Art and Death* (Cambridge, 1993), pp. 49–61.

NOTES

[In the context of seventeenth-century politics and a cultural fascination with suicide and heroic death, as well as of two of her other late works, *Love-Letters between a Nobleman and his Sister*, and *Oroonoko*, Janet Todd discusses Behn's representation of death in *The Widow Ranter*, probably her last written play. The dying rebel hero, Bacon, is an oddly anachronistic figure who, inhabiting a tragicomedy, desires the simplicity of tragedy. In his mingling of grotesque and dignified, he forms a commentary on the tragicomic politics of the last years of James II. Ed.]

1.   *Oroonoko, The Rover*, ed. Janet Todd (Harmondsworth, 1992), p. 256.

2.   *Oroonoko, The Rover*, p. 318.

3.   *Oroonoko, The Rover*, p. 321.

4.   The pamphlet and subsequent ones are reproduced in *Narratives of the Insurrections 1675–1690*, ed. Charles McLean Andrews (New York, 1915). The last quotation is from p. 140. See also Wilcomb E. Washburn, *The Governor and the Rebel: a history of Bacon's rebellion in Virginia* (Chapel Hill, NC, 1957).

5.   *Narratives*, p. 111.

6.   Despite their claim of authenticity, the commissioners provide speeches for their characters, presumably following the methods most associated with the historiography of Thucydides: 'As for the speeches delivered by the several statesmen before and during the war, it is difficult for me to report and exact substance of what was said, whether I heard the speeches myself or learned of them from others. I have therefore made the speakers express primarily what in my own opinion was called for under the successive circumstances, at the same time keeping as close as possible to the general import of what was actually said' (*Thucydides*, trans. John H. Finley Jr [Ann Arbor, MI], pp. 94–5). Restoration drama based on 'history' seems an extension of this practice.

7.   *Narratives*, p. 139.

8.   Mircea Eliade, *The Myth of the Eternal Return; or, Cosmos and History*, trans. Willard R. Trask (Princeton, NJ, 1974), p. 35.

9.   *Oroonoko, The Rover*, p. 268.

5

'But to the touch were soft': Pleasure, Power and Impotence in 'The Disappointment' and 'The Golden Age'

JESSICA MUNNS

INTRODUCTION

Aphra Behn contributed largely to the Restoration's sexual discourse and in this essay I discuss two of her poems in relation to a proliferating literature of sexual anxiety focused on masculine sexual impotence. 'The Disappointment' (1680) is a translation/adaptation of the French poem, 'Sur une Impuissance' (1661) by de Cantenac, significantly altered by Behn as she looks at masculine sexual impotence from a female perspective. The title quotation of this essay is taken from 'The Golden Age' (1684), loosely based on the prologue to Tasso's *Aminta* (1573), in which, I shall argue, Behn offers a route through cultural anxieties centring on the erect or the 'soft' penis read as signs of either male enmeshment in productive labour or inadequacy.[1]

In the seventeenth century, as Roger Thompson has noted, 'masculine impotence or at least inadequacy was a[n] ... obsession'.[2] It is an obsession, of course, which has by no means been limited to the seventeenth century. Masculine impotence provides the stock motif

of many cuckolding tales, which frequently link masculine impotence with wealth. The acquisition of wealth, as in Chaucer's
Merchant's Tale, is often associated with age, age is associated with
sexual decline, and the public power of the older man is undermined by his private inability to satisfy the youth and beauty his
money can purchase. In Restoration literature, alongside these traditional figurations of the power of wealth and the impotence of age,
increased anxieties over the relationships between sex, marriage and
wealth produce new variants on the theme of impotence – new sites
of impotence – and new figurations of what it is about wealth, apart
from age, that produces impotence.

Giles Slade has investigated the combined figure of rake and
eunuch – above all Wycherley's Horner – to argue that 'the centrality of impotence to Restoration discourse of all types, derives ...
from the upheavals following the Civil War which challenged cavalier gender ideology and led to a pervasive insecurity about what
masculinity was'.[3] Undoubtedly, the civil war legacy of social and
political insecurity challenged traditional concepts of authority and,
since political authority was male, masculinity. As J. G. A. Pocock
points out, 'seventeenth-century men were still pre-modern creatures for whom authority and magistracy were part of a natural and
cosmic order', and for whom the 'unimaginable fact [was] that
between 1642 and 1649, authority in England had simply col-
lapsed'.[4] Slade suggests that the demoralising effects of the defeat,
exile, and imprisonment of the cavaliers influenced further generations of young men brought up meditating on their fathers' defeat
and resenting the new powers that masculine defeat and absence
had given their mothers.[5] Slade is surely correct in identifying the
Restoration as a society in 'crisis' over 'masculinity', and in reaction
to a period during which the traditional male ruling class was defeated. I would like to suggest, however, that this societal 'crisis' responded not only to the immediate past of cavalier defeat (and the
ever present traditions of misogyny), but also to the anxieties of a
society in transition from feudal aristocracy to bourgeois capitalism.

In particular, a cavalier/aristocratic and libertine ethos of careless
and free sexuality becomes implicated in the nascent workings of a
market economy that both endorses the free-flow and exchange of
goods and also recommends frugal hoarding and careful expenditure. Richard Braverman examines the relationships between sexual
spending and economic thrift in his discussion of Etherege's lyric
'Cease Anxious World'. Braverman draws attention to the lyric's

anxiety as it propounds a 'cavalier ... antipathy to ... productivity and frugality, countering it with a libertine economy of excessive [sexual] expenditure'. Braverman concludes, however, that the cavalier's 'witty triumph beyond the anxious world of the actual economy is at the same time a measure of his declining status in a society in which real property was more potent than wit'.[6]

Jean-Joseph Goux's discussion of what makes the penis transform into the phallus is relevant to the ideology of cavalier excessive sexual expenditure described by Braverman.[7] For Goux there is a 'structural, genetic, functional correspondence between gold and the penis' and both can become a privileged 'general equivalent' – the Gold Standard, the Phallus. With reference to the privileged status of gold, Goux cites Marx's thesis that gold functions as 'something that can be done without, that does not enter into the satisfaction of immediate needs as an object of consumption nor into the immediate process of production as an agent'. Gold is, in Goux's words, 'pure superfluity, excess par excellence'.[8] For Goux, the penis can similarly transform because it also represents a kind of surplus-value, it is 'the site of unproductive expenditure, that which surpasses immediate needs; it is the site of superfluous (and deferrable) expenditure'.[9] As such a site of excessive expenditure, the penis/phallus fulfils the ideological needs of the cavalier 'antipathy to productivity and frugality'.

For many Restoration writers, however, processes elevating either gold or the penis to a 'general equivalent' above 'immediate needs' have become grounded. The relationship between gold and the penis is present but problematic, sometimes directly and uncomfortably related and not necessarily indicating freedom from need. It was possible to imagine the penis as a site for *productive* expenditure, even labour. Penniless gallants not only work for cash payments but also supply impotent city husbands with needed heirs becoming tools in the sexual and fiscal economy of others.[10] The language of love in Restoration comedies frequently draws on the language of commerce – not least in the various famous 'proviso' scenes.[11] The relationship between sex, marriage and money, or sex, marriage and the processes of exchange is not new or unique to the Restoration, but systems of sex-money-stock-property exchange have become central, widespread, and are an integral part of a very political discourse of impotence, incapacity, and sexual avoidance. The productive labour of the penis can then evoke the Earl of Rochester's aristocratic distaste for those who 'Drudge in fair Aurelia's womb / To get supplies for age and graves' (ll. 17–18).[12]

If masculine sexual potency is equatable with productive labour, coinage, and use-value, then masculine potency and its dominant sign, the phallus, have also become implicated in activities associated with commerce and therefore potentially degrading to a gentleman. The 'purity' of sexual excess – gentlemanly largesse – is in danger of commodification, and with this danger the status of the phallus as a 'general equivalent' is destabilised. Non-productive sex acts, such as the supremely unproductive expenditure of premature ejaculation, or even the failure to achieve erection, become newly problematised sites of concern which are investigated in the 'imperfect enjoyment' genre.[13]

IMPERFECT ENJOYMENT: 'THE DISAPPOINTMENT'

In male 'imperfect enjoyment' poems, the embarrassment of male sexual inadequacy often mingles with mock-heroic raillery, such as addresses to the 'base mettell hanger by your Master's Thigh! / Eternall shame to Prick's heraldry' (ll. 1–2), or reminiscences, as in Rochester's in 'The Imperfect Enjoyment' (1680), of past better encounters when 'This dart of love ... / With virgin blood the thousand maids have dyed' (ll. 37–8).[14] In Sir George Etherege's relatively decorous poem, also entitled 'The Imperfect Enjoyment' (1662), the mock-heroic note is struck as the failed encounter is expressed in terms of siege warfare with the male lover falling 'Dead at the foot of the surrendered wall' (l. 30).[15] The male failing is attributed to female beauty – 'You'd been more happy had you been less fair' (l. 50) – and prudery – 'condemn yourself, not me; / This is the effect of too much modesty' (ll. 41–2). Both excuses draw on conventional constructions of femininity, modest and fair, to explain why the equally conventionally constructed male, vigorous and over-powering, has failed. In both Etherege's and Rochester's poems, a mock-heroic language translates shame into comedy and evokes as well as cancels the traditions of male supremacy. The genre moves uneasily between chivalric glorification and shame, between memories of a better past and the imperfect present, and between self-disgust expressed as mockery and forms of exculpation. In Behn's 'The Disappointment', however, the narrative of masculine conquest temporarily suspended by impotence is reworked into an uncompromising narrative of female frustration.

Behn's poem, situated in an eternal pastoral, is not concerned with the past, and her characters of nymph and swain, Cloris and Lysander, do not bring histories to their encounter.[16] Her poem is less concerned with explaining (away) the male failure than with describing its effect on his female partner. An evocation of female desire replaces the conventional enunciations of male expectation as 'The Disappointment' dwells as much upon Cloris' feelings of aroused desire (stanza 6 is devoted to the topic) as those of her lover, and emphasises *her* 'disappointment' rather than that of her amorous but incapable swain. In contrast to Cloris's 'Resentments' (l. 131), in Rochester's poem his partner, like Bellamira in Sir Charles Sedley's 1687 play of that name, is rather charmingly understanding.[17] When her lover prematurely ejaculates all over her body, 'Smiling, she chides in a kind murmuring noise / And from her body wipes the clammy joys' (ll. 19–20).

Sperm, even if premature and clammy, is still equated with 'joys' and the lady is not so much disappointed as desirous of 'more' (l. 22).[18] The lines in which she asks for 'more' are admirably tactful as she indicates that premature ejaculation is to 'love and rapture's due' (l. 23) – rather than a sign of incapacity. She is not repelled but merely asks, 'Must we not pay a debt to pleasure too?' (l. 24). She is, as it were, an uncritical consumer who is prepared to regard the premature ejaculation as a preview portending further and more mutual pleasures. She is flatteringly confident that her lover has 'more'; nevertheless, her insistence, however charming, that she is still waiting to be paid her measure of sperm and pleasure surely articulates the male fear that *their* 'love' and 'rapture' are not enough for women. It is this apprehension that Rochester's poem both articulates and seeks to cancel.

In Behn's poem premature ejaculation also takes place, but not over the woman's body, rather it is Lysander who feels the consequences of his failure as 'The Insensible fell weeping in his Hand' (l. 90). The relocation is relevant; there are no soft female murmuring noises, no gentle wipes of 'clammy joys', and no requests for 'more'. The male failure is situated in the male body and is regarded as final. Moreover, Behn's Cloris is not sweetly understanding but horrified. When she investigates her lover's limp penis, she rapidly withdraws her fingers as if 'Finding beneath the verdant Leaves a snake' (l. 110). Male imperfect enjoyment poems take off at this point in the narrative of sexual disaster to address their penises, to remind them of past glories and threaten dire punishments.

The form, in fact, is pre-eminently about the penis, who becomes
a character, an old friend but recalcitrant and problematic. The
vagina, if it is mentioned at all, as in Rochester's poem, is crudely
denominated a 'cunt' (ll. 40, 43), or as in the anonymous poem
already cited, 'One Writing Against his Prick', is a 'Port hole' (l. 14)
– basically an empty inert space which it should be possible to penetrate.[19] In 'The Imperfect Enjoyment' Rochester even de-genders the
'cunt' since his imperial penis would 'carelessly invade / Woman or
man / ... Where'er it pierced, a cunt it found or made' (ll. 41–3).
Harold Weber argues that in Rochester's sexual universe, 'men
make women, the penis representative of a phallic power that alone
establishes gender'.[20] These lines, however, which are indifferent
both to procreation and the pleasure of the partner, do not so much
create women with their awkward wombs, but specifically, 'cunts' as
neutral gender-indifferent spaces.

Behn reverses the usual centre of the genre from the penis to the
vagina, for her Cloris does not just possess a convenient orifice but a
luscious vagina described in (clichéd) religious terms as an 'altar'
and a 'paradise' as well as a 'fountain where delight still flows'
(ll. 45, 47, 49). Cloris's vagina is also sensitive and responds to her
emotions. Unlike Rochester's friend, when her lover fails her, she
undergoes an immediate cessation of desire which Behn describes
with anatomical precision: 'The Blood forsook the hinder Place /
And strew'd with Blushes all her Face' (ll. 116–17). Lysander's feelings are described as those of 'Rage and Shame' (l. 97), and are self-
absorbed and self-directed. Cloris's feelings are similarly confused
but different. She feels a mixture of 'Disdain and Shame' (l. 18),
disdain presumably for her lover's incapacity, and shame at having
participated in this fiasco. And, given the centrality of rape in
Restoration discourses of masculine sexuality, there can be few
more humiliating suggestions than the idea that it is male incapacity
and not male rampant vigour that speeds the nymph's steps with
'Fear and Haste ... o'er the Fatal Plain' (l. 130).

The shift from penile absorption to a centring on the female experience is strengthened at the end when the author intervenes to state
that 'The *Nymph's* Resentments none but I / Can well Imagine or
Condole' (ll. 131–2), while Lysander's 'Griefs' are described as un-
knowable (ll. 133–4). In place of the male poems' emphasis on the
male anatomy and sperm as virtual capital – unfortunately wasted,
gratuitously expended in 'clammy joys', and a debt not paid – Behn's
poem shifts the emphasis to the failure to respond and exchange

pleasure for pleasure. The usually cancelled female body is articulated, as are the female physical and emotional sensations of aroused
and unsatisfied desire.

Behn's version of the genre is, indeed, a species of table-turning as
she gives expression to the fears of inadequacy and weakness the
form inscribes but usually seeks to mediate and dissipate through
humour, crudity and deflection. In the lines which describe Cloris
touching her lover's limp penis, the author humorously refers to the
'fabulous Priapus, / That potent god, *as poets feign*' (ll. 105–6, emphasis added), to reveal that the poets, indeed, lie. The military language of sexual conquest is reversed; the plain is 'Fatal' precisely
because it is *not* fatal; no maidenhead has been vanquished, and if
neither combatant has been triumphant, it is Cloris who is up and
running while Lysander lies 'fainting on the Gloomy Bed' (l. 120).
In Behn's poem the unproductive penis cannot be converted into some
other currency of masculine authority. It is neither a well-worn
sword nor a blunted battering ram; it is not a surly old pal or a dis-
dainful aristocrat; Lysander merely has an 'insensible' and 'weeping'
penis and has failed his mistress. In a subversive revision of the
Edenic myth, the penis is a snake from which the nymph recoils and
which brings neither knowledge nor pleasure. Masculine impotence
is the failure to satisfy female desire and defeat cannot be laughed
away, braided into memories of past victories, or, as in the French
original, cancelled out by subsequent success.[21]

In the light of Behn's uncompromising poem of female frustration, male fears that their power and autonomy are threatened by
penile insertion into the demanding and draining vagina/womb are
highlighted. Compared to failure, power is sustained *in absentia* –
unconsumed but also unproved. Giles Slade points out that the combination of the figures of rake and eunuch is significant and argues
that the compensatory behaviours of the rake are an expression of
an utter lack of confidence by contemporary men in their own
manhood.[22] But the eunuch or male who refuses/denies sexual
activity is not simply the lacking figure for which the age found
compensation in the rake. The eunuch, or the male who takes unto
himself the position of the eunuch, is taking up a compensatory position which manifests power through indifference to female
demands. To pleasure a woman plays into her market; to deny her
pleasure conserves the male spermatic treasury. As Goux argues,
'the eunuch (the entrepreneur, or producer) subserviently catering
to the tyrant's (the consumer's) will to *jouissances*, is in fact the

tyrant of the tyrant, though the latter believes he remains the master'.[23] To maintain a position outside the circle of desire, as Pierre does in Thomas Otway's *Venice Preserv'd* (1682) when he refuses sexual intercourse with his mistress but allows her intercourse with her lover, who is also his political opponent, is a position of control. It is, however, a wounded position and control of the sexual economy is bought at a high price. The phallus/penis equation has acquired not so much a slash as question marks, phallus? penis?

PERFECT ENJOYMENT, 'THE GOLDEN AGE'

A solution sought to the conundrums of sexuality, its shifting sites of power, and its implication in a material and social economy of hoarding and spending, was to imagine a golden past when issues of power, authority, and wealth were unknown and when sexuality implied only pleasure – an era, in fact, which if golden was free of gold or guilt. Behn's poem 'The Golden Age' depicts just such an Ovidian era of ease, natural bounty and pleasure. 'The Golden Age' investigates the links between male codes of behaviour, wealth, property, authority, labour and sexual desire, and offers a vision of felicity when all re/productivity was achieved 'Without the aids of men' (l. 35). For although Behn assumes a male voice when she invites a young woman to reassume the Golden Age and confess freely to those desires which 'we can guess' (l. 171), she creates here a very explicitly female paradise.

'The Golden Age' can be seen as positing an alternative rather than a contradictory vision of sexuality to that of 'The Disappointment'. Both are pastorals, but the pastoral of 'The Golden Age' is more complete and carries implications not only of the mutuality of desire but of the mutuality and permeability of gender itself. Behn's Golden Age is also an era in which all the institutions which instantiate masculine power are unknown, unformed, and in which, consequently, concepts of shame which, above all, govern female sexuality are unknown and unformed.

In 'The Disappointment' Cloris' resistance to Lysander is minimal, 'She wants the pow'r to say – *Ah! What d'ye do?*' (l. 20). Nevertheless, her eyes are 'bright and severe' indicating that 'Love and Shame confus'dly strive' (ll. 21–2) and she refers, if not very seriously, to her '*Dearest Honour*' (l. 27) as something she cannot give to Lysander. In 'The Golden Age' the nymphs are less inhibited; the 'Nymphs were free, no nice, no coy disdain, / Deny'd their Joyes, or gave the Lover pain' (ll. 97–8). The only resistance they put up is 'kind' (l. 99), and their physical reactions of 'Trembling and blushing are not marks of shame' (l. 100). The blushing that first indicated Cloris' sexual arousal and was then displaced to her face to signal her shame and anger, is here only to be read as arousal. Love thus uninhibited by societal conventions, 'Nor kept in fear of Gods, no fond Religious Cause, / Nor in Obedience to duller Laws' (ll. 109–10) produces *jouissance*, entirely satisfactory and orgasmic 'Joyes which were everlasting, ever new' (l. 107). The sensations of pleasure and joy are resituated to a non-teleological world of passionate sexuality which is without the taint of shame or the contamination of relations and exchanges in power, wealth, and status.

In Behn's poem, the counter-forces to such a vision of felicity are described through negation in stanzas 3 to 9. The Golden Age is depicted as an era without labour (stanza 3), without war and ambition (stanza 4), without property (stanza 5), and without honour (stanza 8). In the Golden Age there were no rulers, for 'Monarchs were uncreated then' and therefore there were no 'Arbitrary Rulers' and no 'Laws' (4: ll. 51–3). Religion, seen as setting 'the World at Odds', too was unknown and unneeded (4: l. 54), and there was also no need for laws protecting property right for 'bounteous Nature' provided plenty for all (4: ll. 58–64) and 'Right and Property were words since made' (5: l. 65). A detour in stanzas 6 and 7 returns the reader to 'The flowry Meads the Rivers and the Groves' (6: l. 84), asserts the freedom of sexual pleasure in the Golden Age (6: ll. 84–116) prior to 'Politik Curbs' that 'keep man in', and stanza 7 concludes by wondering who but the 'Learned and dull moral Fool / Could gravely have foreseen, man ought to live by Rule?'(7: ll. 112, 115–16).

In a subtle and insightful essay, 'Contestations of Nature', Robert Markley and Molly Rothenberg provide one of the few close readings of this poem. They argue that in 'The Golden Age' Behn's commitment to a patriarchal and aristocratic Tory ideology works against her desire to create a paradise of untrammelled and female sexuality and they point to places where Behn's poem 'discloses contradictions within contemporary constructions of nature, politics, gender, and identity'.[24] Without wishing to impose an ahistorical 'feminism' or a forced consistency on a poem as densely located along complex lines of ideology, my reading of the poem differs from theirs. I wish to suggest that the poem, particularly as seen in the light of my discussion above, offers a subversive vision of female sexuality and desire freed from either the power of the phallus or the failure of the penis.

According to Markley and Rothenberg, Behn 'can neither locate historically nor define theoretically a structure of causation' for the Fall she describes.[25] The logical arrangement of negative elements in the poem, however, is suggestive of a pattern of causation if not historical location. First labour, then war and monarchy, then property, and then honour, are isolated and condemned. As Markley and Rothenberg stress, this pastoral harbours a lie, the lie that, for instance, Raymond Williams argues Ben Jonson's 'To Penshurst' or Thomas Carew's 'To Saxham' harbour with their mystifications of property and status and erasure of labour.[26] Indeed, Markley and Rothenberg argue that Behn recapitulates 'self-aggrandising and aristocratic values' in her description of the prelapsarian swain as 'Lord o'er his own will alone' (4: l. 57).[27] The erasure of labour is, indeed, vital to this, as to many other pastoral poems, since labour unsuitable to the gentle, instantiates just those status differentials, marked by property and wealth, that, however improbably, are being denied. This erasure is achieved by the insistent and visionary depiction of nature so bounteous that labour, and the demarcations of property productive of wealth and status are redundant.

There is nothing original in this pattern; Behn draws both on her original, Tasso's *Aminta* and, surely, on Ovid, as well as the long traditions of Classical and libertine evocations of 'soft' pastoral. With labour erased, what Behn can then depict is a world where the ease and autonomy associated with aristocracy are experienced by all. For in no way is Behn's poem a 'proletarian' pastoral glorifying shared labour and a simple diet of acorns. What she evokes is a world where war, which depends on the property claims produced by labour, and which in turn produces its own ideology of masculine honour, is unknown and, where, therefore, both honour and masculinity, creations of the fallen world, are irrelevant.

Behn distinguishes between this 'natural' aristocracy in which swains are lords of themselves and all that they survey, and the post-lapsarian world where the processes, initiated by labour, have produced a condition of mercantilist struggle marked by invasion and the capture and hoarding of what once was general. It is within these terms of the fallen world as a world of economic struggle where 'Pride and Avarice become a *Trade*', carried on by wars which *'barter'd* wounds and scarrs', seen as *'Merchandize'* (5: ll. 67, 69, 70 emphasis added), that Behn locates the fall of sexuality and the commodification of woman. Behn employs an economic register in her description of the way in which honour inhibits female sexuality, and, in the process, also demystifies honour.

Behn associates honour with the concept of sexual shame for women, 'Honour! thou who first didst damn, / A Woman to the Sin of shame' and, in the process, honour robbed 'us of our gust' (8: ll. 117–18, 19). Specifically, what honour taught woman was to commodify herself by making herself artificially beautiful and hard to obtain. The idea is carried in an image of loosely free-flowing hair imprisoned:

> The Envious Net, and stinted order hold,
> The lovely Curls of Jet and Shining Gold,
> No more neglected on the Shoulders hurl'd:
> Now dressed to Tempt, not gratify the World,
> Thou Miser Honour hoard'st the sacred store,
> And starv'st thyself to keep thy votaries poor.
>
> (ll. 123–7)

Markley and Rothenberg comment on these lines that the woman's 'pre-and post-lapsarian bodies are commodified' since the 'Curls of Jet and Shining Gold define her in economic terms prior to the commercial interest of "Miser Honour"'.[28]

In many ways this reading is correct, and it might be more consistent to compare the black and blonde curls of the Golden Age to tar or straw. The mention of precious objects, however, is commonplace in pastorals and Land of Cokaigne narratives of pre-commercial paradises. Objects, such as jewels, or activities, such as leisure, which register as economically significant in our fallen world, are referred to in paradise texts to stress, as in this text, their unregarded nature in the prelapsarian state. There is always a double inscription at work which presents as a wonder the devaluation of objects or activities which can only be wondered at because they have value. So that even if the curls recall 'Jet' and 'Gold', the point of these terms of value is, surely, that in the happy primal state they lie 'neglected on the Shoulders hurl'd', and only in the fallen world, are they stored in 'stinted order'.[29] Descriptions of the curls as a 'sacred store', reference to lovers as 'Votaries' (l. 137), or to love as a 'sacred Gift' (9: l. 142) might also be felt to be inappropriate to a pre-religious era. In the prelapsarian world Behn imagines, however, that which has now been mystified and made rare to become objects of *unsacred* barter or 'Theft' (9: l. 144) was once both numinous and freely given.

The connection between honour and commodification, indicated by the term 'Miser Honour', is strengthened as the poet banishes honour from sites of poverty 'Shepheards Cottages' (l. 150), and tells it to 'Deal and Chaffer in the Trading Court / The busie Market for Phantastick Things' (ll. 154–5). The lines of connection drawn here are interesting. Honour was frequently subject to satiric attacks, but usually in terms of its 'Phantastick' qualities, such as adherence to a mere word, rather than its integration into a system of trade, exchange and barter. Indeed, honour was attractive (and satires on honour as 'phantastick' are often, in fact, commending it) precisely because it did *not* have a negotiable exchange-value. There is a courtly and aristocratic disdain at work in this poem, as nature's largesse and excess are celebrated, which we would expect from a high Tory poet. There is also a radical and subversive note implicit in the categorical connections between masculinity, property, and the ideological reification of consumerism as honour.

Such reification is impossible in the Golden Age since effortless consumption is the norm in a world of plenty. The landscape description with which 'The Golden Age' opens stresses the lush and endlessly renewing vegetation which invites the 'endless' enactment of love.

> ... an Eternal Spring drest ev'ry Bough,
> And Blossoms fell, by new ones dispossest;
> These their kind Shade affording all below,
> And those a Bed where all below might rest.
> The Groves appear'd all drest with Wreaths of Flowers,
> And from their Leaves dropt Aromatick Showers,
> Whose fragrant Heads in Mystick Twines above,
> Exchang'd their Sweets, and mix'd with thousand Kisses.
> (1: ll. 5–12)

And if lovers are in constant activity under the trees, above them gentle breezes waft perfumed air over the birds, who spend their time in 'Love and Musick' (2: ll. 25–30).

Markley and Rothenberg argue that this is no 'pristine wilderness but an idealised vision of a bucolic English countryside that has already been acted upon (implicitly) by labour'.[30] The Englishness of the countryside is, I think, questionable, and labour is explicitly banished as the poet notes that it is Spring who dresses the boughs and that 'the willing Branches strove / To beautify and shade the Grove'(1: ll. 13–14).[31] This is absurd, but this is paradise and, as suggested earlier, the erasure or displacement of labour is an essential element that enables the erasure of all the other troubling signs that mark the fallen world and which connect sexuality with an economy of power, status and wealth. For Markley and Rothenberg, the dispossession of falling blossoms by new ones suggests 'a violent renewal dependent on usurpation' marking the 'irruption of an economic and political lexicon ("affording", "Exchang'd", "Sacrifice") into an otherwise idyllic and historical description of nature'.[32] The idea of an endlessly self-renewing nature which denies seasonal alteration is a dream at least as old as Homer's Garden of Alcinious. The point of the 'Eternal Spring'(1 : l. 5), so dear to the European imagination, is, surely, that the dispossession of nature, which in the 'real' world signals the hard winter and dearth to follow, is in the happy garden of the Golden Age without fear.

'Eternal Spring' is contrasted with the 'real' world of withering beauty and 'Eternal Night' in the concluding stanza in which Sylvia is urged in Catullian terms to seize the day. Here there is indeed confusion since the Sylvia so abruptly introduced is urged to 'Assume' the 'Golden age' in an era then explicitly described as driven by short time, decay and change – an era, in fact, in which the free sexuality of the Golden Age cannot function. The dispossession of nature, however, is a transformed sign in the Golden Age, precisely marking not usurpation and loss but an extraordinary plenty. Similarly, the exchanges that take place in the branches of 'Sweets' for 'Sweets', and 'Kisses' for 'Kisses', form a continuous and, in a sense, meaningless exchange of sameness. Implicitly, these exchanges are opposed to the more usual forms of barter which depend on the existence of tables of equivalence – kisses for coins, virginity for marriage, money for goods. The language of exchange and dispossession that Behn uses marks not the irruption of an 'economic and political lexicon'; but the distance between our fallen usage and understanding and that lost, best age when all the signs for things we hoard, fear, or covert had free and joyous connotations. Above all, sexuality, contaminated and repressed by the economy of thrift and possession in the fallen world, is freed from economic connotations.[33] This is effected largely by replacing the penis from the processes of reproduction with images of a non-penetrative but fecund sexuality.

Despite the poem's sensual recreation of the pleasures of uninhibited heterosexual activity, a compelling strain of imagery suggests that this golden age and land is polymorphous in its sexuality, and unaware of and indifferent to sexual difference. In stanza 3, as in the Ovidian 'soft pastoral' versions of the Golden Age, the land is described as without husbandry. The earth is unpenetrated, 'The stubborn Plough had then / Made no rude Rapes upon the Virgin Earth' (ll. 31–2). Not only virgin, but also mother, the earth produces 'Without the Aids of men' (l. 34). Behn's earth virgin-mother is self-generating and contains without masculine intervention the principle of all sexuality: 'As if within her Teeming Womb / All Nature, and all Sexes lay' (ll. 35–6). What Behn offers here is a female reinscription of the traditional masculine vision of a land made perfect by its ability to reproduce itself in the absence of women.[34] But where that vision is of an asexuality sustained by a mystical misogyny associating heterosexuality with defilement, Behn's vision is rather of a displacement of an economic defilement of sexuality which then liberates heterosexuality, all sexuality, into free play and pleasure.

In response to Behn's vision of a spontaneous and polymorphous reproduction of nature, Markley and Rothenberg argue that women 'are written out of this myth of undifferentiated procreation'. To be more accurate about the processes of procreation, they argue, and present 'a positive image of unrepressed female desire' would be in seventeenth-century terms to 'confront the consequences of their sexual activity: pregnancy, the bearing of fatherless children, and the resultant challenges to the hereditary distribution of wealth, power and prestige'.[35] But it is not so much that women – or men – are being written out, but rather the cultural practices relating sexuality to the laborious drudgery of reproducing the social economy which are denied through the relocation of reproduction to one virgin womb. Since this womb functions without the intrusion of the penis what is being written out are those 'consequences' which in the fallen world the penis gathers to itself as the phallus. This is visionary, unreal, and in many ways a lie; however, it is a productive lie enabling the celebration of sexuality and procreation without reference to an economy of commodification, which, as I have argued, the entire poem locates as repressive of female desire.

The idea of a spontaneous and non-phallic sexuality is developed in the last lines of the third stanza, which describe the benevolence of the snakes in the paradise. In 'The Disappointment' Cloris withdrew her hand in horror, as from a snake, when she felt Lysander's limp penis. In 'The Golden Age', however, snakes signify neither sin nor masculinity, neither shame nor disdain, and neither the rampant nor the failed penis. Rather, the snakes–penises are revealed as charming toys with which the 'Nymphs did Innocently play' since 'No spightful Venom in the wantons lay; / But to the Touch were Soft, and to the sight were Gay' (3: ll. 46–8). Divorced from the economy of masculine power, the 'Soft' penis is not a mark of male shame and failure. It contains no 'Venom' – that problematic sperm – and it is not the object of female scorn but a thing of tactile pleasure and visual beauty, precisely because it has been removed from reproductive labour and positioned outside a phallocentric system. It does not need to be erect and to penetrate since earth does it all, all alone and on *her* own. In the ideal world Behn has depicted, all the masculine economies of wealth, social position, and sexual domination are bankrupt, or rather they are not yet bankrupt because, happily, they only exist within the sign system of the fallen world. Swain and lord are interchangeable terms, 'Conquerors' are 'Charming' (6: l. 104) not violent and take only what is freely given, and the processes of veiling, hiding, stinting and storing (8: ll. 126, 128, 132, 136) which commodify and repress female sexuality are unknown.

In 'The Golden Age', Behn avoids the contradictory significations that associate pleasure with debt, ejaculation with spending and waste, and inserts sexuality into a material and ideological economy of male power which is then threatened and contaminated by heterosexuality. The passionate physicality of Behn's visionary world of aroused sensual/sexual pleasure may be dependent upon displacing reproduction to the fantasy of spontaneous birth but it also disables the misogyny which is so much a part of sexual discourse which seeks to refuse commodification.[36] The excess associated with aristrocratic ease is retained but feminised as it lies within the 'Teeming Womb' of the virgin earth-mother. The vexed anxieties of denying the penis or fearfully entering the devouring and reproducing womb and either revealing its inadequacies or participating in laborious processes are replaced by images of soft playfulness. In the 'Golden Age', love/sex is polymorphous, 'uncontroul'd' (7: l. 105), and entirely free from the systems of homologous exchange between wealth, status and sexuality which so troubled the age. The clitoris, surely implied by the 'young opening Buds' which 'each moment grew' (3: l. 42), suggests a spontaneous pleasure and renewal dissociated from reproductive labour. 'Right and Property', reduced to 'words', are unknown (ll. 65–6), and 'Snakes securely' dwell 'Not doing harm, nor harm from others felt' (3: ll. 44–5) as Behn imagines an uneconomic era of mutuality and unrationed ever renewable pleasure. It is a world where man's penis is not yet a phallus.

From *Aphra Behn Studies*, ed. Janet Todd (Cambridge, 1996), pp. 178–96.

NOTES

[The article discusses two of Behn's pastoral poems, 'The Disappointment' and 'The Golden Age'. It relates them to a Restoration literature of anxiety over cavalier masculine sexual potency following defeat and the establishment of a new economic order. It argues that Behn offers a route through cultural anxieties centring on the erect or 'soft' penis, read as sign either of male enmeshment in productive labour or of inadequacy. Where 'The Disappointment' reverses conventional expectations, 'The Golden Age' erases all masculine signifiers of control and order, thus liberating women from sexual shame and commodification and allowing for a mutuality of desire and a permeability of gender itself. Ed.]

I am grateful to my colleagues Dianne Sadoff, David Suchoff, Susan Kenney and Gita Rajan, and to my sister Penny Richards, for their thoughtful reading of this essay, which has benefited from their comments. I am also grateful to Janet Todd for her editorial suggestions.

1. The dates given are publication dates. 'The Disappointment' was first published without attribution in *Poems on Several Occasions: By the Right Honourable, the E of R-*, [Antwerpen] 1680. It was reprinted with variations in Behn's *Poems Upon Several Occasions: with a Voyage to the Island of Love*, London, 1684. 'The Golden Age' appears in the same collection. All citations from Behn's poetry are taken from *The Works of Aphra Behn*, ed. Janet Todd, Vol. 1, *Poetry* (Columbus, OH, 1992). Unless otherwise stated, emphasis is as in the text.

2. Roger Thompson, *Unfit for Modest Ears: A Study of Pornographic, Obscene and Bawdy Works Written or Published in England in the Second Half of the Seventeenth Century* (London, 1979), I.105.

3. Giles Slade, 'The two-backed beast: eunuchs and priapus in *The Country Wife*', *Restoration and Eighteenth-Century Theatre Research*, second series, 7, 1 (1992), 23–43, 23.

4. J. G. A. Pocock, *Virtue, Commerce, and History: Essays on Political Thought and History. Chiefly in the Eighteenth Century* (Cambridge, 1985), p. 55. The recycling of Sir Robert Filmer's pre-war *Patriarcha*

(1680), as well as the considerable outpouring of patriarchal sermons, might also be taken as manifestations of crisis and anxiety over masculinity and political authority.

5. Giles Slade, 'The two-backed beast', 25, 27.

6. Richard Braverman, 'Economic "art" In Restoration verse: Etherege's "Cease Anxious World"', *Philological Quarterly*, 69: 3 (Summer 1990), 383–8, 384, 386. The recognition that wit (and birth) are not enough forms the basis of Susanna Centlivre's comedy, *A Bold Stoke for a Wife* (1718) which traces a conflict between various available modes of masculinity on a continuum from frugality to expenditure.

7. For a discussion of the penis/phallus equation see Jane Gallop, *The Daughter's Seduction: Feminism and Psychoanalsysis* (Ithaca, NY, 1982), p. 97. See also Gallop's essay, 'Phallus/penis: same difference', in *Men by Women, Women and Literature*, Vol. 2, n. s., ed. Janet Todd (New York and London, 1981), pp. 243–51.

8. Jean-Joseph Goux, *Symbolic Economies: After Marx and Freud*, trans. Jennifer Curtiss Gage (Ithaca, NY 1990), pp. 27–8.

9. Jean-Joseph Goux, *Symbolic Economies*, pp. 28–9.

10. The reversal of positions was noted in earlier works responding to social reconfigurations in terms of a market economy. In a review of Douglas Bruster's *Drama and the Market in the Age of Shakespeare* (Cambridge, 1992), Peter Bradshaw notes, 'Bruster writes that wives' conjugal duties were seen on and off the stage as a form of sexual labour, which the complaisant cuckold could lease to other men for financial advantage. Thus the eroticism of the pagan "horn of plenty" is transmuted into a cuckold's horn of profitability', *Times Literary Supplement*, 12 February 1993, p. 12. For dramas in which women buy male sexuality, see, for instance, John Dryden's *The Wild Gallant* (1669), Aphra Behn's *The Rover* (1677), and Thomas Otway's *The Souldiers Fortune* (1680).

11. Otway's *Friendship in Fashion* (1677), offers a representative example as a male character explains that men defame women 'to beat down the Market' and a female character warns that men should take care 'lest you over-reach yourselves, and repent of your purchase when 'tis too late' (2. ll. 127, 220–2). See also his brutally financial 'proviso' scene between Sylvia and Courtine in *The Souldiers Fortune* (1680).

12. John Wilmot, Earl of Rochester, 'Song' (1680) from *The Complete Poems of John Wilmot, Earl of Rochester*, ed. David M. Vieth (New Haven and London, 1968). All citations from Rochester's work are taken from this edition.

13. See Richard Quaintance's essay 'French sources of the imperfect enjoyment poems', *Philological Quarterly*, 42 (1963), 190–9.

14. Anon, 'One writing against his prick', *The Penguin Book of Restoration Verse*, ed. Harold Love (Harmondsworth, 1968), p. 184.

15. *The Poems of Sir George Etherege*, ed. James Thorpe (Princeton, NJ, 1963). Etherege's poem is based on Charles Beys's 'La Iovissance Imparfaite. Caprice', published in *Les Oeuvres Poetiques du Sieur Beys* (Paris, 1652).

16. As Janet Todd points out in her notes to the poem, Behn alters the location and situation from the original which takes place in an urban bedroom while the young wife's husband is absent, *The Works of Aphra Behn*, ed. Janet Todd, 1, *Poetry*, p. 393.

17. Bellamira consoles her lover for his impotence by telling him that she likes him 'the better for it' since his failure is due to his faithful love for another woman (IV, vi, 20–2), *Bellamira, or The Mistress*, in *The Poetical and Dramatic Works of Sir Charles Sedley*, 2 vols, ed V. De Sola Pinto (1928; rpt, New York, 1969).

18. As Dustin Griffin notes, 'clammy joys' is 'an elegant periphrasis ... both apt and mock-formal' as the speaker begins to 'poke fun at himself', *Satires Against Man: The Poems of Rochester* (Berkeley, Los Angeles; London, 1973), p. 97. The formality of the mockery inscribes those expectations of control and success which have been so surprisingly denied.

19. Not only in 'imperfect enjoyment' poems, but generally there are numerous derogatory references to the vagina; see, for instance, Rochester's description of Corinna as a 'passive pot for fools to spend in' (*A Ramble in St James's Park*, l. 102).

20. Harold Weber, '"Drudging in fair Aurelia's womb": Constructing Homosexual Economies in Rochester's Poetry', *The Eighteenth Century: Theory and Interpretation*, 33: 2(1992), 99–117.

21. In de Cantenac's poem, the lover returns the next day and satisfactorily makes love to his mistress.

22. Giles Slade, 'The two-backed beast', 31.

23. Jean-Joseph Goux, *Symbolic Economies*, p. 209.

24. Robert Markley and Molly Rothenberg, 'Contestations of nature', in *Rereading Aphra Behn: History, Theory, and Criticism*, ed. Heidi Huttner (Charlottesville and London, 1993), pp. 301–21, 319.

25. Robert Markley and Molly Rothenberg, 'Contestations of nature', p. 307.

26. Raymond Williams, *The Country and the City* (London, 1973), pp. 27–34.

27. Robert Markley and Molly Rothenberg, 'Contestations of nature', pp. 308–9.

28. Markley and Rothenberg, 'Contestations of nature', p. 314.

29. In Sir Charles Sedley's Golden Age poem, *The Happy Pair: or, A Poem on Matrimony* (1702), Adam is indifferent to the wealth that lies around him: 'The Daz'ling Di'mond wanted Influence / Pearls, like the Common Gravel, he contemn'd' (ll. 17–19), *The Poetical and Dramatic Works of Sir Charles Sedley*, vol. 1, pp. 65–73.

30. Robert Markley and Molly Rothenberg, 'Contestations of nature', p. 305.

31. No one in their right minds would see an English spring as affording large opportunities for lolling easily beneath flowering trees. The landscape and the season are conventional and drawn from the Southern European pastorals and bucolics of Theocritus, Ovid, Virgil and Horace. For an example of a specifically English pastoral landscape, see Jonson's 'To Penshurst', which has its own and rather different political agenda.

32. Markley and Rothenberg, 'Contestations of nature', p. 305.

33. In Sedley's *The Happy Pair*, in the fallen world, contemplation of property produces impotence and 'when in Bed he should Embrace his Spouse, / Like a Dull Ox, he's still amongst the Cows' (ll. 267–8).

34. See Harold Weber's discussion of this trope in '"Drudging in fair Aurelia's womb",' 112–13, which draws on James Grantham Turner's *One Flesh: Paradisal Marriage and Sexual Relations in the Age of Milton* (Oxford, 1987).

35. Robert Markley and Molly Rothenberg, 'Contestations of nature', p. 307.

36. See Felicity Nussbaum on the outpouring of misogynistic verse during the Restoration, *The Brink of All We Hate* (Lexington, KY, 1984).

6

Desire and the Uncoupling of Myth in Behn's Erotic Poems

CAROL BARASH

Behn's erotic poems play different mythic narratives off one another to create the possibility of female desire, a place where the female sexual subject enters the fundamentally male traditions of erotic poetry. By 'erotic poems', I mean poems of erotic address, as well as poems that situate themselves as part of ongoing sexual (or sexualised) narratives. One early lyric, 'I led my *Silvia* to a grove', first published in the *Covent Garden Drollery* (1672), speaks from an ungendered but implicitly male point of view:

> I led my *Silvia* to a Grove,
> Where all the Boughs did shade us,
> The sun it self, though it had strove,
> It could not have betray'd us.
>
> ...
>
> A many kisses I did give,
> And she return'd the same,
> Which made her willing to receive
> That which I dare not name.
>
> My greedy eyes no ayds requir'd,
> To tell their amorous Tale:
> On her that was already fir'd,
> 'Twas easie to prevail.

I did but kiss and claspe her round
Whilst they my thoughts exprest,
And laid her gently on the ground:
Oh! who can guess the rest.
　　　　　(ll. 1–4, 13–24)[1]

Based on a manuscript version of this poem called 'A Song for J. H.'
(i.e. John Hoyle) and the poem's elusive ending, Bernard
Duyfhuizen argues that 'I led my Silvia' is a homo-erotic poem,
written to another woman. He also suggests that Behn's 'that which
I dare not name' foreshadows Alfred, Lord Douglas's 'love that dare
not speak its name'.[2] However appealing Duyfhuizen's reading may
be, there is no way to read female-female erotic address from the
poem itself. So that if the poem is (at some personal level) addressed
to another woman, there is no way to mark that as a public
meaning. A later version of the poem, 'The Willing Mistress', first
published in *The Dutch Lover* (1673), explicitly recrafts the story
from the female lover's point of view:

Amyntas *led me to a grove,*
　Where all the Trees did shade us:
　　…

A many kisses he did give,
　And I return'd the same:
Which made me willing to receive,
　That which I dare not name.

His charming eyes no aid requir'd,
　To tell their amorous tale;
On her that was already fir'd,
　'Twas easie to prevail.

He did but kiss, and clasp me round,
　Whilst they his thoughts exprest,
And laid me gently on the ground;
　Ah! who can guess the rest?[3]

While the change to a female speaker heightens the heterosexual
economy of the poem, it also makes possible the inscription of
active female desire.

There is in Behn no natural or universal category 'woman', nor
can women's desire simply be expressed. Her speaker claims in 'On
Desire. A Pindarick' that women veil their desire in order to uphold
'the false disguise' of Honour:

Tell me, yee fair ones, that exchange desire,
  How tis you hid the kindling fire.
  Oh! wou'd you but confess the truth,
It is not real virtue makes you nice:
But when you do resist the pressing youth,
'Tis want of dear desire, to thaw the Virgin Ice.

  ...

And the soft yeilding soul that wishes in your Eyes?
  While to th'admiring crow'd you nice are found;
  Some dear, some secret, youth that gives the wound
Informs you, all your virtu's but a cheat
  And Honour but a false disguise,
  Your modesty a necessary bait
To gain the dull repute of being wise.
                    (ll. 89–94 and 100–6)[4]

The metaphoric language here is similar to 'Oenone to Paris' (the 'kindling fire' of love, the contests between lovers' eyes). 'On Desire' elaborates the doubleness and disguise involved in the contest between desire and honour and links that doubleness to the situation of the woman writer. 'On Desire' has multiple subjects and audiences: desire is addressed as 'Pain', 'spright', 'Phantom', and 'nimble fire'; the poem then speaks to 'Philosophers' and, finally, to women. The speaker of 'On Desire' establishes a community with the female dissemblers described above, and connects her story of desire to theirs:

Deceive the foolish World——deceive it on,
  And veil your passions in your pride;
But now I've found your feebles by my own,
From me the needful fraud you cannot hide.
                    (151; ll. 107–10)

'On Desire' ends by linking the narrator's own desires with the story of Helen and Paris. Once again Behn's speaker is attracted to Helen's dissembling and suggests that admitting the story of Helen's adulterous desire would change the meaning (we might say the cultural history) of desire.

  In what is often read as an explicitly homo-erotic love poem, 'To the fair *Clarinda*, who made Love to me, imagin'd more than Woman', there is no space free from cultural codes, from naming:[5]

Fair lovely Maid, or if that Title be
Too weak, too Feminine for Nobler thee,
Permit a Name that more Approaches Truth:
And let me call thee, Lovely Charming Youth.
This last will justifie my soft complaint,
While that may serve to lessen my constraint;
And without Blushes I the Youth persue,
When so much beauteous Woman is in view.
Against thy Charms we struggle but in vain
With thy deluding Form thou giv'st us pain,
While the bright Nymph betrays us to the Swain.
In pity to our Sex sure thou wer't sent,
That we might Love, and yet be Innocent:
For sure no Crime with thee we can commit;
Or if we shou'd – thy Form excuses it.
For who, that gathers fairest Flowers believes
A Snake lies hid beneath the Fragrant Leaves.
    Thou beauteous Wonder of a different kind,
Soft *Cloris* with the dear *Alexis* join'd;
When e'r the Manly part of thee, wou'd plead
Thou tempts us with the Image of the Maid,
While we the noblest Passions do extend
The love to *Hermes*, *Aphrodite* the Friend.[6]

The relationship between the two women is framed and defined by a world in which gender dualism is law. From the very first line gender is introduced as part of reading and relating to the other, even to another woman: 'Fair lovely Maid, or if that *Title* be | Too weak ... | Permit a *Name* that more Approaches Truth' (emphasis added).[7]

    The speaker heterosexualises her erotic attraction to another woman by imagining first that she herself is a man and Clarinda is a woman. The name Clarinda is itself multiple, troping both on Philips's Orinda and on the source of that name, the female knight Clorinda from Tasso's *Gerusalemme Liberata* (1581). Calling Clarinda a sexually ambiguous 'Charming Youth', Behn's speaker then 'persue[s]' her, breaking social codes about women's 'modesty' or passivity in love. Clarinda's beauty is heightened by the hyper-feminine 'Charms' and metamorphic 'deluding Form' with which she attracts the speaker:

    Against thy Charms we struggle but in vain
    With thy deluding Form thou giv'st us pain,
    While the bright Nymph betrays us to the Swain.

Behn's speaker suggests the more problematic implications of Clarinda's 'deluding Form': while, on the one hand, it is no 'Crime' for a woman to love another woman, even the speaker has not imagined that the female sexual body is snakelike, phallic, or – to be precise – clitoral:

> For sure no Crime with thee we can commit;
> Or if we should – thy Form excuses it.
> For who, that gathers fairest Flowers believes
> A Snake lies hid beneath the Fragrant Leaves.

While the female 'Form' of Clarinda's body seems at first to thwart the speaker's sexual aggression, when that 'Form' is revealed to be female, it proves the relationship sexual after all. The poem moves from name to form to body as that aspect which defines the women's relationship, and it is as textual body that the relationship is finally resolved.

By invoking the mythic pair, Hermes and Aphrodite, at the end of the poem, Behn pushes gender dualism to its logical conclusion, playfully dismantling Ovid's Hermaphroditus into the warring intentions of his/her parents.[8] Where Ovid's myth explains the creation of a body that is sexually both male and female, the desire of Behn's speaker for another woman becomes possible by undoing Ovid's mythical union.[9] Splitting Hermaphroditus into Hermes and Aphrodite allows Behn to transgress the boundaries the speaker invoked earlier between male and female, both to '[gather] ... fairest flowers' and to extend 'noblest passions' to the 'snake ... beneath the Fragrant Leaves'. This love poem to another woman is more clearly encoded in terms of male and female oppositions than any of Behn's heterosexual love poems. The more rigidly gender and sexuality are mapped onto real physical bodies, however, the more manipulable and unstable the categories become. If Clarinda is both maid and youth, both Hermes and Aphrodite, then men and women can no longer be understood as oppositionally 'nymph' and 'swain'. Behn has turned a grammatical either/or into a sexual both/and by dismembering Ovidian myth.[10]

'To the fair *Clarinda*' is one of several poems in which Behn challenges the limits of love in a social and linguistic system that places men and women sexually at war. Almost all of these poems are, on the surface, heterosexual, and Behn is perhaps most daring in inhabiting the male gaze on women so persistently and in so many different guises. Behn's erotic poems construct female subjectivity through strategies of redefining and remapping the relationship between female sexual experience and male-defined linguistic forms and meanings. The dismembering of Ovidian myth in 'To the fair *Clarinda*', the shifting narrative tenses of 'The Disappointment' and 'Oenone to Paris', and the multiple audiences of 'On Desire' all work to multiply and confound cultural narratives of gender and sexuality, and to create positions from which the woman writer can challenge the literary codes she inherits. As Rose Zimbardo correctly shows, the narrator of Behn's fiction is in a position of cultural authority, aligned with modern ways of knowing that distance, objectify, and control by looking.[11] Behn's political poems attempt a similar but more complicated gesture, aligning their authority with the pleasure and spectacle of the female monarch.

From Carol Barash, *English Women's Poetry, 1649–1714: Politics, Community, and Linguistic Authority* (Oxford, 1996), pp. 124–9.

NOTES

[Carol Barash argues that Behn's erotic poems allow the desiring female subject to enter what is traditionally a male preserve. She insists that Behn has no fixed category of 'woman' and that woman's desire cannot simply be expressed. She ends with an analysis of one of Behn's most intriguing and startling poems, 'To the fair Clarinda, who made Love to me, imagin'd more than Woman'. Ed.]

1. G. Thorn-Drury (ed.), *Covent Garden Drollery* (London, 1672; repr. London, 1928, pp. 92–3.

2. Bernard Duyfhuizen, 'That which I dare not name: Aphra Behn's "The Willing Mistress"', *English Literary History*, 58 (1991), 73–5.

3. Aphra Behn, *The Dutch Lover: A Comedy* (London, 1673), pp. 27–8.

4. 'On Desire. A Pindarick', in the poems appended to *Lycidus; or, the Lover in Fashion* (London, 1688), pp. 150–1. Subsequent references to this edition are included in the text; line numbers from Todd, *Complete Works of Aphra Behn* (London, 1992–6), I, 281–4.

5. Behn's emphasis on the material world – and language as part of the material world – is in direct contrast to Katherine Philips's spiritually directed erotic poems. While Philips's poems from 'Orinda' to 'Lucasia' claim that love between women exists separate from marriage, language, and other legal and economic ties to men, the poems

show how her ideal cannot, finally, circumvent the laws of marriage and erotic discourse. In Philips's poems the sexualised 'friendship' between Orinda and Lucasia also figures for the ideal of royalist community in exile. There is not one mythical or cultural space in which 'women's' relationships exist; rather such relationships are situated in relation to the conflicts and inequalities of the larger social order.

6. 'To the fair *Clarinda*' is the last of the poems appended to *Lycidus; or, the Lover in Fashion*, pp. 175–6.

7. Duyfhuizen, 'That which I dare not name', 73–9, suggests that both 'The Willing Mistress' and 'To the fair *Clarinda*' obliquely inscribe the speaker's attraction to other women, 'that which [she] dare not name'; he notes the importance of both looking and naming in several of Behn's erotic poems.

8. Ovid, *Metamorphoses*, iv. 285–388.

9. Behn vigorously rejects the themes of sexual mixing and sexual pollution that pervade Ovid's original. While the idea of the hermaphrodite exists before Ovid (e.g. Plato's *Symposium*), Ovid was the first to narrate the story of the hermaphrodite as the union of Aphrodite and Hermes. See E. F. Kenney, notes to A. D. Melville's translation of Ovid, *Metamorphoses* (Oxford and New York, 1986), p. 398, where he suggests that Ovid makes the story of Salmacis and Hermaphroditus parallel to that of Echo and Narcissus; for the shifting cultural meanings of the hermaphrodite in eighteenth-century Europe, see Julia Epstein, 'Either/Or – Neither/Both: Sexual Ambiguity and the Ideology of Gender', *Genders*, 7 (1990), 99–142.

10. Maureen Duffy, *The Passionate Shepherdess: Aphra Behn 1640–89* (London, 1976), p. 150; and Ros Ballaster, *Seductive Forms: Women's Amatory Fiction from 1684 to 1746* (Oxford, 1992), pp. 75–6, both argue that 'To the fair *Clarinda*' is about a man in drag (perhaps Behn's faithless bisexual lover, John Hoyle). While their readings are plausible and useful, it is important to note that problems of gender and naming introduced in 'To the fair *Clarinda*' are not resolved in the poem itself via references to fact, but by overlapping figurative – and mythic – references. So even if Hoyle – or, more generally, transvestism around the Restoration stage – is the poem's occasion, the literal ultimately provides no linguistic solution to the pleasures of sexual ambiguity described and enacted in the poem.

11. Rose Zimbardo, 'Aphra Behn in Search of a Novel', *Studies in Eighteenth-Century Culture*, 19 (1989) 277.

7

Gender and Narrative in the Fiction of Aphra Behn

JACQUELINE PEARSON

Aphra Behn is still a neglected writer, and even among those critics who have given her work more than a passing acknowledgement there is a striking lack of consensus about the nature and extent of her achievement, especially in her fiction.[1] She has been praised as innovative and original: Robert Adams Day thus finds *Oroonoko* 'entirely original' in its narrative methods and praises its 'astonishing innovations'.[2] On the other hand, many accounts of the rise of the novel ignore or understate her contribution: Ian Watt's classic study, *The Rise of the Novel*, makes only two brief references, and even in a full-length study of Behn's work, F. M. Link finds her fiction unoriginal and concludes that she 'made no significant contribution to the development of the [novel] form'.[3] And if there is little agreement on questions of originality and influence, there is no more on the themes of the novels. *Oroonoko*, for instance, has been seen as expressing 're-publican prejudices', or as demonstrating a strongly royalist viewpoint, or both.[4] There is especially a lack of consensus on Behn's treatment of gender: some critics find her a vigorous feminist, making 'suffragette' claims for women,[5] while others argue that she compromised with a male-dominated literary establishment and that her work consequently displays a 'masculine set of values'.[6]

A high proportion of recent criticism of Behn's fiction adopts a naïvely literalist reading, taking *Oroonoko* and even *The Fair Jilt* and other tales quite simply as self-revelation, as direct autobiography.[7] As a result of, and a reaction against, this kind of reading, the most promising recent reassessments have focused on the role of the narrators.[8] The narrator has been seen to provide circumstantial detail, local colour, a vivid immediacy, and a 'breezy colloquial quality',[9] to offer 'a viable standard of judgement for the readers', to unify the novel and involve the reader emotionally in the narrative, and also 'to attest the truth of the whole story'.[10] I shall argue, however, that the situation is still more complex, and that the narrator, who is not coterminous with 'Aphra Behn', is a complex and subtle part of Behn's treatment, both open and implied, of issues of gender and power. In order to do this, I shall briefly examine the strategies with the narrator in a range of Behn's fiction, before going on to a fuller analysis of the role of the narrator in *Oroonoko*.

I

In Behn's fourteen fictions, the narrator is never definitely male: six give no clue to gender, though she sometimes seems to be female by implication,[11] and in eight, 'The Unfortunate Happy Lady', *Oroonoko*, *The History of the Nun*, 'The Nun', 'The Lucky Mistake', 'The Unfortunate Bride', 'The Wandering Beauty', and 'The Unhappy Mistake', she is definitely female. In the simplest cases the female sex of the narrator lends an authority to her accounts of women's lives and natures, and reflects the empowering of women, or the mockery of men, within the narratives. In more complex tales, the female narrator is depicted, like the female characters, as embedded within patriarchy and limited by it. These women are torn by contradictions, powerful and governing within their fictions, powerless outside them, and their narratives are deeply coloured, even undermined, by these contradictions. What they present as simple narratives, entertaining stories or moral tales, turn out to encode quite different meanings, more sinister, revealing, and subversive, over which the narrators have less perfect control. Narrators are given to Freudian slips, unnoticed and unacknowledged self-contradiction, uncomfortable ambivalences, not fully articulated, about the tales they tell. It is these complex, uncomfortable, flawed, or even duplicitous narrators who are Behn's most effective tool in her analysis of patriarchy.

The most obvious of the contradictions imported by the narrators is their misogyny, paradoxically most apparent in the case of specifically female narrators. Tales may condemn female weakness, like 'The Nun', or celebrate female strength, like 'The Unfortunate Happy Lady', yet in both the female narrator displays an oddly masculine misogyny: 'our Sex seldom wants matter of Tattle', 'how wretched are our Sex, in being the unhappy Occasion of so many fatal Mischiefs', ''tis the humour of our Sex, to deny most eagerly those Grants to Lovers, for which most tenderly we sigh, so contradictory are we to our selves'.[12] The authority of the female narrator is thus used, paradoxically, to give an authoritative insider's view of female weakness, as the female narrator seeks male approval by attacking her own sex or by modest self-deprecation. Such ambiguities are perhaps best understood as the result of the self-divisions – 'so contradictory are we to our selves' – experienced by the female narrator, anxious to succeed within a male-dominated literary establishment and consequently obliged to accept its standards, and yet also, sometimes admittedly, sometimes not, highly critical of that male world and its male inhabitants.

The language of the narrators is important in establishing these contradictions. It is typically marked by apparent humility or self-deprecation, though this is often actually 'a means of self-assertion and a means of commenting upon the limited roles that women are expected to play'.[13] This can be seen especially in the use of apparently or mockingly humble adverbs, like 'perhaps' or 'possibly'. These adverbs appear to create an allegedly female tentativeness,[14] though one very often suspects irony in this apparent self-deprecation, since it actually creates a playful knowingness, often exploited for erotic effect. In 'The Unfortunate Happy Lady' the assumed naïvety of the female narrator's voice touchingly and humorously dramatises the real innocence of her heroine Philadelphia, and we hear simultaneously the two polarised female voices of the tale, the innocent and the experienced: 'She apprehended, that (possibly) her Brother had a Mistress ...' (p. 45). A similar device can be seen in 'The Court of the King of Bantam', where the narrator assumes an apparent coy and tentative tone which is actually playfully revealing and which asserts her authority over even the 'unfeminine' explicitness of the tale: '... her Bed. Where I think fit to leave 'em for the present; for (perhaps) they had some private Business' (pp. 31–2).

Similarly, the narrator's claims to ignorance demonstrate not so much narrative failure as the cool and perfect control of the gentlewoman-amateur, an exasperating mockery of the reader for our need for detail, verisimilitude, and coherent narrative structure:

'The rest I have forgot', 'I had forgot to tell you ...', 'I had forgot to tell my Reader ...'.[15] In light tales like 'The Court of the King of Bantam' the narrator's apparent lack of authority and of certain knowledge on some details serves to comic effect. Here the narrator is not specifically female, and may possibly be, by implication, male ('my Friend the Count', p. 27; 'In less Time than I could have drank a Bottle to my Share', p. 30). If this is so, the apparent imperfection of his narrative authority would serve to parallel the tale's mockery of Sir Would-be King and the travesty of patriarchal authority that he represents. In more serious tales, and where the narrator is more explicitly female, the effect can, as we shall see, be different. The narrator may, for instance, deliberately limit her field of expertise. Thus in *The History of the Nun*, the female narrator concentrates on her story of passion and moral paradox, for 'it is not my business to relate the History of the War' (p. 304) which provides a background; or a possibly female narrator will point out the imperfections and inconsistencies in presumably male authorities – 'Some authors, in the relation of this battle, affirm, that *Philander* quitted his post as soon as the charge was given ...'.[16] Writing in a world where female authorship was the subject of a vigorous and largely hostile scrutiny by the representatives of the dominant culture, Behn has her female narrators humbly accede to the view that female creativity should be confined to certain fields, but this transparently ironic humility does not so much accept the conventional limitations as draw mocking attention to them. 'History' may be the locus of a specifically male authority, but male 'authors' are mocked by implication for the imperfectness of *their* authority.

Behn's narrators also offer a critique of the inequalities encoded in the gendered language of society. Some words are revealed to have different meanings depending on whether applied to male or female subjects. Thus Sylvia would be 'undone' by losing her virginity, while Philander is 'undone' by failing to have sex and proving impotent at his first encounter with her.[17] *Love Letters*, and many other Behn tales and plays, criticise society's language of gender not only by explicit statements of the equality of men and women – they respond to sexual passion with 'equal fire, with equal languishment', with 'equal ravishment' (*LL*, pp. 53, 243) – but also by allowing women to appropriate for their own uses a sexual vocabulary in which they have previously been the objects of male language. Thus men can be 'beautiful' and 'lovely' in the eyes of women as much as women can in the eyes of men,[18] women are conventionally addressed by men as 'charmer', but the word can also, more unconventionally, be used by women of men,[19] and while Behn does not explicitly reject the conventional belief that women are 'the soft ... Sex',[20] she also allows sympathetic males to display 'softness'.[21] *Love Letters* and other tales thus imply a biological equality between the sexes, but also allow their narrators to explore the socially constructed inequalities.

II

Behn's narrators, then, are often specifically female. The implied reader may also be female, as she is invited to enter closed female worlds of nunnery or brothel. A female reader is constructed within the text, by, for instance, Behn's use of the first person plural, which is not the authorial 'we' and contrasts sharply with the narrator's jauntily individualistic 'I', but which implies a female reader and a sympathetic complicity between her and the author – 'how wretched are our sex ...' (A similar device can be found in Behn's plays: in the prologue to her first performed play, *The Forc'd Marriage* (1670), women in the audience are identified as 'Spies' for the 'Poetess'.[22]) Behn's dedication of work to individual women also suggests that she aimed for a female readership: the printed text of *The Feign'd Curtezans* (1679) is dedicated, for instance, to Nell Gwyn, and *The History of the Nun* to Hortense Mancini, Duchess of Mazarine. The historical evidence, fragmentary though it is, also suggests that many women read Behn's work. Almost all women writers between the 1670s and the middle of the eighteenth century are aware of Behn's example and had probably read some of her works: Anne Finch knew Behn's work as a poet, Catherine Trotter had read *Agnes de Castro*, which she adapted for the stage in 1695, Jane Barker had by 1726 read at least *The History of the Nun* and 'The Wandering Beauty', which she retells in *The Lining of the Patchwork Screen*, and many other women writers refer to Behn and her work.[23] Mary Wortley Montagu, whose reading is better documented than that of most women, was acquainted with Behn's *The Emperor of the Moon*, knew her poems well enough to quote two of them, fifteen years apart, and had probably also read *Oroonoko*.[24] In the mid-eighteenth century *Oroonoko* was adapted and included in one of the first women's magazines, thus reaching a still wider middle-class audience.[25] And, to take a final, celebrated example, Mrs Keith of Ravelstone, as a young girl in London in about the

1760s, heard Behn's novels 'read aloud for the amusement of large circles of the first and most creditable society'.[26] The female reader is both constructed within the text and a historical reality outside it.

However, while Behn expected and encouraged women to read her tales, her female narrators sometimes imply, image, or address specifically male readers, often for critical or ironic purposes. The tales are full of female authors, writers, narrators, actors, orators, and painters, producing works which are shown consumed by a specifically male public. Laura Brown, for instance, has read *Oroonoko* as a text crucially on race and on the imperialist commodification of the goods, peoples, and texts of the New World, in which the female narrator and other female characters become the 'consumers' of the 'heroic drama' which centres on Oroonoko.[27] But this tale, and others, rather depict males as consumers of female texts. *Oroonoko* is presented as a text specifically authored by a female and presented to a male readership: 'my Reader, in a World where he finds Diversions for every Minute' (p. 129). Male power operates through a consumption of female texts: the female services but does not alter a male world of power and privilege. The female narrator's gift of Indian clothing is seen as supporting the authority and verisimilitude of male-authored fictions: 'I gave 'em to the *King's Theatre*; it was the Dress of the *Indian Queen* ...' (p. 130). Dryden's play thus consumes female texts, gifts, and clothes, maintaining its own kingly (as the name of the theatre punningly reveals) authority only the more completely since, paradoxically, the centre of the male-authored text is a powerful female, whose power in fiction can be allowed less ambiguous play than that of the 'real' female narrator. Still, if images of female authors and male consumers can offer a glum parallel to a real world of male domination and female oppression, Behn can also use such images more subversively. The narrator entertains Oroonoko by telling him 'the Lives of the *Romans*, and great Men' (p. 175). The balance of power in the previously cited example is reversed: as the male (Dryden) uses the alien 'Other' (the Indian Queen) as the medium of his own authority with the support of the female (the narrator), here the female (the narrator) uses the alien 'Other' (Romans) to maintain her own authority over the male (Oroonoko).

When the English Captain invites Oroonoko aboard his ship and then kidnaps the prince into slavery, the female narrator again adds her own comment directly aimed at the male reader: 'Some have commended this Act, as brave in the Captain; but I will spare my Sense of it, and leave it to my Reader to judge as he pleases'

(p. 162). The female narrator implies a strong moral disapproval, but presents her male readers as less moral, male criteria of judgement being potentially very different from their female equivalents. Behn's female narrator may seem to privilege the male, with her 'incessantly apologetic' tone and 'self-deprecation':[28] but her images of male power dependent on female power, and her attack on male moral judgements, actually mock that apparent privileging, and her male readers themselves.

Other tales also proliferate images of female authors and narrators and their male audiences, especially foolish, impotent, or ineffective male audiences. Thus in 'The Court of the King of Bantam', the foolish Would-be King has developed his delusion because 'it seems [he] had often been told ... either by one of his Nurses, or his own Grandmother, or by some other Gypsy, that he should infallibly be ... a King' (p. 14). Female narrative creates and controls male behaviour. In a more ambiguous example, Miranda in *The Fair Jilt* falsely accuses the Friar of attempted rape, and authors a series of elaborate fictions by which she persuades 'the good men' who hear that 'all she had spoken was Truth' (p. 95). It is a typical Behn irony that as Miranda authors and stages these fictions, she attempts to persuade her male hearers that the innocent Friar is in fact the 'Author' (p. 96) of her suffering.

The tales, then, are full of female authors. The female narrators are themselves specifically authors. Especially in the more tragic tales, they compensate for the failure of their authority in the action by displacing the catastrophic events of their 'real' lives into controllable aesthetic worlds. In 'The Dumb Virgin', where the female narrator cannot prevent the tragic action of incest and death, she takes the name of the doomed hero, Dangerfield, and uses it in 'a Comedy of mine' (p. 429), and in *Oroonoko*, where the 'Authority' (p. 198) of the female narrator fails to save the hero, she none the less is able to take the name of Col. Martin and present him as 'a Character of my new Comedy, by his own Name' (ibid.). Female authority, which fails in the real world, can in autonomous worlds of art convert tragic action into 'Comedy'.

Other female characters also exercise their authority/authorship in literary terms. They naturally reach for 'Pen and Paper' (Maria in 'The Dumb Virgin', p. 436), they own writing-desks (ibid.) and books (Atlante in 'The Lucky Mistake' owns 'a Book ... of the Story of *Ariadne and Theseus*' [p. 381] and 'a very fine Book ... of ... Philosophy' [p. 366], and Sylvia in *Love Letters* is well-read, even taking 'a little novel' with her to read in bed with her latest conquest [p. 413]!). These women gain control of male writings, as Moorea in 'The Unfortunate Bride' intercepts Frankwit's letters, or Sylvia gains control of the 'writings' of Sebastian's estate (p. 301), or has a key to Philander's 'tablets' (p. 42) which enables her to read his letters: such women are directly parallel to the female narrators, who seek also to gain access to literary languages dominated by men. Behn's female characters are inveterate letter-writers, like Sylvia, who not only writes letters but also uses her pen-knife to ward off unwanted suitors (p. 151). Others are poets, like Maria in 'The Dumb Virgin', or Belvira in 'The Unfortunate Bride'.

On the other hand, Behn's female heroes may reflect the activities of the narrator more indirectly, by exercising their authorship not over texts but over the real world, like Miranda in *The Fair Jilt*, or Isabella in *The History of the Nun*, or Arabella in 'The Wandering Beauty', all of whom author elaborate fictions in their own lives: and Arabella is potentially the 'Author' of the 'Happiness' of the man she marries (p. 456). Male authorship is often thwarted or malign: Trefry fails to write his intended biography of Oroonoko, Dangerfield by inadvertent incest is 'the fatal Author of so many Misfortunes' (p. 444), the authority of male authors is uncertain and inconsistent (*Amours*, p. 455), Frankwit's letters to Belvira go astray, and Cesario (= Monmouth) tries to gain forgiveness for his treason but in his letters 'his style was altered, and debased' (*Amours*, p. 458). Male authors fail, female authors gain a control, however ambiguous or contradictory, over literary texts or the world in which they move.

In Behn's fictional worlds, women do not only author texts: they *are* texts. As a cautious woman tells her insistent lover, 'Women enjoy'd, are like Romances read ... which, when found out, you only wonder at your selves for wondering so before at them' (p. 407). The female author creates a female narrator who creates a female poet and letter-writer who fears her lover regards her as a text, consuming her as a commodity without regard to her own desires. The tale in which she appears, 'The Unfortunate Bride', is preoccupied with female power and powerlessness, and Belvira's romance with the man who reads her like a book ends tragically. A slightly more positive example, though also with a tragic ending, can be found in 'The Dumb Virgin', where the mute heroine, who cannot author herself in language, is a 'great Proficient in Painting'. When a famous male painter proves incapable of painting her because he is blinded by her beauty, she is 'vexed' at his 'Weakness', and 'took up his Pencils and the Picture, and ... finished it herself' (p. 425). Maria refuses to be simply the object of art, 'a Wond'rous Piece of Art' (p. 436), as her lover sees her, but insists on being the active subject too, authoring herself as the male painter fails to do. Still, the fates of both these female texts/canvasses/pieces of art are unfortunate; caught between subject and object, between experiencing themselves as active and being seen as consumable commodities, 'Romances read', 'a ... Piece of Art', death seems the only resolution their female narrators can find to these painful self-divisions.

III

Behn's tales, then, proliferate images of female authors and narrators and male readers, and thereby create complex paradoxes about female power and powerlessness. More important, Behn creates narrators who either speak with a consciously ironic voice to reveal the contradictions in the received orthodoxies of gender, or unconsciously reveal themselves as victims of these very contradictions.

One of the most striking roles of the narrator, indeed, is not so much to offer 'a viable standard of judgement'[29] on the fiction and its characters, as to undercut conventional moral judgements even as these are apparently made. For example, in 'The Dumb Virgin; or, The Force of Imagination' the narrator works to subvert the repressive ideologies of gender apparently endorsed by the fiction. The wife of Rinaldo unwisely risks her safety and that of her son by sailing to a resort island; her husband allows her to go although he fears for her safety, 'his love not permitting him the least shew of command' (p. 421). The implication is that women need firm male control. As a result, her ship is attacked by pirates, and her son lost. For women, the 'Force of Imagination' is malign: Maria's mother causes her dumbness and the physical deformity of her sister by the action of her imagination ('Frights and dismal Apprehensions ... Silence and Melancholy', p. 424) on the babies in the womb, and Maria's forceful imagination makes her vulnerable to seduction and inadvertent incest. The tale's message is apparently repressive to women, since female autonomy, for Maria as for her mother, is likely to prove disastrous. At the same time, the presence of the female[30] narrator presents a counter-message, as her powerful imagination creates the text and subverts it.

This tendency of the narrator to undercut the moral apparently offered by her narrative is at its clearest in tales focusing on powerful, wicked women. The surface of the text will condemn them ('the Devil in the Flesh', 'the fair Hypocrite ... the deceiving Fair'[31]), and yet this facile condemnation is likely to be undercut or problematised. A passage in *The Amours of Philander and Sylvia*, spoken by the narrator, begins by condemning the sensual, faithless Sylvia for hypocrisy: 'Thus she spoke, without reminding that this most contemptible quality [i.e. dissimulation] she herself was equally guilty of.' However, the narrator immediately challenges her/his own moralising. Women are 'more excusable' than men in this respect, for their lack of power within society means that dissimulation can be their only resource, while in men, 'whom custom has favoured with an allowance to commit any vices and boast it', it is unnecessary and 'not ... brave' to resort to underhand methods (pp. 321–2). In a world where the sexual double standard operates, the narrator is forced to re-evaluate her/his initial impulse to draw conventional moral conclusions.

Behn's narrators, then, present powerful, wicked, women with an ambiguity that disrupts conventional moralising. Occasionally powerful females are quite simply presented as wicked, like the black woman Moorea in 'The Unfortunate Bride', whose colour is used to 'mean' evil in a way very different from the questioning of such symbolism in *Oroonoko*. But at least on issues of gender the narrative voice of 'The Unfortunate Bride' only *seems* simple. It can be read as endorsing stereotypes that good women are passive and powerless, as Celesia's blindness forcefully images; only bad women are active and dynamic. But in fact there is an active and dynamic female opponent to Moorea: not the good, passive heroines but the female narrator herself, who takes an unusually active role in this fiction, finding the crucial letters which Moorea has intercepted and conveying them 'secretly' (p. 413) to Belvira. Her control of these letters images her control of the narrative, but also introduces a disconcerting sense of identity between the female narrator and female villain in the attempts of both to gain control of male texts. It is perhaps this unacknowledged sense of kinship that causes the female narrator to attack Moorea and her colour with such uncharacteristic vehemence.

The most complex of the narratives centring on the narrator's ambivalent presentation of female 'wickedness' are *The History of the Nun*, *The Fair Jilt*, and *Love Letters*. *The History of the Nun* explores moral paradoxes as a virtuous woman becomes an oath-breaker, an adultress, and a murderess, and it places the female narrator in assured control of these paradoxes. This assurance is possible partly because, like the female narrator of *Oroonoko*, the narrator of *The History of the Nun* is in a situation analogous to her central character. She, like Isabella, was 'design'd an humble Votary in the House of Devotion', but like her had left the convent to re-enter 'the false ungrateful World' (p. 265). As a result, perhaps, of this sense of identification, the female narrator cannot help under-cutting the simple moral she apparently offers. The narrative begins, typically of Behn's fiction, with an authoritative generalisation from the narrator: 'Of all the sins, incident to Human Nature, there is none, of which Heaven has took so particular, visible, and frequent Notice, and Revenge, as on that of *Violated Vows* ...' (p. 263). This is re-emphasised at the end as Isabella, about to be executed, makes an 'Eloquent' speech as a 'warning to the *Vow-Breakers*' (p. 324). The surface moral is simple: Isabella is punished for breaking her monastic and marital vows.

And yet almost from the beginning of the tale, the female narrator also implies a different and contradictory code of values. On the surface, Isabella is guilty: but the narrator's remarks question this by implication, presenting as an alternative to the surface moral scheme of female guilt a disturbing vision of female oppression, of the corruption of female innocence by male example. 'For, without all dispute, Women are by Nature more Constant and Just, than Men ... But Customs of Countries change even Nature her self, and ... The Women are taught, by the Lives of the Men, to live up to all their Vices' (pp. 263–4). Isabella enters the convent when she is too young to decide the course of her whole future life. Neither she nor the female narrator has sufficient power to counter the pressures of society on women to conform to either monastic or marital paradigms:

> I could wish, for the prevention of abundance of Mischief and Miseries, that Nunneries and Marriages were not to be enter'd into, 'till the Maid, so destin'd, were of a mature Age to make her own Choice ... but since I cannot alter Custom, nor shall ever be allow'd to make new Laws, or rectify the old ones, I must leave the Young Nuns inclos'd to their best Endeavours, of making a Virtue of Necessity; and the young Wives, to make the best of a bad Market.
>
> (p. 265)

The fact that women are deprived of authority even over their own lives seems to make it impossible for them, even with the best intentions, to adhere to conventional moral codes. Isabella is 'by Nature innocent' (p. 291), but she cannot resist the power of men and male-dominated institutions. The female narrator, herself similarly handicapped, cannot help unconsciously colluding with the flawed heroine: she thus presents a tissue of paradoxes and contradictions in which, despite the loud proclamation of a moral purpose, the vow-breaking bigamist murderess is also a heroine, praised for her 'Piety and Sanctity of Living' (p. 322), 'Majestic and Charming ... generally Lamented' (p. 324). An apparently simple fable about God's punishment of violated vows – 'perhaps, a moral tale'[32] – in the end becomes something quite different.

Similar effects shape *The Fair Jilt*, where Miranda swashbuckles through the novel's moral world, sexually reckless, amoral, and ambitious. However, the tale begins, not as we might expect with an attack on female vice, but with a celebration of love as 'the most noble and divine Passion of the Soul' (p. 72) and a lengthy satire on men: as in *The History of the Nun*, the moral tale of female weakness is contextualised by an attack on male vice and stupidity. Moreover, the narrator goes on to describe Miranda with an ironic and amused overstatement which undercuts its apparent moralising: 'thousands of People were dying by her Eyes ... Continual Musick ... and Songs of dying Lovers, were sung under her Windows' (p. 77). One register of narratorial voice is overtly moralising – 'the fair Hypocrite ... the deceiving Fair' (p. 106) – but the irony and overstatement elsewhere challenge and mock this tendency to moralise. Behn's narrators are torn between their desire to endorse the moral system that confines them and their sympathy with the female characters who rebel against it. Miranda, despite her sexual immorality and her attempts at rape and murder, finally escapes without punishment, and to the end the narrator's voice works to defuse its own simple moralising. '*They say* Miranda has been very penitent for her Life past ...' (p. 124; my italics): the narrator offers a moral interpretation, but only tentatively, with none of the rich circumstantial detail found elsewhere in the novella, and she disclaims knowledge or responsibility for this part of her narrative, reporting only what 'They say ...'.

The overt and covert narrative voices of this tale are also different in the case of Miranda's husband, Prince Tarquin. The surface register finds him attractive, sympathetic, and good – 'fam'd for all the Excellencies of his Sex', 'this great Man' (p. 97). He is of 'invincible ... Courage' (p. 114), 'Fortitude' (p. 118), faithful to Miranda despite her crimes, 'the perfect man and lover'.[33] And yet the narrator's voice exposes him to irony and ambiguity. She concentrates, for instance, on elaborate technicolour accounts of his clothes and equipage which perhaps hint at a hollowness behind this splendid façade (see, e.g., pp. 98, 101, 119–20). Even his royal title is uncertain and problematic, 'some laughing at his Title, others reverencing it ...' (p. 98). The narrator's rather gushing tone of false naïvety exposes his ambiguities. Miranda recruits him to murder her sister, and his love drives him to attempt it; he fails, the intended victim escapes, and he is left fighting her entourage, 'so invincible was the Courage of this poor unfortunate Gentleman' (p. 114). The discrepancy between this 'Courage' and his cowardly attempt to murder a woman is sharply drawn and exploited for ironic purpose. If in this tale female vice is more sympathetically treated than the narrator is prepared to admit, male heroism is exposed to a colder scrutiny.

Indeed, moral judgements have a strange way of behaving in this novella. The innocent Alcidiana escapes two murder attempts by her sister's instruments, the page Van Brune and Prince Tarquin, while the attempted murderers are sentenced to death. The tale, however, emphasises not the guilt of the attempted murderers and the innocence of their victim, but their essential goodness and her cruelty: '*Alcidiana* had procured her self abundance of Enemies ... , because she might have saved him if she had pleased' (p. 112; cf. p. 115). The tale reveals the guilt of the innocent, the innocence of the guilty; and this problematising of guilt and innocence works covertly on behalf of the guilty Miranda.

A repeated motif in the novella is of a thwarted intention, an incomplete action: both Tarquin and the Page fail in their attempts to murder Miranda's sister, Tarquin's executioner fails to kill him, Miranda fails to keep her monastic vows, as she fails in her attempt to seduce the Friar. This motif of thwarted action is playfully echoed in the narrator's failure to structure the tale as a moral fable. While the surface narrative presents Miranda as a monster of iniquity and Tarquin as a *preux chevalier*, and the fiction within which they move as a moral text, at a deeper level the narrator's voice questions and subverts this facile moral framework and creates a world more complex and disturbing in its ambiguities.

The clearest and most extreme example of the intervention of the narrator to alter the apparent meaning of a text occurs in *Love Letters Between a Nobleman and his Sister* (1684–7). This long *roman à clef* is in three parts, each with a different narrative method. In the first the protagonists Sylvia and Philander tell their own stories in letters with hardly any intervention from the narrator, in the second their letters are connected and contextualised by narrative, and in the third the narrator takes over completely with letters relegated to a very minor role. The sex of the narrator is indeterminate, though there is no sign that a male narrator is intended: indeed its highly critical treatment of the male characters, and its alertness to the workings of the sexual double standard, imply a female identity. The result of the intervention of an objective third-person narrative voice is an increasing complexity in the presentation of character, especially Sylvia's, and an increasing ironic distance between the reader and the characters.

Love Letters has been condemned for its 'feverish self-abandonment' and 'pruriency', its escapism, and Behn's 'rather absurd romantic conception of the story'.[34] But in so far as it is there at all, this romantic escapism is found only in the first part, and it is that of the fictional characters, not of Behn or even her narrator. At least as much as it is a 'novel of passion'[35] it is an ironic critique of passion, and of the society that makes passion the only available locus of female power.

In the first part the characters are self-dramatising, self-conscious in their role-playing. Philander sees himself as Othello (p. 11), and both he and Sylvia express their dilemmas in the clichés of the heroic play, 'tormentingly divided ... between violent love and cruel honour' (p. 17: see also p. 3). (Behn treats the two with scrupulous, and typical, even-handedness: there is no sign that female libertinism is more reprehensible than male.) However, the increasing interventions of the narrator allow us to look behind the heroic façade, at the desperate and shabby appetites for money, sex, and power that motivate the protagonists, and the narrator's use of the language of high romance becomes increasingly ironic or qualified. When the novel ends, the Othello and Cleopatra of the first part have become the anti-heroes of Restoration comedy. Sylvia has become something like the 'jilting wench' Lucetta of *The Rover*, earning a living from her 'conquests' of male 'prey' (p. 461). Philander is exposed to still more devastating undercutting on the part of the narrator. The novel is obsessed with external appearances and the real meanings they reveal or conceal, and the heroic Philander shrinks until he becomes nothing but a splendid exterior concealing an inner vacuum. After his career of betrayal he is ultimately pardoned by the King, and reappears at court 'in as much splendour as ever': but he has gained nothing, for – we are told in a piece of bone-dry narratorial irony – he is 'very well understood by all good men' (p. 461). As the novel continues, the narrator progressively draws our attention to the contradictions in the two heroes. Sylvia is increasingly seen to have 'abundance of disagreeing qualities mixed with her perfections ... Yet she had virtues too that balanced her vices ...' (pp. 259–60), and Philander is increasingly unable to control his own ambiguities: 'tears ... fell from his bright dissembling eyes; and yet so well he dissembled, that he scarce knew himself that he did so' (p. 355). As the narrator reminds us in a playfully authoritative foreshadowing of Dr Johnson, 'there is nothing to be wondered at in the contradictions ... of human nature' (p. 331).

Love Letters, then, shows romance and irony in a complex process of mutual testing. A motif in the narrative itself, indeed, is how meaning is constructed, how a specific narrator or narrative style can alter apparent meanings. Thus in Melinda's correspondence we learn that Sylvia was 'surpris'd' by her repressive family, 'writing' a love-letter to her brother-in-law. Melinda pretends it is in fact her own love-letter to Alexis, and 'all being resolv'd it should be read, ... [Sylvia] herself did it, and turned it so prettily into burlesque love by her manner of reading it, that made Madam, the Duchess, laugh extremely' (pp. 46–7). Narrative meanings are unstable, readily subverted or undercut by female ingenuity. Elsewhere Sylvia exposes the limitations of written language, which again is seen to need a narrative voice to give a 'meaning to little things, which of themselves are of trivial value, and insignificant', but which may be made by tone of voice to 'express' significances 'which their own meaning does not bear' (p. 31). Female narrators and speakers gain power to alter surface 'meaning' by their own vivid control.

Behn has sometimes been compared to her detriment with Richardson, and seen as lacking 'his ability to sustain a psychological analysis within a simple and unified structure'.[36] But this simple unified structure is precisely what Behn does not seek. Her typical narrative develops as a sequence of colliding opposites, as she breaks open apparently simple stories to reveal their encoding of 'the contradictions ... of human nature', especially with regard to the roles of women. Consequently in her plots 'the reader's expectations are constantly being aroused and defeated in the most surprising ways'.[37] A main instrument in this process is the narrator.

The female narrators identify with heroines like Miranda and Isabella precisely in their abilities to author themselves and the world around them. Both heroines manipulate complex fictions, and consequently the female narrators find it impossible not to identify with them. *The Fair Jilt* (pp. 110–11) depicts the parallel methods of composition and authorship of the narrator, writing notes in her 'Journal-Observations', and of the heroine, as she 'caused several Letters to be wrote from Germany, as from the Relations of *Van Brune*', using the same techniques of literary creation and ventriloquism as the narrator herself. The narrators' unwilling, perhaps even unconscious, identification with their female subjects also helps to undercut the surface meanings offered by the narratives.

Elsewhere the female narrator's identification with her heroines can add other complexities to the apparently simple tales she tells. Sometimes the narrator sees herself as analogous to the central figure of the narrative. At its simplest, this sense of identification can enrich the tale by adding a parallel and a deeper level of narrative involvement. This is true even of so light-hearted a tale as 'The Wandering Beauty', perhaps Behn's most charming and high-spirited comic tale with its 'unusually detailed and specific'[38] backgound of the English countryside. But as well as a delightful fairy story it is also a story of female rebellion passed on from one woman to another: 'I was not above twelve Years old, as near as I can remember, when a Lady of my Acquaintance, who was particularly concern'd in many of the Passages, very pleasantly entertain'd me with the Relation of the young Lady *Arabella's* Adventures' (p. 447). Behn here produces a comic version of the analogy between narrator and central character so important in *The History of the Nun* and *The Fair Jilt*. One young woman's quest for unconventional independence and creative power – Arabella adopts disguise and flees from a forced marriage – gives a blueprint and validation to another young woman who will seek an unconventional independence and creative power as a writer.

IV

A final and crucial function of Behn's female narrators is to offer a 'vindication of the woman writer's ability and authority', asserting 'women's equal rights to be recorders of events and interpreters of the world'.[39] Authority and power constitute a central theme in Behn's work, and like her contemporaries she is fascinated by 'fictions of authority'[40] in both public and private spheres. The most intricate in its use of correlations between the public and private worlds is *Love Letters Between a Nobleman and his Sister*. 'Authority' is a keyword in both the private and the political levels of this novel,[41] and one level is used to reflect exactly what happens in the other: Philander betrays both his wife and the sister-in-law whom he has seduced and, in an exact political equivalence, he also betrays both his king and the usurping prince for whom he has betrayed his king.

Behn's fictional worlds are inhabited both by exaggeratedly powerful and exaggeratedly powerless women, and she manipulates both images to allow her narrators to explore, and criticise, the conditions which they and their female creator share. There seems, indeed, always something ambiguous or paradoxical about female powerlessness for Behn's narrators. Women may be bizarrely empowered by their very lack of power: in *Oroonoko* Imoinda protects herself against assault from the Emperor and the slave-owners by simply revealing her vulnerability, so that her 'Modesty and Weeping ... overcame' them (p. 172).

'The Unfortunate Happy Lady' is particularly complex in its paradoxes and their use by the female narrator as a way of coming to terms with her own condition. The paradox of the title reflects the paradoxes of the female powerlessness it depicts. At the beginning Philadelphia the heroine is powerless, imprisoned in a brothel by her brother in an attempt to rob her of her inheritance. Gracelove believes her a whore and tries to buy her favours, but she persuades him of her innocence and they escape together. It is paradoxically her very powerlessness that empowers and protects her by gaining her male support. But the tale goes further, and its second half duplicates the first, but with the power-relations reversed. Whereas Philadelphia was originally poor and powerless, her brother rich and powerful, she gains power as a rich widow, and is able to exercise it over him. While Gracelove tried to buy her in the brothel but generously forebore to use his power over her, she now generously refuses to use her economic power over him. The female-dominated household in the second half counteracts and remakes the female-dominated brothel in the first.

The narrator, though, is somewhat ambivalent in her depiction of female power. Philadelphia is ultimately able to enact an unconventional, quasi-paternal power, but only because another woman, her step-daughter Eugenia, consents to act with conventional submissiveness and be 'wholly ... directed and advis'd by her in all Things'

(p. 63). Moreover, Philadelphia is sympathetic in her exercise of power only as she rescinds it to her chosen husband Gracelove, 'the Man who shall ever command me and my Fortune' (p. 64). The tale presents forcefully polarised images of women, virgins and whores, women of extraordinary power and powerlessness, and in this polarisation the female narrator must find her own place, identifying sometimes with the whores – it is they who remind her that 'our Sex seldom wants matter of Tattle' (p. 43) – sometimes with the chaste heroine. In addition, we must not miss the ironic edge to the apparently misogynist comment. The tale may descend to simple 'Tattle', the narrator be reduced from an assured literary artist to a woman gossiping with her cronies, but this apparent self-deprecation works less against the female narrator than against an imagined reader, and especially a male reader, who is wasting his time by his involvement in female 'Tattle'.

Behn's narrators are preoccupied with issues of female power and powerlessness, especially as they are relevant to the female narrators themselves, who complicate their critiques by identifying, consciously or unconsciously, with their powerful female subjects, but also with powerless women who reflect their own contradictions and ambiguities. Her female narrators find themselves in an apparently 'masculine' position, trying to insert themselves into an androcentric cultural order by gaining control of language and literature. A favourite, and powerful, reflection for this within the texts is provided by a range of images of gender-reversals. As in Behn's plays, the fictions reverse conventional gender-relations. The use of the female narrator, and other devices which empower the female and the female viewpoint, ensure that 'the male character is object, the female subject', and 'it is she who presents, defines and evaluates him' and not vice versa. Behn's systematic use of the female narrator to frame and contextualise her fictions works 'to feminise quite radically the conventional language' of narrative.[42]

One of Behn's simplest devices is to endow her female heroes with male clothes, weapons, language, money, or other symbols of male power. Atlante in 'The Lucky Mistake' opposes Vernole's advances by threatening him with a pistol, and this unmanly male 'apprehended as much Danger from this *Virago*, as he ever did from his own Sex' (p. 382); Sylvia in *Love Letters* behaves in a similar way in a similar situation (pp. 151–2). Sylvia's authority is reflected by domination of the phallic knife and the language which is a parallel instance of male power: it is a *pen*knife, she controls with her 'words' (p. 152), she has been writing and thus shares the activity through which the narrator controls her world. Altogether, indeed, Sylvia's power is extraordinary. She exercises not only the heroic powers of rhetoric and weapons, but also the economic control usually enjoyed by men, the power of pistoles as well as pistols (p. 365). She even assumes a male sexual power as she 'by force compelled him to suffer her kisses and embraces' (p. 366). She is a 'too too powerful maid' (p. 202), and in Philander's eyes, the stereotypical 'weakness of women' is a 'vulgar error', for, in political metaphors typical of Behn's treatment of sexual relations, women are 'fit to rule and reign … born for command and dominion'. It is only 'custom' that gives men 'the name of rule over all', while they are in fact 'slaves and vassals to the almighty sex' (p. 38).

In *Love Letters* the political world is dominated by men, the emotional world by women, and yet the parallelism between the two creates a sense of female power on every level, and the main, male-dominated events are surrounded by a symbolic subtext which emphasises female power: Venus dominates Adonis (p. 201), Armida Rinaldo (pp. 201, 421); and Circe (pp. 289, 426), the Sybils (p. 419), Medea (p. 425), and Queen Elizabeth I (p. 416) all exercise power over men. Parallel heroic images for men tend to be offered ironically, or to develop as images of defeat and betrayal – Theseus (p. 136), Brutus (p. 454), Leander (p. 300), Tarquin (p. 169).

Behn, then, seeks to reverse codes of authority by allowing women to gain control of the symbols of male power, pens and letters, knives and pistols, money and male clothes. The most intelligent and ironic of the narratives that centre on such reversals are *Love Letters* and *The Fair Jilt*. In *Love Letters*, both Sylvia and Calista imitate the literary transvestism of the author by assuming male disguise. Behn, indeed, is unusual in allowing male disguise to express deep psychic truths about her female characters.[43] Sylvia in male disguise is 'pleased with the cavalier in herself' (p. 117), and she enjoys male disguise because it 'gave her a thousand little privileges, which otherwise would have been denied to women, though in a country of much freedom' (p. 118). The two persistent images for Sylvia and her world of fascinatedly self-absorbed appearances are the transvestite disguise and the mirror: Sylvia 'dressed *en chevalier* (and setting her head and feather in good order before the glass …)' (p. 249).

In *Love Letters* the typical relationship is between an immasculated woman and an emasculated man. On the night of their first sexual encounter Philander proves impotent: a symbolic representation of this is the female disguise as Melinda he is wearing at the time to gain access to her. As he leaves he meets the Count who has been trying to seduce Melinda. Taking Philander for her, 'he clapped fifty guineas in a purse into one hand, and something else that shall be nameless into the other, presents that had been both worth *Melinda's* acceptance' (p. 56). In this comic episode Philander is betrayed by the failure of his own virility, and is then subjected to the female role in an uproarious enactment and mockery of male sexual and economic dominance. Later Philander is interrupted in another sexual encounter, and he hides from his pursuers in the basin of a fountain, a traditional symbol for sexual indulgence,[44] and a hilarious and mocking image for the act of ejaculation which Philander has failed to perform. Male impotence is a favourite Behn motif for defusing male power,[45] and a repeated motif in *Love Letters* is the thwarting and mockery of male sexuality. Tomaso (= Shaftesbury) is interrupted in his encounter with 'Nicky-Nacky' and has to hide on 'the tester of the bed' (p. 349), and Sebastian is accidentally shot as he tries to consummate his love for Sylvia: the gun again provides comic and sinister images of ejaculation. This strategy of reversal is repeated in the case of Sylvia's rival Calista, a 'fair *virago*' (p. 318) who adopts male disguise, and when she is stopped by her hated husband, 'shot off her pistol' (ibid.) – another comic and sinister image of the male sexual act which the novel's emasculated men fail to achieve but which is appropriated by its immasculated women.

This reversal of gender roles is most striking within the relationship of the usurping prince Cesario (= Monmouth) and his domineering mistress Hermione. Cesario is 'effeminated into soft woman' (p. 335), 'all effeminacy' (p. 425), for 'love had unmanned his great soul' (p. 456): the analogy of Armida and Renaldo sums up the reversal of roles in their relationship (p. 421). Hermione on the other hand shows 'a grace so masculine' (p. 335), a 'masculine spirit' with 'manliness of ... mind' (p. 417): in a masque she once played the role of Mercury (p. 331). (The unsympathetic presentation of this series of gender-reversals is explained by the fact that most of them are part of the included male narrative of Tomaso, whose own thwarted sexuality and conventional misogyny leads him to a very different view of gender-relations from that of the narrator.)

Apart from *Love Letters*, Behn's most brilliant and witty text of reversed roles is *The Fair Jilt*. Here the multiplicity of viewpoint of the epistolary fiction has been replaced by the dry and ironic voice of the narrator, and the reversal of roles is part of the narrator's subversion of her own text. The story of the sensual, worldly Miranda develops as a sequence of reversed roles, reversed power-polarities, particularly precise and startling in Miranda's encounters with the Friar. In the language of their meeting the narrator hilariously reverses the usual gendered vocabulary:

> he appear'd all that is adorable to the Fair Sex, nor could the misshapen Habit hide from her the lovely Shape it endeavour'd to cover ... She gaz'd upon him ... till she perceiv'd the lovely Friar to blush, and cast his Eyes to the Ground ...
>
> (pp. 78–9)

Sexual roles are wholly reversed: Miranda is female subject, and the male has become nothing but a sex-object. 'The lovely Friar' (a recurrent phrase) blushes and casts down his eyes, and the woman ogles him and undresses him with her eyes. Behn goes a step further than in *Love Letters*: she not only contrives a situation where power structures are reversed, but she uses this reversal to mock a whole system of power which more usually manifests itself in male harassment of women. Miranda does not content herself with ogling, either: she actually attempts rape. The Friar 'could not defend himself from receiving a thousand Kisses' (p. 93), and power relations become very complex and shifty: he 'suffer'd her to force him into his Chair' (p. 92), an odd and ambiguous phrase typical of the whole encounter. She even threatens to 'ruin' (p. 93) the Friar by accusing him of rape, using the verb which in the sexual jargon of the period was standard in referring to a woman's loss of virginity.[46]

These reversals of codes of authority in *The Fair Jilt* help to support the narrator's subversion of the text. Like the female narrator, Miranda usurps male power, power over fictions, over language, and over her life. It is in the narrator's interest to present her dark double without overt condemnation, for by condemning Miranda she condemns herself.

Aphra Behn's fiction, then, creates highly individualised, often female, narrators, and uses them to foreground issues of gender and power by offering ironic and mocking reversals of codes of authority, even by undermining the meaning of the stories as they tell them. These narrators often identify with their subjects, sometimes consciously, sometimes not, and these identifications may result in the narrators' ultimately telling very different stories from the ones they seem to intend. These contradictions are highly revealing of the contradictions faced by women in the late seventeenth century, and perhaps particularly of the female writer and narrators themselves, powerful within the confines of fiction, powerless outside. The most complex text in its manipulation of these contradictions is *Oroonoko*.

V

As in much of Behn's fiction, a central issue in *Oroonoko* is authority: but the subject is complicated by adding to the paradoxical figure of the female narrator, powerful as white imperialist and as narrator, powerless as woman, the exactly analogous figures of the royal slaves Oroonoko and Imoinda. As has been pointed out by some critics, in this tale women are symbolically equivalent to slaves.[47] It is hardly surprising that the ambiguous situations of both Oroonoko and the narrator cause each to suffer from 'Melancholy' (pp. 159, 160, 207). Again the narrator identifies with her protagonist, an identification which complicates the apparent narrative: though, interestingly, in this instance the process of identification complicates not so much the figure of the protagonist as that of the narrator herself.

The 'particularly well-defined narrator'[48] of *Oroonoko* is torn by contradictions on almost every subject; she admires and romanticises Oroonoko but also fears him, and her views of gender and of herself as female narrator are particularly ambivalent. Women are both cowardly and 'of good courage', and she simultaneously apologises for writing with 'only a Female Pen' (p. 169) and wishes that 'a more sublime Wit than mine' (p. 208) could have written his story, and yet claims that the 'Reputation of [her] Pen is considerable enough' (ibid.). She presents herself as willingly servicing a male-dominated culture, giving Indian clothes to be used in Dryden's play and using her 'Female Pen' to 'write [the] praise' of Oroonoko, and yet in many ways she is implicitly in opposition to this culture. For instance, she sees the natural world beyond human civilisation as gendered in a way that casts important reflections on the ambiguous world of civilisation in the novel. The simple, Edenic life of the Indians is praised and is envisaged specifically as female and as superior to the specifically male world of civilisation: 'simple Nature is the most harmless, inoffensive and virtuous Mistress. 'Tis she alone, if she were permitted, that better instructs the World, than all the Inventions of Man' (pp. 131–2).

Female nature is superior to male civilisation: but this female nature, perhaps like the female narrator herself, has a way of behaving with sinister rebelliousness to civilised man. Oroonoko, for instance, demonstrates his male heroism by killing tigers – always, apparently, female. His female companions are cowardly – 'we Women fled' – but so also is Martin, who, although he is a 'Man of great Gallantry' (p. 198), is apparently willing to 'stand aside, or follow the Ladies' as Oroonoko kills the tiger with his sword (p. 180). Gendered pronouns also have an odd way of behaving in the hands of the female narrator. In one exploit Oroonoko 'found the Tyger quit her Prey' and he fights her, ultimately succeeding in thrusting 'his Sword quite through his Breast, down to his very heart ... The dying Beast stretch'd forth her Paw, and ... did him no other Harm than fixing her long Nails in his Flesh very deep' (p. 180). This bizarre tiger is female when strong and aggressive – 'her Prey', 'her long Nails' – male when powerless and defeated. Another 'courageous' female tiger in an extraordinary reversal of gender roles is shown tearing 'a new ravish'd Sheep' (p. 181). The narrator's Freudian slips with pronouns reveal her culturally-constructed anxiety about female power, which will ultimately prevent her from using her own power effectively, but also a compensating fantasy of female power challenging the male world.

The narrator identifies with Oroonoko when he is powerless, 'feminised'[49] by virtue of his exclusion from and opposition to the dominant culture. His woman-like qualities are emphasised, for instance the 'softness' which seventeenth-century ideologies of gender considered as specifically female,[50] and which Oroonoko shares (pp. 135, 201). However, she has difficulties when she sees him as 'masculine', to the extent of making the Oroonoko who 'liked the Company of us Women much above the Men' (p. 175) utter uncharacteristically misogynist remarks about being made 'the Sport of Women' (p. 191) when he gains male power at the head of a slave army. (The words 'men' and 'man', indeed, are often made to carry negative implications: 'a feeble old Man' [p. 157], 'a Man of very little Religion' [p. 160], 'a Man that had no Sense or Notion of the God that he worship'd' [p. 164].)

The narrator's manipulation of point of view also reveals ambiguities. She does not privilege a male, or white, point of view but prefers to adopt the point of view of those excluded from the dominant culture: and this is true even as she acts to support that dominant culture by helping control Oroonoko. Her preference for these usually marginal points of view is obvious in her speaking so explicitly as a woman, and in episodes like the abduction of Oroonoko by the white captain, where the events are seen through the victim, not the proponent, of white imperialism. But it is so marked that in the scene where the white women visit the Indian village we are more aware of how the Indians see them than of how they see the Indians. The naked, 'uncivilised' Indians provide a norm, observing the Europeans, who are dressed with inappropriate elaborateness, 'very glittering and rich' (p. 185), in a way that mocks their secure sense of superiority and presents them as anthropological objects rather than as visiting anthropologists:

> when they saw him therefore, they ... cry'd in their Language, *Oh here's our Tiguamy, and we shall know whether those Things can speak* ... and all ... began to gabble to him, and ask'd, if we had Sense and Wit? If we could talk of Affairs of Life and War, as they could do?
>
> (pp. 185–6)

Throughout the tale, the narrator demonstrates uneasy contradictions about race and also about gender. Women are cowardly, always on the point of fleeing, or absent when they are needed. 'We Women fled' from the tiger; when a slave-revolt is feared, 'Apprehension made all the Females of us fly down the River, to be secured' (p. 198), and the 'Women and Children' (p. 194) of the slaves persuade their men-folk to yield. And yet there is decidedly another face to this, as the narrator emphasises female courage in the action and in metaphors. There are references, for instance, to Amazons (pp. 177, 189), and both the narrator and Imoinda are shown behaving with 'manly' courage. The English are afraid to visit the Indians, but the narrator goes to them with her brother and her 'Woman, Maid of good Courage' (p. 184). 'Heroick *Imoinda*' (p. 195) is, like the female narrator, also powerful and courageous. Pregnant, she is still able to exercise a symbolically phallic power, using 'a Bow and a Quiver full of poisoned Arrows' with which she 'shot the Governor into the Shoulder; of which Wound he had like to have died, but that an *Indian* Woman, his Mistress, sucked the Wound ...' (p. 195). The narrator's tale seems to tell of female defeat, inadequacy, and failure: and yet beneath it is a world of female warriors and healers who, despite material failure, have extraordinary power.

Similar ambiguities appear at their most agonising and extreme around the figure of the female narrator herself. She is an author and also feels she has the right to exercise a political 'Authority' (p. 198), but at the same time she is unable, in the real world, to use it to help the slave-heroes. Oroonoko refers to her as his '*Great Mistress*'

(p. 176), and we perhaps need to remember the way the word 'mistress' implies a purely fictive, metaphorical power at odds with a reality of subordination.[51] She feels she has 'Authority', and yet she is absent on the two crucial occasions when that authority could have been used, when Oroonoko is whipped and when he is executed. In her failure to exercise the capacity for power she has, she exactly mirrors the many other examples of thwarted power and authority in the novel: Oroonoko, though royal, is a slave, Imoinda wounds the Governor but fails to kill him, the narrator's mother and sister are unable to save Oroonoko, Trefry fails to write the life of Oroonoko, King Charles fails to maintain his power over Surinam but loses it to the Dutch, and even her father, appointed 'Lieutenant-General of six and thirty Islands, besides the Continent of *Surinam*' (p. 177), dies before he can take up this powerful position. Like *The Fair Jilt*, this novel presents a world where endeavour is constantly thwarted, good intention prevented and undermined. Benevolent male authority figures are dead or ineffective, like Trefry and the narrator's father, and the only remaining benevolent power is female, however limited or ambiguous. It may be, though, that the narrator emphasises this motif of the thwarting of the good and the victory of the wicked as part of the elaborate process of guilt and self-justification in which she is involved.

I have remarked on the ambiguities of the narrator, her simultaneous view of a world of female powerlessness and her fantasies of a world of female power, her ambiguous status as white (and therefore powerful) but also female (and therefore powerless) which exactly duplicates the position of the royal slaves Oroonoko and Imoinda. These deep divisions result in an odd shiftiness, evasiveness, and even duplicity, which is foreshadowed by the Freudian tricks played by gendered pronouns which I have already mentioned. Otherwise the novel traps the narrator in at least one outright lie, or at least a failure to conceal her own duplicity. Early on the narrator describes the life of the Indians and their relations with the colonising settlers of Surinam:

> So that they being on all Occasions very useful to us, we find it absolutely necessary to caress 'em as Friends, and not to treat 'em as Slaves; nor dare we do otherwise, their Numbers so far surpassing ours in that Continent. Those then whom we make use of to work in our Plantations of Sugar, are *Negroes* ... who are transported thither ...
> (p. 133)

The simple unequivocal statement that it is 'absolutely necessary ... not to treat 'em as Slaves' is, however, completely contradicted later: the Europeans encounter strange Indians, and 'Our *Indian Slaves*, that row'd us, ask'd 'em some Questions ...' (p. 188). The narrator's structures of authority are here seen in total collapse, her evasiveness about race and power finally stripped bare.

Her duplicity about power-relations, or at least her inability to admit to herself unpalatable truths, is indicated also in the significant instability of her pronouns:

> But before I give you the Story of this *Gallant Slave*, 'tis fit I tell you the Manner of bringing them to these new *Colonies*; those they make Use of there, not being *Natives* of the Place: for those we live with in perfect Amity ...
>
> (p. 129)

At one moment the colonists are 'they', at the next 'we' ('they' when enslaving negroes, 'we' when living peacefully with the Indians), and this is typical of the tale. Later we are told that 'They fed him from Day to Day with Promises' (p. 175), although the character we most often see involved in this process is the narrator herself.

The narrator's painful sense of self-division is only exacerbated by the increasing desperateness of the political situation. Because of the settlers' fear of Oroonoko, the narrator allows herself to be used to control him: 'I was oblig'd, by some Persons who fear'd a Mutiny ... to discourse with [Oroonoko and Imoinda] ... they eat with me, and ... I 'oblig'd them in all Things I was capable' (p. 175). The pun on 'oblig'd' (the narrator is 'constrained', Imoinda and Oroonoko 'made indebted') marks her nervous sense of two-facedness and the ambivalence of her own situation: seeming to be in the powerful position of dispensing favours on those without power, she is actually powerless, constrained to prostitute her literary art by using as a method of social control 'Stories of Nuns' and Romans (ibid.). Embarrassment, ambivalence, a self-defensive desire to demonstrate her innocence for the downfall of Oroonoko while still feeling guilt for her collusion in it, these self-divisions deeply colour the narrative and explain the disease of 'Melancholy' (p. 207) she suffers at the end of the tale and which prevents her – she says – from being able to use her 'Authority' to save Oroonoko.

The narrator's contradictory relation to her tale, and to its themes of gender and race, becomes more obvious and disturbing as its appalling end approaches. Gender stereotypes become increasingly extreme as the female narrator's 'Authority' fails and male images become increasingly brutal and inhuman. The slaves 'had lost the divine Quality of Men' (p. 190), while the settlers are not 'worthy the Name of Men' (p. 200). The maleness of those who betray and torture Oroonoko is remorselessly stressed, and so is the femaleness of those – Imoinda, the narrator, her mother and sister – who try to help him. It is a 'Bold English*man*' and a 'wild Irish *Man*' (my italics) who ultimately kill Oroonoko. These men display a 'Barbarity' (pp. 205, 207) greater than that of the 'more civilis'd' (p. 161) Oroonoko, who 'had nothing of Barbarity in his Nature' (p. 135). The polarities of barbarous/civilised are shown as wholly artificial and self-serving. Oroonoko, though, is no longer simply the male hero, for in the ever-increasing exaggeration of gender-stereotypes he has become 'like som Monster' (p. 203), committing not only murder but also a horrific act of self-mutilation uncomfortably analogous to those previously seen among the Indians but then adjudged 'too brutal to be applauded by our *Black* Hero' (p. 188). And yet despite her ambivalences, the narrator continues to present Oroonoko as the nearest her dark world has to a male hero.

Oroonoko is finally castrated and tortured to death. Sympathetic men in this tale must, it seems, be feminised or even emasculated: Trefry fails in authority in exactly the same way as the female narrator, Martin joins the ladies when Oroonoko fights the tiger, and Oroonoko himself is literally emasculated. The tale's women and feminised men carry moral authority, despite the material success of the brutal masculinity of the settlers. The tale begins by questioning gender stereotypes with images of powerless men and powerful women: it ends with the defeat of this modest subversiveness and with a backlash from grotesque and twisted versions of these stereotypes, Imoinda's passive acceptance of death at the hands of Oroonoko, and the images of machismo which, as represented by the settlers, are exaggerated into monstrous forms of barbarism and brutality. It is, perhaps, an attack by exaggeration on the status quo, though its indirectness is the final instance of the narrator's evasiveness, duplicity, and failure of nerve. And yet the novel does not end on quite this note of despair, despite the narrator's agonisingly contradictory attitude to her material, to her own guilt, and to her own role as female author and female authority, for as it ends the narrator reasserts her own power, however ambiguously – 'the Reputation of my Pen is considerable enough' (p. 208), and in fact the tale ends not with the defeat and brutalisation of Oroonoko but with the narrator's praise of her own double, 'the brave, the beautiful, and the constant *Imoinda*' (p. 208).

VI

A study of Aphra Behn's narrators allows, it seems to me, a clearer view than ever before of her real originality in the development of prose fiction. Other Restoration fictions have cynical narrators, detached narrators, and mocking narrators, but the most effective examples – Alexander Oldys's *The Female Gallant* or Congreve's *Incognita* (both 1692), for instance – were produced after Behn's death and were clearly influenced by her. Behn is unique in her period in the complexity and subtlety of her uses of the narrator. Perhaps this is because she writes with a doubleness of vision not available to Oldys or Congreve. As author/narrator she can write herself into the heart of the dominant culture, seeing it from within, but as woman she also views it from the margins; and the ironic contrast between these two viewpoints can produce dazzling effects. Her narrators tell stories that are, for the most part, quite simple in surface terms: but for an intelligent seventeenth-century woman what her culture takes as simple may reveal difficult and painful contradictions. Behn's narrators may intervene to add a consciously ironic critique of plot and characters, as in *Love Letters*, or to undermine conventional ideologies of gender by reversals of gender-role: but the effect may be still more complex, as narrators reveal unconscious contradictions and unacknowledged anxieties. Female narrators may claim to tell a straightforwardly moral tale, as in *The Fair Jilt* or *The History of the Nun*, but this simple tale may then escape from their control, revealing a countertale of female power sympathetically depicted beneath a surface which seems to offer quite simple moral condemnation of dangerous female autonomy. In the most complex case, the female narrator of *Oroonoko* is used as a highly effective part of Behn's critique of subordination, of slaves and of women. Anxious, shifty, duplicitous, divided between sympathy and fear for the royal slaves and doubt and complacency about her own female powers and abilities, between criticism of European colonialism and her desire to earn the approval of the colonists, she reveals, partly by her attempts to conceal, an extra-ordinarily vivid image of the cultural position of seventeenth-century woman.

From *Review of English Studies*, 42: 165–6 (1991), 40–56, 179–90.

NOTES

[Jacqueline Pearson provides an overview of the criticism of Behn's fiction, re-vealing its lack of consensus. She discusses the effect of the narrators of Behn's fourteen tales, noting that eight have female narrators while the others often imply one. This narrator gives authority to the account of women's doings, but sometimes she seems as embedded in the ideologies of the time as her characters. Pearson argues that the device of the flawed and sometimes dupli-citous narrator is an effective tool for Behn's analysis of patriarchy. Behn's stories have real originality in the development of prose fiction. Ed.]

1. References to Behn's works are to *The Works of Aphra Behn*, ed. Montague Summers (London, 1915), Vol. v, except for *Love Letters Between a Nobleman and his Sister*, Parts I and II, and Part III, *The Amours of Philander and Sylvia*, which are to *Love-Letters Between a Nobleman and his Sister*, ed. Maureen Duffy (London, 1987). Behn's fictions were first published after her death in 1689, except for *Love Letters* … (1684–7), *Oroonoko*, *The Fair Jilt*, and *Agnes de Castro* (all 1688).

2. Robert Adams Day, 'Aphra Behn and the Works of the Intellect', in Mary Anne Schofield and Cecilia Macheski (eds), *Fetter'd or Free? British Women, Novelists, 1670–1815* (Athens, OH, 1986), p. 373.

3. Ian Watt, *The Rise of the Novel* (London, 1957, repr. 1972), pp. 20, 36; F. M. Link, *Aphra Behn* (New York, 1968), p. 151.

4. W. J. Cameron, *New Light on Aphra Behn* (Auckland, 1961), p. 20; George Guffey, 'Aphra Behn's *Oroonoko*: Occasion and Accomplish-ment', in Guffey and Andrew Wright, *Two English Novelists: Aphra Behn and Anthony Trollope* (Los Angeles, 1975), esp. pp. 16–17: Laura Brown, 'The Romance of Empire: *Oroonoko* and the Slave Trade', in Felicity Nussbaum and Laura Brown (eds), *The New Eighteenth Century* (London, 1987), pp. 56–8.

5. Donald Bruce, *Topics of Restoration Comedy* (London, 1974), p. 134.

6. Katharine M. Rogers, *Feminism in Eighteenth-Century England* (Brighton, 1983), p. 98.

7. See e.g. Maureen Duffy, *The Passionate Shepherdess: Aphra Behn, 1640–1689* (London, 1977), e.g. p. 34; Angeline Goreau, *Reconstructing*

Aphra: A Social Biography of Aphra Behn (New York, 1980), e.g. pp. 41–69; Cameron, *New Light on Aphra Behn*; Sara Heller Mendelson, *The Mental World of Stuart Women: Three Studies* (Brighton, 1987), e.g. pp. 118–19.

8. E.g. Martine Watson Brownley, 'The Narrator in *Oroonoko*', in *Essays in Literature*, 4/2 (1977), 174–81; Jane Spencer, *The Rise of the Woman Novelist* (Oxford, 1986), esp. pp. 44–52.

9. Day, 'Aphra Behn and the Works of the Intellect', p. 373.

10. Brownley, 'The Narrator in *Oroonoko*', p. 174; Link, *Aphra Behn*, p. 134.

11. In *The Fair Jilt*, for example, the narrator is not explicitly female but shares some of the experiences of the real Aphra Behn – s/he has served in Antwerp in the service of Charles II (p. 98); the narrator of 'The Dumb Virgin' is the confidant of Maria and Belvidera (p. 426), which implies female sex; and in 'The Wandering Beauty' the narrator claims to have been told the story in childhood by 'a Lady of my Acquaintance' (p. 447) which also, perhaps, implies female sex.

12. 'The Unfortunate Happy Lady', p. 43; 'The Nun', p. 341; 'The Unfortunate Bride', p. 404.

13. Larry Carver, 'Aphra Behn: The Poet's Heart in a Woman's Body', in *Papers on Language and Literature*, 14 (1978), 414–24, at p. 423.

14. See e.g. Dale Spender, *Man Made Language* (London, 1980), pp. 6–9.

15. 'The Court of the King of Bantam', p. 33; *Oroonoko*, p. 174; 'The Unfortunate Bride', p. 405.

16. *The Amours of Philander and Sylvia* (*Love-Letters*, p. 455).

17. *Love-Letters*, pp. 53–4.

18. E.g. *The Fair Jilt*, pp. 78, 79, 89, 98, 103, and *The History of the Nun*, pp. 274, 307; and cf. also Jacqueline Pearson, *The Prostituted Muse: Women Dramatists and Images of Women 1640–1737* (Brighton, 1988), p. 163.

19. Used of women, e.g. *Love-Letters*, pp. 57, 82, 311, 334; used of men, e.g. *The Fair Jilt*, p. 92 and 'The Unfortunate Bride', p. 409.

20. 'The Wandering Beauty', p. 447.

21. E.g. *Oroonoko*, p. 135; Frankwit ('The Unfortunate Bride', p. 402); Philander (*Love-Letters*, p. 108).

22. Works, iii. 286.

23. For the formation of a female tradition in writing in the late seventeenth century, and of Behn's central place in it, see Pearson, *The Prostituted Muse*, pp. 21–2.

24. *The Complete Letters of Mary Wortley Montagu*, ed. Robert Halsband (Oxford, 1965–7): *The Emperor of the Moon* mentioned 1 Apr. 1717 (i. 327), the poem 'To Damon' quoted Aug. 1712 (I. 149), and 'A Voyage to the Isle of Love' in July 1727 (II. 81). Her enthusiasm for *Oroonoko* is mentioned c. 3 Feb. 1711 (i. 70) – though the reference might be to Southerne's play rather than Behn's novel.

25. *The Ladies Magazine*: cit. Alison Adburgham, *Women in Print* (London, 1972), p. 107.

26. John Gibson Lockhart, *The Life of Sir Walter Scott* (Edinburgh, 1902–3), VI, 376. Mrs Keith is talking, in 1821, of a time 'sixty years ago'.

27. Brown, 'The Romance of Empire', p. 51.

28. Carver, 'Aphra Behn', p. 423.

29. Brownley, 'The Narrator in *Oroonoko*', p. 174.

30. At least by implication: see n. 11 above.

31. 'The Unfortunate Bride', p. 410; *The Fair Jilt*, p. 106.

32. Paul Salzman, *English Prose Fiction 1558–1700: A Critical History* (Oxford, 1985), p. 315.

33. Link, *Aphra Behn*, p. 138.

34. Ernest A. Baker, *The History of the English Novel* (London, 1929), III, 84; R. A. Day, *Told in Letters: Epistolary Fiction Before Richardson* (Ann Arbor, MI, 1966), p. 190.

35. Natascha Würzbach (ed.), *The Novel in Letters* (London, 1969), p. 199.

36. Link, *Aphra Behn*, p. 135.

37. Day, 'Aphra Behn and the Works of the Intellect', p. 373.

38. Link, *Aphra Behn*, p. 148.

39. Spencer, *The Rise of the Woman Novelist*, pp. 44, 51.

40. Susan Staves, *Players' Sceptres: Fictions of Authority in the Restoration* (Lincoln, NE, 1979).

41. E.g. pp. 15, 195, 276, etc.

42. Edward Burns, *Restoration Comedy: Crises of Desire and Identity* (London, 1987), p. 128.

43. See Pearson, *The Prostituted Muse*, esp. pp. 101–18.

44. E.g. in Spenser, *The Faerie Queene* (1589), Book II, Canto xii, and Tasso, *Gerusalemme Liberata* (1581), xv. 55–62. See Douglas Brooks-Davies, *Spenser's Faerie Queene: A Critical Commentary on Books I and II* (Manchester, 1977), pp. 192–3.

45. Cf. also her poem 'The Disappointment' (*Works*, VI, 178–82).

46. See Pearson, *The Prostituted Muse*, p. 69.

47. Spencer, *The Rise of the Woman Novelist*, pp. 50–1.

48. Guffey, 'Aphra Behn's *Oroonoko*', p. 2.

49. Brown, 'The Romance of Empire', p. 51.

50. For 'softness' as a crucial female virtue in the period see Pearson, *The Prostituted Muse*, pp. 42–3.

51. Robin Lakoff, *Language and Woman's Place* (New York, 1975), p. 29; Pearson, *The Prostituted Muse*, p. 133.

8

Love-Letters: Engendering Desire

ROS BALLASTER

The relationship between the female writing subject and truth-telling is differently articulated in Behn's epistolary fiction from the 'little histories' we have been considering. Behn's fiction owes as much to the *Five Love-Letters from a Nun to a Cavalier* as it does to Madeleine de Scudéry's romances, on the level of plot and form.[1] The challenge of Mariane's love-letters to social taboo is double: first, in that they are an explicit expression of female desire, and second, in that they are written by a woman who is supposed to have repressed her desire in favour of the love of God. Behn, never slow to recognise popular trends, must have realised the potential of the figure of the nun in amatory fiction following the publication of Sir Roger L'Estrange's translation of the *Portuguese Letters* in 1678. Many of her 'little histories' exploit the topos of the desiring nun, and her claim to have told Imoinda stories of nuns in Surinam as early as the mid-1660s might be seen as an artful piece of self-aggrandisement. The heroines of *The Fair Jilt, The History of the Nun, or, The Fair Vow-Breaker,* and *The Nun, or, The Perjur'd Beauty*[2] all break their vows in order to gratify their sexual passion for a lover who courts them at the grate.

The nun represents an erotic challenge. The veil dresses the woman up as an enigma for the lover/reader who pursues her. Behn comments of the order to which her 'Fair Jilt', Miranda, belongs: 'as these Women are ... of the best Quality, and live with the Reputation of being retir'd from the World a little more than ordinary, and because there is a sort of Difficulty to approach 'em, they are the People the most courted, and liable to the greatest Temptations' (p. 75). The attraction of the nun does not lie in her sexual innocence, but rather in her propensity for excessive passion. Her capacity for inordinate and single-minded devotion, evidenced in her religious vows, may be converted to a sexual object. Mariane, the Portuguese nun, in her final letter upbraids her lover on precisely this point:

> methinks, if a body might be allow'd to reason upon the Actions of Love, a man should rather fix upon a Mistress in a Convent than any where else. For they have nothing there to hinder them from being perpetually Intent upon their Passion; Whereas in the World, there are a thousand fooleries, and Amusements, that either take up their Thoughts entirely, or at least divert them.
>
> *(Five Love-Letters*, p. 19)

The nuns in Behn's *The Fair Jilt* turn their religious retirement to their advantage. The nuns' hours are taken up with gallantry and flirting. The veil, far from concealing sexual innocence, is a cover for knowing manipulation of the power of enigmatic femininity: 'there is no sort of Female Arts they are not practis'd in, no Intrigue they are ignorant of, and no Management of which they are not capable' (p. 76). The convent provides a shelter from social and parental observance and censure.

Typically, Behn cannot resist heightening her persona by referring to her own choice not to become a nun, implying that the sexual abstinence prescribed by most convents would be beyond her own powers of endurance. In *The History of the Nun, or, The Fair Vow-Breaker* she comments on the folly of women entering convents before they had reached sexual maturity by referring to her own 'case': 'I once was design'd an humble Votary in the House of Devotion, but fancying my self not endu'd with an obstinacy of Mind, great enough to secure me from the Efforts and Vanities of the World, I rather chose to deny myself that Content I could not certainly promise my self, than to languish (as I have seen some do) in a certain Affliction' (p. 265). Despite the introduction of a first person commentary here, *The Fair Vow-Breaker* is written largely in an impersonal third person voice, a strategy which separates all Behn's 'stories of nuns' from their model, the *Portuguese Letters*. The psychological intensity of the *Portuguese Letters* is not only produced by the plot device of a convent setting. The sense of enclosure provided by the 'frame' of the convent is reinforced by the claustrophobia of an individual psyche struggling to articulate its desire, conveyed by the innovation of the use of a direct first-person narrative.

Despite the insistent presence of a narrative 'I' in Behn's novels, it is an 'I' that can only watch and tell, rather than one that conveys immediacy in sexual passion. Behn habitually employs indirect speech to recount dialogue, but interestingly she shifts into direct speech and an inserted first-person narrative in *The Fair Vow-Breaker* to tell the seduction story of her heroine's friend and fellow-nun, Katteriena. Whereas Isabella is a sexual innocent, Katteriena has been exiled to the convent following a shameful love affair with her father's page. When Isabella finds herself obsessed with Henault, Katteriena's brother, Katteriena recounts her own story in order to persuade her friend that passion can be conquered by separation from the love object. By telling the story in Katteriena's own voice, Behn creates an illusion of immediacy that reported speech generally lacks. Katteriena spares Isabella no details of her psychological and physiological torment: 'my Heart would heave, when e're he came in view; and my disorder'd Breath came doubly from my Bosom; a Shivering seiz'd me, and my Face grew wan; my Thought was at a stand and Sense it self, for that short moment, lost its Faculties' (p. 278). Far from convincing Isabella to abandon her illicit desires, Katteriena's narrative further inflames her. 'No more, no more, (reply'd *Isabella*, throwing her Arms again about the Neck of the transported *Katteriena*) thou blow'st my Flame by thy soft Words, and mak'st me know my Weakness, and my shame' (p. 279). The seduction narrative offered to the reader, then, as a moral warning, teaches her sexual knowledge, and provides surrogate erotic pleasure.

In her prose writing Behn effectively employs two kinds of narrative voice, the first the objectifying, specularising Astrea who (like Scheherazade) accrues power over her audience through her storytelling (*Histories and Novels*); the second, a desirous, subjective, first-person narration put into the mouths of the central actors and providing an intense psychological display (*Love-Letters from a Nobleman to his Sister, The Lover's Watch*). Although the nun stories of the *Histories and Novels* incorporate the thematic concerns of the *Portuguese Letters*, it is Behn's epistolary fiction which is their true heir. Like the *Five Love-Letters*, Behn's epistolary fiction is centrally concerned with the attempt to inscribe and engender sexual desire. These epistolary writings seek both to stimulate desire in the other, lover or reader, and to represent the specific 'difference' of female desire.

As Tania Modleski notes in her analysis of twentieth-century amatory fiction, first-person narrative produces a crisis of authenticity in relation to the speaker's discourse.[3] Without the external 'frame' of an observing narrator, which epistolary form precisely abandons, the reader remains unsure of the integrity of the central protagonist. No third person assures us of the heroine's 'truthfulness' and 'innocence'. We have only her word that she was a victim rather than a manipulator in the game of love.

The *Portuguese Letters* illustrate this dilemma over authenticating or authorising the truth of first-person discourse. As Peggy Kamuf cogently argues in her *Fictions of Feminine Desire*, Mariane's five love-letters document the hysterical woman's coming-to-language as a means of escaping the silent pain of her 'symptomatically convulsed and contorted body' (p. 49). Mariane's first letter expresses the desire 'to convey [her] self in the Place' of the letter (*Five Love-Letters*, p. 6). At this stage, Mariane finds her writing a poor substitute for the totalising mirror function of the language of the gaze, 'Those Eyes that were ten thousand Worlds to [her], and all that [she] desir'd' (p. 5). Her desire to substitute for the letter is not simply one of desire to be in her lover's presence. It signifies a desire to have the rhetorical capacity to put her 'self' down on the page, to convey her subjectivity through writing. The physical symptom becomes her only means of signifying desire.

Mariane repeatedly questions why and for whom she writes, gradually recognising that the real 'addressee' is her self, not her lover. Ultimately her self-analysis allows her to re-enact her own scene of seduction, speak her desire, and liberate herself from her hysteria. In her fourth letter she ceases to construct herself as victim and finds a place in her discourse for the expression of her active desire: ''twas my own precipitate Inclination that seduc'd me', she declares (p. 12). By the end of the fifth letter Mariane can quit her self-created analyst's couch: 'Now do I begin to Phansie that I shall not write to you again for all This; for what Necessity is there that I must be telling of you at every turn how my Pulse beats?' (p. 21).

Doubtless, one of the attractions of the Portuguese style for writers and readers of the late seventeenth century lay in the opportunity that a first-person female narrative voice offered to explore women's relation to writing and the self. As I have argued, Behn's heroines in her *Histories and Novels* are 'written upon', in that they are employed as signifiers of male desire. The epistolary style of the

Portuguese letters enacts a woman's successful endeavours to write her self, rather than reflect an 'other'.

However, there is a paradox at the heart of the Portuguese style, which Aphra Behn was not slow to recognise. Mariane's discourse authenticates itself by its claims to naturalness and spontaneity, by contrast with the supposed artifice and paraphrases of the French romance's amatory language. Yet there is nothing integral to Mariane's language that makes it more authentic than that of the romance. Imitations of the Portuguese letters appear to reduce an originary moment of self-production to a series of rhetorical tropes, different in form from that of the romance to be sure, but no less a 'fiction'. The *Seven Portuguese Letters*, proclaiming themselves 'a Second Part of the Five Love-Letters from a Nun to a Cavalier', repeat tragedy as farce.[4] Supposedly written by 'a Woman of the World, whose Style is very different from that of a Cloystered NUN' (A2), these letters run the whole gamut of Portuguese sentiment as a series of rhetorical poses to the point where the heroine self-consciously directs her reader to her supposed lack of artifice. In her third letter, she comically insists that he 'may be able to judge what disorder [her] mind is in, by the irregularity of this letter' (p. 33).

Whether parody or poor imitation, the *Seven Portuguese Letters* highlight the fact that Mariane's seemingly authentic 'discourse of desire' is indeed nothing more than a fiction of identity, as accessible to the self-interested seducer as the sincere lover. Imitating the *Portuguese Letters* only undermines their integrity. That they can be imitated is the sign of their rhetorical status. By anxiously pointing to the signs of authenticity – narrative disorder, syntactic and se-mantic disturbance – Mariane's imitators incriminate rather than vindicate themselves, proving that their language is not 'all artless speaking, incorrect disorder, and without method' (*Love-Letters*, p. 184), but is, rather, self-regarding, a consciously rhetorical exercise.

Peggy Kamuf observes that Mariane's text relies on the imagina-tive construction of 'the interlocutor as the silent pole through which passes the invention of the writing subject'.[5] It is Aphra Behn, amongst the *Portuguese Letters*' innumerable imitators, who recog-nised that the key to the crisis of authenticity inscribed in Mariane's self-generating narrative lay precisely in the role of the interlocutor. The effectiveness of Mariane's 'cure' (her invention of herself as female writing subject) is predicated on the absence of her lover and the irrelevance of his interpretation of the letters to her project. The self is created in relation to the word, not the other. *Reading* and the

interpretative damage it may do to the claims to authenticity generated by the female writing subject do not enter the equation.

In contrast, Behn's epistolary narratives judge their efficacy by the
extent to which they affect their imagined reader. Behn conceives of
writing, it seems, as narrative act rather than narrative identity. In the
fourth letter of her *Love-Letters to a Gentleman*, the woman concludes: 'Why I write them, I can give no account; 'tis but fooling my
self, perhaps, into an Undoing. I do but (by this soft Entertainment)
rook in my Heart, like a young Gamester, to make it venture its last
Stake' (*Histories and Novels*, p. 406). The economic metaphor is
significant here. Amatory discourse is repeatedly metaphorised in these
letters as a form of economic exchange in which the writer trades,
seeking to 'profit' by eliciting a response from her reader.[6]

Through the course of her eight letters Astrea comes to realise
that language is not a vehicle for desire, bur rather that which constitutes it. In letter eight she determines: 'I will never be wise more;
never make any Vows against my Inclinations, or the little-wing'd
Deity. I do not only see 'tis all in vain, but I really believe they serve
only to augment my Passion' (p. 414). Expanding a metaphor of
economic exchange in letter four she accuses her lover with the
words: 'you would have me give, and you, like a Miser, wou'd dis-
tribute nothing' (p. 406). While her lover commands her to speak
and write, he remains silent.

Silence is the only signifier of lack of desire in epistolary fiction.
Philander's declining affection for Sylvia in *Love-Letters between a
Nobleman and his Sister* is indicated by the brevity of his letters
and the increasingly long silences that punctuate an enforced separation. Sylvia 'reads' his silence correctly, signifying her own continued passion by presenting a lengthy complaint in response to a
cursory note: 'Where is thy heart? And what has it been doing since
it begun my fate? How can it justify thy coldness, and thou this
cruel absence without accounting with me for every parting hour?
My charming dear was wont to find me business for all my lonely
absent ones; and writ the softest letters – loading the paper with
fond vows and wishes' (p. 139). Philander meanwhile writes to
Octavio, the couple's Dutch friend who is infatuated with Sylvia,
and tells him the story of his new love, Calista (who, unbeknownst
to Philander is Octavio's married sister). He too recognises that
writing stimulates desire, in this case on the *writer's* part, when he
apologises: 'Pardon this long history, for it is a sort of acting all
one's joys again, to be telling them to a friend so dear' (p. 246).

The lengthy letter of seduction, or the letter narrating seduction to a friend, is a psychological necessity for the rake, since it is only writing that transforms compulsive appetite, or need, into the more complex and sophisticated delights of desire.

In the second part of the *Love-Letters*, Behn shifts her narrative voice from purely epistolary form to a combination of third person narrative and transcribed letters. Rather than indicating an inability to sustain the epistolary mode on her part, I would argue, this change is a response to the problem of authenticating voice in first-person epistolary writing. Further, it provides a means of drawing attention to the duplicitous ends to which the Portuguese style can be put. The first part of the *Love-Letters* consists of an intense exchange of letters between Philander and Sylvia interrupted only by four letters from other actors in the affair (one from Sylvia's sister and Philander's wife, Myrtilla, another from Sylvia's maid, Melinda, a note from Cesario to Philander, and a proposal of marriage to Sylvia from Philander's rival, Foscario).

The lack of third-person commentary on the nature of the lovers' passion means that the reader has no information about the motivations of the two lovers, other than the accounts they offer, nor the eventual results of the affair. The suspense of this circumstance is in keeping with the history of the novel's writing, in that Behn herself did not know its outcome when she wrote it. The first part was written less than two years after an advertisement appeared in the *London Gazette* (late September 1682) stating that 'Lady Henrietta Berkeley has been absent from her father's house since 20th August last past and it is not known where she is or whether she is alive or dead' (quoted in *Love-Letters*, p. v). Lord Grey of Werke eloped with his sister-in-law and married her to his factotum, one Mr Turner (who appears as Brilliard in the novel). When her father took him to court at the King's Bench on 23 November 1682, Grey was found guilty of debauching the Earl of Berkeley's daughter. However, no sentence was ever passed on Grey since the Earl decided not to press charges, although Henrietta was imprisoned for a night. Less than six months later, the lovers fled to the continent. Grey's flight seems to have been motivated largely by the disclosure of the Rye House Plot to assassinate King Charles in Oxford in late March 1683, in which he had been involved. One of his conspirators, Algernon Sidney, was executed.[7]

Thus, at the time of writing the first part of what amounted to a contemporary scandal novel, Behn could have no resolution to the love 'plot'. On the basis of her known Tory political allegiances, however, it is safe to assume that she would have been unwilling to imply anything good could come out of a Whig rebel absconding with a Tory heiress. The choice of name for her 'hero' is our only clue to his insincerity. His rhetoric is that of the quintessential 'Portuguese' lover.

A letter of proposal from the 'old-fashioned' lover, Foscario, is inserted to highlight the attractions of Philander's language of seduction. Foscario employs the conventions of the French romance. Sylvia's eyes are 'triumphant stars', her mouth 'a storehouse of perfection' from which she can 'pronounce [his] doom'; he will receive her decision 'with that reverence and awe' suited to 'the sentence of the gods', 'the thunderbolts of *Jove*', or 'the revenge of angry *Juno*' (p. 82). In contrast to Foscario's use of martial and classical romantic metaphor, Philander's images echo the eroticised pastoral of Behn's own 'Golden Age'. Secreted in the woods around Sylvia's house, his traditional rakish invocation to the indulgence of 'natural appetite' is couched in a description of pastoral idyll: 'the woods around me blow soft, and mixing with wanton boughs, continually play and kiss; while those, like a coy maid in love, resist, and comply by terms' (p. 28).

Having brought his mistress to the point of submission through the eroticised language of his letters, however, Philander finds himself impotent at their late-night rendezvous. In the letter that follows, Philander seeks to explain his failure. Once again, it is the opposition between writing and vision that functions here. An excess of visual stimulus is located as the cause, and it is only through writing that Philander can regain his desire:

> I saw the ravishing maid as much inflamed as I, she burnt with equal fire, with equal languishment: ... a languishment I never saw till then dwelt in her charming eyes, that contradicted all her little vows ... till quite forgetting all I had faintly promised, and wholly abandoning my soul to joy, I rushed upon her, who, all fainting, lay beneath my useless weight, for on a sudden all my power was fled, swifter than lightning hurried through my enfeebled veins, and vanished all: not the dear lovely beauty which I pressed, the dying charms of that fair face and eyes, the clasps of those soft arms, nor the bewitching accent of her voice, that murmured half love, half smothered in her sighs, nor all my love, my vast, my mighty passion, could call my fugitive passion back again: oh no, the more I looked – the more I touched and saw, the more I was undone.
>
> (pp. 53–4)

As in *The Blind Lady*, if the look is the first stage of desire it is ultimately the cause of its death unless writing intervenes to break the
totalising unity of lovers conjoined. Writing brings about the separation necessary to the creation of desire.

The lovers' elopement presents Behn with a narrative problem.
Once united, it is implausible that they will continue to write to
each other. Part 2 opens with the introduction of new characters,
and takes a new narrative direction by combining an anonymous
third-person narrative with letters, both of which serve to alleviate
this difficulty. By the time Behn came to write this second part, both
love story and political plot that provided its source had to some
extent been resolved. It was published in the same year as Charles
II's death (February 1685), James II's accession, and Monmouth's
rebellion (the battle of Sedgmoor took place on 5–6 July 1685).
However, it makes little or no reference to these events. The only
historical event to which it refers is Lord Grey's documented trip to
Cologne, adding the probably fictional account of Philander's
infidelity with Calista, Sylvia's courtship by a young prince of the
House of Orange, Octavio, and the attempts of her titular husband,
Brilliard, to win her sexual favours by impersonation and disguise.

This kind of action, which comes close to the bedroom farce of
Restoration comedy in which Behn had already proved herself adept,
seems to require a more diverse narrative structure than the psycho-
logical intensity of the Portuguese style could offer. The narrative
voices and perspectives multiply, introducing contributions from
Brilliard, Octavio, Sylvia's maid Antonet, Calista, and her husband
Count Clarinau. Not all write letters and many are given in synopsis.
Increasingly, the specularising and objectifying narrative persona of
Histories and Novels takes control of the interpretation of events.

By the time she published the third part in 1687, Behn had seen
her story reach a suitably dramatic end with Monmouth's plot defeated and himself executed, James seemingly restored to power,
and Lord Grey, consummate hypocrite as ever, escaping retribution
for his involvement in the uprising. In the full knowledge of hindsight, Behn has a free hand to draw out the symbolic implications
of Sylvia's moral decline and education in rakehood in contrast
with Cesario/Monmouth's increasing emasculation and dotage
under the influence of his mistress, Hermione/Lady Wentworth and
her cronies. While Sylvia is educated out of the illusory mirror of
romantic love into social power through manipulation of, rather
than subjection to, the rhetoric of desire, Cesario loses his political

advantages and his 'masculine' honour by falling prey to that same romantic illusion.

Behn's *Love-Letters* produce a version of the invention of the female writing subject which simultaneously imitates and critiques that of the *Portuguese Letters*. In this text, Behn, through her shifts of narrative voice, obliges her reader to recognise that the female writing subject emerges in and through the process of learning to *feign* authenticity as consummately as the male rake. By no other means can she survive in the world of discourse. Sylvia's history is a female version of the rake's progress. Behn leads her heroine through a variety of narratorial positions, from naïve reader (in her affair with Philander) to Portuguese lover (in her response to his desertion of her) to French romance writer (in her seduction of Octavio) to 'feigned' Portuguese lover (in her manipulation of her affair with both men). By the third part, Sylvia has graduated to the narratorial complexity of Behn herself, drawing upon multiple fictional identities and languages in order to secure her control over a lover/reader as sophisticated and cynical as herself (in her affair with the rakish Spaniard Alonzo).

The three parts of the *Love-Letters* effectively cover three of Sylvia's affairs. The first presents her as victim of Philander's seductive rhetoric, deceived by her belief in absolute correspondence between word and feeling, signifier and signified. The letter, for Sylvia, is a transparent mediator of emotion between lovers, a token of an a priori desire. As she puts it, 'to him I venture to say any thing, whose kind and soft imaginations can supply all my wants in the description of the soul' (p. 31).

In the second part, when she discovers her lover's infidelity, Sylvia is at first in despair, convulsed by the hysterical symptoms of a Mariane: 'she many times fainted over the paper, and as she has since said, it was a wonder she ever recovered' (p. 215). However, Sylvia's 'pride and scorn' overcome her 'fits of softness, weeping, raving and tearing' (p. 221). She now turns to 'managing' her new suitor, Octavio, in order to be revenged on Philander. In this case the artifice of the French romance enables Sylvia to escape the hysteria of the Portuguese lover. Sylvia summons Octavio to her presence, carefully preparing a seductive frame suffused with the images habitually associated with the French romance:

> *Sylvia* adorns herself for an absolute conquest, and disposing herself in the most charming, careless, and tempting manner she could

devise, she lay expecting her coming lover on a repose of rich embroidery of gold on blue satin, hung within-side with little amorous pictures of *Venus* descending in her chariot naked to *Adonis*, she embracing, while the youth, more eager of his rural sports, turns half from her in a posture of pursuing his dogs, who are on their chase: another of *Armida*, who is dressing the sleeping warrior up in wreaths of flowers, while a hundred little Loves are playing with his gilded armour; this puts on his helmet too big for his little head, that hides his whole face; another makes a hobby-horse of his sword and lance; another fits on his breast piece, while three or four little *Cupids* are seeming to heave and help him to hold it an end, and all turning the emblems of the hero into ridicule. ... [T]he languishing fair one, ... lay carelessly on her side, her arm leaning on little pillows of point of *Venice*, and a book of amours in her own hand. Every noise alarmed her with trembling hope that her lover was come, and I have heard she says, she verily believed, that acting and feigning the lover possessed her with a tenderness against her knowledge and will.

(pp. 200–1)

In preparing for conquest, Sylvia learns new narcissistic pleasures; like the narrator of *Oroonoko*, Sylvia gains a self-reflexive pleasure by framing herself for the sexually curious gaze. Narcissism here provides an effective means of negotiating hysteria, in which symptoms of repressed desire register on the woman's body, beyond her conscious control.

Sylvia's experiments with amorous representation are, at this stage, unsophisticated, relying on classical pictorial devices rather than the 'artificial naturalness' of the new realism of the Portuguese style. Sylvia's narrative frame, the unmanning of a military hero by the agents of love, clearly inscribes her lover's doom. She is, however, shrewd in her choice of object. In Octavio she finds a reader who wilfully interprets her language according to his own desire.

Octavio does not arrive for this rendezvous. Brilliard's stratagems to bring himself to Sylvia's bed by impersonating Octavio result in a disagreement between the prospective lovers. Sylvia's attempt to conceal her anger in a written response to Octavio's accusation that she is a 'common mistress' is unsuccessful. Behn provides us with a close analysis of Octavio's interpretation of this letter, deftly demonstrating the tension in epistolary exchange between the writer's endeavour to 'effect' the reader, to arouse his sympathy and his passions, and the reader's struggle to discover the writer's 'real' meaning:

He, reading this letter, finished with tears of tender love; but considering it all over, he fancied she had put great constraint upon her natural
high spirit to write in this calm manner to him, and through all he
found dissembled rage, which yet was visible in the middle of the
letter. ... In fine, however calm it was, and however designed, he
found, and at least he thought he found the charming jilt all over; ...
yet, in spite of all this appearing reason, he wishes, and has a secret
hope, either that she is not in fault, or that she will so cozen him into a
belief she is not, that it may serve as well to soothe his willing heart. ...
(pp. 248–9)

It is, then, the desire of the reader that gives writing meaning. The
power of the writer lies in her ability to interpret and manipulate
the reader's desire, and it is this lesson that Behn's Sylvia must learn
if she is to prosper.

By the third part of the novel, Behn is dealing with two pairs of
brother and sister in opposition to each other. Octavio and Calista
follow the only other course open to the deserted lover. Both, like
Sylvia, are victims of seduction, duped into sacrificing their honour,
but their response is retreat into holy orders, here viewed as a voluntary abnegation of discursive power. Sylvia rejects this option, choosing to assume the cynicism of the rake, rather than submit to a regime
of silence and exile from social, personal, and political agency.

Sylvia succeeds for a while in maintaining relations with both
Philander and Octavio, as well as stringing along Octavio's besotted
elderly uncle. She elopes with Philander for a second time but soon
leaves him when he attempts to immure her away in a rustic retreat.
She comes to Brussels and, in need of money, writes to Octavio,
who is now established in a nearby monastery. He is willing to offer
her a pension if she abandons her life of shame. Sylvia's answer is a
deft imitation of the style of Heloise and her Portuguese successor,
Mariane. She writes 'as an humble penitent would write to a ghostly
Father ... and if ever she mentioned love, it was as if her heart had
violently, and against her will, burst out into softness, as she still
retained there' (p. 433).

In her pursuit of Don Alonzo, Sylvia's new facility in amatory representation is fully tried and tested. Travelling to Brussels disguised
as a man, she is obliged to pass a night in the same bed as Alonzo.
During their late night conversation, Alonzo freely admits to his
'male' companion the rakish nature of his desire: 'I have burnt and
raved an hour and two, or so; pursued, and gazed, and laid seiges,
till I had overcome; but, what is this to love? Did I ever make a

second visit, unless upon necessity, or gratitude? (p. 411). Sylvia sets about winning this coveted second visit by laying siege to the young Spaniard in Brussels, providing tantalising glimpses of herself in the guise of two different women at public events. Finally, she arranges for him to visit her lodgings and fascinates him with a series of quick changes: 'he sees, he hears, this is the same lovely youth, who lay in bed with him at the village *cabaret*; and then no longer thinks her woman: he hears and sees it is the same face, and voice, and hands he saw on the *Tour*, and in the park, and then believes her woman' (p. 441).

Sylvia's strategies appear on one level to be a simple imitation of those of her first lover, Philander, and his ability to manipulate amatory language in pursuit of sexual gratification. However, she introduces a new twist to this linguistic facility by her peculiarly feminine exploitation of enigmatic identity. Sylvia's feigned identities allow her to retain her male lover's interest and constantly renew her own. In brief, Sylvia learns the tricks of the professional woman writer of amatory fiction, generating fictions around the figure of the woman that withhold identity while they appear to reveal it. In contrast, Mariane's epistolary struggles might be interpreted as those of the amateur woman writer learning to speak her desires through the device of the absent lover. Mariane's history begins and ends in silence; Sylvia's moves on to another fiction. Behn informs us that, despite being expelled from Brussels by the governor for 'ruin[ing] the fortune' of Alonzo, Sylvia continues to roam the continent 'and daily makes considerable conquests wherever she shews the charmer' (p. 461).

Like all Behn's prose fiction, the *Love-Letters* is a heady compound of sexual and party politics. From this and her other works, Behn emerges as a mistress of the art of disguise. Like her author, Sylvia is an anti-heroine, a survivor who in her ceaseless pursuit of social, sexual, and linguistic agency adapts every available resource to hand. Behn presents her readers with a critique of women's enslavement to a variety of fictions of feminine identity, and offers an escape route beyond retreat into silence and spurious claims to authenticity. The novelty of the novel seems to have provided Behn with the ideal platform for the elaboration of a new relationship of the female writing subject to feminine identity. It is not insignificant that Behn's earliest experiments in literature were in the drama, another literary genre in which women, in the shape of Restoration actresses, had obtained a new means of turning amatory representation to profit.

The refusal on the part of Aphra Behn critics to forsake the hermeneutic endeavour to discover her authentic voice has deflected attention from her literary complexities to the thin and unsatisfactory threads of her biography. Her fictions are indeed 'imagin'd more than Woman' in their challenge to the amatory forms traditionally associated with the woman writer. In the attempt to carve out a place for the woman writer in the newly competitive literary market, Behn's fiction turns to a radical questioning of the relationship between gender identity and fiction. These amatory narratives appropriate for the woman writer the power of representation by exposing gender identity, the dichotomy of masculine and feminine, as in itself a fiction. Like her own Clarinda, Behn poses herself to her readers as an erotic enigma in order to maintain her representational power: 'When e'er the Manly part of [her] would plead | She tempts us with the Image of the Maid' (*Works*, VI, 363).

From Ros Ballaster, *Seductive Forms: Women's Amatory Fiction from 1684 to 1746* (Oxford, 1992), pp. 100–13.

NOTES

[Ros Ballaster argues that *Love-Letters between a Nobleman and his Sister*, 'Love Letters to a Gentleman', and several of the short stories, such as *The Fair Jilt* and *The History of the Nun*, radically question the relationship between gender identity and fiction. In *Love-Letters*, in particular, Behn is concerned with the attempt to inscribe and engender sexual desire; in the process she presents her readers with a critique of women's enslavement to a variety of fictions and to feminine identity. The heroine Sylvia learns the tricks of the professional woman writer of amatory fiction, generating fictions around the figure of the woman that withholds identity whilst appearing to reveal it. Like her author, Sylvia becomes a mistress of disguise. Ed.]

1. *Five Love-Letters from a Nun to a Cavalier* (1678) was a translation by Roger L'Estrange of the French *Lettres Portugaises* purported to be letters from a Portuguese nun, Mariane, to a French army officer who had seduced and abandoned her. Madeleine de Scudéry (1607–1701) was the writer of lengthy heroic romances such as *Clelia* (1654–61) in 10 volumes.

2. References to Behn's works are to *The Works of Aphra Behn*, ed. Montague Summers (London, 1915), vol. V.

3. Tania Modleski, *Loving with a Vengeance: Mass-Produced Fantasies for Women* (New York, 1982), pp. 54–5.

4. *Seven Portuguese Letters, being a Second Part* to the *Five Love-Letters from a Nun to a Cavalier, One of the most Passionate Pieces, That Possibly Ever Has Been Extant* (London, 1681). The letters were published in France by Barbin in 1669, a few months after he had produced the *Lettres Portugaises*, to capitalise on the latter's success.

5. Peggy Kamuf, *Fictions of Feminine Desire: Disclosures of Heloïse* (Lincoln, NA, 1982), p. 56.

6. At this stage in the history of the postal service, moreover, receivers rather than senders were required to pay the duty on letters mailed within the city. The return of an unopened letter by an unresponsive mistress or lover takes on a peculiarly economic motive under these circumstances. See Ruth Perry, *Women, Letters and the Novel* (New York, 1980), pp. 63–4 and R. W. Chapman, 'The Course of the Post in the Eighteenth Century', *Notes and Queries*, 183 (1942), 67–9.

7. Angeline Goreau, *Reconstructing Aphra: A Social Biography of Aphra Behn* (New York, 1980), pp. 274–8.

9

Beyond Incest: Gender and the Politics of Transgression in Aphra Behn's *Love-Letters between a Nobleman and His Sister*

ELLEN POLLAK

Expressly incestuous and deeply embedded in the politics of regicide and political rebellion, Aphra Behn's *Love-Letters between a Nobleman and His Sister* is also a text insistently preoccupied with questions and gender, identity, and representation. Published in three parts between 1684 and 1687, Behn's novel is based loosely on an affair between Ford, Lord Grey of Werke, and his wife's sister, Lady Henrietta Berkeley, a scandal that broke in London in 1682, when Lady Berkeley's father published an advertisement in the *London Gazette* announcing the disappearance of his daughter. Lady Berkeley had in fact run off with Grey, the well-known anti-monarchist figure whom Dryden alluded to as 'cold Caleb' in *Absalom and Achitophel* (1681) and who serves Behn here as a model for her character Philander. Prosecuted by Lord Berkeley for abducting and seducing his daughter, Grey was eventually found guilty of 'debauchery' but never sentenced.[1] Shortly thereafter, he was also implicated in the Rye House Plot to murder Charles II and was later active in Monmouth's rebellion against Charles's brother,

James. In Behn's fiction Grey figures as a political follower and friend of Cesario, the French prince of Condé, whose failed attempt to overthrow his king is modelled on the parallel exploits of Charles's bastard son. Lady Berkeley is Sylvia, the dutiful royalist daughter whom Philander seduces and corrupts. Like the crown for Cesario, she is for Philander a sign of male prerogative and desire, her body the theatre across which several dramas of masculine rivalry are played out.

It is not surprising that a text situated so expressly within the political context of the Duke of Monmouth's rebellion against the royal authority of both his father and his uncle should structure itself around the repetition of a series of analogously configured masculine rivalries. Through her elaborate foregrounding of the figure of a woman, however, Behn adds a dimension to this drama of political and familial succession that is manifestly absent from such comparable royalist efforts as *Absalom and Achitophel*. To what extent Behn's choice to develop the love interest here was motivated by her recognition of the greater acceptability for a woman of the role of romance historian over that of political poet, we cannot know for sure,[2] but when Lady Berkeley's father published his advertisement announcing her disappearance and offering £200 for her return, Behn clearly perceived an opportunity to explore the narrative possibilities (as well as discursive instabilities) inherent in comparing stolen daughters with stolen crowns.

Behn incorporates the scandalous historical fact of the Berkeley–Grey affair into the political, thematic, and figural dimensions of her fiction by situating Philander's justifications for his adulterous and incestuous desire for Sylvia squarely within the context of Restoration debates over the relationship and relative authority of nature and conventional morality. As Susan Staves has amply demonstrated, an increasing dissociation of natural law theory from theology during the second half of the seventeenth century effectively established the conditions both for changes in the institutional treatment of moral crimes and for the emergence of a new brand of heroism in the imaginative literature of the age. Herculean and libertine stage heroes captured the popular imagination through their bold allegiance to a nature defined not in accordance with, but in opposition to, religion, law, custom, and conventional morality. Such heroes appealed to nature to justify a range of behaviours traditionally regarded as crimes against nature as well as God. Along with adultery, sodomy, and parricide, the deployment of incest as a figure for rebellion against traditional forms of authority became a favourite device on the Restoration stage for articulating cultural anxieties and for giving dramatic play to the multiple tensions inherent in contemporary efforts to rethink the connections between the laws of nature, religion, and social morality.[3]

Behn's libertine hero, Philander, fits the profile of this new literary type in his elaboration of natural justifications for his socially criminal desire for Sylvia. From as early as his very first letter, he invokes the liberatory ethos of a return to original pleasures. The legal institutions of kinship and of marriage, he insists, are mere practical creations inspired by material interests, while his own incestuous and adulterous passion has a primacy that transcends the prudent imperatives of tradition. Philander uses the fact that his relation to Sylvia is affinal (a legal relation created through his marriage to her sister) as opposed to consanguineal (a blood relation) to further question the natural basis for the rules that prohibit his having sex with her: 'What kin, my charming *Sylvia*, are you to me? No ties of blood forbid my passion; and what's a ceremony imposed on man by custom! ... What alliance can that create? Why should a trick devised by the wary old, only to make provision for posterity, tie me to an eternal slavery?'[4] In point of legal fact, as Sybil Wolfram's work has shown, because the English concept of marriage in the seventeenth century was based on the legal and religious doctrine of the unity of husband and wife, 'intercourse between affinal relations was ... on a footing with and as much incest as intercourse between close blood relations'.[5] But Philander represents an emergent strain of thought that radically questioned the received assumption that incest controverted natural law.

Scripture itself had become a site of theoretical controversy among seventeenth-century moral philosophers, especially at those points where God appeared arbitrarily to command behaviour elsewhere prohibited by His law. Staves cites the story of Abraham's divinely ordered murder of Isaac as one scriptural conundrum that seemed to focus the crisis of authority experienced by moralists,[6] but there were also numerous instances of apparent biblical inconsistency regarding the legitimacy of incestuous practices. One of the most pervasively cited involved a perceived discrepancy between the injunctions of Leviticus, which forbade incest, and those of Genesis, which bade Adam and Eve (whom most commentators regarded as siblings) to increase and multiply.

Thus, in 1625 Hugo Grotius asserted that, although marriages between brothers and sisters are illegal, they are forbidden by divine command and not (as appeared to be the case with parent–child marriages) by 'the pure law of nature'.[7] Here Grotius accepts the Jewish teaching that the prohibition against sibling marriage was given to Adam 'at the same time with the laws to worship God, to administer justice, not to shed blood, [etc.] ... ; but with the condition that the laws regulating marriage should not have effect until after the human race had multiplied sufficiently'.[8] Jeremy Taylor echoed Grotius thirty-five years later when he asserted that, by contrast to parent–child incest, sibling marriages are only 'next to an unnatural mixture'; for 'if they had been unnatural, they could not have been necessary' as 'it is not imaginable that God ... would have built up mankind by that which is contrary to Humane Nature'.[9] And in 1672, Richard Cumberland took a similarly relative position on the question of sibling incest, arguing that marriages between brothers and sisters 'in the first Age of the World' were '*necessary* to propagate that Race of Men, and to raise those Families, which Reason now endeavours to *Preserve*, by *prohibiting*'.[10]

Behn's Philander does not emerge ex nihilo, therefore, when he invokes Genesis to justify his incestuous desires. In a manner typically modern and predictably Whig, he disdains the beaten track of conventional morality to assert the prerogatives of an originary state: 'Let us ... scorn the dull *beaten road*, but let us love like the first race of men, nearest allied to God, promiscuously they loved, and possessed, father and daughter, brother and sister met, and reaped the joys of love without control, and counted it religious coupling, and 'twas encouraged too by heaven itself' (p. 4). As Ruth Perry has observed, Philander speaks for the authenticity of nature over the artifice of social codes. Posing as the ultimate pastoral lover, he emulates the freedom of creatures in the natural world. There is 'no troublesome honour, amongst the pretty inhabitants of the woods and streams, fondly to give laws to nature', he insists, 'but uncontrolled they play, and sing, and love; no parents checking their dear delights, no slavish matrimonial ties to restrain their nobler flame' (p. 28). Only 'man ... is bound up to rules, fetter'd by the nice decencies of honour' (p. 29).[11]

Given Behn's royalist politics, Philander's defence of incest may seem at first blush a simple alignment of Whiggism with transgression, the act of regicide – as René Girard has noted in another context – constituting an equivalent in the political realm of parricide or incest within the family.[12] Those who violate loyalties to their king, Behn seems to want to say, are also apt to violate the other bonds on which the social order and its civilising systems of difference depend.[13] Behn's creation of a heroine of royalist birth who draws the better part of her appeal from her success in outdoing Philander at the game of transgressiveness, however, destabilises this easy, politicised opposition between authority and rebellion and suggests a more complex and heterogeneous notion of transgression than a simply negative political coding would allow.[14] As more than one critic has noted, Behn's treatment of gender often seems to complicate and refract, if not indeed to contradict, her party politics, creating in her work the sense of multiple and incommensurate ideological agenda.[15] *Love-Letters* exemplifies this tendency through its own rhetorical excess, inviting itself to be read with a certain burlesquing tongue-in-cheekiness, as if it wants to make us ask – and it does make us ask – why (if this is first and foremost a political scandal novel) Behn would choose to defend the royal cause through so protracted a portrait of untamed female insubordination.

Is it true, as Janet Todd and Maureen Duffy both suggest, that Behn wants to promote the values of sincerity and authenticity as they are embodied in the figure of Philander's friend and rival, Octavio, by showing us that Philander's appeal to nature is nothing more than base hypocrisy?[16] Perhaps, at the most manifest level; but why then does her narrative read so much like a celebration of the pleasures and powers of role-playing and artifice whereby the indomitable Sylvia sacrifices Octavio to her revenge against Philander? If, as Perry suggests, Behn's characters are designed to show us 'where disrespect for law and order can lead', why does Behn's relation to her heroine's depravity seem so very fraught with irony?[17] The narrator tells us that Sylvia is imperious, proud, vain, opinionated, obstinate, censorious, amorously inclined, and indiscreet (pp. 259–60), and yet Behn seems to revel in the emotional resilience the heroine's duplicity affords. Jane Austen rarely assumes a more heteroglot relation to her heroines than Behn does when, reflecting on the ease with which Sylvia is able to transfer her affection from one lover to the next, she writes: 'Nature is not inclined to hurt itself; and there are but few who find it necessary to die for the disease of love. Of this sort was our *Sylvia*, though to give her her due, never any person who did not indeed die, ever languished under the torments of love, as did that charming and afflicted maid'

(p. 261). The nature appealed to here is elusively construed, gesturing ironically toward an unstable opposition between female nature and artifice in a world where a natural female impulse toward self-preservation requires the performance, nearly unto death, of the artifice of languishing femininity.[18]

Feminist critics have taken differing positions regarding the significance of the incest in Behn's text. To Janet Todd, it is merely a sensationalist device meant to keep Behn's book in print but not an important theme developed at any length.[19] For Judith Kegan Gardiner, on the other hand, Sylvia's willing participation in an incestuous adultery with her brother-in-law is the paradigmatic instance of her transgressiveness as a heroine and the conceptual point of departure for a complex reconfiguration of literary history.[20] Reading *Love-Letters* as a story of brother–sister incest that does not follow a familiar and traditionally valorised oedipal logic but instead avoids 'both father–son and mother–daughter paradigms for a transgressive sexuality in which the woman is not exclusively a victim but a willing and desiring agent',[21] Gardiner makes the case that a revaluation of the importance of Behn's text in the history of the novel genre opens the way to imagining an alternative paradigm of literary history, one that displaces an oedipal by what she calls 'an incestuous model of the novel's origins'.[22]

But is Behn's heroine stably figured as a willing agent of incestuous desire? Does the text of *Love-Letters* in fact support Gardiner's assessment that incest functions for Sylvia, as it does for Philander, as the expression of a liberatory eros? Behn may indeed refuse an oedipal model of female desire, but does she therefore necessarily embrace an incestuous ideal of feminine transgression? I shall argue that, on the contrary, far from replacing an oedipal with an incestuous ideal, Behn's narrative effectively displaces the conceptual grounds of a heterosexual matrix of assumptions that encodes incestuous desire as a form of freedom from patriarchal law.

There is a great deal more at stake here than a subtle difference of reading. Where we locate the transgressiveness of Behn's heroine has critical implications not just for the place Behn will occupy in contemporary conceptions of aesthetics and of literary history but also for a feminist analysis of narrative representations of incestuous desire, especially for recent efforts to theorise the role of incest in modern discursive inscriptions of female desire.[23] In making the case for Sylvia's incestuous agency without taking into account how she is located specifically as a female subject in relation both to incest and to the law that produces it as an object of repression – without regard, that is, to the patriarchal power structure within which incest derives its meaning and transgressive force to begin with – Gardiner allows a dangerous slippage to occur in her argument. Assuming that incest always inevitably constitutes transgression (indeed reading incest as the ultimate transgression), she relies on a characteristically modern discursive coding of incestuous desire as natural – an emergent cultural inscription in seventeenth-century England, as we have seen, but one that I would argue Behn's narrative actively refuses to underwrite.

In fact, I would suggest, far from elaborating a simple equivalence or correspondence between incest and transgression, Behn uses both categories to register the shifting positionality of gendered subjectivities, producing a variable model of the transgressiveness of incest and the incestuousness of transgression for her male and female characters. Rather than inscribing incest as a stable and univocal marker of transgression, she destabilises incest as a trope of liberation by exposing the ways it is differently constituted for her hero and heroine. In the process, she radically problematises the question of desire's origins, representing what Gardiner reads as original desire in Sylvia not as an intrinsic essence but as an effect of power.[24] Sylvia's transgressiveness as a heroine is situated not in her incestuous agency but elsewhere; it emerges rather in a conceptual and performative space made available to her only by the eventual recognition that Philander's exaltation of incest as a liberation from prohibitive patriarchal law actually functions as an instrument of power. Incest operates in Behn's text, in other words, not as a simple figure for transgression but as a complex discursive site where the oppositional ideologies of patriarchy and individualism intersect, at once confronting each other and, in the process, exposing their joint complicity in (and their shared dependence on) the appropriation and cooptation of female desire.

This is hardly to revert to Todd's assessment of the essential insignificance of the incest in Behn's text. On the contrary, it is to read Sylvia's incest as a necessary part of Behn's complex critique of Whig libertarian politics. At the level of plot, after all, the incest does take Sylvia outside her father's house; it thus establishes the conditions within which Behn is able to show that that outside is always already inside – always on the verge of reinscribing the very law it would subvert. To be successfully transgressive on Behn's terms, Sylvia will have to move beyond the illusory liberation of naturalised incestuous desire – *outside* the outside of an oedipal dyad in which women are mere theatres for the playing out of male desire. The serial nature of *Love-Letters* allows Behn to effect these consecutive displacements compellingly, by creating an opportunity for her to write her heroine out of and beyond the limits of the typical romantic plot.[25]

PHILANDER'S 'PHALLIC HANDSHAKE' AND THE LIMITS OF THE LIBERTINE CRITIQUE OF PATRIARCHY

I approach my subject through a reading of several key episodes that help to establish the context within which the incest in Behn's narrative acquires meaning. My aim is to illuminate the extent to which the incestuous relation between Philander and Sylvia is conditioned by the dynamics of a system of homosocial exchange in which the daughter's desire functions not as a locus of agency but as a site of confrontation between paternal and fraternal interests. Because familial conflict is coded politically in Behn's novel, this reading also necessarily involves discussion of the way Sylvia's body functions in a double symbolic register as a political as well as familial battleground.

This is not to say that Sylvia entirely lacks transgressive agency. It is rather to suggest that we must first understand the structuring homosocial frame within which her incest is enacted ultimately to appreciate the process whereby she manages to move beyond the possibilities for transgression it delimits into a space subversively generated by a parodic repetition of its terms. For, however paradoxically, it is only after Sylvia comes to recognise her status as a sign within a drama of masculine rivalry, to understand that as a woman she is always already a representation within a homosocial matrix of desire, that she opens herself to the possibility of taking performative control of her enactment of desire and gendered subjectivity.

I take as my point of entry Philander's account of an episode that occurs relatively early in part one, immediately after his first nocturnal tryst with Sylvia. As a dutiful royalist daughter, Sylvia early expresses considerable anguish over Philander's attempts to prevail upon her 'honour'; she finally concedes, nevertheless, to a private interview, which she justifies as a trial of her virtue and resolution. And as Philander's letter recounting the details of their first night alone together reveals, Sylvia does remain 'a maid' despite the opportunity for physical conquest on his part.

The cause of Philander's forbearance, as he explains, is neither his regard for Sylvia's honour (on the contrary, he says, her resistance inflames him all the more) nor her physical attractions (these, he insists, are overwhelming) but a fit of sexual impotence brought on by a state of overstimulation. Having 'overcome all difficulties, all the fatigues and toils of love's long seiges, vanquish'd the mighty phantom of the fair, the giant honour, and routed all the numerous host of women's little reasonings, passed all the bounds of peevish modesty; nay, even all the loose and silken counterscarps that fenced the sacred fort', instead of receiving 'the yielding treasure', Philander had fallen 'fainting before the surrendering gates', a circumstance he goes on to associate with the weakness of old age. In a rhetorical manoeuvre that underscores his physical prowess even as it acknowledges a lapse in his '(till then) never failing power', he attributes his attack of impotence to the envy of the gods; one 'malicious at [his] glory', he suggests, has left him full of 'mad desires', but 'all inactive, as age or death itself, as cold and feeble, as unfit for joy, as if [his] youthful fire had long been past, or *Sylvia* had never been blest with charms'. Indeed, the excess of passion has so paralysed Philander that he curses his youth and implores the gods to give him 'old age, for that has some excuse but youth has none' (pp. 50–1).

The dialectic of youthful vigour and old age within which Philander here encodes what amounts to an averted incestuous consummation is, as we have to some extent already seen, precisely the dialectic within which he has attempted to justify his incestuous and adulterous desire from the start. From as early as his very first letter to Sylvia, he has idealised his affection for her by casting the older generation as guardians of a threatened domain of power, invested only in the jealous retention of control over the future. The institutions of kinship and of marriage are mere 'trick[s] devised by the wary old' (p. 4), who, like the gods, arbitrarily wield the reins of political power even as they fear and envy Philander's authentic passion and youthful virility.

Philander reproduces this dialectic at a more literal level in his reference later in the same letter to a parallel sexual plot involving another male predator and another 'reluctant maid'. For even as Philander – 'the young, the brisk and gay' (p. 51) – is engineering an interview with Sylvia, Sylvia's father – that 'brisk old gentleman' (p. 56) – has been counting on a garden assignation with Melinda, her refreshingly worldly serving maid. Few readers will forget the hilarious 'accident' by which plot and comic subplot here intersect,

enabling Behn to play irreverently with the ironies, multiple meanings, and shifting power relations produced when the 'maid' Sylvia,
'mistress' of Melinda, plays 'mistress' to Philander while her 'maid',
Melinda, plays 'mistress' to Sylvia's father. Much as Defoe would
later point to the ironies inherent in the homonymous relation contained within the honorific *Madam*, Behn here uses the shifting and
multiplying of subject positions to baldly expose the illusory forms
of power invested in all varieties of mistresses and maids.[26]

According to Philander, no consummation takes place between
master and 'mistress' here any more than between Philander and
Sylvia. Alarmed by a noise that makes the young lovers fear discovery, Philander steals into the garden disguised in Melinda's night-
gown and headress, only to be mistaken for Melinda by the eager
old gentleman. Here is his account of events as they unfold:
'*Monsieur* the Count, ... taking me for Melinda, ... caught hold of
my gown as I would have passed him, and cried, "Now *Melinda*, I
see you are a maid of honour, – come, retire with me into the grove,
where I have a present of a heart and something else to make you"'
(p. 55). It is now Philander's turn to play the role of reluctant maid:
'With that I pulled back and whispered – "Heavens! Would you
make a mistress of me?" – Says he – "A mistress, what woulds't thou
be, a cherubin?" Then I replied as before – "I am no whore, sir," –
"No", cries he, "but I can quickly make thee one, I have my tools
about me, sweet-heart; therefore let us lose no time, but fall to
work," ... With that he clapped fifty guineas in a purse into one
hand, and something else that shall be nameless into the other, presents that had been both worth *Melinda's* acceptance' (p. 56).

Combining many of the key motifs and topoi of *Love-Letters*
(among them masquerade, gender reversal, class and generational
encounter, and homosocial exchange of a most literal variety) – all
within an epistolary frame – Philander's garden adventure offers a
veritable object lesson in the problematics of reading Behn. It is possible to take Philander's narrative at face value, to accept the hero at
his word, as Gardiner does when she reads Philander's disguise as
providing a sort of comic externalisation of his demeaning impotence. Philander, as she sees him here, is a whining buffoon – 'a ludi-
crously declassed and feminised figure' – whose exposure through
Behn's publication of his private correspondence realises his own
worst fear, as he expresses it in his letter, of being publicly ridiculed
('Where shall I hide my head when this lewd story's told?' [p. 51]).
In Philander's account of his comic adventure with Beralti, Gardiner

suggests, Behn not only casts doubt on the virility of the notoriously promiscuous Lord Grey but 'undercuts the admiration accorded to Don Juans generally. His withdrawal from the garden, which leaves his father-in-law in a state of sexual frustration, is, Gardiner argues, a burlesque of 'his own frustrated romantic seduction of Sylvia'.[27]

But Gardiner's reading does little justice to the hermeneutic instabilities generated by the epistolary nature of Behn's text, instabilities that produce the immanent possibility – if not the eminent probability – that Philander is only feigning impotence. The only grounds we have for validating what really happened on that disappointing night are, after all, Philander's words – his own dubious representation of events. And in light of the strategies of seduction he has deployed up to this point, it makes perfect sense to read his attack of impotence not as a fact but as a performance (or what might more appropriately be termed a magnificent anti-performance in this case). Far from constituting a form of humiliation, this episode actually helps Philander to consolidate his power over Sylvia.[28]

Philander's 'retreat' from consummation at this moment of peak excitement and opportunity is thoroughly in keeping with the strategies of deferral by which he has gained entry into Sylvia's bedchamber in the first place. From the outset, he has moved with a certain deft belatedness. As early as her third letter, Sylvia pines for word from Philander: 'Not yet? – not yet?' she laments, 'oh ye dull tedious hours, when will you glide away? and bring that happy moment on, in which I shall at least hear from my *Philander*; ... Perhaps *Philander's* making a trial of virtue by this silence' (p. 14). In her next, still waiting ('Another night, oh heavens, and yet no letter come!' [p. 16]), she even entertains the thought that Philander may in fact be toying with her: 'Is it a trick, a cold fit, only assum'd to try how much I love you?' (p. 16). Predictably, Philander has an excuse, although in presenting it he also betrays a certain disingenuity: 'When I had sealed the enclosed, *Brilliard* told me you were this morning come from *Bellfont*, and with infinite impatience have expected seeing you here; which deferred my sending this to the old place; and I am so vain (oh adorable *Sylvia!*) as to believe my fancied silence has given you disquiets; but sure, my *Sylvia* could not charge me with neglect?' (pp. 11–12).

It may be revenge for Sylvia's ambivalence about surrendering herself to him, indeed for the tenacity with which she clings to the imperatives of honour, that drives Philander to these delays. For although Sylvia often longs for him, she is just as often grateful for his neglect: 'Let me alone, let me be ruin'd with honour, if I must be ruin'd. – For oh! 'twere much happier I were no more, than that I should be more than *Philander's* sister; or he than *Sylvia's* brother: oh let me ever call you by that cold name' (p. 14). Philander, however, will be satisfied with gaining nothing less than absolute control over the representation of Sylvia's desire. Early on she describes herself as the very embodiment of disorder and indeterminacy: 'Could you but imagine how I am tormentingly divided, how unresolved between violent love and cruel honour, you would say 'twere impossible to fix me any where; or be the same thing for a moment together' (p. 17). Onto this doubt and indecision, Philander fixes his own desire, reading Sylvia as he wishes – like Adam, dreaming her doubt into desire for his advances and then naming it as love (pp. 7–8). 'I know you love', writes Philander to Sylvia (p. 24). 'He soon taught her to understand it was love', asserts the narrator in the novel's 'Argument'; 'thou art the first that ever did inform me that there was such a sort of wish about me', writes Sylvia to Philander (p. 61). Such phrases echo as a refrain throughout part one. And Sylvia does at last defer to the authority of Philander's reading of her, both in finally accepting his diagnosis of her alienation from desire and in conceding to his accusations of her fickleness and inconstancy along the way.

In the context of this series of deferrals, Philander's impotence simply constitutes a culminating moment in the production of desire in Sylvia. Although in prior letters she had vacillated wildly between attraction to her brother-in-law and a perfectly catechismal defence of patriarchal honour, in the two letters that she writes in quick succession immediately following Philander's 'lapse' in potency, she describes herself as experiencing a degree of desire she has previously not known. 'I have wishes, new, unwonted wishes', she writes, 'at every thought of thee I find a strange disorder in my blood, that pants and burns in every vein, and makes me blush and sigh, and grow impatient, ashamed and angry' (p. 63). She now further concedes that her previous 'coldness' must have been dissembled, as she was 'not mistress of' it (p. 63). (This concession by Sylvia is of interest for our reading of Philander, as it admits the possibility that coldness may be feigned.) Sylvia continues, 'there lies a woman's art, there all her boasted virtue, it is but well dissembling, and no more – but mine, alas, is gone, for ever fled' (p. 63). In the process of increasingly surrendering to Philander's 'cause', Sylvia now begins in several instances to echo his very words and arguments, mirroring his early references to 'fond custom' and 'phantom honour' as well as the opportunistic and somewhat desperate arguments he had used to justify his commitment to the political interests of the treacherous Cesario. Just as he had there described himself as being 'in past a retreat' (p. 40) and declared that 'though the glorious falling weight should crush me, it is great to attempt' (p. 41), so Sylvia now casts herself in the role of heroic martyr to her love: 'I am plunged in, past hope of a retreat; and since my fate has pointed me out for ruin, I cannot fall more gloriously. Take then, *Philander*, to your dear arms, a maid that can no longer resist, who is disarmed of all defensive power: she yields, she yields, and does confess it too' (p. 65). Sylvia's response to Philander's impotence, in short, is to renounce every doctrine she has hitherto been taught by the 'grave and wise' (p. 62). He induces her to give up a 'coldness she is not mistress of' by, in effect, being master of his own. One more instance of deferral (occasioned this time by Cesario's calling him away) will secure his romantic victory; to prove his passion, Philander will offer to disregard the summons, but Sylvia – now thoroughly identified with his interests – insists that he respond, promising that Philander's obedience to the commands of Cesario (whom earlier she had regarded as a rival) will be rewarded in her arms (pp. 68–9).

If, as Sylvia is here driven to presuppose, affecting coldness is 'a woman's art' – a prerogative or sign of femininity – then feigning impotence is for Philander, in more than one sense, 'putting on' the maid. It is a way both of putting Sylvia on (i.e., controlling her through deception) and of doing so by performing a woman's part (affecting coldness), a strategy made literal in Philander's garden performance as Melinda.[29] Appropriating to himself a dissembled coldness that he identifies as a female strategy, Philander does not invite Sylvia to become a better mistress of her own standoffishness, but instead manoeuvres her into accepting the coercive fiction of her own natural desire for him. Her longing for him is thus understood not as the effect of a performance on his part but as an essence intrinsic to her, a 'natural propensity' (p. 60) poorly masked in her case by a shabby cloak of artificial virtue. As she does at several other points throughout her text, Behn here problematises the question of desire's origins in depicting Sylvia's grasping after a causal narrative: 'I am the aggressor', she declares eventually, 'the fault is in me, and thou art innocent' (p. 60).[30] Thus does Philander take control rhetorically of their courtship by inducing Sylvia to own an 'unaccountable' passion (p. 61) over which she has neither prior knowledge nor control.

It remains, however, to determine the role of Philander's garden performance as a reluctant maid in his project of displacing all traces of reluctance in Sylvia. I have argued that what to Gardiner is whining and buffoonery on Philander's part can also, if we refuse to assume the hero's authenticity, be understood as a form of strategic self-dramatisation whereby Philander acquires power by performing impotence. Philander's account of his 'pleasant adventure' in the garden similarly serves his ends with Sylvia by enlisting her collusion as a reader in a comic undermining of paternal authority. By reducing the count to a rather embarrassing travesty of the predatory excesses of youth, it offers a repetition and amplification of Philander's successful manipulation of the signs of impotence and femininity to establish the conditions of sexual victory.[31] It is not just that Philander has prior knowledge from Melinda of Beralti's sexual indiscretions while Beralti himself remains ignorant of Philander's dalliance with his daughter. There is also the fact that the old man is prepared to pay for Melinda's services, a detail that, while it bespeaks Beralti's economic prowess, also makes him compare unfavourably with Philander. The fifty guineas intended for Melinda may stand as a mark of Bellfont's class as well as gender supremacy, but they are also a sign of his maid's affective indifference to him – an indifference that, as we have seen, stands in stark contrast to the passion Philander arouses in Sylvia (despite, if not indeed because of, his temporary lapse in potency). In fact, the comic circumstance of Melinda's physical absence at the moment when the fifty guineas is bestowed makes an utter mockery of the count's physical power over her. The scene in which the father both literally and figuratively attempts to impose the phallus is also the scene in which the paternal phallus is inadvertently exposed, not simply to the laughter of the son-in-law but, through him, to the daughter's laughter too.

But Beralti's garden vigil for the daughter's maid takes place at the very moment when Philander is preparing the stage for the theft of the daughter's maidenhead. The identity of role between Philander and the count as predatory males is thus complicated by their status as rivals. They are not simply mirrors of one another – males in quest of separate objects of desire – but competitors for control of Sylvia. (Could not Beralti's dalliance with the maid in fact be read as a phantasmatic rendering of the eroticised relation between father and daughter that underpins the entire sexual drama of part one?)[32] To the extent that they situate Sylvia's alienation

from her father within the context of a drama of masculine rivalry
in which she figures not as an agent but a sign, the familial dynamics
here are critical. Philander's inclination to flout paternal authority
and to infringe upon the father's right of rule is an aspect of his political character as a follower of the regicidal Cesario. But the link
does not end there. Like Cesario, Philander functions in the capacity
of a son, a role that he has acquired by his marriage to Sylvia's
sister, Myrtilla, and one that involves not just the acquisition of
certain privileges but also the institution of specific prohibitions.
The rules of kinship that give Philander freedom of access to
Beralti's daughters also presuppose the assumption of countervailing
filial responsibilities. Sylvia alludes to both these prerogatives and
their limits when she contemplates the consequences of her father's
discovery of their affair: 'my father being rash, and extremely
jealous, and the more so of me, by how much more he is fond of
me, and nothing would enrage him like the discovery of an interview like this; though you have the liberty to range the house of
Bellfont as a son, and are indeed at home there; but ... when he
shall find his son and virgin daughter, the brother and the sister so
retired, so entertained, – What but death can ensue? Or what is
worse, eternal ... confusion on my honour?' (p. 43). In seducing
Sylvia (by, in effect, usurping the father's prerogative to dispose of
her virginity), Philander violates the authority invested in him as a
brother – an 'authority' that, as the following passage testifies, Sylvia
recognises as 'lawful'. Describing herself as impaled by a sense of familial obligation in the face of his advances, as 'a maid that cannot
fly', she entertains a moment of regret: 'Why did you take advantage
of those freedoms I gave you as a brother? ... but for my sister's
sake, I play'd with you, suffer'd your hands and lips to wander
where I dare not now; all which I thought a sister might allow a
brother, and knew not all the while the treachery of love: oh none,
but under that intimate title of a brother, could have had the opportunity to have ruin'd me ... by degrees so subtle, and an authority so
lawful, you won me out of all' (pp. 14–15).[33]
   Within the discursive economy of Behn's text, in short, Sylvia's
honour – represented both by her virgin body and her desire to fulfil
her f(am)ilial obligations – becomes Philander's political battle-ground.
As 'daughter to the great *Beralti*, and sister to *Myrtilla*, a yet unspotted
maid, fit to produce a race of glorious heroes', Sylvia recognises that
all her actions reflect on the honour of 'the noble house of the *Beralti*'
and that Philander seeks 'to build the trophies of [his] conquests on

the ruin of both *Myrtilla's* fame and [her own]' (p. 18). From a political perspective, it is not sufficient that he ruin Myrtilla only, as Sylvia
yet remains to 'redeem the bleeding [royalist] honour of [her] family'
(p. 22). As Myrtilla puts it in her one admonitory missive to her sister,
Sylvia is 'the darling child, the joy of all, the last hope left, the refuge'
of 'the most unhappy [family] of all the race of old nobility' (p. 71).
Philander's corruption of Beralti's dutiful younger daughter through
the illicit appropriation of sexual rights over her in this sense constitutes a Whig usurpation of the royalist right of rule.

One sees here, better perhaps than at any other point in her text,
the logic of Behn's interweaving of sexual and political narratives;
for what Behn's complex structuring of her tale makes evident is the
profound interimplication – indeed the mutually constitutive nature
– of sexuality and politics. The relationship between plots here is
more than merely analogical, more than the simple matter of a
metaphor in which sexual conquest serves as a figure at the level of
private life for a more public, political form of victory. It is rather a
relationship of discursive interdependence in which the categories of
the private and the public, materiality and meaning, desire and the
law reveal their inherently contingent and unstable identities.
Gardiner accepts the efficacy of a stable distinction between private
and public life when she rests her reading on the difference between
Philander's positive political power and his lack of familial authority
over Sylvia. But this is precisely the distinction Behn destabilises
when she exposes the intensely political nature of individual desire.
Philander's binary opposition between private and public life is, she
suggests, an illusion created to sustain the liberatory fiction that
legitimates the operations of masculine privilege.

Philander represents his incestuous love for Sylvia as an expression of unconstrained desire that marks a liberation from a material-
ist economy of sexual exchange. Against the institution of marriage –
'a trick devised by the wary old only to make provision for posterity'
(p. 4) – he urges the authenticity of 'pleasures vast and unconfin'd'
(p. 20). And eventually, in the invective against marriage to which
she devotes her penultimate letter in part one, Sylvia too comes to
embrace such a libertine philosophy, asserting that only adulterous
love can occasion genuine heterosexual reciprocity ('That's a heav-
enly match', she writes, 'when two souls touched with equal passion
meet, ... when no base interest makes the hasty bargain, ... and ...
both understand to take and pay' [p. 109]). Ultimately, however,
by showing how the very act of erotic transgression that Philander

proffers as an individualist solution to the problem of hierarchical repression ultimately reinscribes Sylvia's specular status in reciprocal relations between men, Behn exposes the limits of the libertine critique of patriarchy.

The asymmetrical and nonreciprocal character of Sylvia and Philander's relationship will become increasingly clear, both to Sylvia and to the reader, as the events of parts two and three of the narrative – especially those involving the relationship between Philander and Octavio – unfold. But even within the limits of the love plot of part one, that inadvertent 'phallic handshake' between father and son-in-law in the garden – a savage burlesque of the gentleman's agreement by which the gift of the daughter is legitimately exchanged – reveals (even as it figures the bypassing of legitimate succession) the homosocial ground of both patriarchal law and its transgression. Fifty guineas and that 'nameless' entity, the father's penis, may be 'presents ... both worth *Melinda's* acceptance', but only Sylvia – phallic representative of the Father's Name and Law – is worth Philander's. Just as Sylvia's ensuing marriage to Philander's 'property', Brilliard, will expose the underlying ironies of the libertine's dependence on the legal artifice of marriage to secure control over the body of his lover, so Behn here shows that an incestuous challenge to the law of patriarchal prerogative does not necessarily constitute a challenge to the law of masculine privilege.

From *Rereading Aphra Behn: History, Theory and Criticism*, ed. Heidi Hutner (Charlottesvilla, VA, 1993), pp. 151–66.

NOTES

[Seeing *Love-Letters* as something of a celebration of the body of Sylvia, Ellen Pollak argues that the work, which is overtly about incest and state politics, is much concerned with questions of gender, identity, and representation. Behn destabilises incest as a trope of liberation since it is differently constituted for men and women, and she radically problematises the question of desire's origins. Pollak makes her points through the episode in which Philander suffers a fit of sexual impotence and is then accosted in female dress by his father-in-law. Ed.]

1. For further discussion of the Berkeley–Ford affair, see Maureen Duffy, *The Passionate Shepherdess: Aphra Behn, 1640–89* (London, 1977), pp. 221–4; and Angeline Goreau, *Reconstructing Aphra: A Social Biography of Aphra Behn* (New York, 1980), pp. 273–8). For an

account of the trial, see William Cobbett, *State Trials* (London, 1811), 9: 127–86. For the probable identification of Dryden's Caleb as Grey, see Cecil Price, *Cold Caleb: The Scandalous Life of Ford Grey, First Earl of Tankerville, 1655–1701* (London, 1956), p. 71.

2. Ros Ballaster discusses the effect on Behn of conventions regarding 'appropriate' female forms in her *Seductive Forms: Women's Amatory Fiction, 1684–1740* (Oxford, 1992), pp. 71–81.

3. Susan Staves, *Players' Scepters: Fictions of Authority in the Restoration* (Lincoln and London, 1979), ch. 5. For other discussions of the dissociation between theology and natural law theory in the seventeenth and eighteenth centuries, see Bruce Boehrer, '"Nice Philosophy": *'Tis Pity She's a Whore* and the Two Books of God', *SEL*, 24 (1984), 355–71; Alfred Owen Aldridge, 'The Meaning of Incest from Hutcheson to Gibbon', *Ethics*, 61 (1951), 309–13; and W. Daniel Wilson, 'Science, Natural Law, and Unwitting Sibling Incest in Eighteenth-Century Literature', *Studies in Eighteenth-Century Culture*, 13 (1984), 249–70.

4. Aphra Behn, *Love-Letters between a Nobleman and His Sister*, ed. Maureen Duffy (London, 1987), p. 4. Subsequent references to this edition will be cited parenthetically in the text by page number.

5. Sybil Wolfram, *In-Laws and Outlaws: Kinship and Marriage in England* (London and Sydney, 1987), p. 43. On the status of the in-law relationship with respect to incest in England, see also Jack Goody, 'A Comparative Approach to Incest and Adultery', *British Journal of Sociology*, 7 (1956), 291; and Staves, *Players' Scepters*, p. 304. Behn's Myrtilla in effect assumes affinal as well as consanguineal ties in the inlaw relation when she suggests to Sylvia that the existence of her child by Philander strengthens his connections to Sylvia both by relation and by blood. Philander, she writes, 'has lain by thy unhappy sister's side so many tender years, by whom he has a dear and lovely offspring, by which he has *more fixed himself to thee by relation and blood*' (p. 70; italics added). The doctrine of 'one flesh' that underlay the British concept of marriage became the basis also for arguments regarding the illegality of sexual relations between stepson and stepmother. See, for example, Jeremy Taylor, who argues that 'she that is one flesh with my Father is as neer to me as my Father, and thats as neer as my own Mother' (*Ductor Dubitantium: or The Rule of Conscience* [London, 1660] bk. 2, ch. 2, rule 3, n. 29).

6. Staves, *Players' Scepters*, p. 263–4.

7. Hugo Grotius, *The Law of War and Peace (De Jure Belli ac Paci Libri Tres)*, trans. Francis W. Kelsey (Indianapolis and New York, 1925), bk. 2, ch. 5, sect. 13, par. I, p. 242. Grotius observed the difficulty, if not impossibility, of assigning 'definite natural causes' for the unlawfulness of incestuous marriages within any degree of affinity or consanguinity (bk. 2, ch. 5, sect. 12, par. I, p. 239).

8. Grotius, *The Law of War and Peace*, bk. 2, ch. 5, sec. 13, para. 5, p. 244.

9. Taylor, *Ductor Dubitantium*, 2.2.24–5.

10. Richard Cumberland, *De Legibus Naturae*, trans. as *A Treatise of the Laws of Nature* by John Maxwell (London, 1727); facsimile reprint in *British Philosophers and Theologians of the Seventeenth and Eighteenth Centuries*, ed. René Wellek (New York and London, 1978), ch. 8, sec. 9, p. 338. The implications of this incipient questioning of the natural basis of the incest prohibition would be extended in the mid-eighteenth century by Henry St John Bolingbroke, who went so far as to construe Eve as Adam's daughter: 'Eve was in some sort the daughter of Adam. She was literally bone of his bone, and flesh of his flesh, by birth, if I may call it so, whereas other husbands and wives are so in an allegorical manner only. But to pass this over, the children of the first couple were certainly brothers and sisters, and by these conjunctions, declared afterward incestuous, the human species was first propagated' ('Fragments, or Minutes of Essays', in *Works*, 8 vols (London, 1809), 7:497–8). Another instance where scripture seemed to sanctify parent–child incest on the grounds of necessity or good intentions was in its account of Lot's daughters. See, Bolingbroke, *Works*, 7:416–17; and Simon Patrick, *A Commentary Upon the Historical Books of the Old Testament* (London, 1727), Gen. 19:32.

11. Ruth Perry, *Women, Letters, and the Novel* (New York, 1980), p. 24.

12. René Girard, *Violence and the Sacred*, trans. Patrick Gregory (Baltimore and London, 1977), p. 74.

13. Such an association of seditious rebellion with incest was not unique in royalist discourse of the Restoration. Like sorcery, incest was associated with the sanctioning of alternative (and therefore illegitimate) sources of authority. Thus, for example, when George Hickes undertook in 1678 to recount the trial and conviction of the seditious conventicle preacher James Mitchell for his attempt on the life of the archbishop of St Andrews, there seemed reason enough to feature Mitchell's tenuous association with the unsavoury figure of Thomas Weir by appending to the record of Mitchell's trial the story of Weir's own earlier trial and execution for adultery, incest, sorcery, and bestiality. See *Ravillac Redivivus: Being a Narrative of the late Tryal of Mr. James Mitchel ... , to which is Annexed, an Account of the Tryal of that most wicked Pharisee Major Thomas Weir ...* (London, 1678). Weir had been tried and executed in 1670. Hickes, a nonjuror, was personal chaplain to the duke of Lauderdale. An expanded second edition of his narrative was published in 1682. In 1710, Curll also brought out an amplified version under the title 'The Spirit of Fanaticism Exemplified'. On the association of incest and sorcery (both of which figure significantly in *Love-Letters*), see Mary Douglas, *Purity and Danger: An*

Analysis of the Concepts of Pollution and Taboo (London, 1966), pp. 107–13; David M. Schneider, 'The Meaning of Incest', *Journal of Polynesian Society*, 85 (1976), 149–69; and Judith Lewis Herman, *Father–Daughter Incest* (Cambridge and London, 1981), p. 50.

14. Grey, his Whig allegiances notwithstanding, was as of royalist birth. 'Consider, my lord', writes Sylvia, 'you are born noble, from parents of untainted loyalty' (p. 33).

15. See, for example, Goreau, *Reconstructing Aphra*, pp. 272–3; Ballaster, *Seductive Forms*, pp. 78–9; Robert Markley, '"Be impudent, be saucy, forward, bold, touzing, and leud": The Politics of Masculine Sexuality and Feminine Desire in Behn's Tory Comedies', in *Revisionist Readings of the Restoration and Eighteenth-Century Theatre*, ed. J. Douglas Canfield and Deborah Payne (forthcoming); and Robert Markley and Molly Rothenberg, 'Contestations of Nature: Aphra Behn's "The Golden Age" and the Sexualizing of Politics', in *Rereading Aphra Behn* (1993).

16. Janet Todd, *The Sign of Angellica: Women, Writing, and Fiction, 1660–1800* (New York, 1989), p. 83; Maureen Duffy, Introduction to Virago edition of *Love-Letters*, p. xi–xii.

17. Perry, *Women, Letters, and the Novel*, p. 25.

18. On the topic of self-preservation in seventeenth-century natural law theory, see Maximillian E. Novak, *Defoe and the Nature of Man* (London, 1963).

19. Todd, *The Sign of Angellica*, pp. 79–82.

20. Judith Kegan Gardiner, 'The First English Novel: Aphra Behn's *Love Letters*, the Canon, and Women's Tastes', *Tulsa Studies in Women's Literature*, 8 (Fall 1989), 201–22.

21. Ibid., p. 207.

22. Ibid., p. 218. For a fuller discussion of oedipal models of the novel's origins, especially Ian Watt's, see also Laurie Langbauer, *Women and Romance: The Consolations of Gender in the English Novel* (Ithaca and London, 1990), pp. 28–30.

23. See, for example, Judith Butler, 'Prohibition, Psychoanalysis, and the Heterosexual Matrix', in her *Gender Trouble: Feminism and the Subversion of Identity* (New York and London, 1990), ch. 2.

24. This question, in the form of debate about whether Henrietta Berkeley had been a consenting party in leaving her father's house, was also an important issue in Grey's trial. See Cobbett, *State Trials*, 9: 127–86; and Price, *Cold Caleb*, pp. 98–100.

25. For a theoretical consideration of such destabilising narrative strategies in twentieth-century women's writing, see Rachel Blau DuPlessis,

Writing beyond the Ending: Narrative Strategies of Twentieth-Century Women Writers (Bloomington, IN, 1985).

26. Others have fruitfully discussed Behn's characteristic multiplying of subject positions. See, for example, Ballaster, *Seductive Forms*, ch. 3; and Jessica Munns, '"I by a Double Right Thy Bounties Claim": Aphra Behn and Sexual Space', in *Curtain Calls: British and American Women and the Theater, 1660–1820*, ed. Mary Anne Schofield and Cecelia Macheski (Athens, OH, 1991), pp. 193–210.

27. Gardiner, 'The First English Novel', pp. 212–13.

28. Duffy's assertion that Philander's impotence is a symptom of syphilis and thus a 'tell-tale signal' of his sexual promiscuity (Introduction to *Love-Letters*, p. xii), a possibility Todd is also willing to entertain (*The Sign of Angelica*, p. 81), is an interesting but largely unfounded speculation.

29. Although I use it in a different sense, I borrow the impulse to characterise gender performance and cross-dressing as potential put-ons from Kristina Straub's recent work on female theatrical cross-dressing and the parodic performance of masculinity in the career and writing of Charlotte Charke in *Sexual Suspects: Eighteenth-Century Players and Sexual Ideology* (Princeton, NJ, 1992), ch. 7; a version of this chapter, entitled 'The Guilty Pleasures of Female Theatrical Cross-Dressing and the Autobiography of Charlotte Charke', also appears in *Body Guards: The Cultural Politics of Gender Ambiguity*, ed. Julia Epstein and Kristina Straub (New York and London), pp. 142–66.

30. Gardiner simplifies what Behn makes problematic, it seems to me, when she reads these assertions by Sylvia as 'subversive of traditional gender roles' in that they characterise the heroine as a desiring subject who 'glories in her new desires' ('The First English Novel', p. 213).

31. This is not to deny Philander's account of his garden escapade either its comic hilarity or its status as Behn's satire of Philander/Grey. One cannot help but agree with Gardiner that Perry (who bases her reading solely on part one of the narrative) is wrong in her assertion that 'there is no gaiety about [the] truancy' of Philander and Sylvia (Gardiner, 'The First English Novel', p. 213; Perry, *Women, Letters, and the Novel*, p. 25). But is the gaiety of the episode generated solely or even primarily by Behn's wicked delight in humiliating Philander/Grey? Or is there some other, competing source of comedy at work? There is a question of audience at issue here, because Philander (to the extent that he functions as a character rather than a mere surrogate for Behn) controls the narration, which he offers as entertainment to Sylvia. What is at stake for Philander in this relation? He claims a simple, practical motive – that of feeding Sylvia information Melinda will need to cover for him with the count. But if Philander were so utterly ashamed of the

impotence Gardiner sees re-enacted in the scene, why would he bother to give so elaborate an account of those events to Sylvia? Surely, if Beralti's garden tryst with the disguised Philander is a parodic repetition of the youthful upstairs encounter between Philander and Sylvia, its effect is less to burlesque Philander than the count.

32. That Sylvia and 'the maid' are surrogates for one another is suggested at several other points, e.g., when Sylvia claims to be inditing for Melinda or when she puts (or at least attempts to put) Antonet to bed in her place with Octavio.

33. Once again, my reading here diverges from that of Gardiner, who insists that because Philander is Sylvia's brother 'in law', as opposed to her father or her brother, he 'has no authority over her', despite the fact that he is 'politically more powerful' than she is ('The First English Novel', p. 218).

10

The Romance of Empire: *Oroonoko* and the Trade in Slaves

LAURA BROWN

> Our victims know us by their scars and by their chains, and it is this
> that makes their evidence irrefutable. It is enough that they show us
> what we have made of them for us to realise what we have made of
> ourselves.
>
> (Jean-Paul Sartre, Preface to Frantz Fanon's *The Wretched of the
> Earth*)[1]

Aphra Behn's novella *Oroonoko: Or, the Royal Slave*, written and
published in the summer of the year of the 1688 revolution in
England,[2] no longer needs an extensive introduction for students of
Restoration and eighteenth-century literature, or even for many
critics in other fields. *Oroonoko* has almost entered the canon, as
works by Behn and other women writers have been recovered by
Anglo-American feminist criticism. The novella *Oroonoko* and the
dramatic satire *The Rover*, Behn's two most important works, both
saw new printings in the late 1960s and early 1970s.[3] And Behn
herself has recently been the subject of two critical biographies, by
Maureen Duffy and Angeline Goreau – the first significant studies
since George Woodcock's *Incomparable Aphra* in 1948.[4] But
Woodcock was clearly an anomaly: an anarchist critic in the early
stages of the Cold War, exploring issues of feminism and racism
while others in the field were consolidating the New Critical paradigm. The only prior attention to Behn had been a brief skirmish

initiated by Ernest Bernbaum in 1913 about the historical question of Behn's trip to Guiana, the geographical setting of *Oroonoko*.[5]

Now we can find *Oroonoko* even in the undergraduate curriculum on occasion, and according to the *MLA Bibliography* two or three articles on Behn appear each year – treating matters of gender and genre.[6] Feminist criticism has opened up *Oroonoko* to readers who twenty-five years ago would have stuck to Dryden, Rochester, or Congreve. But even though that feminist revision has been significant – especially for projects in political criticism like this one – the recovery of *Oroonoko* was quite unnecessary. In another tradition of cultural criticism apparently inaccessible to the feminist revisionists who 'recovered' Behn for students of literature, *Oroonoko* has long held a prominent place. The novella has been recognised as a seminal work in the tradition of antislavery writings from the time of its publication down to our own period. The story of Behn's 'royal slave' occupied the English stage for almost a century, in dramatic redactions by Thomas Southerne (*Oroonoko*, 1696) and John Hawkesworth (a revision of Southerne's play, 1759). And its sentimental authenticity was confirmed and augmented by the famous occasion in 1749 when an African 'prince' and his companion, previously sold into slavery but ransomed by the British government and received in state in London, attended a performance of Southerne's *Oroonoko*: affected 'with that generous grief which pure nature always feels, and which art had not yet taught them to suppress; the young prince was so far overcome, that he was obliged to retire at the end of the fourth act. His companion remained, but wept the whole time; a circumstance which affected the audience yet more than the play, and doubled the tears which were shed for *Oroonoko* and *Imoinda*.'[7] Historians of slavery have never neglected *Oroonoko*. In the two most important accounts of literary treatments of slavery that deal with eighteenth-century England, Wylie Sypher's *Guinea's Captive Kings* (1942) and David Brion Davis's *The Problem of Slavery in Western Culture* (1966), Oroonoko figures prominently as a significant and even prototypical character in 'a vast literature depicting noble African slaves' (Davis, p. 473), a crucial early text in the sentimental, antislavery tradition that grew steadily throughout the eighteenth century.[8]

Perhaps the feminist failure to attend to the primary concern of *Oroonoko* is partially due to the general neglect of race and slavery among critics of eighteenth-century literature. This is the period of the largest slave trade in history, when at least six million human beings were forcibly transported across an ocean, to produce a massive new workforce on two continents and in the islands of the West Indies. England's economic participation in the slave trade, especially after the Peace of Utrecht in 1713 and the acquisition of the Asiento – the exclusive right to supply slaves to the West Indies – has been extensively documented.[9] For over forty years literary critics have had access to Sypher's exhaustive description of the pervasive references to slavery in the literature of the period, from William Dodd and Thomas Bellamy to Daniel Defoe and James Thomson. If critics in the field have been almost universally oblivious to race, feminists have only followed suit.

Thus, while *Oroonoko* is certainly a crucial text in the tradition of women's literature and in the development of the novel; while it supplies us with an interesting early example of the problematic stance of a self-consciously female narrator; and while it demonstrates almost programmatically the tensions that arise when romance is brought together with realism; it demands at this conjuncture a broader political re-evaluation. *Oroonoko* can serve as a theoretical test case for the necessary connection of race and gender – a model for the mutual interaction of the positions of the oppressed in the literary discourse of its own age, and a mirror for modern criticism in which one political reading can be seen to reflect another, one revisionist school a plurality of revisions. Sartre's juxtaposition in the epigraph to this essay – 'what we have made of them' and 'what we have made of ourselves' – suggests the reciprocal movement necessary for such a political revisionism, both within the treatment of specific texts and in the discipline of literary studies at large. In Sartre's reading of Fanon, that reciprocity is the prerequisite for a relationship of mutual knowledge between the coloniser and the colonised. In this reading of *Oroonoko*, the figure of the woman in the imperialist narrative – a sign of 'what we have made of ourselves' – provides the point of contact through which the violence of colonial history – 'what we have made of them' – can be represented.

The conjunction of race and gender in the study of ideology and literary culture might seem almost automatic, since recent work on colonial and third-world literature has been so strongly dependent on the same analytical category that has underwritten much contemporary feminist theory: the notion of the 'other'. The staging of the relationship of alterity has taken many forms in contemporary theory. Beginning perhaps with the Hegelian scenario – and the paradigmatic play between master and slave – the 'other' can be internalised as a dimension of the psychological dynamic, or externalised as an account of social forms – producing, on the one hand, psychic models like that of the conscious and unconscious or the imaginary and symbolic, or sociological or anthropological paradigms like that of the in-group and the out-group or the cooked and the raw. Feminist critics have drawn widely from these interconnected dualisms to describe the position of women in patriarchal culture. More recently, third-world critics have consistently utilised the category of the 'other' in accounts of the relationship of coloniser and colonised, Occident and Orient, European and native, white and black. But with the exception of Gayatri Chakravorty Spivak, neither group has used the concurrence of terms as the occasion for a congruence of critiques. The force of Spivak's work, in this context, has been in her insistence on the distortions that occur when a feminist approach fails to take cognisance of colonialism and, reciprocally, in her reading of the literary culture of coloniser and colonised through the figure of the woman.[10] For most recent critics of colonial and neocolonial literature, however, gender enters not at all into the analysis of imperialist ideology. Such a striking irony is perhaps symptomatic of constraint implicit in these dualisms – a binary logic that militates against the dialectical argument at which this essay aims.

In addition to forestalling the conjunction of critical accounts of race and gender, the category of the 'other' works to hold apart the historical categories of imperialist and native. This dualism is in part politically necessary: it enables Edward Said to detail the massive, diffuse spectrum of discursive power controlled by the coloniser, and gives Frantz Fanon a powerful terminology in which to advocate revolutionary struggle. For Said 'Orientalism' is a discourse of power, a 'distribution of geopolitical awareness' into various cultural forms – 'aesthetic, scholarly, economic, sociological, historical, and philological' – by which the Occident creates and concurrently intends to understand, 'control, manipulate, even to incorporate' the Oriental 'other'.[11] His study, then, documents and demystifies the discourse of the Occident from the perspective of the Third World, just as, from the same perspective but with the alternative strategy, Fanon's writings articulate the interests of the colonised – recounting, theorising, and ultimately advocating a struggle to the death, through the absolute and violent conflict in the colonial world between the settler and the native.[12]

Following Fanon, Abdul JanMohamed provides perhaps the most schematic model for the role of the 'other' in the critique of colonialism. He argues that 'the dominant model of power- and interest-relations in all colonial societies is the manichean opposition between the putative superiority of the European and the supposed inferiority of the native'.[13] For JanMohamed, colonialist ideology and literary culture are constituted by a choice of identity with or difference from the 'other', and Tzvetan Todorov, in his account of 'the conquest of America' – an account, in his words, of 'the discovery the *self* makes of the *other*'[14] – depends, perhaps more systematically than any other critic of colonialism, upon the argument from alterity. For Todorov, Columbus, like 'every colonist in his relations to the colonised', conceives of the native according to the 'two component parts' of alterity, absolute identity or absolute difference (p. 42).

Said, Fanon, JanMohamed, and Todorov locate the 'other' in the historical struggle between the coloniser and the native. Homi Bhabha focuses instead upon an intrinsic otherness, the difference within the colonial subject, whether coloniser or colonised. When the dominant discourse of colonialism attempts the representation of the native, 'other "denied" knowledges enter upon the dominant discourse and estrange the basis of its authority'.[15] Thus although Bhabha argues directly against a 'power struggle between self and Other, or ... mother culture and alien cultures' (p. 153), he does posit within the colonial subject a division that reproduces the dualism we have already observed. This position raises the problem of the status of opposition for some critics who adopt the perspective of alterity. Though Bhabha claims that 'the discursive conditions of dominance [turn] into the grounds of intervention' (p. 154), his argument suggests that opposition is contained within the production of colonial power, that the only autonomy that remains for the native 'other' resides within the dominant colonial discourse. This notion of the pervasive, pre-emptive nature of power is often evoked by American Foucauldian critics and is defined by Stephen Greenblatt in a recent essay on Shakespeare's second *Henriad*. Discussing the 'alien voices', the 'alien interpretations' encountered by the first English settlers in Virginia, Greenblatt claims that 'subversiveness, as I have argued, was produced by the colonial power in its own interest'.[16] Here the category of the 'other' privileges the position of power while minimising the possibility of resistance.

Productive and important as this binary opposition has proven, then, it seems nevertheless to have stymied a genuinely dialectical critique of colonial culture. It forecloses an approach that works through alterity to the interaction that may occur even in an oppressive relationship. And it sometimes also precludes finding a place for the struggles of the native in the complex edifices of power that seem to contain all resistance.[17] But the ideal of moving beyond absolute difference has been raised repeatedly by recent critics. Todorov ends with the hopeful assertion that 'self-knowledge develops through knowledge of the Other' (p. 254). He seeks ultimately to locate a position beyond difference: 'We need not be confined within a sterile alternative: either to justify colonial wars ... or to reject all interaction with a foreign power ... Nonviolent communication exists, and we can defend it as a value' (p. 182). JanMohamed too imagines a 'syncretic possibility', theoretically available through the dialectic upon which his manichean opposition is founded, but present in practice only as an unrealised negative example ('Economy', p. 65), symptomatic of the difficulty of transcending alterity. In the same way, Said turns to the 'human' at the end of the *Orientalism*: 'I consider Orientalism's failure to have been a human as much as an intellectual one ... Orientalism failed to identify with human experience, failed also to see it as human experience.' 'Without "the Orient" there would be scholars, critics, intellectuals, human beings, for whom the racial, ethnic, and national distinctions were less important than the common enterprise of promoting human community' (p. 328). 'Communication', 'syncretic possibility', 'human community' – however it is named, this gesture outside the 'other' is at best an adjunctive, utopian moment, attractive but obviously extraneous to the argument from alterity. It gives us a sentiment without a method; we can derive from these examples inspiration, but not critical practice.

My treatment of *Oroonoko* is extensively indebted to these critics, but it seeks to avoid what I see as the theoretical pitfalls of the 'other' and to substitute the dialectical notion of what Johannes Fabian, in a critique of modern anthropological writing, calls 'radical contemporaneity' (p. xi). Focusing on the discipline's constitutive use of time as a distancing mechanism, on temporalisations placing the native in the 'primitive' past or in a 'passage from savagery to civilisation, from peasant to industrial society' (p. 95), Fabian argues that this systematic 'denial of coevalness' (p. 31) has operated in the ideological service of colonialism and neocolonialism by concealing the fact that 'anthropology's Other is, ultimately, other people who are our contemporaries' (p. 143). Fabian proposes that anthropologists 'seek ways to meet the Other on the same ground, in the same Time' (p. 164). His notion of radical contemporaneity is based on the Marxian theory of history as embodied in the formations of the present, on a view of 'the totality of historical forces, including their contemporality at any given time' (p. 158). Radical contemporaneity serves 'as the condition for truly dialectical confrontation between persons as well as societies. It militates against false conceptions of dialectics – all those watered-down binary abstractions which are passed off as oppositions: left vs right, past vs present, primitive vs modern. ... What are opposed, in conflict, in fact, locked in antagonistic struggle, are not the same societies at different stages of development, but different societies facing each other at the same Time' (p. 155). For Fabian 'the anthropologist and his interlocutors only "know" when they meet each other in one and the same contemporality' (p. 164).

The critic of literary culture can rarely argue that either she or the colonialist author and her characters 'meet the Other on the same ground, in the same Time' (p. 164). But from the perspective of radical contemporaneity, the texts of colonialism reveal signs of the dialectical confrontations embodied in the historical formations of the period. Though the colonialist and the native may never 'know' one another or their historical present, we can perhaps come to know something of both. The aim of this critical project, then, is to demonstrate the contemporaneity of issues of race and gender in a particular stage in the history of British capitalism associated broadly with commodity exchange and colonialist exploitation. Their conjunction in this particular text is sufficient to demonstrate the value of a pragmatic dialectical criticism, and indeed the political importance of refusing to posit any opposition as absolute.

II

As a test case for 'radical contemporaneity', *Oroonoko* may seem at first to provide a rather recalcitrant model: the novella lends itself with great readiness to the argument from alterity. Indeed, Behn's opening description of 'royal slave', Oroonoko, is a *locus classicus* of the trope of sentimental identification, by which the native 'other' is naturalised as a European aristocrat. In physical appearance, the narrator can barely distinguish her native prince from those of England.

[Oroonoko] was pretty tall, but of a Shape the most exact that can be fancy'd: The most famous Statuary could not form the Figure of a Man more admirably turn'd from head to foot ... His Nose was rising and *Roman*, instead of *African* and flat. His mouth the finest shaped that could be seen; far from those great turn'd Lips, which are so natural to the rest of the Negroes. The whole Proportion and Air of his Face was so nobly and exactly form'd, that bating his Colour, there could be nothing in Nature more beautiful, agreeable and Handsome.

(p. 8)

If this account of Oroonoko's classical European beauty makes it possible to forget his face, the narrator's description of his character and accomplishments further elaborates the act of absolute identity through which he is initially represented:

Nor did the Perfections of his Mind come short of those of his Person; and whoever had heard him speak, wou'd have been convinced of their Errors, that all fine Wit is confined to the white Men, especially to those of Christendom ... 'twas amazing to imagine ... where 'twas he got that real Greatness of Soul, those refined Notions of true Honour, that absolute Generosity, and that Softness that was capable of the highest Passions of Love and Gallantry. ... the most illustrious Courts could not have produced a braver Man, both for Greatness of Courage and Mind, a Judgment more solid, a Wit more quick, and a Conversation more sweet and diverting. He knew almost as much as if he had read much: He had heard of and admired the *Romans:* He had heard of the late Civil Wars in *England*, and the deplorable Death of our great Monarch; and wow'd discourse of it with all the Sense and Abhorrence of the Injustice imaginable. He had an extreme good and graceful Mien, and all the Civility of a well-bred great Man. He had nothing of Barbarity in his Nature, but in all Points address'd himself as if his Education had been in some *European* Court.

(pp. 8, 7)

Oroonoko is thus not only a natural European and aristocrat, but a natural neoclassicist and Royalist as well, an absurdity generated by the desire for an intimate identification with the 'royal slave'. Like Columbus in Todorov's account, Behn's narrator seems to have only two choices: to imagine the 'other' either as absolutely different and hence inferior, or as identical and hence equal. The obvious mystification involved in Behn's depiction of Oroonoko as a European aristocrat in blackface does not necessarily damage the novella's emancipationist reputation: precisely this kind of sentimental identification was in fact the staple component of antislavery narratives for the next century and a half, in England and America. But the failure of Behn's novella to see beyond the mirror of its own culture here raises the question of Behn's relationship with the African slave.

For not only is the novella's protagonist an aristocratic hero, but his story is largely constructed in the tradition of heroic romance. Briefly, Oroonoko, a noble African prince, falls in love with Imoinda, the daughter of his aristocratic foster-father. The two are divided first by the intervention of the King, Oroonoko's grandfather, who covets Imoinda for himself, and then by their independent sale into slavery. Reunited in Surinam, the British colony in Guiana where Behn was a visitor, Oroonoko and Imoinda are at first promised their freedom, then lead a slave rebellion, and finally die – Imoinda at the hands of Oroonoko, Oroonoko (known, as a slave, by the name of Caesar) executed by the colonists. Oroonoko's exploits follow closely the pattern outlined by Eugene Waith for the 'Herculean hero', the superhuman epic protagonist who plays a major role in heroic form from the classical period through the Renaissance.[18] Oroonoko is invincible in battle, doing singlehandedly 'such things as will not be believed that Human Strength could perform' (p. 30). He is also a man of wit and address, governed absolutely by his allegiance to the conventional aristocratic code of love and honour. When he declares his love to Imoinda, for instance, it is voiced entirely in the familiar terms of heroic romance: 'Most happily, some new, and, till then, unknown Power instructed his Heart and Tongue in the Language of Love. ... his Flame aim'd at nothing but Honour, if such a distinction may be made in Love' (p. 10).

This formula is typical of the dramatic heroic romances by Davenant, Orrery, Dryden, and Lee that were prominent on the English stage especially from the Restoration through the 1670s. Behn made her own contribution to this genre in *Abdelazer*, a heroic tragedy produced and published in 1677. The main direct source of heroic convention in *Oroonoko*, then, is the aristocratic coterie theatre of the Restoration. When Oroonoko swears his loyalty to 'his charming Imoinda' (p. 71):

> they mutually protested, that even Fetters and Slavery were soft and easy, and would be supported with Joy and Pleasure, while they cou'd be so happy to possess each other, and to be able to make good their Vows. *Caesar* swore he disdained the Empire of the World, while he could behold his *Imoinda*.
>
> (p. 44)

This abdication of empire for love is one of the most persistent motifs of late heroic drama, exemplified most prominently by Dryden's Antony in *All for Love* (1677): 'Give to your boy, your Caesar, / This rattle of the globe to play withal, ... I'll not be pleased with less than Cleopatra.'[19]

The hierarchical and rigid conventions of heroic romance made it particularly useful in the representation of the alien scenes of West Indian slavery. In a discussion of nineteenth-century travel writing, Mary Louise Pratt analyses the strategy of 'reductive normalising', through which the alien figure of the native is textualised and contained by the imperialist observer. She finds this textual device typical of writing about the imperial frontier, 'where Europeans confront not only unfamiliar Others but unfamiliar selves', and where 'they engage in not just the reproduction of the capitalist mode of production but its expansion through displacement of previously established modes'.[20] In Behn's text 'reductive normalising' is carried out through literary convention, and specifically through that very convention most effectively able to fix and codify the experience of radical alterity, the arbitrary love and honour codes of heroic romance.

Emerging directly from this mystification is the persistent presence of the figure of the woman in *Oroonoko*. In heroic romance, of course, the desirable woman serves invariably as the motive and ultimate prize for male adventures. As this ideology evolved in the seventeenth-century French prose tradition, dominated by women writers like Madeleine de Scudéry and Madame de LaFayette, women became increasingly central to the romantic action. Behn's novellas, like other English prose works of the Restoration and early eighteenth century, draw extensively upon this French material, and the foregrounding of female authorship in *Oroonoko* through the explicit interventions of the female narrator signals the prevalent feminisation of the genre.

This narrative must have women: it generates female figures at every turn. Not only is the protagonist represented as especially fond of the company of women (p. 46), but female figures – either Imoinda or the narrator and her surrogates – appear as incentives or witnesses for almost all of Oroonoko's exploits. He fights a monstrous, purportedly immortal tiger for the romantic approval of his female admirers: '*What Trophies and Garlands, Ladies, will you make me, if I bring you home the Heart of this ravenous Beast ...* We all promis'd he should be rewarded at all our hands' (p. 51). He kills the first tiger in defence of a group of four women – who 'fled as fast as we could' (p. 50) – and an unidentified, symptomatically faceless Englishman, who effaces himself further by following the ladies in their flight (p. 50). On the trip to the Indian tribes over which Oroonoko presides as expedition leader, the female figure is again the centre of attention. Along with the narrator and her 'Woman, a Maid of good Courage' (p. 4), only one man agrees to accompany Oroonoko to the Indian town, and once there, the '*White* people', surrounded by the naked natives, stage a scene of cultural difference in which the fully clothed woman is the central spectacle.

> They were all naked; and we were dress'd ... very glittering and rich; so that we appear'd extremely fine: my own Hair was cut short, and I had a taffety Cap, with black Feathers on my Head. ... from gazing upon us round, they touch'd us, laying their Hands upon all the Features of our Faces, feeling our Breasts and Arms, taking up one Petticoat, then wondering to see another; admiring our Shoes and Stockings, but more our Garters, which we gave 'em, and they ty'd about their Legs.
>
> (p. 55)

Even at the scene of Oroonoko's death, the narrator informs us, though she herself was absent, 'my Mother and Sister were by him' (p. 77).

The narrator herself makes it still more evident that the romantic hero is the production and expression of a female sensibility, of 'only a Female Pen' (p. 40). The narrator's act of modest self-effacement here, and again on the last page of the novella, signals the special relevance she claims for the female figure, in contrast to the 'sublime' masculine wit that would have omitted the crucial naturalness and simplicity (p. 1) of the tale for which the female pen has an innate affinity:

> Thus died this great Man, worthy of a better Fate, and a more sublime Wit than mine to write his Praise: Yet, I hope, the Reputation of my pen is considerable enough to make his glorious Name to survive to all Ages, with that of the brave, the beautiful, and the constant *Imoinda*.
>
> (p. 78)

As the female narrator, along with the proliferative female characters who serve as her proxies, produces Oroonoko's heroic drama, so that they become in turn its consumers, Oroonoko also is represented as a consumer of the romantic form he enacts. He keeps company with the women in the colony, in preference to the men, and in their conversations he and Imoinda are 'entertained ... with the Loves of the *Romans*' (p. 46), a pastime that incidentally serves to forestall Oroonoko's complaints about his captivity. In the end, then, even Oroonoko himself is feminised, incorporated into the circular system by which the figure of the woman becomes both object and beneficiary of romantic form.

III

But the 'normalising' model of heroic romance does not account for all the material in Behn's representation of West Indian slavery. In fact, neither the theme of slavery nor the romantic action would seem to explain the extended account of the Caribs, the native Americans of Guiana, with which Behn begins. This opening description deploys another set of discursive conventions than those of romance: the natives are the novella's noble savages. The notion of natural innocence, which civilisation and laws can only destroy, is obviously incompatible with the hierarchical aristocratic ideology of heroic form; Oroonoko, educated by a Frenchman, is admirable for his connection with – not his distance from – European civilisation. The account of the Indians belongs partly to the tradition of travel narrative, by Behn's period a popular mode describing voyages and colonial expeditions to the new world and including detailed reports of marvels ranging from accurate botanical and ethnographic records to pure invention.[21]

Behn's opening description of the Indians establishes her credibility in this context, but in its almost exclusive emphasis on trade with the natives, it also indicates the economic backdrop of the history of the 'royal slave':

> trading with them for their Fish, Venison, Buffalo's Skins, and little Rarities; as *Marmosets* ... *Cousheries*. ... Then for little *Paraketoes*, great *Parrots, Muckaws*, and a thousand other Birds and Beasts of wonderful and surprizing Forms and Colours. For Skins of prodigious Snakes ... also some rare Flies, of amazing Forms and Colours ... Then we trade for Feathers, which they order into all Shapes, make themselves little short Habits of 'em, and glorious Wreaths for their Heads, Necks, Arms and Legs, whose Tinctures are unconceivable. I

> had a Set of these presented to me, and I gave 'em to the King's
> Theatre, and it was the Dress of the *Indian Queen*, infinitely admired
> by Persons of Quality; and was unimitable. Besides these, a thousand
> little Knacks, and Rarities in Nature; and some of Art, as their
> Baskets, Weapons, Aprons.
>
> (p. 2)

The marvels here are all movable objects, readily transportable to a
European setting, where they implicitly appear as exotic and desirable acquisitions. Behn's enumeration of these goods is typical of the
age's economic and literary language, where the mere act of listing,
the evocation of brilliant colours, and the sense of an incalculable
numerousness express the period's fascination with imperialist accumulation.[22] But the Indians' goods are at best a small factor in the
real economic connection between England and the West Indies;
they serve primarily as a synecdoche for imperialist exploitation.

This opening context is centred upon the feathered habit which
the narrator acquires, and which, she claims, became upon her
return to England the dress of the Indian Queen in Dryden's heroic
play of the same name (1664), an artifact of imperialism displayed
in the most spectacular manner possible – adorning the female
figure of a contemporary actress on the real stage of the Theatre
Royal in Bridges Street. The foregrounding of female dress parallels
the scene of the expedition to the Indian village, where the spectacle
of the narrator's clothing is similarly privileged. And in general, the
items in the opening account of imperialist trade reflect the acquisitive instincts of a specifically female sensibility – dress, skins, and
exotic pets. Pets, indeed, in particular birds, were both sign and
product of the expansion and commercialisation of English society
in the eighteenth century.[23] Even more important, the association of
women with the products of mercantile capitalism, and particularly
the obsession with female adornment, is a strong cultural motif in
this period of England's first major imperial expansion.[24] Addison's
image of the woman fitted out in the fruits of empire evokes the
ideology to which Behn's account belongs:

> I consider woman as a beautiful, romantic animal, that may be
> adorned with furs and feathers, pearls and diamonds, ores and silks.
> The lynx shall cast its skin at her feet to make her a tippet; the
> peacock, parrot, and swan shall *pay contribution* to her muff; the sea
> shall be searched for shells, and the rocks for gems; and every part of
> nature furnish out its share towards the embellishment of a creature
> that is the most consummate work of it.[25]

Dressed in the products of imperialist accumulation, women are, by metonymy, identified not only with those products, but ultimately with the whole fascinating enterprise of trade itself.

And of course the substantial trade and real profit was not in the Indians' buffalo skins, *Paraketoes*, or feathers, but in sugar and slaves. Behn's description of the slave trade, highly accurate in many of its details, is the shaping economic and historical context of *Oroonoko*. A letter written in 1663 to Sir Robert Harley – at whose house at St John's Hill (p. 49) the narrator claims to have resided – from one William Yearworth, his steward, may describe the arrival of the slave ship which Behn would have witnessed during her visit to the colony:[26]

> Theare is A genney man [a slave ship from the Guinea Coast] Ariued heare in This riuer of ye 24th of [January] This Instant att Sande poynt. Shee hase 130 nigroes one Borde; ye Comanders name [is] Joseph John Woode; shee has lost 54 negroes in ye viage. The Ladeyes that are heare liue att St Johnes hill.[27]

Behn recounts the participation of African tribal leaders in collecting and selling slaves to European traders, the prearranged agreements for lots in the colonies, the deliberate dispersal of members of the same tribe around the plantations, the situation of the Negro towns, the imminence of rebellion, and the aggressive character of the Koromantyn (in Behn, Coramantien) slaves – the name given to the Gold Coast tribes from which Oroonoko comes.[28]

Behn's account of the black uprising – an obvious consequence of the slave trade – has no specific historical confirmation, but the situation is typical. Revolts and runaways, or marronage, were commonplace in the West Indies and Guiana throughout this period. In Jamaica rebellions and guerrilla warfare, predominantly led by Koromantyn ex-slaves, were virtually continuous from 1665 to 1740.[29] Marronage was common in Guiana as well during the period when *Oroonoko* is set: while Behn was in Surinam a group of escaped slaves led by a Koromantyn known as Jermes had an established base in the region of Para, from which they attacked local plantations.[30] And Wylie Sypher has documented several cases like Oroonoko's, in which the offspring of African tribal leaders were betrayed into slavery, often on their way to obtain an education in England.[31]

The powerful act of 'reductive normalising' performed by the romantic narrative is somewhat countered, then, by a similarly powerful historical contextualisation in Behn's account of trade. Not that the representation of trade in *Oroonoko* is outside ideology; far from it. As we have seen, the position it assigns to women in imperialist accumulation helps rationalise the expansionist impulses of mercantile capitalism. We could also examine the novella's assumption – partly produced by the crossover from the code of romantic horror – that blacks captured in war make legitimate objects for the slave trade. We cannot read Behn's colonialist history uncritically, any more than we can her heroic romance. But we can read them together because they are oriented around the same governing point of reference – the figure of the woman. In the paradigm of heroic romance, women are the objects and arbiters of male adventurism, just as, in the ideology of imperialist accumulation, women are the emblems and proxies of the whole male enterprise of colonialism. The female narrator and her proliferative surrogates connect romance and trade in *Oroonoko*, motivating the hero's exploits, validating his romantic appeal, and witnessing his tragic fate. Simultaneously they dress themselves in the products of imperialist acquisition, enacting the colonialist paradigm of exploitation and consumption, not only of the Indians' feathers and skins, and the many marvels of the new world, but of slaves as well, and the adventure of the 'royal slave' himself.

These two paradigms intersect in Oroonoko's antislavery speech:

> *And why* (said he) *my dear Friends and Fellow-sufferers, should we be Slaves to an unknown People? Have they vanquished us nobly in Fight? Have they won us in Honourable Battle? And are we by the Chance of War become their Slaves? This wou'd not anger a noble Heart; this would not animate a Soldier's Soul: no, but we are bought and sold like Apes or Monkeys, to be the sport of women, Fools and Cowards.*
>
> (p. 61)

The attack on slavery is voiced in part through the codes of heroic romance: the trade in slaves is unjust only if and when slaves are not honourably conquered in battle. But these lines also allude to the other ideology of *Oroonoko*, the feminisation of trade that we have associated primarily with the Indians. Oroonoko's resentment at being 'bought and sold like Apes or Monkeys ... the sport of women' is plausible given the prominent opening description of the animals and birds traded by the Indians, in particular of the little 'Marmosets, a sort of Monkey, as big as a Rat or Weasel, but of a marvellous and delicate shape, having Face and Hands like a Human Creature' (p. 2). In conjunction with the image of the pet monkey, Oroonoko's critique of slavery reveals the critique of colonialist ideology in one of its most powerful redactions – the representation of female consumption, of monkeys and men.

In grounding the parallel systems of romance and trade, the female figure in Behn's novella plays a role like that outlined by Myra Jehlen, the role of 'Archimedes' lever' – the famous paradoxical machine that could move the earth, if only it could have a place to stand.[32] Though they are marginal and subordinate to men, women have no extrinsic perspective, no objective status, in this narrative, either as the arbiters of romance or as the beneficiaries of colonialism. But though they have no independent place to stand, in their mediatory role between heroic romance and mercantile imperialism, they anchor the interaction of these two otherwise incompatible discourses. They make possible the superimposition of aristocratic and bourgeois systems – the ideological contradiction that dominates the novella. And in that contradiction we can locate a site beyond alterity, a point of critique and sympathy produced by the radical contemporaneity of issues of gender with those of romance and race.

IV

On the face of it, the treatment of slavery in *Oroonoko* is neither coherent nor fully critical. The romance motifs, with their elitist focus on the fate of African 'princes', entail an ambiguous attack on the institution of slavery, and adumbrate the sentimental antislavery position of the eighteenth century. But the representation of trade and consumption, readily extended to the trade in slaves and the consumption of Oroonoko himself, and specifically imagined through a female sensibility, renders colonialism unambiguously attractive. This incoherence could be explored in further detail: in the narrative's confusion about the enslavement of Indians and the contradictory reasons given for their freedom; in the narrator's vacillation between friendship with and fear of the 'royal slave'; in the dubious role she plays in 'diverting' Oroonoko with romantic tales so as to maintain his belief that he will be returned to Africa, her collusion in the assignment of spies to attend him in his meetings with the other slaves, and the quite explicit threat she uses to keep him from

fomenting rebellion; and even in the fascination with dismember-
ment that pervades the novella's relation with the native 'other' –
both Indian and African – and that suggests a perverse connection
between the female narrator and Oroonoko's brutal executioners.

A deeper critique of slavery emerges at the climactic moment in the
ideological contradiction that dominates the novella. This insight
originates in the hidden contemporary political referent of the narrative: the party quarrels in the West Indies and Guiana at the time of
Behn's visit. Though the novella's account is sketchy, Behn names
historical persons and evokes animosities traceable to the political
tensions that emigrated to the colonies during the revolution and
after the Restoration.[33] The relative political neutrality of the West
Indies and Guiana attracted Royalists during the revolution and
Parliamentarians and radicals after the Restoration. The rendering of
the colonists' council (p. 69), and the account of the contests for juris-
diction over Oroonoko reflect the reigning atmosphere of political
tension in Surinam during the time of Behn's visit in 1663 and 1664,
though without assigning political labels to the disputants. In fact, the
Lord Governor of Surinam to whom the novella refers is Francis,
Lord Willoughby of Parham, intimate of the royal family and of Lord
Clarendon and constant conspirator against the Protectorate, who
had received his commission for settlements in Guiana and elsewhere
in the Caribbean from Charles II, at his court in exile. Willoughby is
absent during Behn's narrative, but the current governor of the
colony, William Byam, who orders Oroonoko's execution, was a key
figure in the Royalist struggle for control of Barbados in the previous
decade, and likewise in Surinam engaged in a continuous battle
with the contingent of Parliamentarians in the colony. In 1662,
immediately before Behn's arrival, Byam had accused a group of
Independents, led by Robert Sandford, of conspiracy, summarily
trying and ejecting them from the colony. Sandford was the owner of
the plantation neighbouring Sir Robert Harley's, St John's Hill, the
narrator's residence. Harley also was a Royalist and had been a friend
of Willoughby, though a quarrel between the two during Harley's
chancellorship of Barbados resulted in Willoughby's expulsion from
that colony in 1664. There were few firm friendships beyond the Line
in this tumultuous period of colonial adventurism. Indeed in 1665,
shortly after Behn left Surinam, Willoughby himself, in a visit to
Guiana meant to restore orderly government to the colony, was
nearly assassinated by John Allen, who resented his recent prosecution for blasphemy and duelling.

Behn herself may have been engaged with these volatile politics through an alliance with a radical named William Scot, who went to the colony to escape prosecution for high treason in England, and whose father Thomas figured prominently on the Parliamentary side during the revolution and Commonwealth.[34] The radical connection makes some sense in that Byam, the notoriously ardent and high handed Royalist, is clearly the villain of the piece, and Colonel George Martin, Parliamentarian and brother to 'Harry Martin the great *Oliverian*' (p. 50), deplores the inhumanity of Oroonoko's execution. But its relevance need not be directly personal. The first substantial antislavery statements were voiced by the radical Puritans in the 1660s,[35] there was a Quaker colony in Surinam during this period; and George Fox made a visit to the West Indies in 1671, where he urged the inclusion of blacks at Friends' meetings.[36] Though as a group the Quakers in the New World were ambivalent about slave ownership and often profited from the slave trade themselves, individual Friends throughout this period enlarged upon Fox's early example. William Edmundson spoke against slavery in both the West Indies and New England.[37] Planters in Barbados charged that Edmundson's practice of holding meetings for blacks in Quaker homes raised threats of rebellion, and in 1676 the colonial government passed a law to prevent 'Quakers from bringing Negroes to their meetings' and allowing slaves to attend Quaker schools.[38] Though modern readers often assume that the early attack on slavery voiced in *Oroonoko* arose from a natural humanitarianism, the Puritan precedent suggests that Behn's position had an historical context. Such sentiments were 'natural' only to a specific group.

But there is no simple political allegory in Behn's novella. Though the Royalist Byam is Oroonoko's enemy, Behn describes Trefry, Oroonoko's friend, as Willoughby's overseer in Surinam; although he has not been historically identified, Trefry must have been a Royalist. His open struggle with Byam over Oroonoko's fate might allude to divisions within the Royalist camp, divisions which were frequent and intense in Barbados, for instance, when Willoughby came to power in that colony. More important than direct political correspondences, however, is the tenor of political experience in the West Indies and Guiana in this period. For Behn and others, the colonies stage an historical anachronism, the repetition of the English revolution, and the political endpoint of Behn's narrative is the re-enactment of the most traumatic event of the revolution, the execution of Charles I.

From almost the instant of his beheading, the King's last days, and the climactic drama of his death, were memoralised by Royalist writers in a language that established the discourse of Charles's suffering as heroic tragedy. *The Life of Charles I*, written just after the Restoration and close to the year in which Oroonoko's story is set, suggests the tenor of this discourse.

> He entred this ignominious and gastly Theatre with the same mind as He used to carry His Throne, shewing no fear of death ... [Bloody trophies from the execution were distributed among the King's murderers at the execution and immediately thereafter] ... some out of a brutish malice would have them as spoiles and trophees of their hatred to their Lawfull Sovereign ... He that had nothing Common in His Life and Fortune is almost profaned by a Vulgar pen. The attempt, I confess, admits no Apology but this, That it was fit that Posterity, when they read His Works ... should also be told that His Actions were as Heroick as His Writings ... Which not being undertaken by some Noble hand ... I was by Importunity prevailed upon to imitate those affectionate Slaves, who would gather up the scattered limbs of some great Person that had been their Lord, yet fell at the pleasure of his Enemies.[39]

Related images appear in a version published in 1681, shortly before the writing of *Oroonoko*:

> these Barbarous Regicides ... his Bloody Murtherers ... built a Scaffold for his Murther, before the Great Gate at *White Hall*, whereunto they fixed several Staples of Iron, and prepared Cords, to tye him down to the Block, had he made any resistance to that Cruel and Bloody stroke ... And then, most Christianly forgiving all, praying for his Enemies, he meekly submitted to the stroke of the Axe ... he suffered as an Heroick Champion ... by his patient enduring the many insolent affronts of this subtile, false, cruel and most implacable Generation, in their Barbarous manner of conventing, and Condemning him to Death; and to see his most bloodthirsty Enemies then Triumph over him. ... they have made him *Glorious* in his Memory, throughout the World, by a Great, Universal and most durable Fame.[40]

Charles I was a powerful presence for Behn at the writing of *Oroonoko*, even though the story was composed only shortly before its publication in 1688, long after Charles's death, the Restoration, and even the intervening death of Charles II – the monarch with whom Behn's acquaintance was much more personal. Oroonoko's heroism is attached to that of Charles I not just generically – in the affinity of 'Great Men' of 'mighty Actions' and 'large Souls' (pp. 7, 47)

– but directly. Behn's slave name for Oroonoko – Caesar – is the same she repeatedly used for the Stuart monarchs: Charles II is Caesar in her poem 'A Farewell to Celladon on His Going Into Ireland' (1684), as is James II and her 'Poem to Her Sacred Majesty Queen Mary' (1689).[41] Oroonoko, as we have seen, is defined by his sympathy for Charles's 'deplorable Death' (p. 7). Sentenced, like Charles in these royalist accounts, by the decree of a Council of 'notorious Villains' (p. 69) and irreverent swearers, and murdered by Banister, a 'Fellow of absolute Barbarity, and fit to execute any Villainy' (p. 76), 'this great Man' (p. 78), another royal martyr, endures his death patiently, 'without a Groan, or a Reproach' (p. 77). Even the narrator's final apology – though it refers specifically to female authorship – reproduces the conventional humble stance of the chroniclers of the King's death: 'Thus died this great Man, worthy of a better Fate, and a more sublime Wit than mine to write his Praise; Yet, I hope, the Reputation of my pen is considerable enough to make his glorious Name to survive to all Ages' (p. 78). 'The Spectacle ... of a mangled King' (p. 77), at the close of the narrative,[42] when Oroonoko is quartered and his remains distributed around the colony, evokes with surprising vividness the tragic drama of Charles Stuart's violent death. The sense of momentous loss generated on behalf of the 'royal slave' is the product of the hidden figuration in Oroonoko's death of the culminating moment of the English revolution.

But the tragedy is double in a larger sense. Abstractly speaking, both Charles I and Oroonoko are victims of the same historical phenomenon – those new forces in English society loosely associated with an antiabsolutist mercantile imperialism. The rapid rise of colonisation and trade coincided with the defeat of absolutism in the seventeenth century. In a mediated sense the death of Charles I makes that of Oroonoko possible, and Oroonoko's death stands as a reminder of the massive historical shift that destroyed Charles Stuart and made England a modern imperialist power. Ironically, in this context, both King Charles and the African slave in the New World are victims of the same historical force.

We might imagine that the account of Oroonoko's death represents the moment of greatest mystification in the narrative, the proof of an absolute alterity in the confrontation between the colonialist and the native 'other'. What could be more divergent than the fate of Charles Stuart and that of an African slave? But the violent yoking of these two figures provides the occasion for the most brutally visceral contact that Behn's narrative makes with the historical experience of slavery in the West Indies and Guiana. Merely the information that Oroonoko is a Koromantyn (p. 5) connects his story to eighteenth-century testimony on slavery and rebellion in the colonies. Bryan Edwards describes the character of slaves from this area:

> The circumstances which distinguish the Koromantyn, or Gold Coast, Negroes, from all others, are firmness both of body and mind; a ferociousness of disposition; but withal, activity, courage, and a stubbornness, or what an ancient Roman would have deemed an elevation, of soul, which prompts them to enterprizes of difficulty and danger; and enables them to meet death, in its most horrible shape, with fortitude or indifference. ... It is not wonderful that such men should endeavour, even by means the most desperate, to regain the freedom of which they have been deprived; nor do I conceive that any further circumstances are necessary to prompt them to action, than that of being sold into captivity in a distant country.[43]

Edwards is obviously drawn to epic romanticisation, but his historical account suggests the experience behind the romance in Behn's narrative. So common was rebellion among the Koromantyns, that Gold Coast slave imports were cut off by the late eighteenth century to reduce the risk of insurrection.

Edwards recounts one such rebellion in Jamaica in 1760, which 'arose at the instigation of a Koromantyn Negro of the name of Tacky, who had been a chief in Guiney' (II, 59–60). He details the execution of the rebel leaders, who were killed, like Oroonoko, to make 'an Example to all the Negroes, to fright 'em from daring to threaten their Betters' (*Oroonoko*, p. 70):

> The wretch that was burned was made to sit on the ground, and his body being chained to an iron stake, the fire was applied to his feet. He uttered not a groan, and saw his legs reduced to ashes with the utmost firmness and composure; after which one of his arms by some means getting loose, he snatched a brand from the fire that was consuming him, and flung it in the face of the executioner.
>
> (II, 61)

A correspondent from Jamaica to the *London Magazine* in 1767 provides a similar account:

> Such of them [rebel Negroes] as fell into our hands, were burnt alive on a slow fire, beginning at their feet, and burning upwards. It would have surprized you to see with what resolution and firmness they bore the

torture, smiling with an air of disdain at their executioners, and those about them.[44]

And John Stedman, the period's most detailed reporter of the executions of rebel maroons, recounts the request of a man who had been broken on the rack: 'I imagined him dead, and felt happy; till the magistrates stirring to depart, he writhed himself from the cross ... rested his head on part of the timber, and asked the by-standers for a pipe of tobacco.'[45]

In this context, Oroonoko's death takes on a significance entirely different from that conferred upon it through the paradigm of heroic romance or the figuration of Charles's death:

> [he] assur'd them, they need not tie him, for he would stand fix'd like a Rock, and endure Death so as should encourage them to die ... He had learn'd to take Tobacco; and when he was assur'd he should die, he desir'd they should give him a Pipe in his Mouth, ready lighted; which they did: And the executioner came, and first cut off his Members, and threw them into the Fire; after that, with an ill-favour'd Knife, they cut off his Ears and his Nose, and burn'd them; he still smoak'd on, as if nothing had touch'd him; then they hack'd off one of his Arms, and still he bore up, and held his Pipe; but at the cutting off the other arm, his Head sunk, and his Pipe dropt and he gave up the Ghost, without a Groan, or a Reproach.
>
> (p. 77)

As far as this horrible fictional scene takes us from the image of Dryden's Antony or that of Charles Stuart, those radically irrelevant figures are the means by which the narrative finds its way to the historical experience of the Koromantyn slave – the means by which the passage offers not merely a fascination with the brutality depicted here and in the other historical materials I have cited, but a sympathetic memorialisation of those human beings whose sufferings these words recall.

V

In *Oroonoko* the superimposition of two modes of mystification – romantic and imperialist – crucially conjoined by the figure of the woman, produces an historical insight and a critical sympathy that the argument from alterity cannot explain. This is not to say that Behn herself is any more unambivalent an emancipationist than we had originally suspected. But it does suggest that even though Behn can see colonialism only in the mirror of her own culture, that occluded vision has a critical dimension. As the 'normalising' figure of alterity, the romantic hero, opens up the experience of the 'other', we can glimpse, in the contradictions of colonialist ideology, the workings of a radical contemporaneity.

I have tried to exemplify the notion of radical contemporaneity variously in this reading of Behn's novella. In Charles Stuart and Oroonoko we have seen two creatures who could never meet in this world joined as historical contemporaries through the contradictory logic of Behn's imperialist romance. We have used a feminist reading of colonialist ideology, which places women at the centre of the structures of rationalisation that justify mercantile expansion, to ground the account of the contradictions surrounding the representation of race in this work. And we have juxtaposed the figure of the woman – ideological implement of a colonialist culture – with the figure of the slave – economic implement of the same system. Though Behn never clearly sees herself in the place of the African slave, the mediation of the figure of the woman between the two contradictory paradigms upon which her narrative depends uncovers a mutuality beyond her conscious control.

These relationships of contemporaneity spring from the failures of discursive coherence in *Oroonoko*, from the interaction of the contradictory aristocratic and bourgeois paradigms that shape the novella. This interaction is the dialectical process that my reading of *Oroonoko* has aimed to define, the process by which we may 'meet the Other on the same ground, in the same Time'. By this means, we can position the African slave in Behn's novella not as a projection of colonialist discourse, contained or incorporated by a dominant power, but as an historical force in his own right and his own body. The notion of a relatively autonomous native position, of a site of resistance that is not produced and controlled by the ideological apparatuses of colonialist power, has crucial consequences for our conclusions about colonialist ideology, the critique of colonialism, and ideology critique in general. It suggests that we can read the literature of those in power not only for the massive and elaborate means by which power is exercised, but also as a source of leverage for those in opposition, that while sites of resistance may be produced within a dominant ideology, they are not produced by it, and they do not serve it. They are produced despite it, and they serve to locate opposition in a body and a language that even the people of the colonialist metropole can be made to understand.

From *The New Eighteenth Century*, ed. Laura Brown and Felicity Nussbaum (New York, 1987), pp. 40–61.

NOTES

[Laura Brown aims not simply to reread the problem of race and gender as independent lines of inquiry but to demonstrate the contemporaneity of both issues in the context of a particular moment in the history of British capitalism. She discusses *Oroonoko*'s debt to the traditions of heroic romance and coterie aristocratic drama and analyses the way in which Behn uses romance conventions to reduce the hero's otherness. She argues that, in this 'mystificatory' process, the figure of the woman as narrative producer and consumer (audience-reader) is crucial. Ed.]

I would like to thank Walter Cohen, Judy Frank, Jeff Nunokawa, Felicity Nussbaum and Mark Seltzer for their help with early versions of this article.

1. Jean-Paul Sartre, Preface to *The Wretched of the Earth*, by Frantz Fanon, trans. Constance Farrington (New York, 1968), p. 13.

2. For the date of composition, see George Guffey, 'Aphra Behn's *Oroonoko*: Occasion and Accomplishment', in *Two English Novelists: Aphra Behn and Anthony Trollope*, by Guffey and Andrew Wright (Los Angeles, 1975), pp. 15–16.

3. *The Rover*, ed. Frederick M. Link (Lincoln, NE, 1967); *Oroonoko; or, The Royal Slave*, introduction by Lore Metzger (New York, 1973). Subsequent references to *Oroonoko* will be to this edition; page numbers are inserted parenthetically in the text.

4. Marureen Duffy, *The Passionate Shepherdess: Aphra Behn, 1640–89* (London, 1977); Angeline Goreau, *Reconstructing Aphra: A Social Biography of Aphra Behn* (New York, 1980); George Woodcock, *The Incomparable Aphra* (London, 1948). In addition to these works, book-length treatment of Behn in this century includes a brief biography by Victoria Sackville-West, *Aphra Behn: The Incomparable Astrea* (New York, 1928); an historical monograph by William J. Cameron, *New Light on Aphra Behn: An Investigation into the Facts and Fictions Surrounding Her Journey to Surinam in 1663 and Her Activities as a Spy in Flanders in 1666* (Auckland, 1961); and a Twayne study by Frederick M. Link, *Aphra Behn* (New York, 1968).

5. Ernest Berbaum, 'Mrs. Behn's Biography, a Fiction', *PMLA*, 28 (1913), 432–53, and 'Mrs. Behn's *Oroonoko*', *Anniversary Papers by Colleagues*

and Pupils of George Lyman Kittredge (Boston, 1913). For the refutations of Bernbaum's claim that Behn owes her account of Guiana entirely to George Warren's *Impartial Description of Surinam* (1667), see Harrison Grau Platt, 'Astrea and Celadon: An Untouched Portrait of Aphra Behn', *PMLA*, 49 (1934), 544–59; and especially Goreau, *Reconstructing Aphra*, pp. 41–69.

6. Judith Gardiner, 'Aphra Behn: Sexuality and Self-Respect', *Women's Studies*, 7 (1980), 67–78; William Spengemann, 'The Earliest American Novel: Aphra Behn's *Oroonoko*', *Nineteenth-Century Fiction*, 38 (1984), 384–414; Larry Carver, 'Aphra Behn: The Poet's Heart in a Woman's Body', *Papers on Language and Literature*, 14 (1978), 414–24.

7. *The Gentleman's Magazine*, 19 (Thursday, 16 February 1749), 89–90. See also *The London Magazine*, 18 (February, 1749), 94. This event is described by David Brion Davis, *The Problem of Slavery in Western Culture* (Ithaca, NY, 1966), p. 477; and Wylie Sypher, 'The African Prince in London', *Journal of the History of Ideas*, 2 (1941), 242, among others. Page numbers for subsequent references to Davis's book and to Sypher's article are inserted parenthetically in the text.

8. Wylie Sypher, *Guinea's Captive Kings: British Anti-Slavery Literature of the XVIIIth Century* (Chapel Hill, NC, 1942), Page numbers for subsequent references are inserted parenthetically in the text.

9. E.g. Richard B. Sheridan, *Sugar and Slavery: An Economic History of the British West Indies 1623–1775* (Baltimore, MD, 1974), esp. pp. 249–53.

10. See Gayatri Chakravorty Spivak, 'French Feminism in an International Frame', *Yale French Studies*, 62 (1981), 73–87; '"Draupadi" by Mahasweta Devi', in *Writing and Sexual Difference*, ed. Elizabeth Abel (Chicago, 1982); and 'Three Women's Texts and a Critique of Imperialism', *Critical Inquiry*, 12 (1985), 243–61.

11. Edward W. Said, *Orientalism* (New York, 1979), p. 13.

12. See Frantz Fanon, *The Wretched of the Earth*, trans. Constance Farrington (New York, 1968).

13. Abdul JanMohamed, *Manichean Aesthetics: The Politics of Literature in Colonial Africa* (Amherst, MA, 1983), and 'The Economy of Manichean Allegory: The Function of Racial Difference in Colonialist Literature', *Critical Inquiry*, 12 (1985), 59–87; the quoted passage is on p. 63. Page numbers for subsequent references are inserted parenthetically in the text.

14. Tzvetan Todorov, *The Conquest of America: The Question of the Other* (*La conquête de l'Amérique: La question de l'autre*, 1982), trans.

Richard Howard (New York, 1984), p. 4. Page numbers for subsequent references are inserted parenthetically in the text.

15. Homi K. Bhabha, 'Signs Taken for Wonders: Questions of Ambivalence and Authority under a Tree Outside Delhi, May 1817', *Critical Inquiry*, 12 (1985), 144–65; the quoted passage is on p. 156. Page numbers for subsequent citations are inserted parenthetically in the text. See also Bhabha's 'The Other Question – The Stereotype and Colonial Discourse', *Screen*, 24 (1983), 18–36.

16. Stephen Greenblatt, 'Invisible Bullets: Renaissance Authority and its Subversion, Henry IV and Henry V', in *Political Shakespeare: New Essays in Cultural Materialism*, ed. Jonathan Dollimore and Alan Sinfield (Ithaca, NY, 1985), pp. 18–47; the quoted passage is on p. 24.

17. Johannes Fabian, *Time and the Other: How Anthropology Makes Its Object* (New York, 1983). Page numbers for subsequent references are inserted parenthetically in the text.

18. Eugene M. Waith, *The Herculean Hero in Marlowe, Chapman, Shakespeare and Dryden* (New York, 1962).

19. John Dryden, *All for Love*, ed. David Vieth (Lincoln, NE, 1972), II, 442–6.

20. Mary Louise Pratt, 'Scratches on the Face of the Country; or, What Mr. Barrow Saw in the Land of the Bushmen', *Critical Inquiry*, 12 (1985), 119–43; the quoted passage is on p. 121. Page numbers for subsequent references are inserted parenthetically in the text.

21. In the earlier period, Richard Hakluyt's *Principall Navigations* (1589) and Samuel Purchas's *Purchas his Pilgrimes* (1625); in the later period Sir Hans Sloane, *A Voyage To the Islands Madera, Barbados, Nieves, S. Christophers and Jamaica ...* , 2 vols (London, 1707); Churchill's *A Collection of Voyages and Travels* (London, 1732).

22. See Laura Brown, *Alexander Pope* (Oxford, 1985), ch. 1.

23. J. H. Plumb, 'The Acceptance of Modernity', in *The Birth of a Consumer Society: The Commercialization of Eighteenth-Century England*, ed. Neil McKendrick, John Brewer, and Plumb (Bloomington, IN, 1982), pp. 316–34; the reference to exotic birds appears on pp. 321–2.

24. Neil McKendrick, 'The Commercialization of Fashion', in *The Birth of a Consumer Society*, pp. 34–99, esp. p. 51.

25. Joseph Addison, *Spectator 69*, 19 May 1711, in *The Spectator Papers*, ed. Donald F. Bond (Oxford, 1965), I, 295.

26. See Goreau, *Reconstructing Aphra*, p. 56.

27. 'Letters to Sir Robert Harley from the Stewards of His Plantations in Surinam. (1663–4)', reprinted in *Colonising Expeditions to the West Indies and Guiana, 1623–1667*, ed. V. T. Harlow (London, 1925), p. 90.

28. Koromantyn or Coromantijn is a name derived from the Dutch fort at Koromantyn on the Gold Coast; in Surinam it designated slaves from the Fanti, Ashanti, and other interior Gold Coast tribes. For background and statistics on the tribal origins of the Bush Negroes of Guiana, see Richard Price, *The Guiana Maroons: A Historical and Bibliographical Introduction* (Baltimore, MD, 1976), pp. 12–16.

29. Orlando Patterson, 'Slavery and Slave Revolts: A Sociohistorical Analysis of the First Maroon War, 1665–1740', in *Maroon Societies: Rebel Slave Communities in the Americas*, ed. Richard Price, 1973; 2nd edn (Baltimore, MD, 1979), pp. 246–92, esp. pp. 256–70.

30. Price, *Guiana Maroons*, p. 23.

31. Sypher, 'The African Prince in London', *Journal of the History of Ideas*, 2 (1941), 237–47.

32. Myra Jehlen, 'Archimedes and the Paradox of Feminist Criticism', in *The 'Signs' Reader: Women, Gender and Scholarship*, ed. Elizabeth Abel and Emily K. Abel (Chicago, 1983), pp. 69–95.

33. See the documents under 'Guiana' in the Hakluyt Society's *Colonising Expeditions to the West Indies and Guiana, 1623–1667*, esp. 'The Discription of Guyana', 'To ye Right Honourable ye Lords of His Majesties most Honorable Privy Councel, The Case of ye Proscripts from Surinam with all Humility is briefely but most truely stated. 1662', and 'Letters to Sir Robert Harley from the Stewards of his Plantations in Surinam. 1663–1664'; V. T. Harlow's detailed introduction to this reprint collection, esp. pp. xxvii–1v and 1xvi–xcv; Goreau, *Reconstructing Aphra*, pp. 66–9; and Cyril Hamshere, *The British in the Caribbean* (Cambridge, MA, 1972), pp. 64–5.

34. Goreau, *Reconstructing Aphra*, pp. 66–9.

35. Richard Baxter, *A Christian Directory, or, a Summ of Practical Theologie, and Cases of Conscience* (London, 1673), pp. 557–60. Cited in Thomas E. Drake, *Quakers and Slavery in America* (New Haven, CT, 1950), p. 3. Drake dates the section on slavery to 1664–65. Also sympathetic, though less explicitly antislavery, is George Fox, 'To Friends Beyond the Sea That have Blacks and Indian Slaves' (1657), in *A Collection of Many Select and Christian Epistles, Letters and Testimonies* (London, 1698), Epistle No. 153; cited in Drake, *Quakers and Slavery*, p. 5. On Quakers see also Davis, *The Problem of Slavery*, pp. 304–26; Carl and Roberta Bridenbaugh, *No Peace Beyond the Line: The English in the Caribbean 1624–1690*

(New York, 1972), pp. 357–9; and Herbert Aptheker, 'The Quakers and Negro Slavery', *Journal of Negro History*, 26 (1940), 331–62. An even earlier, unambiguous antislavery statement from the radical Puritans appears in the Digger pamphlet *Tyranipocrit Discovered* (1649), quoted in *The World Turned Upside Down: Radical Ideas during the English Revolution*, by Christopher Hill (Harmondsworth, 1975), p. 337.

36. See Drake, *Quakers and Slavery*, p. 6 for an account of Fox's recorded sermons at this time. See also Bridenbaugh, *No Peace Beyond the Line*, p. 357.

37. Cited in Drake, *Quakers and Slavery*, pp. 9–10: copy of a letter of William Edmundson, dated at Newport, the 19th 7th Mo 1676, in records of New England Yearly Meeting, vol. 400, a ms. volume entitled 'Antient Epistles, Minutes and Advices, or Discipline'. See Drake for other examples of early Quaker statements.

38. Cited in Drake, *Quakers and Slavery*, p. 8; see also Bridenbaugh, *No Peace Beyond the Line*, p. 358.

39. Richard Perrinchiefe, *The Life of Charles I in the Workes of King Charles The Martyr* (London, 1662), pp. 92–3, 118.

40. William Dugdale, *A Short View of the Late Troubles in England* (Oxford, 1681), pp. 371–75.

41. Spengemann, 'The Earliest American Novel', p. 401.

42. I am indebted to Adela Pinch (Department of English, Cornell University) for my reading of these lines.

43. Bryan Edwards, *The History, Civil and Commercial, of the British Colonies in the West Indies*, 2 vols (Dublin, 1793), rpt. (New York, 1972), II, 59. Most of the detailed accounts of slavery in the West Indies and Guiana date from the later eighteenth century. But there is ample evidence of marronage, rebellion, and judicial torture throughout the West Indies and including Surinam from Behn's period on. Surinam passed out of British hands in 1667, and thus the fullest documentation of the treatment of rebel slaves in that country describes conditions under the Dutch. There is every reason to believe, however, in a continuity from British to Dutch practices historically in Surinam, just as there is every evidence of the same continuity throughout the West Indies and Guiana – British or Dutch – at any given moment in the long century and a half of active slave trade. For further documentation, in addition to the works cited in subsequent notes, see George Warren, *An Impartial Description of Surinam upon the Continent of Guiana in America* (London, 1667); *Historical Essay on the Colony of Surinam*, 1788, trans. Simon Cohen, ed. Jacob R. Marcus and Stanley F. Chyet (New York, 1974); Price, *Guiana Maroons*; Price, ed., *Maroon Societies*.

44. *London Magazine* 36 (May 1767): 94. Also cited in Davis, *The Problem of Slavery*, p. 477.

45. John Stedman, *Narrative of a Five Years' Expedition Against the Revolted Negroes of Surinam* (1796; rpt. Amherst, MA, 1972), p. 382. Stedman's book contains the fullest account available in this period of the punishments for maroons in the West Indies and Guiana. Price finds Stedman's descriptions 'to have a solid grounding in fact', and he also shows that Surinam was the most brutal of the major plantation colonies of the New World (*Guiana Maroons*, pp. 25, 9).

11

Juggling the Categories of Race, Class and Gender: Aphra Behn's *Oroonoko*

MARGARET FERGUSON

Feminist literary scholars working in the field of Renaissance culture and trained mostly in US and Canadian universities have until recently defined their analytic focus more often with reference to problems of gender and class than with reference to race.[1] With some notable exceptions such as Karen Newman's recent essay on *Othello*, Laura Brown's study of Aphra Benh's *Oroonoko*, and Ania Loomba's *Gender, Race, Renaissance Drama*, I know of little recent work by feminist students of early modern literature which directly attempts to *theorise* the relation between either historical or contemporary critical concepts of gender, race, and class.[2] Without claiming to untangle the various knots signalled by the conjunction of these terms in my title, I do want to reflect briefly on some of the questions that conjunction raises for feminist critical thinking now, before turning to Aphra Behn.

If feminist literary scholars of the Renaissance are at a relatively early stage in defining race as an analytic category and conceiving of research programmes that would explicitly address its constellation of problems, we need, at the very least, to join Joan Kelly's famous question – Did women have a Renaissance? – with versions of that question for groups *other* than white European women, recognising, however, that the different 'versions' of the questions may not turn out to be neatly analogous.[3] Though analogies, even identities,

may be a useful place to begin expanding a critical frame of reference – as I was reminded when an undergraduate in one of my
classes on Behn's *Oroonoko* referred to the white female narrator of
that work as a 'member of the female race' – we need to work
against as well as with the grain of our desire for parallels. We can
see Joan Kelly herself trying to do this in a passage written in 1979,
a passage which uses parenthetical phrases to signal both an awareness that the feminist scholar needs to constitute her object of study
with reference to questions of race and an uncertainty about just
how she should do so: 'What we see are not two spheres of social
reality but two (or three) sets of social relations. For now I would
call them relations of work and sex (or of class and race, and
sex/gender).[4] Kelly's key dichotomies keep threatening to break into
trichotomies, but they don't quite. A feminist-Marxist paradigm
is clearly at work in her effort to define the object of study as a set
of relations pertaining, broadly speaking, to the 'parallel' realms of
economic production, on the one hand – work – and the realm of
the sex/gender system, on the other, that realm which feminist social
scientists in the 1970s were defining in order to stress the cultural
rather than biological determinations of 'female nature'.[5] But where
does race fit into this paradigm? It doesn't, or doesn't very clearly.
Why break the category of *work* down into 'class' and 'race', and
what's the possible relation between these two subcategories and the
apparently parallel subdivision Kelly parenthetically offers for sex,
namely the two terms 'sex/gender', separated however by an oblique
stroke, not an 'and'? Obviously, race doesn't stand in anything like
the relation to class that gender, in Kelly's formulation, stands to
sex.

I call attention to this formulation first because it's symptomatic
of a continuing problem in Renaissance feminist studies and
arguably in literary feminist scholarship by whites in the academy,
more generally. I use Kelly also because her formulation points to a
somewhat paradoxical and necessarily provisional solution that I
want to propose, and briefly illustrate, in this chapter. The solution
can be put first in a negative formulation: it is *not* to attempt to fix a
definition of the terms or of their mode of correlation; such defini-
tional work should not in any case be done in the abstract but rather
with reference to specific historical instances. Just think, for
example, of the complex ways in which the three categories are
linked, conceptually and with material effects, in the well-known
convention of American racial ideology whereby a white woman can

give birth to a black child but a black woman cannot have a white child.[6] Another description of this convention stresses the idea of social status rather than gender: children of mixed marriages in twentieth-century US society are affiliated, regardless of their biological phenotype, with the racial group of the lower-ranking parent, Marvin Harris remarks in an encyclopedia article on 'Race'.[7] This consequential bit of ideology clearly solicits analysis with respect both to gender and to class, and indeed both categories, broadly construed, have interacted historically to shape, and sometimes abruptly alter, our culture's legal definitions of race. David Brion Davis notes for instance, that the state of Maryland reversed the old convention of *partus sequitur ventrum* (the child follows the mother) in the late seventeenth century in order to 'inhibit the lustful desires of white women'.[8] Here white women as a group are characterised as prone to behaviour that blurs socially important racial distinctions (the Maryland statute was generated by a discussion of how to classify mulattoes). An eighteenth-century document, however, displays a fear of female sexuality that is yoked with, or channelled through, an ideology of class: 'The lower class of the women of England', wrote the noted historian of Jamaica, Edward Long, 'are remarkably fond of the blacks, for reasons too brutal to mention; they would connect themselves with horses and asses, if the law permitted them.'[9]

To illustrate the variability – across temporal and geographical boundaries – of ideological conceptions of race, the American historian Barbara Fields tells a lovely story about an American journalist who allegedly asked Haiti's Papa Doc Duvalier what percentage of his country's population was white. 'Ninety-eight percent', Papa Doc responded.

> Struggling to make sense of this incredible piece of information, the American finally asked Duvalier: 'How do you define white?' Duvalier answered the question with a question: 'How do you define black in your country?' Receiving the explanation that in the United States anyone with any black blood was considered black, Duvalier nodded and said, 'Well, that's the way we define white in my country.'[10]

This anecdote leads me to a more positive formulation of my provisional solution: a plea to scholars to suspend their own assumptions about what a category like race means or meant to members of a different culture. Encountering the classic epistemological problem

– which is also, inevitably, an ethical and political problem – of the 'First World' anthropologist seeking to interpret a 'native' cultural concept,[11] scholars who work with concepts of class, race, and gender might do well to keep all three terms floating, as it were, in an ideological liquid – a solution, I might venture to say – without assuming that we have any a priori understanding of what they mean even in our own by no means homogeneous academic sub-culture, much less what the terms may have meant for textual producers and receivers in different historical and cultural milieux than our own.

A certain kind of historicist scholar, of either the so-called 'old' historicist or the radical Foucauldian 'new' stripe, might object to my proposed (non) solution on the grounds that each of the categories of social thought I'm invoking here is in some sense anachronistic for Renaissance studies. While it is certainly true that the terms 'race', 'class', and 'gender' had demonstrably different *dominant* meanings in Renaissance English than they do today, they are nonetheless significant areas of semantic overlap: Renaissance references to the 'human' or the 'English' race, for instance, don't entail the obsession with pigmentation differences typical of nineteenth- and twentieth-century notions of race, but the earlier usage does display the 'ideological device', still common in many contemporary racial categorisations, of securing group identity by a (frequently mythical) set of genealogical rules.[12] The historicist objection against anachronism can be useful if it helps us avoid simplistic conflations, but the objection should not prevent us from seeking evidence pertaining to the *types* of systemic social inequities frequently signalled – whether inadvertently or critically – by the uses of one or more of these terms in post-Renaissance discourses. To stop the search for significant traces of such inequities is to accept an academic argument for hermeneutic 'purity' that is arguably an ideological defence against seeing continuities between systemic injustices in past societies – including those partly shaped and largely represented by European intellectuals – and in our own. The effort of *interrogating* modern notions of race, class, and gender by comparing them (as it were) to earlier historical versions of these notions – and vice versa – seems to me crucial to the intellectual work of US feminism in the 1990s.

That work has been powerfully though also controversially begun by a number of recent scholars. Among them are Teresa de Lauretis in her book *Technologies of Gender* (1987), which argues that

gender is a *representation*, not an essence fundamentally determined, for instance, by 'sexual differences', and which further
argues that 'gender represents not an individual but a relation, and a
social relation';[13] Barbara Fields, in the article from which I drew
the Papa Doc story, an article entitled 'Ideology and Race in
American History' (1982), which argues provocatively for a
demystified understanding of race as a category derived from historical circumstances and racist ideologies rather than from some
imputed 'reality' of biological face; and the Marxist scholars
Stephen Resnick and Richard Wolff, who argue for a non-essential-
ist conception of class in *Knowledge and Class* (1989). Defining class
not primarily as a categorising system for social groups but rather as
a *process* by which 'unpaid labour is pumped out of direct producers', they stress that this process is 'overdetermined' (in a phrase
they borrow, with caveats, from Louis Althusser, who borrowed it
from psychoanalytic discourse) by other processes such as 'labour
transforming nature', 'exerting and obeying authority among
persons', 'giving and gaining access to property', and, last but not
least, language.[14] This approach to class is useful, first because it
mitigates many of the problems raised by historians and literary
scholars concerned with anachronism (i.e., should one speak of
'classes' before the full development of capitalism and/or before
class consciousness exists on the part of a given group?);[15] and
second because it insists that any given individual may occupy more
than one 'position' relative to the 'class process'.

Let us look, now, at some of the ways in which the categories of
race, class, and gender, understood as historically contingent and
relational rather than foundational concepts, work in a mutually
determining fashion in Behn's *Oroonoko* (1688) and in what we can
reconstruct of the various historical discourses and shifting configuration of material life from which her book derives and to which it
contributed substantially – most obviously by limning an image of
the 'Noble Negro' in ways that made it, as Laura Brown observes, 'a
crucial early text in the sentimental, antislavery tradition that grew
steadily throughout the eighteenth century'.[16]

Whatever the 'facts' of Aphra Behn's birth (conflicting theories construct her as the illegitimate daughter of an aristocrat, male or female,
or as the child of a barber or a wetnurse), the single most important
determinant of her multiple class positions was arguably her access to,
and later her deployment of, the skills of literacy.[17] Her lack of a classical education meant that she was not 'fully' literate in her culture's

terms, but her ability to read and write English and several other European languages nonetheless allowed her to earn her living by her pen, first as a spy for Charles II and later as the author of plays, poems, novellas, and translations. Though classic Marxist theory does not consider intellectual work 'direct production', the writer in the early modern era, as a member of an emergent class or caste of secular intellectuals ambiguously placed between their sometimes relatively humble origins and the nobility whom they frequently served and with whom they often imaginatively identified, was in many cases a producer of commodities for the market. Indeed the energy with which many humanist writers sought to distinguish their labour from 'merely' clerkly or artisanal work suggests how fraught with anxiety (then as now) was the self-definition of persons who occupied the ambiguous class position of intellectual worker.[18] If, from one perspective and in certain circumstances, the writer was himself (or much more rarely, herself) a worker from whose labour surplus was extracted by others (as, for instance, occurred when one worked for fixed wages as the secretary or accountant for an aristocratic plantation owner), from another perspective, the writer was often a (relatively) privileged beneficiary of the process whereby early capitalists profited from the forced labour (say) of indentured white servants or black or Indian slaves. My examples are of course chosen to highlight the multiple ambiguities that arise when one seeks to specify how a figure like Aphra Behn participated in the process of extracting surplus in Britain's early colonial economy. At this point, I will insist only on foregrounding the fact that she *did* participate, as a producer of verbal commodities who explicitly if intermittently defined herself as oppressed by and financially dependent on wealthy men, but also as a member of an English 'family' of slave-owners (as it were) and as such, one who directly and 'naturally' profited from others' labour.

The peculiarities of her multiple and shifting class positions are inextricably linked to, indeed partly determined by, the anomalies of her situation as a *female* writer, one who sold her wares to male patrons as a prostitute sells her body to clients. As Catherine Gallagher has brilliantly shown, Behn herself elaborated the prostitute-woman writer analogy along with an even more ideologically mystified one of the female writer as an absolutist monarch.[19] In *Oroonoko*, set in the early 1660s, before Behn's rather mysterious marriage to a Dutch merchant, but written in 1688, long after she had ceased to be a wife, she defines her status as formed in crucial ways by her gender; she refers explicitly to her 'female pen', and frequently presents herself as a heroine with features drawn from literary codes of romance and Petrarchan lyric.[20] Lurking behind her portrait of the author as a young, unmarried lady with great verbal facility is a complex body of cultural discourse on Woman and the forms of behaviour she should eschew (talking and writing in public, which behaviour is often equated with prostitution) and embrace (obedience to fathers and husbands being a prime command).[21] An emerging cultural discourse about women who went to the colonies – often, allegedly, to acquire the husbands they'd not found in England, or worse, to satisfy their 'natural' lust with men of colour – also lurks behind Behn's self-portrait.[22] This cultural subtext, made into an explicit subplot of Thomas Southerne's 1696 stage version of *Oronooko*, seems particularly germane to Behn since, as Angeline Goreau has argued, her (adoptive?) father left her without a dowry when he died *en route* to Surinam.[23] Her novella at once partly reproduces the negative cultural subtext(s) of female gender and seeks to refute them.

Her social status is also defined as a function of her race, or, more precisely and provisionally, of her membership in a group of colonising English white people who owned black slaves imported from Africa and who uneasily shared Surinam with another group of non-white persons, the native Indians. We can conveniently trace some of the contradictions in the narrator's social identity, with its multiple 'subject positions' created in part by competing allegiances according to race, class, and gender, if we examine the narrative 'I' in relation to the text's different uses of the pronoun 'we'. With whom does the 'I' align itself?[24]

The first stage of an answer is to say that the 'I' aligns itself sometimes with a 'we' composed of women: in these cases the 'I' is definitely a 'she'. At other times, however, the 'I' aligns – or in political terms, allies – itself with a 'we' composed of property-owning English colonists defending themselves against an 'other' (a 'them') composed of African slaves or of native Indians, and sometimes of both. In these cases, the gender of the 'I' is evidently less salient than are nationality, membership in a surplus-extracting group, and colour. Within these two basically contradictory subject positions, however, other configurations appear and disappear. 'We' women, for instance, are sometimes opposed to cruel and powerful white men, and this opposition clearly participates in the interrogation of the institution of marriage which many of Behn's plays mount and which texts by other seventeenth-century Englishwomen pursue as well: Lady Mary

Chudleigh, for instance, in a poem 'To the Ladies', of 1703, wrote that 'Wife and servant are the same, / But only differ in the name'.[25] An opposition drawn along lines of gender within the British community allows – in the peculiar circumstances of colonialism – for an unusual alliance to flourish between white females, notably the narrator and her mother and sister, and the black slave Oroonoko: a community of the unjustly oppressed is thus formed, and indeed unjust oppression comes to be associated with a state of effeminacy figured, interestingly, as male impotence.[26]

The analogy between white women and Oroonoko, and particularly the alliance between the narrator and her hero, is, however, extremely volatile, partly because it posed an obvious double-pronged threat to the colonial social hierarchy in which white men occupied the top place. The narrator, as the unmarried daughter (so she claims) of the man who was supposed to govern the colony had he not died *en route* to his post, threatens the ideologies of patriarchy in some of the ways that Queen Elizabeth had done a hundred years before Behn wrote her book. To claim, as Behn does in her prefatory letter to an aristocratic patron, that there was 'none above me in that Country', and to depict herself as living in 'the best house' in the colony (p. 49), is to engage in imaginative competition with the man who actually stood in for Behn's father, one Colonel William Byam, who is painted as a brutal tyrant in the text and who cordially despised Aphra Behn, according to the historical record.[27] Wielding an instrument of writing which she and her society saw as belonging to masculine prerogative, the narrator courts notoriety by representing herself as the sympathetic confidante of a black male slave who had, in his native land, been a prince engaged in erotic and by implication political rivalry with his grandfather and king.[28] The narrator and Caesar are allied in a multifaceted league of potential subversion.

As if to defuse that threat, the narrative counters the 'we' composed of white women and Oroonoko with a stereotypical configuration, familiar from the Renaissance drama, which pits sexually vulnerable (and valuable) Englishwomen against a black man imagined as a villainous rapist.[29] One can see the 'we' shifting in a striking fashion between these two poles in a passage that occurs near the end of the tale immediately after a description of how Caesar – as the narrator announces she is compelled to call Oroonoko after he assumes his slave identity in Surinam (p. 40) – leads a slave rebellion, is deserted by all but one of the other slaves, and is recaptured and brutally punished by white male property-owners. The narrator interrupts the plot's temporal progression to return to a point in the just-recounted story when the outcome of Oroonoko's rebellion was still uncertain. That uncertainty is oddly preserved for Behn's readers by her shift from the simple past tense to a subjunctive formulation that mixes past, present, and the possibility of a different future:

> You must know, that when the News was brought ... that Caesar had betaken himself to the Woods, and carry'd with him all the Negroes, we were possess'd with extreme Fear, which no Persuasions could dissipate, that he would secure himself till night and then, that he would come down and cut all our throats. This Apprehension made all the Females of us fly down the River to be secured; and while we were away, they acted this Cruelty; for I suppose I had Authority and Interest enough there, had I suspected any such thing, to have pre-vented it: but we had not gone many Leagues, but the News overtook us, that Caesar was taken and whipped like a common Slave.
>
> (pp. 67–8)

In this passage, the authorial 'I' seems at once extraordinarily lucid and disturbingly blind about her own complicity in her hero's capture and humiliating punishment. Had she been present, she 'supposes' she could have prevented the cruelty which 'they' – white men – wrought upon the black male slave.[30] Her claim to possess some singular social authority, however, is belied by her representation of herself as part of a group of weak females, a passive group possessed – and the play on that word is rich – not by men, black or white, but rather by an agent named Fear and quickly renamed Apprehension. That oddly abstract agent, however, turns out, if we look closely, to be a product of some-thing the passage twice calls 'News' – a mode of verbal production that is often defined as unreliable in this text, and that belongs, significantly, to a semantic complex that names crucial features of Behn's own discourse in *Oroonoko*. The novella's opening pages an-nounce that this is a 'true eyewitness' account of things that happened in the 'new Colonies', and the author advertising her wares, along with the lands her words represent, is well aware that she must offer 'Novelty' to pique her English reader's interest, for 'where there is no Novelty, there can be no Curiosity' (p. 3).[31] The author herself, it would seem, is both a producer and a consumer of 'news', and in the passage about her roles in Oroonoko's aborted rebellion she repre-sents her identity – and her agency – as an ambiguous function of the *circulation* of information.

Here, as in many other parts of the book, the narrative oscillates between criticising and profiting from a 'system' of circulation which includes not only words, among them the lies characteristic of male Christian slave-traders, but bodies as well. In this disturbing oscillation, which has obviously contributed to the utter lack of critical consensus about whether Behn's book supports or attacks the institution of slavery, we can see the lineaments, I believe, of a more complex model of European colonisation than Tzvetan Todorov posits in his book on *The Conquest of America*.[32] In contrast to Todorov's book and most instances of Renaissance travel literature I've read, Behn's novella construes the relation between Old World and New not only in terms of a binary opposition between self and 'other' but also in terms of a highly unstable triangular model which, in its simplest version, draws relations of sameness and difference among a black African slave, a white Englishwoman, and a group of Native Americans who are described, in the book's opening pages, as innocents 'so unadorned' and beautiful that they resemble 'our first parents before the fall' (p. 3). Neither the white Englishwoman nor the black African man share the Indians' (imputed) quality of primeval innocence. The narrator and Oroonoko-Caesar have both received European educations, albeit less good, we may suppose, than those accorded to privileged white men; and both are at once victims and beneficiaries of socioeconomic systems that discriminate kings from commoners and support the privileges of the nobility with the profits of the slave-trade. Oroonoko is described as having captured and sold black slaves in African wars before he was himself enslaved by a dastardly lying Christian; and the narrator not only belongs to a slave-owning class but clearly supports the nationalistic colonising enterprise which fuelled and depended on the African slave-trade.[33] She laments the loss of Surinam to the Dutch a few years after the events of the novella take place (interestingly, the English traded that colony for New Amsterdam, in 'our' America, in 1667) and even uses a lush description of a gold-prospecting river trip to suggest the desirability – in 1688, on the eve of William of Orange's accession to the British throne – of retaking the lost colony and its lost profits: 'And 'tis to be bemoaned what his majesty lost by losing that part of America', she adds (p. 59).[34] By thus presenting a narrator and a hero who are both victims and beneficiaries of the international system of the slave-trade, and by contrasting and comparing both characters, at different moments, to the exotic and 'innocent' Indians, Behn provides a perspective on 'the Conquest of

America' that complicates, among other binary oppositions, the ethical one, infinitely labile in the literature of the imperial venture, between 'we' as 'good' and 'them' as 'evil' – or vice versa.

What even this account of the complexity of Behn's novella leaves out, however, is the ideological force of the 'other' black slave in the story – Imoinda, Oroonoko's beloved, whom the English rename Clemene. Imoinda is doubly enslaved – to the whites, male and female, who have bought her and also, as the narrative insists, to her black husband. In striking contrast to the unmarried narrator, who stands, in relation to Oroonoko, as a queen or Petrarchan lady-lord to a vassal – a 'Great Mistress' (p. 46) – Imoinda is an uncanny amalgam of European ideals of wifely subservience and European fantasies about wives of 'Oriental' despots. She is thus the perfect embodiment, with the exception of her dark hue, of an image of the ideal that the English author holds up to this example of the 'other'; such wives

> have a respect for their Husbands equal to what other People pay a Deity; and when a Man finds any occasion to quit his Wife, if he love her, she dies by his hand; if not he sells her, or suffers some other to kill her.
>
> (p. 72)

This passage occurs late in the tale, immediately after Oroonoko has resolved to kill his pregnant wife for reasons that show him to be no less obsessed than Othello by a sexual jealousy intricately bound up with ideologies of property possession: 'his great heart', the narrator approvingly explains, 'could not endure the Thought' that Imoinda might, after his death, 'become a Slave to the enraged Multitude', that is, be 'ravished by every Brute' (p. 71). So, with Imoinda's joyful consent (she's considerably more compliant in her fate than Desdemona), he 'sever[s] her yet smiling Face from that delicate Body, pregnant as it was with the fruits of tenderest Love' (p. 72).

Even this brief glance at Imoinda's death scene should suggest how odd it is that Imoinda's specificity as a *black wife* should be effaced not only from most critical narratives on Behn but also from the cover of the only inexpensive modern edition of the text, the Norton paperback edited by Lore Metzger. This object solicits the attention of potential readers with a cover picture that evokes the titillating cultural image of miscegenous romance in general and, in particular, the best-known high-cultural instance of such romance for Anglo-American readers, namely Shakespeare's *Othello*. The cover shows a black man on a tropical shore holding a knife histrionically pointed toward the bare throat of a *white* woman. A note on the Norton edition's back cover informs us that the frontispiece reproduces one from a 1735 edition of *Oroonoko* – not, however, Aphra Behn's novella, but rather the play published in 1696 by Thomas Southerne. Although some critics have treated Behn's and Southerne's versions as interchangeable, there are in fact crucial differences between them.[35] In addition to making his Oroonoko a much less severe critic of slavery than Behn's hero is, Southerne replaces Behn's idealised but distinctly black heroine with a beautiful white girl. This change may perhaps be explained as Southerne's bow to a strikingly gendered and also coloured convention of the Restoration stage which I'm still trying to understand, namely that male English actors could appear in blackface but actresses evidently could not.[36]

Whatever the reasons for Southerne's recolouring Behn's Imoinda, they can't be reduced to the exigencies of stage convention since he was criticised by contemporaries for not giving her a dark hue to match Oroonoko's – a hue the critic specifically terms 'Indian' in a confusion typical of primitivist ideology.[37] Among Southerne's motives, I suspect, was a desire to capitalise on a rumour titillatingly mentioned and denied in the anonymous biography included in her 1696 *Histories and Novels*, a rumour that during her stay in Surinam Behn had a romance with Oroonoko.[38] The continuing circulation of this rumour through the medium of modern books, even though most critics don't credit it, is a commercial fact that needs more discussion than I have space for here. I do, however, want to open some questions about that fact, and our participation in it is as mostly First World-born and mostly white readers, or potential buyer-readers, of *Oroonoko*. Behn's text offers an ambiguous reflection on the role of intellectual producers and consumers in an expanding international market which included in the seventeenth century, as it still does in ours, books and bodies among its prime commodities. Behn's reflection on (and of) this market has many facets, one of which, uncannily but I think instructively, seems to anticipate the titillating representation of differently gendered and coloured bodies that would advertise her story (but the possessive pronoun points to problems in the very conception of authorial 'ownership') in the eighteenth century and again in the late twentieth.

The facet of Behn's 'market representation' to which I'm referring is her textual staging of an implicit *competition* between the
white English female author and the black African female slave-
wife-mother-to-be. The competition is for Oroonoko's body and
its power to engender something in the future, something that will
outlive it. That power remains latent – impotent, one might say –
without a female counterpart for which Behn offers two opposing
images: Imoinda's pregnant body, holding a potential slave-
labourer ('for', as the text reminds us, 'all the Breed is theirs to
whom the Parents belong'); and, alternatively, the author's 'female
pen', which she deploys to describe, with an unnerving blend of
relish and horror, the scenes of Oroonoko's bodily dismember-
ment and eventual death following his leading of a slave revolt.
She uses that pen also, as she tells the reader in the final paragraph, in hopes of making Oroonoko's 'glorious Name to survive
all Ages' (p. 78).

The narrator of course wins the competition. Through her pen
flow at least some of the prerogatives of the English empire and its
language, a language she has shown herself using, in one remarkable
scene, as a potent instrument of sexual and political domination. In
this scene, which explicitly pits an image of politically 'dangerous'
biological reproduction against an image of 'safe' verbal production,
the author presents herself most paradoxically as both a servant and
a beneficiary of the eroticised socioeconomic *system* of domination
she describes. When some unnamed English authority figures perceive that Oroonoko is growing sullen because of the 'Thought' that
this child will belong not to him but to his owners, the narrator is
'obliged', she tells us, to use her fiction-making powers to 'divert'
Oroonoko (and Imoinda too) from thoughts of 'Mutiny'. Mutiny is
specifically tied to a problem in population management, a problem
about which Behn's text – like much colonialist discourse, including
chilling debates on whether it is better to 'buy or breed' one's slaves
– is fundamentally, and necessarily, ambivalent.[39] Mutiny, the narrator observes, 'is very fatal sometimes in those Colonies that abound
so with Slaves, that they exceed the Whites in vast numbers' (p. 46).
It is to abort the potential mutiny that the narrator is 'obliged' to
'discourse with Caesar, and to give him all the Satisfaction I possibly
could' – which she does, entertaining him with stories about 'the
Loves of the Romans and great Men, which charmed him to my
company'. In an interestingly gendered division of narrative goods,
she tells Imoinda stories about nuns.[40]

Playing a version of Othello's role to an audience comprised of her slaves, Behn dramatises a complex mode of authorial 'ownership' of characters cast in the role of enthralled audience. In so doing, she represents herself creating a paradoxical *facsimile* of freedom, for herself, her immediate audience, and by implication, her largely female English readers as well, in which servitude is rendered tolerable by being eroticised, fantasised, 'diverted' from activities, either sexual or military, that might work to dislodge the English from their precarious lordship of this New World land. Just how precarious their possession was the narrative acknowledges by repeatedly lamenting their loss of the land to the Dutch; but the deeper problems of the logic of colonialism are also signalled, albeit confusedly, by the contrast between the description of slave mutiny quoted above and the explanation offered early in the story for why the British do *not* enslave the native Indians, a group which, like the Africans, are essential to the colonialists' welfare; 'they being on all occasions very useful to us', the narrator says, 'we find it absolutely necessary to caress 'em as Friends, and not to treat 'em as Slaves, nor dare we do other, their numbers so far surpassing ours in that Continent' (p. 5).[41] This passage sheds an ironic light on the later moment when the narrator uses stories to divert Oroonoko from thoughts of mutiny, for we see that one logical solution to the mutiny problem, a solution that her stories to Oroonoko suppress but which her larger narrative only partially represses, is the possibility of *not* enslaving a group of 'others' who outnumber you. Such a solution, with respect both to Africans and to Indians, had been recommended by a few early critics of the colonial enterprise; but Behn is far from joining the tiny group who voiced criticisms of the whole system of international trade based on forced labour by persons of many skin colours including freckled Irish white.[42]

In its characteristically disturbing way, Behn's novel shows us just enough about the author's competition with Imoinda, and the enmeshment of that competition within a larger socio-sexual-economic system, to make us uneasy when we hold the book *Oroonoko* in our hands and realise that the text itself invites us to see the book as a safe-sex substitute for the potentially mutinous but also economically valuable black slave-child Oroonoko might have had with Imoinda. In a bizarre twisting of the old trope of book as child, Behn offers her contemporary English readers, and us too, a representation of an economy in which the white woman's book is born, quite starkly, from the death and silencing of black persons, one of them pregnant. Behind the scene of Oroonoko's final torture, which gruesomely anticipates Alice Walker's description, in her story of a cross-race rape during the US Civil Rights struggle, of 'white folks standing in a circle roasting something that had talked to them in their own language before they tore out its tongue', is the murder-sacrifice of the black woman and her unborn child.[43] And the threat represented by the black woman, I would suggest, is obscurely acknowledged to be even greater than the threat represented by the black man, so that the text finally has to enlist him, through enticements of European codes of masculine honour and Petrarchan romance, to suppress the one character who actually uses physical force rather than words to attack the highest legal representative of the colonial system, namely the male Lieutenant-Governor. Reversing the Renaissance commonplace that defined deeds as masculine, words as feminine, Imoinda wounds Byam, the narrator tells us, with a poisoned arrow; he is saved, however – though the narrator clearly regrets this – by his Indian mistress, who sucks the venom from his wound. The white female narrator's own ambivalent relation to male English authority is figured here by the device of splitting 'other' women into two roles: one rebellious and one erotically complicitous.

Imoinda's rebellious power – and the need to destroy it – are figured most strikingly, I think, in the two juxtaposed episodes where Oroonoko first kills a mother tiger and lays the whelp at the author's feet (p. 51) and then kills a property-destroying tiger – again female – and extracts her bullet-ridden heart to give to the English audience. At this moment Oroonoko is most transparently shown as a figure for the author of *Oroonoko*, a repository of novel curiosities which Behn offers to her readers as he offers the tiger's cub, and then its heart, to his owner-admirers:

> This heart the conqueror brought up to us, and 'twas a very great curiosity, which all the country came to see, and which gave Caesar occasion of making many fine Discourses, of Accidents in War, and strange Escapes.
>
> (p. 53)

Here Behn deliberately constructs her hero from echoes of Shakespeare; Oroonoko woos her and other British ladies as Othello wooed Desdemona with his eloquent story of his 'most disastrous chances … moving accidents … hair breadth-scapes i' th' imminent deadly breach' (I.iii. 134–6).[44] With respect to the power relation between a narrator and an audience, this scene offers a mirror reversal of the one in which the narrator entertains her sullen, potentially mutinous hero with *her* culture's stories of 'great [Roman] men'. We can now see even more clearly that the 'ground' of both scenes, the 'material', as it were, from which the production and reception of exotic stories derive, is the silent figure of the black woman – silent but by no means safe, as is suggested by the image of the female tiger and the narrative device of duplicating it.

Perhaps, then, the Norton cover is an ironically apt representation of the complex of problems centring on property – sexual, economic, and intellectual – that Behn's book at once exposes and effaces. For the white woman who stands in Imoinda's place might well be Behn herself, the literate white woman who spoke *for* some oppressed black slaves but who did so with extreme partiality, discriminating among them according to status (the novel sympathises with *noble* slaves only, depicting common ones as 'natural' servants and traitors to Oroonoko's cause) and also according to gender. Laura Brown has remarked that Behn's representation of Oroonoko is full of the ironies of the colonialist version of the self-other dialectic, in which the 'other' can only be recognised as an image of the European self.[45] Brown does not, however, explore how Behn's narrative includes the 'other other' of Imoinda in that dialectic, or rather, at once includes and occludes the multiple differences between the figure named Imoinda/Clemene and her black husband, her white 'mistress', and, of course, her historical 'self', the woman, or more precisely, women, who were Indians and Africans both and who did not speak English, much less the idiom of heroic romance Behn favours, until the Renaissance, as we call it, brought Europeans to African and American territories. The last word of Behn's book is 'Imoinda'. I want to suggest, by way of a necessarily open-ended conclusion, that a quest for the historical and contemporary meanings of that name – with its teasing plays on 'I', 'moi' [me], 'am', 'Indian' – will require more attention to modalities of identification and difference than most feminist, Marxist, deconstructionist, psychoanalytic, or new historicist critics have yet expended.

The importance of that task can perhaps be better appreciated when one thinks of how insistently the colonising of the New World was figured as a project of erotic possession (as, for instance, in

Donne's famous lines apostrophising his naked mistress as 'O My America, my New Found-land'), and, more specifically, as a project rife with fantasies of miscegenation – a mixing of ostensibly distinct categories that was just beginning, in the mid-seventeenth century, to be legally prohibited in the American colonies and which was for that reason acquiring a new erotic charge.[46] Indeed one might well want to pursue Imoinda's cultural significance by studying the odd symmetries and dissonances between the representations of both Africa and America as female bodies, the former repeatedly described as inaccessible, the latter as easily penetrable at first, but later often dangerous.[47]

If I end by suggesting that more work needs to be done on Imoinda's symbolic and material existences, I do so because I'm well aware that my own essay has only begun to formulate, much less answer, questions about the *blanks* on the maps which many of us use to explore the temporal and spatial terrain we term the Renaissance. In attempting a kind of interpretation that seeks to grasp relations of gender, race, and class through – and against – the material of a specific historical text read in a 'context' impossible to delimit with certainty much less to master intellectually, I've sought to keep all three of my key category terms in play, not reducing any one to another, noticing how they sometimes supplement, sometimes fracture each other. I'm aware, however, that I'm a juggler who can't begin to handle enough balls: I've left out of this discussion many other categories of social thought that operate in Behn's text, among them religion and a powerful monarchist political ideology that arguably both drives and limits the story's investment in the oxymoronic figure of the *royal* slave.[48] Despite the gaps in my narrative, I hope I've done enough to suggest not only the difficulties but some of the pleasures of working with conceptual categories that lie squarely in the centre of battlefields, historical and contemporary. Working with such categories spurs me to think about my own implication in an economic and ideological system that has some salient continuities with the system inhibited and represented by Aphra Behn, a white woman writer whose gender allowed her to belong only eccentrically to the emerging caste of travelling intellectuals serving, representing, and sometimes critically anatomising Europe's early imperial enterprises.

From *Women, 'Race', and Writing in the Early Modern Period*, ed. Margo Hendricks and Patricia Parker (London, 1994), pp. 209–24.

NOTES

[Margaret Ferguson investigates the categories of gender, race and class in a study of Behn's *Oroonoko*, noting how the tale avoids the binary opposites of us and them, good and bad, innocent and corrupt. She observes the multiple and shifting class positions held by the white female writer, as well as the volatile analogy between narrator and hero. Behn's narrator oscillates between criticising and profiting from the colonial circulation of both goods and words and, Ferguson argues, is in implicit competition with the black woman Imoinda for Oroonoko as man and text. Ed.]

Many colleagues and students have helped me with this essay; I owe special thanks to Judy Berman, Ann R. Jones, Mary Poovey, David Simpson, Valerie Smith, and Liz Wiesen. An earlier version of this essay was written for a special issue of *Women's Studies: An Interdisciplinary Journal* (Spring 1991), ed. Ann R. Jones and Betty Travitsky. I am grateful to Wendy Martin, editor of *Women's Studies*, for allowing me to reuse materials that originally appeared in that special issue.

1. For cogent, bibliographically useful discussions of the historical and conceptual problems implicit in the varying popular and academic understanding of each of these terms see Henry Louis Gates, Jr, 'Writing "Race" and the Difference it Makes', pp. 1–20, and Anthony Appiah, 'The Uncompleted Argument: Du Bois and the Illusion of Race', both in *'Race,' Writing, and Difference*, ed. Henry Louis Gates, Jr, *Critical Inquiry*, 12 (Autumn 1985); Joan Wallach Scott, 'Gender: A Useful Category of Historical Analysis,' in her *Gender and the Politics of History* (New York, 1988), pp. 28–50; Raymond Williams's discussion of ambiguities in both Marxist and non-Marxist notions of class in *Keywords* (New York, 1976), pp. 51–9; Constance Jordan, 'Renaissance Women and the Question of Class', in *Sexuality and Gender in Early Modern Europe*, ed. James G. Turner (Cambridge, 1993), pp. 90–106; and Stephen A. Resnick and Richard D. Wolff, *Knowledge and Class* (Chicago, 1987).

2. See Karen Newman, '"And wash the Ethiop white": Femininity and the Monstrous', in *Fashioning Femininity and the English Renaissance Drama* (Chicago, 1991); Laura Brown, 'The Romance of Empire: *Oroonoko* and the Trade in Slaves', in *The New Eighteenth Century*, ed. L. Brown and Felicity Nussbaum (New York, 1987), pp. 40–61; and Ania Loomba, *Gender, Race, Renaissance Drama* (Manchester, 1989).

3. See Joan Kelly, 'Did Women Have a Renaissance?' (1977); rpt. in *Women, History, and Theory: The Essays of Joan Kelly* (Chicago, 1984), pp. 19–50.

4. Kelly, 'The Doubled Vision of Feminist Theory', in *Women, History, and Theory*, pp. 51–64; the quotation is from p. 58.

5. For a pioneering effort to define a 'sex/gender' system (a phrase she prefers to 'patriarchy' or 'mode of reproduction'), see Gayle Rubin, 'The Traffic in Women', in *Toward an Anthropology of Women*, ed. Rayna R. Reiter (New York and London, 1975), pp. 157–210, esp. pp. 159, 167. More recently, some feminists have criticised this concept as granting an overly 'transparent' determination to the body (what Rubin calls 'anatomical sex difference'); see, e.g., Moira Gatens, 'A Critique of the Sex/Gender Distinction', in *Beyond Marxism?*, ed. J. Allen and P. Patton (Leichhardt, NSW, 1985), pp. 143–60; and also Teresa de Lauretis, *Technologies of Gender: Essays on Theory, Film, and Fiction* (Bloomington, IN, 1987), p. 9 (on why she prefers the term *gender* to sex/gender system).

6. See Barbara Fields, 'Ideology and Race in American History', in *Region, Race and Reconstruction*, ed. J. Morgan Kousser and James M. McPherson (New York, 1982), p. 149.

7. *International Encyclopedia of Social Sciences*, ed. David L. Sills (New York, 1968), 13: 264.

8. David Brion Davis, *The Problem of Slavery in Western Culture* (Ithaca, NY, 1966), p. 277.

9. Edward Long, *Candid Reflections upon the Judgement Lately Awarded by the Court of King's Bench … on What is Commonly Called the Negro Cause* (London, 1772; cited in Davis, *The Problem of Slavery*, p. 277); see also Natalie Zemon Davis's discussion of the ideological and sometimes political associations between 'unruly' women and lower-class men during the Renaissance, in 'Women on Top', *Society and Culture in Early Modern France* (Stanford, CA, 1975), pp. 124–51.

10. Fields, 'Ideology and Race', p. 146.

11. For an interesting discussion of this problem see Wendy James, 'The Anthropologist as Reluctant Imperialist', in *Anthropology and the Colonial Encounter*, ed. Talal Asad (New York, 1973), pp. 41–69, and other essays in that volume, including Asad's Introduction.

12. The *OED* gives numerous illustrations from Renaissance texts of the definitions of race as 'Mankind' (1.5a) or as 'A limited group of persons descended from a common ancestor' (1.2), though it cites no examples of meanings stressing physical differences and a general taxonomic division of all humans according to race (1.2d: 'One of the great divisions of mankind, having certain physical differences in common') until 1774; the first reference to race as a liability (implicitly) of dark colour is Emerson's remark, in *English Traits* (1856), that 'Race in the Negro is of appalling importance' (1.6b). It is instructive to read the *OED*'s highly selective diachronic narrative on race in conjunction with Marvin Harris's discussion of the synchronically various uses of the term and its 'ethnosemantic glosses', which are applied 'to human

populations organised along an astonishing variety of principles'. To illustrate that variety, he remarks that in some societies where the group identity is not secured through the 'ideological device' of genealogical rules, categorisations will tend to rely *more* on visible signs of difference such as skin colour than they do when 'the idea of descent' is paramount. In Bahia, for instance, where descent rules are absent, 'full siblings whose phenotypes markedly differ from each other are assigned ... to contrastive racial categories' and 'pronounced disagreements concerning the identity of individuals frequently occur' ('Race', *International Encyclopedia of Social Sciences*, 13:263, 264).

13. See de Lauretis, *Technologies of Gender*, pp. 2–3.

14. Resnick and Wolff, *Knowledge and Class*, pp. 115, 117.

15. In *Keywords* Raymond Williams suggests that the term 'class' acquired its modern sense designating divisions of social groups (in contrast to divisions among things like plants) during the period between 1770 and 1840 (p. 61). For discussion of the problems of using 'class' in analysing early and pre-modern social formations, see E. P. Thompson, 'Eighteenth-Century English Society: Class Struggle Without Class?' *Social History*, 3 (1978), 133–65. See also Constance Jordan's important recent essay 'Renaissance Women and the Question of Class' (cited above, n. 1).

16. Brown, 'The Romance of Empire', p. 42.

17. According to Behn's first biographer, she was a 'Gentlewoman, by Birth, of a good Family in the City of Canterbury in Kent' (*Memoirs of the Life of Mrs. Behn. Written by a Gentlewoman of her Acquaintance*, in *Histories and Novels*, London: printed for S. Briscoe, 1696, sig. A₇v, quoted from the British Library copy). Not until the late nineteenth century did anyone seek publicly to refashion Behn's biography; Sir Edward Gosse then lowered her social status on the evidence of a scribbled note, 'Mrs Behn was daughter to a barber', in the margin of a recently discovered MS by Anne Finch, the Countess of Winchelsea. Goreau provides an account of Gosse's 'discovery' (given authority in his *Dictionary of National Biography* article on her) and subsequent biographical arguments on pp. 8–10 of *Reconstructing Aphra: A Social Biography of Aphra Behn* (New York, 1980). For further discussions of the 'mystery' of Behn's birth and the manifold speculations it has engendered, see Goreau, pp. 11–13, 42–3; Sara Mendelson, *The Mental World of Stuart Women: Three Studies* (Brighton, 1987), pp. 116–20; and Maureen Duffy, *The Passionate Shepherdess: Aphra Behn, 1640–89* (London, 1977), ch. 1. See Goreau, *Reconstructing Aphra*, pp. 12–13, for a discussion of the importance of Behn's (anomalous) education for her social status.

18. See Wlad Godzich, 'The Culture of Illiteracy', *Enclitic*, 8 (Fall 1984), 27–35, on humanist intellectuals as servants of the emerging nation

JUGGLING RACE, CLASS AND GENDER 229

states and the expanding international market of the early modern era. See also the chapter on Joachim de Bellay in Margaret Ferguson, *Trials of Desire: Renaissance Defenses of Poetry* (New Haven, CT, 1983).

19. I am grateful to Catherine Gallagher for letting me see her chapters, 'Who Was That Masked Woman? The Prostitute and the Playwright in the Comedies of Aphra Behn' and 'The Author Monarch and the Royal Slave: Oroonoko and the Blackness of Representation', in her forthcoming book *British Women Writers and the Literary Marketplace from 1670–1820*. A version of 'Who Was That Masked Woman?' appears in *Last Laughs: Perspectives on Women and Comedy*, ed. Regina B. Barecca (New York, 1988).

20. For the date of *Oroonoko*'s composition see George Guffey, 'Aphra Behn's *Oroonoko*: Occasion and Accomplishment', in *Two English Novelists: Aphra Behn and Anthony Trollope*, co-authored with Andrew White (Los Angeles, 1975), pp. 15–16. All quotations from *Oroonoko* are from the text edited by Lore Metzger (New York, 1973). The reference to the female pen is from p. 40. See Laura Brown. 'The Romance of Empire', esp. 48–51, for a discussion of the story's debt to the traditions of heroic romance and, in particular, coterie aristocratic drama.

21. For an excellent account and bibliography of the Renaissance ideology of normative femininity, see Ann Rosalind Jones, *The Currency of Eros: Women's Love Lyric in Europe, 1540–1620* (Bloomington, IN, 1990), ch. I.

22. For examples of this gendered 'colonial' cultural discourse see the passages cited above from Davis, *The Problem of Slavery*, and Goreau, *Reconstructing Aphra*, pp. 48–9 (on the fears of 'sodomy' that kept one lady living in Antigua housebound, and on the repercussions of the fact that men in the colonies greatly outnumbered women).

23. On Behn's situation after her father died, impoverished but also freer of paternal constraint than was thought proper, see Goreau, *Reconstructing Aphra*, p. 42.

24. My account of the multiple alignments of the 'I' is indebted to questions prepared by Judy Berman for a graduate seminar at the University of California, Berkeley, in the spring of 1988.

25. Chudleigh's text, from her *Poems on Several Occasions* (London, 1703), is quoted from *First Feminists: British Women Writers 1578–1799*, ed. Moira Ferguson (Bloomington and Old Westbury, 1985), p. 237. Cf. the statement in a famous pamphlet entitled *The Levellers*, also from 1703, that 'Matrimony is indeed become a meer Trade [.] They carry their Daughters to *Smithfield* as they do Horses, and sell to the highest bidder.' Quoted in Maximillian E. Novak and David Stuart Rodes's edition of Thomas Southerne's *Oroonoko* (Lincoln, 1976), p. xxiv.

26. Behn offers a more literal and comic representation of impotence in the
   first part of the novella, where Imoinda is taken from Oroonoko by his
   tyrannical but impotent grandfather; she also represents male impotence
   in many of her plays and in her witty poem 'The Disappointment'.

27. The quotation is from the 'Epistle Dedicatory' to Lord Maitland,
   included in the edition of *Oroonoko* by Adelaide P. Amore (Washington,
   DC, 1987), p. 3, but not in the Norton edition. See Goreau,
   Reconstructing Aphra, pp. 68–9, for Byam's reasons for disliking Behn
   and his snide reference to her as 'Astrea' in a letter to a friend in England.

28. See her Preface to *The Lucky Chance*, where she requests 'the
   Priviledge for my Masculine Part the Poet in me (if any such you will
   allow me) to tread in those successful Paths my Predecessors have so
   long thriv'd in' (*The Works of Aphra Behn*, ed. Montague Summers,
   6 vols [1915; rpt. New York, 1967], 3, p. 187).

29. For a fine discussion of this stereotypical confrontation across colour
   and gender lines, see Anthony Barthelemy, *Black Face, Maligned Race:
   The Representation of Blacks in English Drama from Shakespeare to
   Southerne* (Baton Rouge, LA, 1987), esp. ch. 4. Behn herself, in
   Abdelazar: Or the Moor's Revenge (1677), her adaptation for the
   Restoration stage of Dekker's *Lust's Dominion*, exploits the conven-
   tional image of the threateningly sexual black man.

30. Note that the most logical syntactic antecedent of 'they' would be a
   group of *black* men composed of Oroonoko and his band, perpetrating
   the rape which one might easily construe as the referent for 'this
   cruelty'. The grammatical ambiguity arguably points to the struggle
   between the narrator's original perception of danger and her 'cor-
   rected' but guiltily impotent retroactive perception that the white men,
   not the black ones, were her true enemies.

31. Cf. the passage where the white male character Trefry is said to be
   'infinitely well pleased' with the 'novel' of Oroonoko's and Imoinda's
   reunion (p. 44).

32. See, for instance, the diametrically opposed interpretations of George
   Guffey and Angeline Goreau on the issue of Behn's representation of
   black slaves. For Guffey, who reads confidently 'through' the sign of
   Oroonoko's blackness to an English political subtext, the novella's
   ideological argument is not anti-slavery but against the enslavement
   of *kings*, specifically the Stuart King tenuously on England's throne
   in 1688 ('Aphra Behn's *Oroonoko*: Occasion and Accomplishment',
   pp. 16–17). Goreau, in contrast (and equally confidently), sees Behn's
   'impassioned attack on the condition of slavery and defence of human
   rights' as 'perhaps the first important abolitionist statement in the
   history of English literature' (*Reconstructing Aphra*, p. 289). See
   Tzvetan Todorov, *The Conquest of America: The Question of the Other*
   (New York, 1984).

33. The text is, however, significantly ambiguous about whether Behn could or did own slaves in her own right, as an unfathered, unmarried woman. In her prefatory letter to Maitland, she refers to Oroonoko as 'my Slave', but she suggests, in the course of the story, that she lacked the power to dispose of her chattel property: she relates that she 'assured' him falsely, as it turns out, that he would be freed when the governor arrived (p. 45).

34. Cf. p. 48, where the narrator laments that 'certainly had his late Majesty [Charles II], of sacred Memory, but seen and known what a vast and charming World he had been Master of in that Continent, he would never have parted so easily with it to the Dutch'; the passage goes on to advertise the natural riches of the (once and future) colony. On the British loss of Surinam in exchange for New York, see Eric Williams, *From Columbus to Castro: The History of the Caribbean* (1970; rpt. New York, 1984), p. 81.

35. See, for example, Lore Metzger's introduction to the Norton *Oroonoko*, pp. ix–x and Eric Williams, *From Columbus to Castro*, p. 207: 'Oroonoko opposed the revolts of the slaves as did his creator, Mrs Behn'. That statement seems to rely more on Southerne's version, where Oroonoko is made to speak in favour of the institution of slavery and lead a revolt only with great reluctance, than on Behn's, where the hero passionately leads the slaves to revolt and defends their right to regain their liberty (p. 61).

36. In *Guinea's Captive Kings: British Anti-Slavery Literature of the XVIIIth Century* (Chapel Hill, NC, 1942), p. 21, Wylie Sypher suggests that it was more acceptable for theatre audiences that Imoinda be white. Queen Anne and her ladies had been criticised for wearing blackface in Jonson's *Masque of Blackness*, but Englishwomen representing Moors had evidently worn black masks and make-up in the Lord Mayor's pageants in London after the Restoration; see Anthony Barthelemy, *Black Face, Maligned Race*, esp. ch. 3.

37. For the poem attacking Southerne for failing to give Imoinda an '*Indian*' hue', see Maximillian E. Novak and David S. Rodes's Introduction to their edition of Southerne's *Oroonoko*, p. xxxvii. In *The Problem of Slavery*, Davis discusses the tendency to conflate Amerindians and African blacks in a discourse of 'primitivism' (p. 480).

38. See *Memoirs on the Life of Mrs. Behn* (cited above, n. 17), sig. B₁r; the rumour is also mentioned by Lore Metzger in her Introduction to *Oroonoko*, p. x; most modern biographers prefer another story (which has some documentary support) that Behn had an affair with a white Republican, William Scott, during her stay in Surinam (see Goreau, *Reconstructing Aphra*, pp. 66–8).

39. On the 'buy or breed' debates, see Daniel P. Mannix in collaboration with Malcolm Cowley, *Black Cargoes: A History of the Atlantic Slave Trade 1518–1865* (New York, 1962), p. 52.

40. See Amore, 'Introduction to *Oroonoko*, for the hypothesis that this detail testifies to Behn's piety and possible Catholicism. Accepting the likelihood that she was indeed a Catholic, I wouldn't assume that the stories designed for Imoinda by the narrator are any more pious than Behn's own racy stories about nuns; indeed there may well be a bit of authorial self-reference (or even witty self-advertisement) here. See Behn's *History of the Nun, or, The Fair Vow Breaker* and *The Nun, or The Perjur'd Beauty*, both in *The Works of Aphra Behn*, ed. Montague Summers, vol. 5.

41. Since the blacks also greatly outnumbered the whites in the colony, Behn's explanation for the distinction in the English treatment of the two non-white groups is clearly problematic. The matter continues to be a site of debate in modern histories of slavery in the New World, for even though Indians *were* frequently enslaved, all of the colonial powers came, eventually, to *prefer* African to Amerindian slaves for reasons that confusingly blended economic, theological, and cultural explanations. Some modern historians, for instance Winthrop Jordan, in *White over Black: American Attitudes toward the Negro, 1550–1812* (Chapel Hill, NC, 1968), invoke colour difference as an explanation for why Africans came (eventually) to be seen as better (more 'natural') slaves than Indians, but this view, cited and refuted by Fields, p. 11, seems anachronistic and reductive. More satisfactory discussions are given by Davis, *The Problem of Slavery*, who sees the distinction as an 'outgrowth of the practical demands of trade and diplomacy' (p. 178) bolstered by ideological fictions about blackness (the biblical colour of evil) and 'noble savages'; and by William D. Phillips, Jr, *Slavery from Roman Times to the Early Transatlantic Trade* (Minneapolis, 1985), who, in discussing the commonly cited adage that 'one Negro is worth four Indians' in terms of labour power, suggests that the difference between the Africans' experience in agricultural societies and the Amerindians' in mainly hunting-gathering cultures helps account for this sobering ideological distinction (p. 184) that makes a person's *economic* value stand in antithetical relation to his or her *moral* value (in European eyes, at least, which equated freedom with 'natural' nobility).

42. For discussions of early critics of slavery such as Las Casas (who came only late in life to decry the enslavement of blacks as well as Indians) and Albornoz, see Davis, *The Problem of Slavery*, p. 189 and *passim*; Eric Williams, *From Columbus to Castro*, pp. 43–4; and Goreau, *Reconstructing Aphra*, p. 289 (on the Quaker George Fox's opposition to the system of slavery).

43. Alice Walker, 'Advancing Luna – and Ida B. Wells', in *You Can't Keep a Good Woman Down* (New York, 1981), p. 93.

44. Quoted from *Othello*, ed. Alvin Kernan (New York, 1963), p. 55.

45. See Brown, 'The Romance of Empire', pp. 47–8, where she comments astutely on Behn's description of Oroonoko as a perfect European hero ('his nose was rising and Roman, instead of African and flat', Norton edn, p. 8).

46. Elegy 19, 'To his Mistris Going To Bed', quoted from *John Donne: Poetry and Prose*, ed. Frank Warnke (New York, 1967), p. 96. See Mannix and Cowley, *Black Cargoes*, p. 60, on the Maryland Assembly's early (1663) law against racial intermarriages, a law specifically directed against Englishwomen; cf. Davis's observation, in *The Problem of Slavery*, that the North American colonies adopted 'harsh penalties for whites who had sexual relations with Negroes, and the punishments were usually more severe for white women' (p. 277, n. 27).

47. See Barthelemy, *Black Face*, ch. 3, for a rich account of personifications of Africa on English maps and in pageants; and see also Louis Montrose, 'The Work of Gender in the Discourse of Discovery', *Representations*, 33 (Winter 1991), 1–41.

48. See Maureen Duffy and George Guffey for different versions, both I think reductive, of a topical interpretation of *Oroonoko* which takes Behn's hero as an allegorical figure for various Stuart monarchs, especially the 'martyred' Charles I and the soon-to-be-deposed James II. Catherine Gallagher offers a more nuanced reading of the novella in terms of absolutist political ideology in her forthcoming *British Women Writers and the Literary Marketplace*.

Further Reading

Andrade, Susan Z., 'White Skin, Black Masks: Colonialism and the Sexual Politics of *Oroonoko*', *Cultural Critique* (Spring 1994), 189–214.

Ballaster, Ros, *Seductive Forms: Women's Amatory Fiction from 1684 to 1740* (Oxford: Clarendon Press, 1992).

——, 'Pretences of State: Aphra Behn and the Female Plot', *Rereading Aphra Behn*, ed. Heidi Hutner (Charlottesville: University of Virginia Press, 1993), pp. 187–211.

Barash, Carol, *English Women's Poetry, 1649–1714: Politics, Community, and Linguistic Authority* (Oxford: Clarendon Press, 1996).

Boehrer, Bruce Thomas, 'Behn's "Disappointment" and Nashe's "Choice of Valentines": Pornographic Poetry and the Influence of Anxiety', *Essays in Literature*, 16 (1989), 172–87.

Brown, Laura, 'The romance of empire: *Oroonoko* and the trade in slaves', *The New Eighteenth Century: Theory, Politics, English Literature*, ed. Felicity Nussbaum and Laura Brown (New York: Methuen, 1987), pp. 41–61.

Brownley, Martine Watson, 'The Narrator in *Oroonoko*', *Essays in Literature*, 4 (1977), 174–81.

Canfield, J. Douglas, *Tricksters & Estates: On the Ideology of Restoration Comedy* (Lexington: University of Kentucky Press, 1997).

Carlson, Susan, 'Aphra Behn's *The Emperor of the Moon*: Staging Seventeenth-Century Farce for Twentieth-Century Tastes', *Essays in Theatre*, 14 (May 1996), 117–30.

Chernaik, Warren, 'Unguarded Hearts: Trangression and Epistolary Form in Aphra Behn's *Love-Letters* and the *Portuguese Letters*', *Journal of English and Germanic Philology*, 97 (January 1998), 13–33.

Chibka, Robert, '"Oh! Do Not Fear a Woman's Invention": Truth, Falsehood, and Fiction in Aphra Behn's *Oroonoko*', *Tulsa Studies in Literature and Language*, 30 (1988), 510–37.

Copeland, Nancy, '"Once a whore and ever"? Whore and Virgin in *The Rover* and its Antecedents', *Restoration*, 16 (1992), 20–7.

Diamond, Elin, '*Gestus* and Signature in Aphra Behn's *The Rover*', *English Literary History*, 56 (1989), 519–41.

Davis, Lennard, *Factual Fictions: The Origins of the English Novel* (New York: Columbia University Press, 1983).

Day, Robert Adams, 'Aphra Behn and the Works of Intellect', *Fetter'd or Free? British Women Novelists 1670–1815*, ed. Mary Ann Schofield and Cecilia Macheski (Athens, OH: Ohio University Press, 1986), pp. 372–82.

Duffy, Maureen, *The Passionate Shepherdess: Aphra Behn 1640–1689* (London: Cape, 1977).

Duyfhuizen, Bernard, '"That which I dare not name": Aphra Behn's "The Willing Mistress"', *English Literary History*, 58 (1991), 63–82.

Ferguson, Margaret, 'Juggling the categories of race, class, and gender: Aphra Behn's *Oroonoko*', *Women's Studies*, 19 (1991), 159–81. Rpt. *Women, Race and Writing in the Early Modern Period* (London: Routledge, 1994), pp. 209–24.

Ferguson, Moira, '*Oroonoko*, Birth of a Paradigm', *New Literary History*, 23(2) (1992), 339–59.

Finke, Laurie, 'Aphra Behn and the Ideological Construction of Restoration Literary Theory', *Rereading Aphra Behn*, ed. Heidi Hutner (Charlottesville: University of Virginia Press, 1993), pp. 17–43.

Gallagher, Catherine, 'Who was That Masked Woman? The Prostitute and the Playwright in the Comedies of Aphra Behn', *Last Laughs: Perspectives on Women and Comedy*, ed. Regina Barreca (New York: Gordon Breach, 1988).

——, 'Oroonoko's Blackness', *Aphra Behn Studies*, ed. Janet Todd (Cambridge: Cambridge University Press, 1996), pp. 235–58.

Gardiner, Judith Kegan, 'The First English Novel: Aphra Behn's *Love-Letters*, the Canon, and Women's Tastes', *Tulsa Studies in Women's Literature* (Fall 1989), 201–22.

Goreau, Angeline, *Reconstructing Aphra: A Social Biography of Aphra Behn* (New York: Dial, 1980).

Green, Susan, 'Semiotic Modalities of the Female Body in Aphra Behn's *The Dutch Lover*', *Rereading Aphra Behn*, ed. Heidi Hutner (Charlottesville: University of Virginia Press, 1993), pp. 121–47.

Greer, Germaine (ed.), *The Uncollected Verse of Aphra Behn* (Stump Cross: Stump Cross Books, 1989).

Hendricks, Margo, 'Civility, Barbarism, and Aphra Behn's The Widow Ranter', *Women, 'Race', and Writing in the Early Modern Period* (London: Routledge, 1994), pp. 225–39.

Hobby, Elaine, *Virtue of Necessity: English Women's Writing 1649–88* (London: Virgo, 1988).

Hughes, Derek, *English Drama 1660–1700* (Oxford: Clarendon Press, 1996).

Hutner, Heidi, 'Revisioning the Female Body: Aphra Behn's *The Rover*, Parts I and II', *Rereading Aphra Behn*, ed. Heidi Hutner (Charlottesville: University of Virginia Press, 1993), pp. 102–20.

Jacobs, Naomi, 'The Seduction of Aphra Behn', *Women's Studies*, 18(4) (1991), 395–403.

Kavenik, Frances M., 'Aphra Behn: The Playwright as "Breeches Part"', *Curtain Calls: British and American Women Writers and the Theater, 1660–1820*, ed. Mary Anne Schofield and Cecilia Macheski (Athens, OH: Ohio University Press, 1991), pp. 178–91.

Kubek, Elizabeth Bennett, '"Night Mares of the Commonwealth": Royalist Passion and Female Ambition in Aphra Behn's *The Roundheads*', *Restoration*, 17 (1993), 88–103.

Lewcock, Dawn, 'More for seeing than hearing: Behn and the use of theatre', *Aphra Behn Studies*, ed. Janet Todd (Cambridge: Cambridge University press, 1996), pp. 66–83.

Lipking, Joanna, 'Confusing matters: searching the backgrounds of *Oroonoko*', *Aphra Behn Studies*, ed. Janet Todd (Cambridge: Cambridge University Press, 1996), pp. 259–81.

Lussier, Mark, '"The Vile Merchandize of Fortune": Women, Economy, and Desire in Aphra Behn', *Women's Studies*, 18 (1990), 370–93.

Markley, Robert and Molly Rothenburg, 'Contestations of Nature: Aphra Behn's "The Golden Age" and the Sexualizing of Politics', *Rereading Aphra Behn*, ed. Heidi Hutner (Charlottesville: University of Virginia Press, 1993).

Markley, Robert, 'Be Impudent, be saucy, forward, bold, touzing and leud: The Politics of Masculine Sexuality and Feminine Desire in Behn's Tory Comedies', *Cultural Readings of Restoration and Eighteenth-Century English Theater*, ed. J. Douglas Canfield and Deborah C. Payne (Athens, GA: University of Georgia Press, 1995).

Mendelson, Sara Heller, *The Mental World of Stuart Women: Three Studies* (Brighton: Harvester, 1987).

Mermin, Dorothy, 'Women becoming poets: Katherine Philips, Aphra Behn, Anne Finch', *English Literary History*, 57 (1990), 335–56.

Munns, Jessica, '"But to the touch were soft": pleasure, power, and impotence in "The Disappointment" and "The Golden Age"', *Aphra Behn Studies*, ed. Janet Todd (Cambridge: Cambridge University Press, 1996), pp. 178–96.

——, 'Barton and Behn's *The Rover*: or, the Text transpos'd', *Restoration and Eighteenth Century Theatre Research* (1988), pp. 11–22.

O'Donnell, Mary Ann, *Aphra Behn: An Annotated Bibliography of Primary and Secondary Sources* (New York: Garland, 1986).

Owen, Susan J., *Restoration Theatre in Crisis* (Oxford: Clarendon Press, 1996).

Pacheco, Anita, 'Rape and the Female Subject in Aphra Behn's *The Rover*', *English Literary History*, 65 (1998), 323–45.

Payne, Deborah C., '"And poets shall by patron-princes live": Aphra Behn and Patronage', *Curtain Calls: British and American Women Writers and the Theater, 1660–1820*, ed. Mary Anne Schofield and Cecilia Macheski (Athens, OH: Ohio University Press, 1991), pp. 105–19.

Pearson, Jacqueline, *The Prostituted Muse: Images of Women and Women Dramatists 1642–1737* (Brighton: Harvester, 1988).

——, 'Gender and Narrative in the Fiction of Aphra Behn', *Review of English Studies*, 42 (165–6)(1991), 40–56, 179–90.

Pollak, Ellen, 'Beyond Incest: Gender and the Politics of Transgression in Aphra Behn's *Love-Letters between a Nobleman and His Sister*', *Rereading Aphra Behn: History, Theory, and Criticism*, ed. Heidi Hutner (Charlottesville: University of Virginia Press, 1993).

Rogers, Katharine M., 'Fact and Fiction in Aphra Behn's *Oroonoko*', *Studies in the Novel*, 20 (1988), 1–15.

Root, Robert L. Jnr, 'Aphra Behn, Arranged Marriage, and Restoration Comedy', *Women and Literature*, 5 (1977), 3–14.

Rosenthal, Laura J., 'Owning Oroonoko: Behn, Southerne, and the Contingencies of Property', *Renaissance Drama*, 23 (1992), 25–38.

Salzman, Paul, 'Aphra Behn: Poetry and Masquerade', *Aphra Behn Studies*, ed. Janet Todd (Cambridge: Cambridge University Press, 1996), pp. 109–29.

Schafer, Elizabeth, 'Appropriating Aphra', *Australasian Studies*, 19 (1991), 39–49.

Spearing, Elizabeth, 'Aphra Behn: the Politics of Translation', *Aphra Behn Studies*, ed. Janet Todd (Cambridge: Cambridge University Press, 1996), pp. 154–77.

Spencer, Jane, *The Rise of the Woman Novelist: From Aphra Behn to Jane Austen* (Oxford: Blackwell, 1986).

——, '"Deceit, Dissembling, all that's Woman": Comic Plot and Female Action in *The Feigned Courtesans*', *Rereading Aphra Behn: History, Theory and Criticism*, ed. Heidi Hutner (Charlottesville: University Press of Virginia, 1993), pp. 86–101.

——, '*The Rover* and the Eighteenth Century', *Aphra Behn Studies*, ed. Janet Todd (Cambridge: Cambridge University Press, 1996), pp. 84–106.

Spengemann, William C., 'The Earliest American Novel: Aphra Behn's *Oroonoko*', *Nineteenth-Century Fiction*, 38 (1984), 384–414.

Stiebel, Arlene, 'Subversive Sexuality: Masking the Erotic in Poems by Katherine Philips and Aphra Behn', *Renaissance Discourses of Desire*, ed. Claude J. Summers and Ted-Larry Pebworth (Columbia: University of Missouri Press, 1993), pp. 223–36.

Sullivan, David M., 'The Female Will in Aphra Behn', *Women's Studies*, 22 (1993), 335–47.

Taetzsch, Lynne, 'Romantic Love Replaces Kinship Exchange in Aphra Behn's Restoration Drama', *Restoration*, 17 (1993), 30–8.

Thomas, Susie, 'This Thing of Darkness I Acknowledge Mine: Aphra Behn's *Abdelazar, or, The Moor's Revenge*', *Restoration*, 22(1) (Spring 1998), 18–39.

Todd, Janet (ed.), *The Sign of Angellica: Women, Writing and Fiction 1660–1800* (London: Virago, 1989).

——, ed. *The Complete Works of Aphra Behn* (London: Pickering & Chatto, 1994–6).

——, *The Secret Life of Aphra Behn* (London: Andre Deutsch, 1996).

Woodcock, G., *The Incomparable Aphra* (London: Boardman, 1948).

Woolf, Virginia, *A Room of One's Own* (London: Hogarth Press, 1928).

Young, Elizabeth V., 'Aphra Behn, Gender, and Pastoral', *Studies in English Literature*, 33 (1993), 523–43.

——, 'Aphra Behn's Elegies', *Genre*, 28 (Spring/Summer 1995), 211–36.

Zimbardo, Rose, 'Aphra Behn in Search of a Novel', *Studies in Eighteenth-Century Culture*, 19 (1989), 277–87.

——, 'The Late Seventeenth-Century Dilemma in Discourse: Dryden's *Don Sebastian* and Behn's *Oroonoko*', *Rhetorics of Order Ordering Rhetorics in English Neoclassical Literature*, ed. J. Douglas Canfield and J. Paul Hunter (Newark: University of Delaware Press, 1989), pp. 46–67.

Notes on Contributors

Ros Ballaster is Fellow in English Literature at Mansfield College, Oxford University. She is the editor of Delarivier Manley's *New Atalantis* and Jane Austen's *Sense and Sensibility* and author of several articles on seventeenth- and eighteenth-century women's writing.

Carol Barash is the author of *Desire and the Uncoupling of Myth in Behn's Erotic Poems* and editor of *An Olive Schreiner Reader: Writings on Women and South Africa*.

Laura Brown is Professor of English at Cornell University, and most recently author of *Ends of Empire: Women and Ideology in Early Eighteenth-Century English Literature*.

Elin Diamond is Associate Professor of English at Rutgers University, New Brunswick. She is the author of *Unmaking Mimesis* and *Pinter's Comic Play* and editor of *Performance and Cultural Politics*. Her articles on performance and feminist theory have appeared in journals and anthologies.

Margaret Ferguson is Professor of English at the University of California at Davis. She has co-edited *The Tragedy of Mariam*, by Elizabeth Cary, *Feminism and Postmodernism*, and *Rewriting the Renaissance: The Discourses of Sexual Difference*. She has published several articles on Aphra Behn and is currently completing a book entitled *Female Literacies and Emergent Empires: France and England, 1400–1688*.

Catherine Gallagher is Professor of English at the University of California, Berkeley. She has written several books including *Industrial Reformation of English Fiction*, and *Nobody's Story* and edited *The Making of the Modern Body*.

Jessica Munns is Professor of Literature at the University of New Orleans, and Director of the Women's Studies Program. Her publications include *Restoration Politics and Drama, The Plays of Thomas Otway, 1675–1682* and *A Cultural Studies Reader: History, Theory, Practice*, co-edited with Gita Rajan.

Susan Owen is Lecturer in English Literature at the University of Sheffield. She is the author of *Restoration Theatre and Crisis*, and of ten articles on Restoration drama and one on chaos theory. She is working on a survey of drama from 1660 to 1714 and an edition of four Exclusion Crisis plays as well as editing a book of essays, *Drink, Drinkers and Drinking Places in Literature.*

Jacqueline Pearson is Senior Lecturer in English at the University of Manchester, England. She is the author of *John Webster's Tragicomic Endings, The Prostituted Muse: Images of Women and Women Dramatists 1642–1737* and many articles. She has recently completed *Women's Reading in Britain 1750–1834: A Dangerous Recreation.*

Ellen Pollak is the author of *The Poetics of Sexual Myth: Gender and Ideology in the Verse of Swift and Pope* and of numerous articles on eighteenth-century literature and culture. Her essay in this volume is part of a book she is completing on gender, incest and representation in the eighteenth-century novel. She teaches at Michigan State University.

Janet Todd is Professor of English at the University of East Anglia. She is the author of *The Sign of Angellica: Women, Writing and Fiction 1660–1800* and most recently *The Secret Life of Aphra Behn.*

Index